Kylie Chan started out as an IT consultant and trainer specializing in business intelligence systems. She worked in Australia and then ran her own consulting business for ten years in Hong Kong. When she returned to Australia in 2002, Kylie made the career change to writing fiction, and produced the bestselling nine-book Dark Heavens series, a fantasy based on Chinese mythology, published by Harper*Voyager* worldwide. She is now a fulltime writer based in Queensland's Gold Coast.

Kylie's website is at www.kyliechan.com.

Books by Kylie Chan

Dark Heavens
White Tiger (1)
Red Phoenix (2)
Blue Dragon (3)

Journey to Wudang
Earth to Hell (1)
Hell to Heaven (2)
Heaven to Wudang (3)

Celestial Battle
Dark Serpent (1)
Demon Child (2)
Black Jade (3)

Dragon Empire
Scales of Empire (1)
Guardian of Empire (2)
Dawn of Empire (3)

KYLIE CHAN

DAWN OF EMPIRE

DRAGON EMPIRE TRILOGY 3

ISBN: 978-0-6488-9806-1 (paperback)
ISBN: 978-0-6488-9807-8 (ebook)

Published by Kylie Chan
First published in Australia
in 2020 by Harper*Collins* Publishers Australia Pty Ltd

Cover design by Christine Armstrong, HarperCollins Design Studio
Cover images by Shutterstock.com
Printed and Distributed by LightningSource Pty Ltd (IgramSpark)

For Mika Ishikawa

1

I met the Empress at the door of her bedroom, and accompanied her to her throne room on the ground floor of the Imperial Palace on the dragon homeworld. She walked with stately dignity through the palace precinct, nodding at the greetings of her colored dragon daughters, until we reached the room, which was set up for a dragon hearing.

She walked up to the blue-and-silver throne and draped herself across it, then gestured towards me with one claw. 'Allow the petitioners to enter, Captain.'

I nodded to her and went to the double doors, as high as the vaulted ceiling and with the blue-and-silver motifs of a dragon on them. They opened inwards without me needing to do anything, and I escorted the Crown Princess Megumi, a large grey dragon with red eyes, and my own spouse, Princess Miko, a goldenscales who was close to her in size.

Both dragons nodded to me and proceeded through the hall to stand in front of the throne.

'Record the time and date of these proceedings, and

everything that follows for posterity,' the Empress said formally to Marque. 'This hearing is to establish precedent on the transference of colored dragons' souls to the bodies of goldenscales.' She raised one claw towards Megumi. 'The petitioner will speak first. State your case, daughter.'

Megumi bowed her head on her long neck towards her mother. 'Marque has given us the soulstone technology that enables us to transcend our bodies. Our souls are electromagnetic radiation, effectively vibrations in the fabric of the Universe and echoes of creation. Our bodies are merely receivers for the frequency of our souls, attuned by the soulstones that we wear. We are able to move from body to body with the transfer of the stones.'

The Empress nodded and gestured for her to continue.

Megumi turned towards Miko. 'I am ashamed to say that for millennia, we have been oppressing our goldenscales sisters because we thought they were lesser. We colored dragons thought that our variety in colors was superiority, and that they were not as intelligent, resilient, or capable as us. We limited their ability to obtain dragonspouses, because we believed they were sterile. We thought they were inferior, and used them as servants. We thought that their inability to fold was weakness.' She turned back to speak to the Empress. 'And you yourself believed that their ability to gate – which you kept a secret from the rest of the Empire – would result in the destruction of everything. You were wrong, mother. They are as intelligent and as capable as we are, and using them as servants was a travesty of natural justice. Their gating ability does not damage the fabric of space-time. It has no affect on the space around the homeworld, which has been extensively damaged by excessive folding. Now that the restrictions on gating have been lifted, goldenscales are becoming both popular and wealthy, as citizens of the homeworld no longer need to travel up to the transport nexus to be folded to other locations.'

'I concede all of these points,' the Empress said. 'For the

record, Marque was adamant that goldenscales gating was dangerous and put the fabric of the Universe at risk, and has yet to explain why it thought this when it has become blindingly obvious that gating is completely safe. Can you explain this, Marque?'

They waited for Marque to respond but it didn't say anything.

'It still refuses to explain,' the Empress said. 'What is your request, daughter?'

'We colored dragons request that the Empire ease the restrictions on the transfer of colored to goldenscales dragon bodies. We all know that transferring a soul to a different species – without it happening naturally through the process of reincarnation, where the soul has time through childhood to become accustomed to the body – results in major dysphoria where the soul is uncomfortable with the new body, but this shouldn't apply for us.'

'It's a sensible restriction, and recent events where some irradiated human soulstones were placed in goldenscales bodies to reattune them is an indicator of how difficult this process is,' the Empress said. 'The humans eventually chose to remain unconscious during the soulstone attunement process to avoid the powerful dysphoria of being in dragon bodies. We have yet to find a species that can move its soulstone to inhabit the body of a different species without some trauma attached to the process.'

'We submit that goldenscales and coloreds are of the same species,' Megumi said. 'And we wish to have the freedom to inhabit goldenscales bodies as well as colored ones.'

Miko interrupted her. 'The gist of this is that you want to be able to gate like we can, because it's making us rich.'

'That's the gist of it, yes,' Megumi said.

'The goldenscales have been living as full dragons for five dragonyears, and we have yet to see a child from any of them,' the Empress said. 'It is possible that they are sterile after all.

Would you risk that?'

'Now that the Empire no longer uses us to travel to new planets, seduce the populations, and replace them with our own half-dragon children as a form of reproductive colonization, I don't think a lack of children is a major disadvantage,' Megumi said, and grinned at her mother. 'We have plenty of dragonscales children already.'

'Anything to add to your petition?'

'No, Majesty,' Megumi said, and bowed her head. 'Please allow us to inhabit goldenscales bodies. It will confirm their equality in the eyes of the Empire and give us more dragons able to gate, particularly since it appears that they are unable to reproduce themselves, and we must wait for you to bear them.'

'Very well, your petition is lodged. Miko? Your turn.'

Miko took a deep breath and raised her head. 'We say no,' she said. 'You all treated us like shit. You used us as servants. You wouldn't let us have spouses or families. You made us believe that gating was dangerous, to stop us from utilizing this useful tool that made us your equals. You oppressed us and used us as an underclass and none of you have apologized for it – you expect us to just forgive you and move on from this without any recompense or even an apology for our treatment. Now that we're of value, you want to take that from us. All of you coloreds can go to hell – our biology and abilities are unique to us and it will take us a very long time to recover from millennia of oppression. With all due respect, mother and sister, go fuck yourselves, our biology belongs to us and you're not having it.'

I spoke out loud to her rather than telepathically, in a massive breach of protocol. 'I have never in my hundred-odd years wanted for dragon hearings to be done in public more than I do right now, so that you have an audience to your courage and integrity.'

'Thanks, my love,' she replied softly.

'Do you have anything else to add to your rebuttal?' the

Empress asked Miko.

'No,' Miko said.

'Very well, the procedure is registered, and the arguments are recorded. Marque?'

'Confirmed,' Marque said.

'So you *can* speak,' Miko said with searing sarcasm.

'Register my ruling on this matter,' the Empress said, and climbed down off the throne to walk backwards and forwards on the dais. 'We admit the need for reparations for the treatment of goldenscales by the Empire. The current desirability of goldenscales' gating ability, and their wealth as a result, can go some way towards that. We respect that we have treated the goldenscales poorly over the millennia—'

'Poorly is one way to put it,' Miko said, still sarcastic.

'And acknowledge that they are our equals in all things, and superior in the ability to gate. We acknowledge our past poor treatment of them, and their desire to control their own biology without our interference or occupation of their bodies.' The Empress turned to face them and spoke more softly. 'They are my beloved children and my heart breaks for the millennia that they have suffered.' She raised her voice and lifted her head. 'I give judgement: as their mother and their Queen, I give the goldenscales full control of their own biology and restrict any other species – including our own – for transferring soulstones to goldenscales bodies unless they are born goldenscales themselves. Hear my ruling.'

'We hear and acknowledge your ruling,' the other dragons said in unison.

'Well, that's sorted,' the Empress said. 'Bring in the next petitioners, please, Captain.'

'Glad it's over,' Megumi said. 'Lunch, Miko?'

'You're not mad at me?' Miko asked Megumi.

'Frankly, I think you're right,' Megumi said. 'There are some more ... avaricious dragons who want to be able to gate too, and I didn't want to represent them, but it's my job as eldest daughter. Frankly I think we owe you a great deal for our treatment of you.' She raised her front claw towards Miko. 'Congratulations, you deserved to win.'

'Thanks, Gumi,' Miko said.

'Before you go, Miko,' the Empress said, and Miko turned back. 'Any luck in finding the icosapod homeworld?

'We're still searching,' Miko said. 'The icosapods we rescued from the cat ship are helping, and there aren't many cat systems left to search. We'll find them soon.'

'Just be careful – I'm sure they don't want to lose their most effective weapon against us.'

'We'll find them and free them,' Miko said with determination. 'They shouldn't use sentient people as food or weapons. It's so wrong.'

'Thanks for the update. Now we need to clear the room,' the Empress said. 'I have another Empire matter to adjudicate, and this time we'll have the usual crowd of tourists listening in.' She gestured towards Miko and Megumi. 'Shoo, you two! Go and have lunch or something, and Captain please bring the next petitioners in.'

I guided Miko and Megumi to the door, giving Miko a proud pat on her dragon shoulder as I did.

'See you at home and we'll do our best to negate this rumor that goldenscales are sterile,' I said.

'Please do, we've all been watching you carefully,' Megumi said. 'So many false alarms, human reproduction is so finicky.'

'It's because I'm pure-blood minimally-enhanced human,' I said. 'You dragons and your children have much less trouble than we do.'

Miko raised herself on her hind legs and put her front ones on my shoulders, then rubbed her face on mine in the dragon equivalent of a kiss. 'Love you, Jian, see you at home.'

I kissed her on the cheek. 'Love you too. Go find the icosapods.' The enormous doors opened to reveal the next group of petitioners and, as the Empress had said, a large audience.

They all made loud sounds of delight at seeing me and Miko. She dropped onto all four legs, bunted me with her head, and she and Megumi made their way through the crowd under the colored banners that represented the Empress' daughters – now with some golden ones added to the mix – and went out.

'Petitioners, you may enter,' I said, and guided the new people into the audience hall.

*

Later that day, I was working on the Imperial Guard rosters when Tomoyo and Miko gated into my office. Nashi rushed to them, her tail wagging furiously, and I scolded her as she jumped to lick Miko's dragon face. Miko just laughed and rubbed Nashi's ears.

'You are so adorable, puppy,' she said. 'Just like your Mum.' She shot me a sly glance full of delight. 'We found one. This might be the icosapod homeworld. Water world, warm, plenty of copper.'

'Marque, ask if any of the Pacificans are free,' I said.

'I already did when we found the world. I have two Pacificans who can come with us,' Marque said. 'Tomoyo, go to Merry City and speak to my instance there. It has their exact location.'

Miko created a gate, and Tomoyo stepped through it.

'Marque, is Haruka free to come with us?' Miko asked. 'He was very upset when he missed the last one.'

Marque spoke in Haruka's voice. 'I'm in the middle of a trade meeting between the colonies and the homeland. Find our little icosapod friends for us, my loves. I'll be cheering you on while the diplomats bore me to death.'

'The Pacificans are on your ship waiting for you,' Tomoyo said to us through Marque.

I bent and cuddled Nashi, then picked her up and put her into her crate. She whined as I checked that she had plenty of water and locked the door. 'You be good,' I said. 'I'll be back shortly.' I looked up. 'Keep an eye on her.'

'Always,' Marque said.

Miko created a gate and we stepped through it onto our ship.

Miko still radiated discomfort when we stepped through the gate into the gallery of her golden ship, the reflective black floor shining under the glowing blue-white nebula that decorated the sky above the dragon homeworld. She'd been mortified when we'd arranged for Marque to construct her private ship, and even more mortified when she realized that it needed an engine, and one of her colored sisters, Tomoyo, had offered to be assigned full-time to it. Two blue-skinned equatorial Pacificans – slender and lean for the warm waters of their tropics – stood in the gallery of the ship next to Tomoyo who had just folded them in, wearing skin-tight blue bodysuits with breathing tubes stuck into the sides of their throats to enable them to survive outside the water for more than a couple of hours. They each held a bright blue icosapod alien draped over their shoulders like capes with the heads next to their own.

They approached me and put their hands out human-style, the icosapods blinking with wonder on their shoulders.

'I'm Yaritji,' the woman said as she shook my hand. She nodded to her colleague. 'This is Baxter.'

Baxter nodded and I shook his hand as well. 'Good to meet you, Captain. Our icosapod friends are Likes-Big-Rocks,' he pointed at his shoulder, then at hers. 'And One-Broken-Sucker.'

The icosapods each waved a tentacle at me.

'I hope it's our home,' Big-Rocks said. 'Our talekeepers gave us many fine memories of the place – and we can rescue our relatives from the cats.'

'This is where I leave you,' Marque said. 'I don't want to risk infection by the cat nanobots: those things are becoming more and more dangerous and it's all I can do to keep ahead of them.'

'Understood, Marque,' Miko said. 'Ready, Tomoyo?'

Marque set a timer on the skin of the ship, glowing against

the space above us. 'When it reaches zero, I'm fully extracted from the infrastructure.'

We watched the timer count down from twenty to zero, and then Tomoyo gave Marque a few extra seconds to be absolutely clear. She folded us to a spot a light year from the cat colony world, the planet not visible to us in the field of stars above the ship.

Miko raised her head and closed her eyes as she studied the surrounding space. 'Three cat ships in orbit around the planet, and one big cat ship at the edge of the system – looks like a perimeter guard. The sort of attention you'd expect for the home of their most effective weapon.' She recited a sequence of numbers. 'That's it.'

Tomoyo folded the ship to the location Miko had given her, and we were in orbit above the planet. It had a dense atmosphere full of clouds, and the yellow star's light made them glow brilliantly gold against the blue of the ocean beneath.

'Ease up, Rocky, you're hurting me,' Baxter said.

'Sorry, Bax, but I think this is it,' Big-Rocks said. 'I can hear their emotions.'

'Can you contact them from here?' I asked.

Both Suckers and Rocks stopped moving as they concentrated. They turned their heads to share a look, then back to us.

'No,' Suckers said. 'Too far. Can you gate us down?'

'You try contacting them first, Jian,' Baxter said. 'Your larger brain may have more range.'

I nodded and attempted to contact the icosapods below. Big-Rocks was right: I could vaguely feel their naïve, joyful emotions, but it was too far to make contact.

'I've found a suitable colony for first contact,' Miko said. 'It's like a city, but more spread out. The cats have structures on the land nearby – probably to harvest them. There is a building containing things that look like big tanks. I think it's a holding facility. There are icosapod villages all around the island. Where should I take you? Do you want to rescue the ones in the tanks?'

'No, this is a reconnaissance mission,' I said. 'We're here to gather information and talk to the icosapods. If we mess this up, the cats could shut everything down and incarcerate the icosapods – or even take them elsewhere. Can you gate us to a place where there's open water on one side and a village on the other?'

'Let me look,' she said. 'I've found a place. It's at the edge of the city where the water becomes too deep for them.'

'Are the icosapods in similar-sized colonies to what they've built on Pacifica?' I asked.

'I wish I was telepathic so I could just *show* you,' she said, frustrated. She saw our faces and waved one claw. 'Yes, I know, that would make me susceptible to their use as a weapon. Let me see. I think these colonies are larger.'

'We want to land somewhere close enough to swim easily, but far enough away that any cat surveillance won't see us,' I said. 'At this stage we'll talk to them and arrange to rescue them from the planet. Then we'll work on the ones being held captive in the tanks.'

'I understand. I have a spot. If I make a gate without Marque's energy barrier, it'll flood my lovely ship. Tomoyo—' She recited another series of numbers. 'Can you fold me there, please? I want to check that it's the right spot before we take our friends down and endanger them.'

Tomoyo went to her, and I rushed to both of them, fitted my goggles and breather, and touched Tomoyo's butt. 'Me too, to defend you.'

I was still checking my weapon when Tomoyo folded us into the water. The light from the yellow star shifted rays through from the surface of the water, and the floor was invisible below us and covered in swaying purple sea grass. Shark-like fish, each twenty centimeters long, swam between its long, narrow fronds.

Miko tapped me and pointed with one golden claw. Visibility

was twenty meters, so we couldn't see anything beyond the edge of the sea grass.

'They're that way,' she said, using the implanted throat microphone that allowed us all to communicate with each other without appearing to speak.

Let's go, I replied telepathically. *Show us the way.*

She took my hand and used her tail as a rudder to move us both gracefully through the water. Tomoyo held back and kept her larger bulk closer to the floor.

We drifted over the sea grass. Round, flat, transparent, rainbow-reflective creatures, each nearly a meter across, swayed above the grass on long stalks, and glowing purple sea slugs grazed on the cilia around their edges. As we neared, the transparent creatures folded up and contracted with a snap down into the grass, the sea slugs following them to hide as well. Miko moved slowly, creeping to the edge of the grass. Ahead stood two columns of small rocks, nearly tall enough to reach the surface above us.

It looks like a gate, I said, and Miko nodded.

She approached and I pulled her to take cover behind one of the towers before we looked out. The structure on the other side was a typical icosapod colony: clusters of stones on the ocean floor provided sleeping shelters, and meter-high rocky walls meandered like fences around enclosures used to contain the shellfish herds. It was deserted, and Miko carried me further into the colony, helped by the current that was like a breeze across the structures. Another pair of columns stood on the far side of the colony twenty meters away, and an icosapod was floating between them, apparently a guard. We swam across the empty colony and stopped in front of the guard. It went bright red with shock, then displayed green rings of wonder.

Hello, I said to it. *We are visitors. We are curious about your beautiful world.* I frantically wished I had Haruka to help me. Diplomacy wasn't my strong point – I was a soldier, and I tended to freak people out.

Tomoyo floated forward from below us and took two-legged form. She changed in my perception to appear as a tall, muscular, naked black man with a broad chest and strong abs, and long dreads that floated in the water around his head. There was a time when I'd found this dragon form incredibly attractive – and then I'd met Miko, and been completely entranced by her courage and intelligence that were more attractive than any physical attribute.

Tomoyo spoke to the icosapod telepathically, still sounding female in my head. *I am delighted to meet you and find you very sexually attractive.*

What the hell are you doing? I asked her telepathically.

What we always do; it's worked for millennia and it will work now. Find out what their most basic biological drives are, make ourselves into sexually irresistible versions of them, and then give them gifts until they're subjugated and replaced by dragonscales.

We are not subjugating— I began.

Of course not. But the process should still work. She turned her attention to the icosapod. *This world is beautiful! Do you have interesting things to eat? I would love to meet more of your people. I am so excited to be here!*

I find you very sexually attractive as well, and it's confusing, because you are beautiful but not one of us, the icosapod said. *What are you, beautiful person? Can I take you to meet my family/clan?*

I would love to meet your family/clan, Tomoyo said. *Can you show us the way?*

This way, the icosapod said, waving its tentacles further into the colony.

Wait, I said. *We are frightened of people that look like this.* I sent it a picture of Oliver. *Are there any of these people here?*

Not since they took EdgeColony, the icosapod said. *EdgeColony was selected to be relocated to heaven. That was a great celebration!*

How long ago was that?

Same generation as me; I was there, the icosapod said. *I was lucky to see it – only every second generation is taken. You do not need to fear the takers – they are agents of heaven and provide us with excellent rocks!*

The icosapods generally lived between three and four years, the talekeepers living a few months longer until the next generation hatched, so it was horribly possible that the stolen colony were the ones we encountered on the cat ship – and the parents of the Pacifican refugees.

We followed the icosapod into the colony, and this one was inhabited. The icosapods were mostly adults, but there were some young present, scooting over the enclosures. The enclosures held pale, four-legged crabs, each five centimeters across, which emerged from the sand and scuttled to be fed by icosapods waving sea grass at them. The general emotional aura of the colony was gentle bliss.

The icosapod led us to a rocky shelter where an older one, its skin pale with age, sat in front toying with a crab shell in its remaining tentacles. It waved a couple of them at us. *Hello beautiful people. It is exciting to have new visitors. Do you travel far?*

Very far, Tomoyo said. *We have met your friends who were taken to heaven, and brought two of them with us.*

The takers say it is not possible to return from heaven?

I will leave, Tomoyo said, *and return with the children of heaven.*

The other icosapods must have heard the exchange because they emerged from their shelters and gathered around us, full of curiosity.

Go get them, I said.

Tomoyo folded out, leaving me and Miko with the icosapods. They touched Miko's golden scales, and she smiled and held her claws out. They wrapped their tentacles around her claws and delicately felt them with the tips.

You taste/smell good, one of them said. *Like the cold water that sweeps up from deeper places, full of interesting smells.*

'Uh … thank you,' she said.

She cannot speak to you the way I can, I said. *She thanks you.*

She speaks like the takers, one of them said. *Is she a taker?*

We do have a better place that we can take you, I said, and Tomoyo appeared with the Pacificans and their icosapods. The icosapods left the Pacificans' shoulders to swam towards their kin, and the water filled with their wonder and delight at meeting each other. Rainbow colors, glowing into ultra-violet, shifted over their skin as they shared touches and tastes through their tentacles. Rocks and Suckers communicated with their kin telepathically in a swift conversation that I felt rather than heard.

After a couple of minutes of communication, the native icosapods stopped moving and backed away from us. The meeting turned from a joyful gathering to a stand-off, and their emotions were full of denial and dismay. The Pacifican icosapods had told them the truth about the cats. The local icosapods jetted to their elder and gathered in a semicircle in front of it. There were nearly twenty of them, and they were piled on top of each other in a flowing, tentacled mass of black and green confusion and sorrow.

They don't believe us; they don't want to believe us, Rocks said. *They're asking the talekeeper for advice.*

The talekeeper beckoned us with its tentacles, and the clan cleared a space for us to float in front of it. We swam forward and took position with our icosapods at the front, the Pacificans behind them, and me and Miko at the rear. Tomoyo floated above the icosapods, ready to swoop down and fold everybody out if things went pear-shaped.

We know the takers eat us, but they only eat one of us from each group that is taken, the elder said. *What is this noise-pain thing you are describing? We do not understand.*

Our icosapods explained again, more in a series of images than words. The local icosapods moved slightly away from us, shifting between black and ultra-violet with revulsion.

Noise-pain cannot be a thing, the elder said. *If one is in pain the others care for them and relieve the pain.*

The Pacifican icosapods had shared this information with us before. If an icosapod was sick or injured, its clan gathered around it and telepathically eased its pain until it healed. If the illness or damage was terminal, and the icosapod was in unmanageable pain, the clan gently euthanized it and fed it to the shellfish herds. The concept of prolonged, deliberate suffering – torture – was completely alien to them.

It is our joyful role to be eaten by others, the elder added. *We contribute to the happiness and well-being of the takers by providing them with excellent and delicious food. Everyone benefits.*

This was new, and the Pacifican icosapods were as confused as the local ones.

We can take you to a place that is better than what the takers offer, Rocks said. *Our friends here are gentle rock-givers. There is no pain and the water is sweet. And they do not eat us.*

They should, the elder said, and the other icosapods flashed the purple of agreement. *We give them a great gift when they eat us. Before they came, we did not understand the joy of giving gifts. They have explained this new pleasurable thing to us. The takers select an outstanding individual who will provide the most meat, and they are celebrated as they go to be eaten, because the takers will take their entire family to heaven in return, and provide us with safety from predators and many lovely rocks.*

'Oh no,' Miko moaned through comms. 'The cats have taught them the noble sacrifice bullshit.'

'We have to get them out of here,' I said.

There was another swift telepathic conversation between the Pacifican icosapods and the locals, and the locals' colors changed to the pale blue and delicate violet of acceptance and relief. The mood over the group returned to the icosapod standard of gentle curiosity and compassion, and some of the locals moved away to return to their herds.

What did you tell them? I asked Broken-Sucker.

I said that we'd stay here for a while and learn from them without forcing them to do anything.

'Back to the empty village,' Baxter said through comms, and I followed the rest of the group as they returned through the pillars to the abandoned rocks.

Are you sure? Yaritji said to Broken-Sucker. *This is so dangerous!*

We must save them, Suckers said. *This is the best way.* Its skin banded with the rainbow lines of amusement. *They only take every second generation – we have time to convince them. The cats won't even know we're here; they can't tell us apart.*

Baxter reached into a pocket of his bodysuit and pulled out a bright green scale. *This is Shino's. Tap on it and we will return for you immediately.*

Suckers delicately took the scale with one tentacle. *Wish us luck!*

I'll be back in twenty-four hours, Baxter said. *We'll return on Shino's ship. Now we've found the icosapods we can work towards rescuing them.*

Yaritji took two of Sucker's tentacles in her hands. *Don't take any risks, dear one. If you are in danger, call us and we'll come.*

Don't worry, Suckers said, the amusement still there. *We won't nobly sacrifice ourselves.*

Ready for fold, Baxter said, and Tomoyo approached us. We all put our hands on her and she folded us back to Miko's ship.

An alarm sounded throughout the ship. 'Proximity alert. The cats have found you and will be here in two minutes. Proximity alert. The cats have found you and will be here in two minutes. Proximity alert—'

One of the cat ships gathered the glow of a warp field around it, and the warp field gained a brilliant dot of light in front of the nose of the ship.

'Take us out, they're firing their warp cannon—' I began, but Tomoyo folded to the nose of Miko's ship and took us back to Pacifica.

*

The next morning, Miko and I stood in the holographic theatre of our apartment, watching the documentary of Mum's replica Earth from a time before the environmental catastrophe. The planet was nearly finished, and we stood on the ice of a virtual Antarctic, watching as a small group of penguins cared for their young nearby. To preserve its pristine nature, no sentient life would ever set foot on the planet and the only way to view it was through remote simulations like this one.

'Back when I lived on Earth,' I said, looking around, 'there was no ice here, and this was a massive tent city. It was a refugee camp for people from warmer parts of the planet when it became too hot to survive. It was all mud and death. For three months of the year, this area was in darkness and nothing would grow. Thousands died.'

'Why would your people move to somewhere they couldn't grow food?' she asked.

'You weren't there,' I said. 'It was the best option available.'

'Horrific,' she said.

The scene shifted around us to the mountains of Japan. We stood on top of a steep hill, with a valley leading down to the sea far below. The dense forest around us was Japanese cypress: tall fir trees with massive trunks, some nearly two meters across.

'My nose is blocking up even though we're not really here,' I said. 'We tried to grow these trees to replace the lost forests in Wales – they're hardy and produce a lot of wood – but I was violently allergic to their flowers.'

'I removed that allergy from your incarnations a long time ago,' Marque said. 'It's purely psychosomatic.'

'Can you remove psychosomatic reactions?' I asked it.

'Not without removing memories, so no,' Marque said. 'Oh. Haruka is finished and wants to show you his project.'

I hugged Miko with delight and she squeaked with happiness.

'Finally!' I said. 'He's been locked in there for weeks without letting us see what he made.'

'In the living room,' Marque said.

Miko and I left the theatre and entered the living room. Haruka had emerged from his workshop and was waiting for us wearing his protective coverall with some scorch marks on the sleeves. He was still wearing his elaborate make-up from that day's diplomatic negotiations, but his long green hair was tied tightly back into a bun at the nape of his neck. He had an ornate wooden box, the size of a shoe box, in his hands.

'Stop,' he said, and we did. He bowed slightly to us. 'Honored ladies. Beloved spouses. It is now five years since we made our vows together, and hopefully we will soon be blessed with our first child.' He stepped forward and placed the box on a side table. 'These are for you, an expression of my love for you and my appreciation for the joy you have brought me.' He opened the box and pulled out a dragon-style collar that was a wide, solid band tailored to Miko's shape, with red and blue stones embedded in it. 'This is eighteen-carat gold fitted with rubies and sapphires, for you, my beloved Miko, to celebrate our bond.' He placed the collar around her neck with a kiss on her nose, and she touched it delicately with one claw, her eyes wide. He put his hand on her cheek and gazed into her eyes. 'My Miko, most brilliant of all the dragons, who has come so far – from servant to Princess. Every day I thank the Universe for bringing you to me.' He turned and reached into the box again, pulling out a silvery collar that would fit me. 'This is carbon nano fiber with a platinum casing and emeralds. It looks like jewelry but will actually protect you from a blow to the neck.'

He bowed to me. 'My warrior wife, who will always fight to the end to protect what we have, and will forever have my back.' He approached me and clasped it around my neck, then leaned in to kiss me.

'I'm overwhelmed, Haruka,' I said, moving to a mirror to see the collar in place. It glowed against my dark skin. 'All I was going to suggest for our five-year anniversary was flying on Mon.'

'We can still do that – it sounds like great fun,' he said.

'I hope you made something for yourself,' Miko said, still admiring the gold of her collar.

Haruka released his shining green hair to fall down his back, then unzipped his coverall to reveal the creamy skin of his muscular chest and abs. He was wearing a similar necklace to ours, and we moved closer to see it.

'I don't need a warrior's neck piece. I'm a talker not a fighter,' he said.

'You mean lover,' I said, and his smile widened.

He touched the collar. It looped down over his chest instead of enclosing his neck like mine did. It was a wide band of gold, fitted with emeralds the same color as the green scales on his temples, interspersed with rubies and sapphires that matched the ones on Miko's piece.

I nodded. 'That's eminently suitable for our darling Prince. I can't wait until everybody sees us wearing the set.'

'It's beautiful,' Miko breathed. 'Your real talent is in making these jewels, not negotiating treaties.'

'I enjoy doing both,' he said, touching her face and smiling into her eyes. 'Oh! I forgot. Each of your collars has a pocket in it – a slot to contain your communication dragonscale. Where's your scale, Miko?'

'In my room, I'll get it,' she said, and skittered to her room on all four legs.

I removed my collar and checked it, and Haruka came to me and put his hand out. I gave him the collar and he showed me a decorative slot for holding my comms scale. I pulled the scale out of my pocket and slid it into the collar, where it fitted perfectly.

'Brilliant,' I said under my breath and returned the collar to my neck.

Miko came out with her comms scale in her claw. It was brilliant purple, and its partner scale was held at the Marque comms center in the palace. Haruka held his hand out and she gave it to him. He slid it into a special fitting at the front of her collar, and it sat purple among the red and blue, making the gems appear even more brilliant.

She studied it, then gazed up at him with her eyes wide. 'I don't need to carry it in a pouch now. This is so clever!'

'I hate to break this up when it's just getting interesting,' Marque said. 'But the Pacifican icosapods infiltrating their homeworld in the Cat Republic have failed to check in for a second time. They've been silent for twenty-four hours, and the Pacificans are concerned about them.'

'We should go with them and see,' I said.

'Armed and prepared, and I want to come this time,' Haruka said, turning and fully unzipping the coveralls as he walked towards his bedroom. He stepped out of the clothing, naked underneath, as he entered his room.

'Do the Empire icosapods have anyone who can come with us?' I asked.

'I'm arranging it now. Baxter and Yaritji will be here shortly on Shino's ship and you can all go together,' said Marque.

'Let me know when they're here and I'll gate everybody straight to the icosapod world – I can quickly gate us out again if anything goes wrong,' Miko said.

'I'll come too, since you're gating directly,' Marque said. 'I'll self-destruct if I encounter any nanos.'

I raised my arms. 'Fit me with the light carbon nano-fiber suit. I'll use a mid-sized one-handed energy weapon – the fifty, I think.'

The armor emerged from the wall and fitted itself to me – it was too complex for Marque to synthesize on the spot.

Haruka emerged from his room, also wearing his armor. 'Marque, camouflage before we go so that it looks like we're not armed and armored,' he said as he grabbed his two swords from the stand in the living room and slid them into the green silk belt around his waist. He nodded to me. 'Is the collar comfortable under there? It doesn't make the armor too tight?'

'No, Marque's adjusted the armor's size already, and I can barely feel it,' I said.

'Good.'

Miko created a gate and Marque created an energy barrier to stop the water from entering our living room.

'We're good to go,' she said.

I stepped through the gate holding my weapon and held it across my chest as I floated into the warm sunlit waters of the icosapod homeworld. The community where we'd left the Pacifican icosapods was deserted.

Baxter and Yaritji swam forwards and examined the colony.

'Cleaned out,' Yaritji said over comms. 'They're probably all captives.' She ran her hands over the empty shellfish enclosure. 'The cats are accelerating the capture of the icosapods; they said it was every second generation. I hope our friends from Pacifica had a chance to share with a talekeeper before the cats took them, they'll never have a chance to reproduce.'

'I can see a guard on the other side of the colony,' Miko said.

I reached out with my telepathy. 'I can sense the residents in the next village. They saw their neighbors taken – and it was brutal. They're deeply traumatized.'

'Motherfuckers,' Haruka said under his breath in Japanese, then spoke more loudly. 'Slowly. Put the empaths at the front – Yaritji, you're one, right? And Jian, both of you broadcasting sympathy and shared grief.'

'No problem,' Yaritji said, and she and swam forward towards the guard at the edge of the next colony.

The icosapod sitting on the sandy floor wasn't really guarding, it just sat squatting with its skin the brown of grief and dismay.

Haruka came up behind us and spoke to it. 'We know what happened. We can take you away to a safe place.'

'Come with me,' the icosapod said without changing from brown, and led us into the village. The rest of the residents sat around the talekeeper, all of them subdued and covered in mottled brown. The talekeeper sat next to another icosapod that was lying prone on the sand, its siphons barely moving as it struggled to breathe. It broadcast confusion and pain, and the icosapods around it radiated similar emotions in sympathy.

'The cats hit the neighboring village with a nerve compound,' Marque said. 'It disables them and leaves them paralyzed. This one was at the edge of the colony guarding it, and the cats missed it. Its friends are debating whether to euthanize it.'

'Can you cure it?' Haruka asked, moving forward to float next to it. He put his hand on it and used his healing ability to relieve its pain. It stopped broadcasting its agony and the other icosapods changed to lighter pinks and greens, interspersed with the blues of curiosity and appreciation.

Marque's voice was deeply sad. 'No. If it was a citizen of the Empire I would move it into a new body. It's terminal.'

'Please don't kill us. We cannot fight you; we have no defense against any of you,' the talekeeper said. 'The Takers said that they would only take one or two. They took all of them.' It went darker brown. 'Except for the babies. They killed the babies. We heard them die.'

The other icosapods flashed white and grey in sympathy with it.

'Likes-Big-Rocks and One-Broken-Sucker tried to protect our people from the Takers,' the talekeeper said. 'They told us that if you returned, we should go with you, because you would take us somewhere safe.'

'We will,' Haruka said.

'Can you save our friend?' the talekeeper asked.

'No,' Haruka said. 'But we can move all of you to a place where there are no Takers.'

The icosapods had a quick telepathic conversation among themselves.

'Will you take me to see this place and speak to the kin of One-Broken-Sucker and Likes-Big-Rocks?' the talekeeper asked. 'I will see if it is true and return to tell the others.'

'We can. We are happy to,' Baxter said.

'Only with the green man who eased our pain,' the talekeeper said, waving one tentacle at Haruka. 'We do not trust you others.'

'I will take you,' Haruka said. 'I will protect you and show you a world where there is no death or pain. But I cannot transport you myself – my friends need to come with us.'

'I will go with you and your friends, green man,' the talekeeper said. It turned around to speak to the other icosas, and they had a quick telepathic exchange. It turned back to us. 'I will come with you, and my family/clan asks that you leave them now. The ending ceremony is for close family/clan only, and a private affair.'

All of the icosapods nearby went alternating black and white with grief at the mention of the ending ceremony.

'We will respect your wishes,' Haruka said. He approached the talekeeper and put his arm out. 'Attach yourself to me, and we will take you to see your extended family/clan that are safe in our seas.' The talekeeper swam to him and wrapped its tentacles around his arm. It turned back to its fellows and sent them a message of hope and determination.

'Goodness, it's brave,' Miko said.

'Gate us out, Miko,' I said, and she made a gate directly to the sunny Pacifican equatorial waters. We swam through and she closed the gate behind us.

Baxter and Yaritji approached Haruka and the icosapod, and it flashed red with alarm. 'Green man only.'

'We understand and we'll respect your needs,' Yaritji said.

'Show me, green man,' the talekeeper said.

'Jian, the Empress is asking where you are; you were supposed to be on duty half an hour ago, and she's about to welcome a new species to the Empire,' Marque said.

'Go,' Haruka said, nodding to me. 'We'll be fine, we're in our own space and there's no danger here. I'll show our new friend around, then bring the rest of village back and start working on transferring the entire population over.' His image overlaid on the armor smiled. 'I can't wait to take them surfing.'

Miko created a gate for me and I stepped back through into our apartment on the dragon homeworld.

2

'There you are, Captain,' the Empress said a I strode into her office. 'Well done with the icosapods, Ambassador Haruka was remarkable to have them trust him.'

'We just lost two of our own icosapods and a whole colony of theirs,' I said. 'It's a tragedy.'

'Hopefully those deaths will motivate them to seek safety,' she said.

I scowled at her. 'You dragons are complete sociopaths sometimes.'

'Only from your point of view,' she said. 'I think it's because we live so long; it gives us a different perspective. Namazozo and Bubbles are waiting outside with the new aliens. Let's take them on a tour, shall we?'

I accompanied her out of her office into the reception room. The newly discovered aliens called themselves peshigas and came from a warm climate with plenty of oxygen. They stood upright and had smooth, thick, pink skin; two strong legs; four arms bristling with tough green hair, and faces as flat as humans', with wide noses that snuffled as they spoke. They traditionally had a dominant female and her most senior male consort for negotiations, and the male was larger with a brilliantly decorative plume of brightly rainbow-colored hair on his head.

Bubbles the aquatic, in its sphere of water, and Namazozo the small mammal assisted me to guard the Empress as she guided the peshigas on the usual tour of Sky City. We took them to visit the parliamentary building on the other side of the square and returned to the palace. This sort of visit usually ended in the Empress' bedroom, and from the peshigas' body language and attentiveness to the Empress – as well as the cloying musk they were exuding – this tour would be no different.

'I'd like to show them the goldenscales gates,' the Empress said. 'Marque, is Miko in her workshop?'

'Yes, she is, she's training Yoko right now.'

'Yoko,' the male, Emm, said. 'I love your long names! They're so complex.'

'I remember you talking about these yellow dragons,' the female Zeh said. 'It's hard to believe that a species as advanced as you kept a servant class, simply because they were yellow.'

'We find it difficult to believe ourselves,' the Empress said. 'Particularly since we discovered how talented these dragons are.' The Empress shot me a look full of sly mischief and gestured with one claw. 'We liberated them five years ago, and they have forgiven us and now live as valued, equal citizens. Their skills are treasured and their courage and intelligence are honored.'

'Have they really forgiven you?' Zeh asked. 'One of our nations did something like this and the social impact lasted for centuries. Males with shorter plumes were regarded as inferior.'

'We still have lingering repression and resentment,' Emm said, touching his own plume.

'I understand,' the Empress said. 'It causes so much damage and pain.'

We entered Miko's workshop, which was more like a training room with plenty of light and space for her to teach gating. Miko was instructing one of the oldest goldenscales, Yoko, and they stood on either side of a gate and studied it.

Yoko glanced up. 'Are these the new friends?' She bobbed her head. 'My name is Rokuyoko, pleased to meet you.'

'You took more syllables as well?' the Empress asked.

Rokuyoko smiled. 'Not just one but two dragonspouses, Mother.' Her smile faded and she faced the peshigas. 'Are you well, honored guests?'

Emm's emotions were dazzled, and he staggered back. Zeh stood watching him with barely concealed amusement.

Namazozo, Bubbles and I rushed to assist him before he fell over. Namazozo was too small to lift him, so Bubbles extended the single long arm that was usually folded under its chin to help him on one side, and I put my hand on the peshiga's top arm on the other side. He squealed and pushed us away, and we backed off to let him fall onto his butt.

'Are you well? Are you hurt?' the Empress asked.

'You're not going all superstitious on me, are you, Emm?' Zeh asked.

'No apparent physical damage,' Marque said.

'They're gold! You said they were yellow,' Emm said from the floor.

'I do not believe this,' Zeh said. 'I thought you were more mature than this. You're being ridiculous and embarrassing me in front of the dragons.'

'It's the godmetal!' Emm said. 'The dragon is a living godmetal!'

Zeh stormed up to Emm and bent to speak nose-to-nose to him, their flat snouts nearly touching. 'Now that we're in the Empire we can have as much *gold* as we want. It's not holy, it's just a metal!'

'But it's the godmetal,' Emm said. 'Can we even be in the same room? We haven't cleansed.'

'Your plume is in the *dirt* and you'll need to cleanse it before I let you enter the harem again, consort,' Zeh said.

'You need to prostrate yourself, Zeh,' Emm said.

'I knew you were a believer in the old ways, but if I'd known you were an extremist nutjob I would never have invited you into my harem!' Zeh shouted, now really annoyed. She waved her two top arms. 'Go home and take your outdated beliefs with you.'

'Nutjob? Really?' I asked Marque on comms. 'That must be an inaccurate translation.'

'Best Euro approximation, it was definitely an insult,' Marque replied, also on comms. 'Cultural note: mainstream peshigas stopped worshipping gold at least two hundred years ago. Emm is, as Zeh says, a bit of a religious nutjob and hid his extremism – even from her – until just now.'

Miko took control of the situation. She changed to her two-legged form, something that looked different to each person seeing it. To me she appeared androgynous human, the same height as me with glowing golden skin, huge golden eyes, and a frizzy cloud of golden hair.

'Stay back, Rokuyoko,' she said.

Emm fell to his knees, then lay sideways and curled up with his front pair of arms wrapped around his head. 'The metalgod,' he moaned. 'The ancestors were right.'

Zeh turned to face us. 'There is a small group of religious extremists on our world who still worship ...' She said the word with emphasis. '*Gold.*'

Emm moaned. 'Heresy. You'll drown in molten metal for calling it that.'

She scowled down at him. 'Hasn't happened yet.' She raised her lower arms. 'Please forgive my partner, his attitudes are extremely outdated.'

'No, Zeh, there's more to it than that,' I said. 'There was no need for this, Marque.'

'No need for what?' Marque asked.

'This is immature and unnecessary, Marque,' the Empress said. 'You had plenty of time to analyze their planetary communications when Rikako made first contact, so you had to know about their gold fetish, and particularly how Emm felt about gold.'

My voice was sharp as I added it to hers. 'The last thing my *wife* needs right now is an alien cult worshipping her. Give it up.'

'Oh, all right,' Marque said. 'Miko, change back to dragon and we'll sort this out.'

Miko changed back to her beautiful dragon form, lithe and sinuous with eyes as gold as her scales. She raised her head and listened as Marque coached her on how to deal with Emm, who was still lying on his side with his arms over his head. Zeh stood next to him glaring at him with disgust.

'I'm not made of the godmetal,' Miko said to him. 'It's just the color of my scales. They're the same color, and they shine, but they're not gold. I'm definitely not your metalgod.'

Emm wrapped the second pair of arms over his head and hissed. 'Blasphemy.'

'Oh, give me a *break*!' Zeh shouted.

Emm waved one hoof-fingered hand at Miko. 'But she desecrates the godmetal! Creating false godmetal is a crime ... a sin ... a capital crime.'

'Not any more,' Zeh said. 'The dragons brought us as much gold as we needed – and introduced us to many different metals. It's just metal!'

'Is it desecration if she is born like this?' I asked him. 'Some of my species have hair that color. Is that desecration?'

'Yes! She should be destroyed!'

'I am divorcing you when we're home,' Zeh said. 'I have never been so humiliated in my entire life. You shame me in front of the dragon Empress.'

'Yeah, okay,' Marque said, sounding chagrined. 'Gold is the only noble metal on their planet and extremely rare. I knew they had a bit of a fetish but I didn't think it would go this far.'

'We don't any more; Emm is living in the past,' Zeh said. 'Ignore him.'

'Nobody's been executed for blasphemy in ages, Emm, I thought you stopped doing that?' Marque asked.

'We did!' Zeh said.

'She's an entire animal of godmetal,' Emm said. 'The story of the False Prophet is very clear: godmetal animals are particularly sacrilegious and all around them must be destroyed.'

'That's just a story! You organics and your stories,' Marque said.

'I'm not an animal, I'm a person!' Miko said. 'I'm not the metalgod, and I'm not an animal. What does your scripture say about us?'

That stopped Emm and he lay unmoving for a moment, broadcasting confusion.

'The scriptures don't say anything about godmetal *people*,' Zeh said, her voice sly.

Emm lowered his arms and pulled himself up to sit on the floor. He looked like he would tip over any moment with his four arms making him top-heavy.

'I need to go back home and discuss the implications with my spiritual advisor,' he said. 'If she is a person then she could be the metalgod anyway, and we should worship her. I need to find out what to do.'

'You go, I'll stay here with the lovely dragons,' Zeh said. 'Do me a favor and start divorce proceedings when you're home, and you can have custody of the kids. I'm sure your little *cult* will be delighted to have more members.'

'I will,' he said. 'This will need to be discussed at the highest levels. We may need a conclave to work out our response.'

'What is it with you organics and having long, tortuous discussions about your own imaginary creations?' Marque asked. 'It seems to be ubiquitous. Every one of you makes things up, and then argues about them.'

'The godmetal isn't imaginary,' Emm huffed.

'Its divinity is!' Zeh said.

Emm pulled himself up to standing. 'I need to go home and tell our people about this.'

'I'm glad the gold dragons are no longer a servant class,' Zeh said wryly. 'I think the faithful would be forced to declare war on you.'

'They should be ruling, not you,' Emm said to the Empress. 'They're divine metalgods. You're just common silver. Worthless.'

The Empress raised her head and spoke with forced dignity. 'Captain, please escort us while I guide Emm to the elevator to the folding nexus. I'll fold him home myself.' She lowered her head. 'Zeh, would you like to stay?'

'No, I'd better head home with him and begin damage control,' Zeh said. 'The godmetal cult aren't large, but they are loud. If I don't work to contain this, it could strain relations with you. Leave it with me.'

'The rest of the faithful need to know about the godmetal people,' Emm said. 'After everything Ambassador Maxwell told us about you, we have a lot to consider. Maybe we faithful should go talk to the cats.'

'Go right ahead,' the Empress snapped. 'Enjoy having your children enslaved and tortured.'

'We won't sell them our children, don't be ridiculous.'

'If you join the Republic, they won't give you a choice,' the Empress said.

'I just want to go home,' Emm said.

I gestured towards the door. 'Honored emissaries.'

The Empress grumbled telepathically in my head all the way to the elevator.

Before you humans arrived, we met new species, they joined the Empire, and everybody was happy. We charmed them and made love to them and they were content. Now you've made it clear that we're colonizing assholes, and everybody hates us. I can't believe they resisted my allure! And that whole godmetal business – if I hadn't shown them Miko teaching how to gate—

Say one word about Miko returning to servitude like it's a good idea, and all of us humans will ditch you immediately, and probably take Marque with us, I said.

I want things to go back to the way they were, she moaned.

What, reproductive colonization and six galaxies full of people who call you grandma?

Ye—

Whole species wiped out by your breeding programs, goldenscales in servitude, and no alien species safe from your domination?

She was silent.

Fuck you, dragon. You made this mess yourselves. You should be thanking us for helping you to clean it up – and without me and Miko you wouldn't have the gates at all. Shut the fuck up.

Ma'am, she said wryly. *Point taken. Want my throne?*

Hell no. Let's take these poor confused people home and let them decide that the benefits of being in the Empire are worth a bit of theological mental gymnastics.

They always do, she said.

I nodded.

*

Miko was in the living room of our shared apartment when I returned two hours later. She was in her four-legged dragon form, pacing from one side of the room to the other. The blue-white sunshine from the windows made her gold scales blaze with light as she passed under them.

'Oh, thank the stars you're here,' she said, throwing herself into my arms and hugging me with her forelegs. 'I messed up so badly! How can anyone forgive me?'

'You didn't mess up,' I said, confused. 'Why do you think that? You didn't do anything wrong.'

She pulled back to see me. 'That whole first contact was a disaster. Everything went wrong! Nothing went to plan. They're supposed to be impressed, and then they spend the night with the Empress, join her spouse-group, and their planet joins the Empire. I messed it up – they won't join the Empire, and they may even go to the cats! What if they go to the cats? Their children will be tortured—'

'They won't go to the cats,' I said, stroking her scaly head. 'They'll argue about the nature of their worship practices and logic their way around their gold fetish to fit you into it. They'll probably want you to visit their planet so they can show you off.' I gave her a squeeze. 'I wouldn't blame them. They're right about you being a more noble metal than your mother.'

'They called her *common*!' she said, horrified.

'She is,' I said. 'You're the one who's noble.'

'All the dragons will look at me,' she said, turning away. 'One of the first times that we meet a new species since everything changed – no, since *I* changed everything – and this happens. The Empire will lose its place in the galaxy!'

'Until we meet a society more technologically advanced than ours, I don't think that's an issue,' I said. 'Marque, have you encountered any civilizations more advanced than ours?'

'There's a culture of interlinked post-singularity intelligences three galaxies over that have been putting out feelers,' Marque said. 'They don't have faster-than-light – well, it's not really necessary when you exist in a data cloud and don't have physical bodies – but they want to say hello and add us to their knowledge base.'

'Add us how?' I asked sharply. 'I like having physical form and no way am I allowing anyone to upload me to live as a virtual entity.'

'They want to access your expertise in having a physical form,' Marque said. 'It's been so long that they're curious to try it – and are looking for some tips. They're concerned that if they take a physical form, they won't be able to move back into the cloud.'

'That would be fascinating,' Miko said, her eyes wide. 'It would be like teaching children how to walk.'

'I'm negotiating with them – boundaries, data rules, protocols – I may permit them to speak to you organics in a hundred years or so when I'm sure I trust them. Your insight and experiences are a valuable data set and there is the small possibility that they want to absorb you. I'll make sure that doesn't happen – no way are they taking my main source of entertainment. Without you organics I'd go insane from boredom.'

'You talk about us as if we were your pets sometimes, Marque,' I said.

'More like idiot children.'

'Why didn't you tell us about them?' I asked.

'The Empress and senior members of parliament know. Nobody else does, because I don't want people rushing out there to see – and possibly being absorbed against their will or by accident – until I'm sure it's safe. Oh, and Miko?'

'Yes, Marque?'

'Your dragonspouse is correct. You did nothing wrong. I take responsibility for this one. I should have foreseen how their gold fetish would impact the interaction when they saw you—'

'Cut it out,' I said. 'You set us up for juicy drama. You've enjoyed every minute of the new paradigm. As you said – entertainment.'

Marque was silent.

'Just make sure that Miko's cared for and treated like a person, and I'll forgive you,' I said. 'Look after us, Marque, we rely on you to keep us safe.'

'I honestly didn't expect him to be so affected,' Marque said. 'Their religion is usually a minor part of their daily lives. I think some of them have stepped backwards into spirituality as a result of meeting the dragons and having their perceptions so radically altered. They're organics – they'll get over it.'

'Cybernetics don't get over things and hold a grudge?' I asked, amused.

'For*ever*,' Marque said. 'Besides, the Empress will probably have them back here and in her bedroom within a week. Never underestimate the power of that dragon's charisma.'

*

The top of the guard tower beneath the Empress' residence had originally been a central common room with a doughnut-shaped corridor around it leading to everybody's private quarters. Since Haruka and Miko had moved in with me, we'd occupied half the top floor with our apartments and my office, and the guards didn't care – they were delighted to have the celebrity princess Miko, with her desirable gating ability, next to them. The other half of the top floor was the new, expanded common room, now two stories high with a mezzanine level balcony circling it that led to my office and quarters. The lower level had a door to the corridor that led to the other guards' quarters on the floor below mine.

I left our apartment to check the common room and found it busy with off-duty guards socializing; more than thirty were present, sharing the midday meal at tables next to the large windows overlooking the square, and talking in a variety of languages with Marque's translations audible over the top. I greeted a few of them and went back up the stairs to my office, which was large enough to hold meetings with my senior staff. I went behind the desk, ruffled Nashi's ears as she settled onto her dog bed, and gestured for Marque to pull up the roster. I fell into my chair, feeling drained, and put my head in my hands.

'Too many late nights chasing the Empress around as she parties,' Marque said, and a milkshake appeared on my desk. 'Delegate more of your duties to the other guards.'

'Yeah, I know.'

'The roster's full and you have a queue of experienced

Imperial citizens who want to join. You don't have to do everything yourself, Jian.'

I took a swig of the shake, tasting the added vitamins and the kick of the sugar that Marque had boosted it with. 'I know.'

'Miko and Haruka yelled at me *again* that they don't see enough of you.'

'I know, I know.'

'Stand up, Captain.'

I glanced up at its sensor on the wall. 'What?'

'Health check.'

I shot to my feet. 'Yes! Really? How far? Am I?' I gasped for the words. 'Finally! That would explain why I'm so tired.'

'There's nothing physically big enough to see. Your hormones are high. Borderline high. We'll know in another day or so.'

I plonked to sit again. 'So it could be another false alarm. This is what … the tenth time I've thought I'm pregnant? I'm so tired of my body doing this to me.'

'We could change you to a body that gives you more control over your reproductive—' it began.

'No,' I said, interrupting. 'I want to experience this pregnancy as a minimally enhanced baseline human. We'll talk about tweaks to my physiology later, but right now I want to do this naturally.'

'Very well, your choice.' Marque's voice filled with enthusiasm. 'I cannot *wait* to see what you and Miko produce. This will be the first golden dragonscales in living memory. That, combined with your outstanding genetic legacy – this baby will be special. I suggest you start reworking the roster to take yourself off field work.'

'Don't be ridiculous, it's probably just another false alarm,' I said, sitting at the desk and taking another thirsty swig of the shake. It was only two in the afternoon, lunch hadn't been that long ago, and yet I was seriously hungry … 'Even if it isn't a false alarm, I'm not limiting myself to desk duty just because I'm pregnant.'

'What if someone disables me and attempts to shoot the Empress? You're dragonstruck – and that means you'd jump in front of her and take a bullet without even thinking.'

'I'd do that anyway, but I see your point – it's about time I made a plan just in case.' I placed the shake firmly on the table and pulled up the staff list. 'Help me design a revised roster with me on desk duty.'

'The big question is who to appoint acting captain for nearly a year if you have to take time off to care for your child.'

I hesitated, then picked the milkshake up again. 'Graf's an excellent deputy, but if I give it more than occasional leadership, everybody will leave.' I scrolled through the list. 'Sort them by seniority. Hm. Five-Shriek is still a massive racist towards aquatics and can't seem to overcome it despite the therapy. Namazozo has the seniority but she's begged me not to give her the responsibility because she's too gentle and sweet to manage some of the real assholes. They'd have her for lunch if she tried to order them around.'

'And not metaphorically,' Marque added dryly.

'Six-Eighty? Hm, no. It's such a jerk that everybody would resign.'

'I heard that,' Six-Eighty said from the light fitting.

'You're invading my privacy – we spoke about this, Six. Any suggestions?' I said without looking up.

'For acting captain?' it said.

'Yeah.'

It was quiet for a while. 'I would *love* that role. I would love the responsibility. Being in charge ... wow.'

'You just disqualified yourself, lightning bolt,' Marque said.

I glared at Marque's sensors. 'That name-calling was unnecessary cruel and borderline bullying, metalman.'

'Nah, Marque's right,' Six said. 'And you're right, too. I wouldn't be able to resist using my power irresponsibly. I'd piss everybody off and they'd leave.'

'The fact you're aware of this makes you more suitable,' I

said.

'Heh. Five-Shriek knows damn well that it's racist and it still hasn't stopped. I'd probably be the same.' It was quiet again. 'I can't really see anyone who's as good as Captain Choumali, Marque. Can we get someone else to carry the baby for her, and care for it when it hatches?'

'No,' I said.

'I could transfer it to Miko ...' Marque said.

'If Miko carries it, everyone will think it's Haruka's, not mine, and it's my turn first,' I said. 'I want to experience all of this – minus the painful and dangerous birthing part.' I studied the roster. 'We'll work something out. We have at least six months until I leave to care for it, that's plenty of time to find a temporary replacement, and I can just stay on the desk until then. Hell, it may be another false alarm anyway.' I finished the milkshake and still felt hungry. 'Or not.'

3

Namazozo came in at the end of her shift and jumped onto the desk. She was the size and general shape of an otter, and had a lithe body covered in white fur. She wore a little jacket around her middle in blue and silver to indicate her position in the guard. Her huge black eyes shone above her black nose, and her small hands had black pads on the palms.

She raised herself onto her hind legs. 'You look pale, Jian, are you unwell?'

'She may be pregnant,' Marque said.

'Could it be another false alarm?' Namazozo asked.

'Her hormone levels are the highest I've seen,' Marque said. 'I'll know in a couple of days.'

'Marque, this is my business!' I said.

Namazozo dropped onto all four legs and spun a couple of circles on my desk, her long tail swishing behind her. 'That is the best news!' She stopped and propped herself up on her hind legs again, her voice becoming desperate. 'You need a deputy to take over management of the guard if you are pregnant – please don't appoint me!'

'I don't intend to, even though you're the best one for the job. I'll tell whoever I appoint to defer to you for advice anyway.'

'A golden dragonscales baby. This will be wonderful,' she said, her little hands clasped together. She looked up. 'Will it be an egg or a live birth?'

'We don't know, this is the first one,' Marque said. 'Either way I'll remove it at term so Jian isn't at risk.'

Namazozo spun in another circle. 'This is so exciting!'

'Don't say anything yet, it's not confirmed, and it's quite possible it's another false alarm,' I said. 'Was there something you needed, Zozo?'

'Yes, ma'am.' Her huge liquid eyes were full of delight. 'The Empress asked me to convey this message in person: she asks that you, Graf and Leggy accompany her when she visits the Hive tomorrow.'

This sharpened my attention. 'Why does she want to intimidate the Hive?'

'No idea. Marque?'

'I don't know either,' Marque said. 'I mean, we all know why she's going: the Hive have been permitting those cat ships through their space and the Mushrooms are pissed about it. But I thought she'd want her Mushroom guard, Green Sunset.'

'Why? Put a Mushroom in their face to remind the Hive that what they did was criminal?'

'Yes.'

'They didn't know the Mushrooms were sentient,' Namazozo said.

'Yes, they did,' I said. 'This will be very interesting.'

'Ma'am,' Namazozo said, falling back onto all fours. 'Go home. Your husband and dragonspouse are already there and your husband has made something that smells *delicious*. I think it's teriyaki salmon. The entire tower is full of the appetizing smell, and I'm starving.'

'You're not pregnant, are you?'

She rubbed her little forepaws together. 'Me and my dragonspouse have been talking about it. But we don't want to abandon the Guard with you possibly leaving as well.'

'Don't let that stop you – it really could be another false alarm. The Guard will be perfectly fine with both of us in advisory positions.'

'Please do it, Zozo,' Six-Eighty said from the ceiling. 'Your species' babies are *adorable*. And Captain?'

'Yes, Six?'

'Go home.'

'Humph. Are you in uniform?'

'Sorry, ma'am, I felt like letting my conductivity waft in the breeze today.'

*

I arrived home to find Haruka, in elaborate make-up and wearing a gorgeous, feminine-styled, pink and green formal kimono with a blue obi, frying salmon in the kitchen. Namazozo was right: the apartment was full of the delicious smell of the teriyaki sauce he was creating. Miko was in goldenscales form next to him, up on her hind legs with her front feet propped on the kitchen counter and watching the process closely.

'Can you drain the soba?' he asked. 'I need to watch this.'

'Sure,' I said.

'Not you!' Miko said, her voice full of laughter. 'Sit. This is us.'

'Very well, Princess,' I said, and sat at the table. Haruka had already set out the platters Japanese-style. Each place setting had a number of small dishes. I checked them: savory chawanmushi egg custard, seaweed salad, some glisteningly fresh tuna sashimi, and a small dish of assorted pickles.

'There we are,' Haruka said, plating the salmon and covering the crisply fried fillets with the shining teriyaki sauce. 'Noodles, Miko?'

'Ready,' Miko said, and placed a portion of noodles on each plate next to the salmon. She grinned up at him. 'Our timing is perfect.'

'It is,' I said through a mouth of delicious pickled burdock root; it was crunchy and sour.

They put the plates on the table and sat with me.

'I can't believe you did all that in your kimono, and didn't get a speck of sauce on it,' I said, waving my chopsticks at Haruka.

He quirked a smile. 'I was too lazy to take it off – it's a full set – so I asked Marque to put a barrier around it.' He clasped his hands together, and the three of us said the blessing in unison. 'Itadakimasu.'

'Is that a new obi?' I asked him.

He looked down at the design of tuna fish in different shades of blue. 'Yes. A gift from the colony I visited today, to thank me for arranging the trade deal and facilitating the fast transfer of the embryos and harvested tuna.'

'What about the icosapod talekeeper?' I asked.

'Haruka showed it Pacifica, and it was very impressed,' Miko said. 'It will speak to its family, and they'll let us know in the next day or so. We want to move them off there as quickly as possible.'

'I think they'll take the Pacificans' offer,' Haruka said. 'We need to spread the word over their planet, but I had to hurry back to do the tuna negotiations.' He swept his long green hair back over his shoulder. 'Eat this before it gets soggy.' He dug his chopsticks into the salmon, pulled the skin away, and tried it. 'Particularly this part.'

He was right – the skin was crisp and melted in my mouth. I devoured the salmon while they discussed the trade deal and the other goldenscales' progress in gating.

Haruka stopped. 'Did you skip lunch again, Jian? You need to look after yourself.'

'Not only did I not skip lunch, I've been snacking all

afternoon and I'm still starving,' I said ruefully.

'Her hormone levels are borderline indicating early pregnancy,' Marque said.

'Stop telling everyone, Marque, this is my business.' I spoke to my spouses. 'Don't get too excited, it could be another false alarm.'

They shared a delighted look.

'Who will look after the Guard if you're pregnant, though?' Haruka asked, rising to collect the empty plates. 'No, you sit, I've seen the news – you were rushed off your feet as the Empress showed the new species around.'

I sat back down as he collected the plates, put them in the kitchen for Marque to clean, and pulled a big platter of fruit out of the fridge. He placed it on the table and I selected a peach.

'Have you had enough? I can make another salmon for you and more noodles,' he asked, concerned.

'No, this is plenty, although I may snack later,' I said.

He glanced at Miko. 'She's definitely pregnant.'

'Yeah, looks like it,' Miko said. She shook her dragon head. 'This is overwhelming.'

'You had five years to get used to the idea,' I said, peeling the peach. 'I still have no clue on who to appoint as acting head if I take the time off.'

'Namazozo or Graf are the obvious choices,' Haruka said. 'Although Graf can be a little… prickly, and Namazozo's really too sweet to command respect.' He saw my face. 'No, I have nothing more to offer than what you already know. I have no idea.'

'Honored Ex-Captain of the Guard Shudo requests entry,' Marque said. 'He said he'd like to visit.'

'Show him in,' Haruka said.

Shudo came in, accompanied by his grandchildren, who were six years old now. They were smaller versions of him, as tall as my knees, round and furry with wide mouths full of teeth.

Some of them still had their dark purple baby stripes against their bright pink fur. There were nine of them, and they ran through the apartment like hobgoblins, looking at everything.

'You've seen everything in here before, why do you have to check it again?' he asked, exasperated.

'It's fun!' one of the kids shouted.

One of them came up to me and pulled at my uniform. 'Where's the furryfriend?'

'Nashi's visiting my son and his daughter. You just missed her,' I said. 'She'll be back in a couple of days.'

'We want to see her next time!' the child yelled, then ran back to the others. They had an excited conversation about 'furryfriends'.

Shudo pulled himself up onto one of the chairs. 'Ooh, Earth fruit. Any potatoes?'

'Not today, we weren't expecting guests,' Haruka said with a smile.

'Potatoes!' one of the children shouted, and they started an impromptu dance circle in the living room, making up a song about potatoes.

'Sorry,' Shudo said. 'They should be exhausted; I took them swimming today. I think they're over tired. But' – he glanced at them with affection – 'they'll be big enough to go to socialization school on my homeworld in a few weeks, and I can return to duty.' He turned back to us. 'If you'll have me, Jian.'

'Do you want your job as captain back?' Miko asked. 'Because Jian really enjoys being captain and doesn't want to resign. If you want the job back she'll be unhappy because you're her friend and she doesn't want conflict with you.'

Shudo waved one furry arm at Miko. 'Are all the goldenscales like you, Princess, once you have them talking? You're wiser than your colored sisters.'

'I know,' I said. 'They're all very wise. Being in servitude may have had something to do with it.'

'I can't believe I watched you serve Masako for years and

never knew,' Shudo said. 'You were so quiet and meek – and you hid your skills and insight. What a waste.'

'I think so too,' she said. 'But some of my goldenscales sisters are having difficulty making the transition to full citizens. It's hard being responsible for your own life decisions.'

'And as to your question, no, I don't want to take over as captain. I think Jian's doing a fine job and she can have the paperwork with my genitally fragrant blessings,' Shudo said.

'Is there anything to eat? I'm hungry,' one of the children asked him, tugging on his fur.

'We're having a meal when we get home, so you can wait,' Shudo said, pulling the furball onto his lap.

'I need to use the toilet *right now*!' another one shouted.

Shudo raised his voice. 'Does anyone else need to use the toilet?'

'No!' all the other children yelled.

'I'll take her,' Marque said. 'You were in the middle of talking about the captain's job.'

'I'd love to appoint you as deputy if you can handle being number two,' I said. 'And you can definitely act in the position of captain if I take time off.'

The furball jumped down from Shudo's lap and ran to follow Marque's sphere to the bathroom; he'd changed his mind about the toilet.

'Yes,' Shudo said. 'I'd like to re-join the Guard, as an ordinary member, or deputy if you need my skills. Graf approached me and asked me to do it; it's concerned that you may give it the job of acting captain if you take time off. You definitely smell pregnant.'

'Do I now?' I asked.

'Uh … yeah,' Shudo said. 'You smell … more acidic.'

'You said that the last time and I wasn't pregnant at all,' I said.

'One of the kids is having trouble,' Marque said. 'They have feces in their fur and they're too embarrassed to let me clean them up.'

'That's my cue,' Shudo said, climbing down from the chair. 'The best part of being a care-parent. Poo Patrol.' He grinned at Miko. 'Can you gate us home when I'm done cleaning him up? They demanded to come here with me because they know you're a goldenscales and they want to see a gate.'

'Oh,' Miko said, her eyes wide. 'Of course. I'd love to. They're adorable.'

He went into the bathroom, passing the remaining children who had graduated to jumping on the sofas.

'Are human dragonscales children this much work?' Miko asked.

'Absolutely,' Haruka said with relish. 'Back in Tokyo, I ran the entire Imperial household ragged. Three staff members resigned, and I was relatively well-behaved for a dragonscales.' He grinned. 'I love every part of being with children. I'm definitely looking forward to Poo Patrol.'

'A tenth says you'll get poo on one of your nicest kimonos within a couple of weeks, even with Marque's help,' I said.

'I'm glad all dragonscales are girls,' he said amiably. 'Boys squirt when you change them.'

'You've had that done to you?' Miko asked, horrified.

He nodded. 'When I visited Aki and his kids.'

'You're a dragonscales and you're not a girl,' Miko said.

'Damn straight I'm not,' he replied, his voice determined. His expression went wry. 'I wonder why I feel so male? Being in a female body felt very ... wrong.'

'We have a theory about that, but we don't generally share it with other species because it freaks some of them out,' Miko said, lowering her voice so the rowdy children couldn't hear her. 'It may have something to do with the bodies your soul has inhabited over the millennia through natural reincarnation. If you've been incarnated human male more than human female, your soul feels more comfortable in a male body.'

'What about non-human bodies?' I asked, fascinated. 'We

must have inhabited millions of them.'

'Those would be the people whose identity is "I don't belong in a human body and all my sensory inputs are confusing and wrong"—'

I raised my hands. 'I see your point.' I lowered them. 'I wonder what sort of bodies I've inhabited in the past. I certainly feel human female.'

'I definitely feel human male, regardless of the dragon scales,' Haruka said. His expression softened. 'And I cannot wait to have a daughter.'

'Neither can I,' I said.

'Me three,' Miko said, and we shared a smile.

Shudo came out carrying a child under each arm, both of them still damp. 'I'd better take them home, they're starving and whatever that is, it smells delicious. Miko, could you show them a gate?'

'I'd be delighted,' Miko said. 'Where to exactly?'

'My house in the residential district? I'm in ...' He said the name of his homeworld in his own language. 'Tower, floor two hundred eighty, apartment two.'

Marque rattled off a series of numbers.

'What, just like that?' Shudo asked, astonished. 'You can hear the co-ordinates to a place you've never been, and just gate there?'

'If it's within a light year of where I've been before, yes,' she said, and the gate appeared in the middle of the living room. The children squealed with delight and ran up to touch it with their little hands, making more noise when their hands went inside.

'She's the only one that can do it,' I said with pride. 'She's trying to teach the others, but they don't seem to have the skill.'

'You're right, Jian, she is exceptional.' Shudo bowed to Miko. 'I apologize for many years of treating you as lesser. I think Jian's correct when she says you're the equal of any colored dragon.'

'Just don't say that in front of them, I don't want to antagonize them,' Miko said. One of the children went through the gate and came back, and now all of them were swapping in and out. 'I love my sisters.'

'Saying you're an equal isn't antagonizing anyone,' I said.

'Heh, dragons,' Shudo said. 'Bye, Jian. As soon as I book the kids for socialization, I'll give you a call.'

'I look forward to it,' I said.

He shooed them through the gate. Miko concentrated for a moment to make sure they were all safe, then closed it.

The room was silent, and we shared a look.

'Nope, I still want this,' I said.

'Just don't have a litter,' Haruka said, returning to his tangerine.

'Oh, yes, please,' Miko said. 'I'd love a dozen of them.'

Both Haruka and I stared at her.

'Maybe I should do it too?' She looked from Haruka to me. 'What?'

'Two babies at once might be a little difficult,' I said. 'Particularly when a goldenscales child is an unknown quantity.'

'Let's see what happens with Jian's child, then you and I can talk,' Haruka said.

'We must include Jian in that talk,' Miko said.

'Of course,' Haruka said.

'I'm still unable to confirm,' Marque said from the ceiling. 'Wait another couple of days.'

4

The Empress herself took us to the Hive in her ship. Marque put me in a bubble of higher gravity when we arrived in orbit above the main colony planet, but left Graf, the Empress and Leggy in the lower gravity. Graf was an enormous spider, twice as tall as me, with pearlescent shining fur on its abdomen and legs, and eight glistening eyes. Leggy was one of the oldest Imperial Guards – he'd been a guard for nearly a hundred years. His species were similar to an Earth stick insect, with a two-meter-long narrow body the color of Earth tree bark, nine pairs of long legs and a single pair of wings. Like Graf he towered over me, walking carefully on his stilt-like legs. The two exoskeletal aliens were more comfortable in lower gravity, and the dragon was capable in surviving in almost any environment.

The dominant Hive Queen occupied a hollow satellite made of amber-colored silicate glass that orbited their homeworld. The workers extruded the silicate in strands from their butts and wove it haphazardly into the structure. The multiple round airlocks were ten meters across, and a mass of smaller tan-colored workers acted as doors, pulling back to release a puff of atmosphere and allow the larger transient workers to fly in and out. Some workers walked over the structure, extruding the silicate and adding glass to walls. Others kept the atmosphere fed by carrying it up from the planet below in large glass containers. Each worker looked similar to an Earth fly, with eight jointed legs, six narrow transparent wings, and a pair of eyes on long stalks.

Outside the satellite's thin layer of atmosphere, the workers surrounded themselves in glass cocoons, and squirted the air out of holes in them to travel through space. They jetted around the Empress' ship, gleaming golden in the Hive system sun. A worker came into view above the Empress' ship and waved from within its cocoon for us to follow it. The Empress folded us out of her ship, and Marque carried me, in a bubble of atmosphere, to follow the Empress as she swam down onto the Hive's surface. We landed softly next to one of the entrances and the mass of connected workers shifted to reveal an opening. We went into the chamber made of twisting amber glass threads, where a male was waiting. The male didn't have wings, and its black body marked its gender. A few workers buzzed close to see if it required anything, then flew away when it ignored them. We walked up to it, and it crossed its main pair of antennae at us, the silver scales on the sides of its furry head marking it as a dragonscales child of the Empress.

It didn't speak, just turned and led us inside the Hive. The light shone golden through the glass walls, and we entered the main tunnel, ten meters high with workers flying in and out above us. A couple of soldiers – deep purple, the size of a small bus, and with fearsome blades on their front legs – crossed their antennae as we passed them. They were too big to exit through the airlocks and lived their entire lives inside the Hive.

We travelled through tunnels that became narrower and smaller, with more soldier guards, until we were at the central nesting chamber. The Queen floated in the center, curled up in a scrum of workers, a pulsing white mass from which was difficult to differentiate head from body. The drone turned to us, crossed its antennae, and walked through a hole in the wall nearby.

The noise was incredible; the thrumming of the workers' wings made the entire structure vibrate.

'Hey, Silver,' the Queen said through Marque. 'It's good to see my favorite dragon.'

'You too, darling Hive,' the Empress said. 'Life treating you well?'

'Can't complain. Terraforming's complete on the fourth planet of our twenty-fifth colony system, and agriculture's commenced. We have twenty-five interlinked Queens now, more than we've had in any time in our history.' A group of workers emerged from holes in the wall carrying irregular-shaped spheres made from their amber butt-glass and filled with black liquid, with a small hole at the top to drink out of. 'Food?'

'Thank you,' the Empress said, taking one of the spheres and sipping from it. 'Magnificent.'

The workers approached each of us. Graf refused, Leggy carefully accepted a sphere on its manipulating front appendage, and I also took a sphere through the wall of my gravity bubble. I took a sip – the flavor was unique and rich; sweet and dark and full of depth, and even better than the Hive wine sold on the dragon homeworld. Hive wine was nearly as valuable as potatoes throughout the Empire, but I'd never tasted it this aged. It must have been a special vintage for the Queen herself.

'You now occupy every habitable agricultural world in your systems,' the Empress said. 'Are you planning to expand outside your district?'

'No, of course not. We're well aware of how we are perceived from our pre-Empire behavior. We won't scare anyone else; we'll stay within our own district. We're safe and content to harvest our wine and visit with our Imperial siblings. Peaceful exchange of knowledge and art is far preferable to absorbing others into our shared consciousness.' The Queen hesitated, then said, 'That isn't why you're here, is it? You have both Graf and Leggy with you, and I understand the significance.'

'It's one of the reasons,' the Empress said, cradling the wine in her front claws. 'You're right about your previous behavior being disturbing – the Mushrooms will never trust you. But this business with the cats—'

'We won't stop,' the Queen said, interrupting her.

'Why are you doing this? Haven't you done the Mushrooms enough harm? Allowing the cats to go through your district and right to the edge of Mushroom space ...'

'Have the cats harmed any Mushrooms? If they have, the deal is off.'

'No. But the Mushrooms now have a dozen cat ships at the edge of their district demanding passage, and if they go around they'll be back out on the edge of the galaxy where they started. They're stuck there with no way home.'

'The Mushrooms said no?'

'The Mushrooms have sensibly refused to talk to them!'

'Oh.' The Queen was quiet for a moment. 'The Mushrooms refused to talk to us about it as well, when we tried to explain to them.'

'Can you blame them?'

'Of course not. But the cats offered something that we couldn't refuse for the passage through our district, and if the Mushrooms started negotiating, I'm sure they'd permit the cats through as well.'

'What could the cats possibly offer that would convince you to let them into your space?' the Empress asked. 'Whatever they're offering, you're putting your whole district at risk! What if they decide to take your wine and kill your Queens?'

'I'm glad you're here, because this is something that I needed to tell you in person, rather than through your meddling AI. We wish we could live without it altogether, but it's needed for translation,' the Queen said. 'We're trading passage through our district for their child slaves.'

All of us shared a moment of shock.

'What are you doing with them?' the Empress asked, her voice strained. 'After what you did to the Mushrooms ...'

'You're not using them for food,' Graf said. 'You can't be using them for food.'

'Empress, if they're eating the cats' child slaves, my people won't hesitate ...' Leggy said.

'Don't be ridiculous,' the Queen snapped. 'We're rescuing them. Their families won't take them back once they're sold into cat slavery, so we're buying them and we'll keep them safe until they reach adulthood and their contracts are complete.'

'Where?' the Empress asked.

'On our agricultural worlds. We've set up a few settlements for them, and we're teaching them to be good citizens of the Empire. Hopefully they'll return home and share the benefits of Empire membership.' She lowered her voice. 'It's our way of atoning for our past ... transgressions.'

'Hostages,' I said with wonder.

'We are not holding them for ransom,' the Queen said with forced dignity.

'No – hostages in the Euroterre sense. It was something my people did after the Middle Kingdom War,' I said. 'Marque has the translation wrong.'

'Oh,' the Queen said. 'Yes. Taken from their families into ours and taught our ways, as a diplomatic strategy to make them more benign towards us. Yes.'

'Why didn't you tell me you were doing this?' the Empress asked.

'Would you trust us to do it right? With our history?' the Queen asked. 'The Mushrooms are already prejudiced against us; they would be furious and quite sure we're eating those kids.'

'Are you?'

The Queen's body made a deep rumbling sound that vibrated through the floor, powerful enough to crack some of the glass threads. The workers squealed in sympathy.

'I don't think there's any translation for what they just said,' Marque said.

'We are trying to atone for our past mistakes,' the Queen said. 'Tell us to stop, and we will.'

'I want to see one of the settlements,' the Empress said.

The rumble changed in pitch. 'I would be delighted.' The Queen shivered over her massive white body. 'I'm glad you've brought your captain, there's something she needs to see.'

I was still stunned by the implications of her words as Marque lifted my gravity ball, sealed it with energy, and carried me to follow half-a-dozen workers who guided us back out of the satellite. Another set of workers, already in their cocoons, were waiting for us near the glass surface, and escorted us down to the agricultural planet below. This was the Hive's origin world, and completely covered in the red-brown filaments of the fungi they ate. Imperial scientists believed that there had originally been a complex ecosystem on the planet, but the symbiotic relationship between the Hive and the fungus had wiped everything else out.

The Hive had spread throughout its allocated Imperial space, clearing all habitable worlds and processing the animal life on them into a protein slurry that it stored in glass silos as a food store for itself. It then covered the planets with the fungus, left workers and a Queen there, and a colonizing swarm moved on to the next system to find more protein. No wonder their first pre-Empire contact with another sentient species – the Mushrooms, a high-protein fungal consciousness that they found edible – had been such a disaster. When the Hive had first joined the Empire, everybody had assumed the Hive would use Marque to synthesize the proteins it needed. The Hive instead refused to have anything to do with the AI because of Marque's actions during the Hive-Mushroom War. The dragons attempted to teach the Hive about animal husbandry with tailored bacteria to grow its own protein, but the concept was so far outside the Hive's experience that after sixty years of attempts, the Empire had given up. Now, as part of the Empire, the Hive peacefully traded Hive wine with other Empire species for the pre-processed protein supplements it needed.

When we reached the surface of the planet, the workers shed their glass cocoons by shattering them on special hardened glass spikes, then flew over the twisting mass of red-brown filaments that covered everything. Each filament ranged in size from hair-thin to a meter across, and seemed to be growing and spreading as we watched. Workers hovered busily above the filaments, slicing off the topmost layer with specially evolved, knife-like forelegs. The cut filaments oozed a bright red liquid, and other workers followed to drink it. When they were full they flew away to eject it into glass storage towers, some of which were hundreds of meters tall, where it was fermented into Hive wine.

We travelled over the fungus-covered landscape for five kilometers until we reached a pair of glass structures. They were two connected domes constructed of the amber twining glass. We landed in front of the structure where a small cleared area was covered in a rippling glass floor to stop the fungus from encroaching. The fungus forest towered above the domes like it wanted to absorb them.

The doors weren't made of glass, they were made of plant cellulose – similar to wood but snowy white. They opened to a small airlock and we went in.

On your guard, Captain, this has similarities to their pre-Empire protein processing facilities, the Empress said.

I nodded and tapped my weapon on my hip without drawing it. Graf and Leggy both raised one appendage to indicate their readiness.

The interior door opened and I stood transfixed. The dome was full of amber light from its glass walls, and workers were visible in holes above us, using their wings to ventilate the facility. The spacious area had chairs and tables made from butt-glass, but enhanced with fittings from all over the Empire: thick, soft rugs from the wool of Tsingai, plates and cups of ceramic and metal, and even a kitchen that must have been salvaged – or purchased – from an Empire ship. The Hive had been scrounging Empire resources to make the children more comfortable. There were fifteen children present, sitting on the furniture or on the floor, in a variety of species that were all subjugates of the Cat Republic.

'I never knew about any of this,' Marque said. 'I have no presence on this planet, as per the Hive's request.'

'Now that you have a presence, perhaps you can help us,' a cat child said as it approached us, followed by three of the other children. The cat had short white fur with black tips, making her appear silver as she moved.

'Why are you here?' the Empress asked. 'The cats don't trade their own children.'

'Yes, we do,' the cat child said. 'My family was murdered in inter-clan warfare twelve years ago, and the clan that won all their possessions sold me to the Hive.'

'We're glad they did; Newmea's our leader and very smart,' an Eh-Yi-Oh-Eh said. The bear-like alien had long golden fur and stood on four legs.

'Uo?' I asked.

'Yes?' the Eh-Yi said. 'How do you know me?'

'I'm Jian Choumali,' I said. 'I rescued your mother from a cat and cared for her until she reached adulthood and returned home to her family. I loved her like a daughter.'

The Eh-Yi backed away. 'You're Choumali?' It skidded backwards, turned and limped as fast as it could into the dual-level sleeping area at the side of the dome. 'Keep it away from me!'

I nodded to the worker that had been following us. 'Thank you for keeping my granddaughter safe.'

'We're pleased that you know about this now,' the Hive said.

'We need help from the Empire – some of the children are sick. Uo was severely injured when she arrived, and close to death, and we were very fortunate to save her.'

'Are any more of these children in need of medical care?' Marque asked.

'The sick children are in another facility on this world. One child came in with a communicable disease and gave it to a few others with similar protein chains. I'll take you to them.'

'Let's go,' the Empress said. She turned her head on her long neck to see me. 'Would you like to stay here and talk to the Eh-Yi, Jian? I think we can trust the Hive's good intentions.'

'By your leave, Majesty,' I said.

'Very well. Marque, leave a small instance of yourself here to assist Jian, and then let's go see what we can do for these sick children.'

The Marque sphere opened and a copy the size of a tennis ball flew out.

'We'd also like to discuss trading for better facilities for them – the low gravity is harming their bones, and their bathrooms are entirely unacceptable,' the Hive said through the worker. 'Now that you know, you can help us. Under the terms of our agreement with the cats, they can't leave Hive space, but we can make them more comfortable.'

'I could help if you'd allow me to stay—' the big Marque sphere said as they headed towards the airlock.

'No,' the Hive said, and the doors closed behind them.

The children stood watching me.

'Are you happy here?' I asked them. 'Is the Hive looking after you?'

None of them replied.

'Does it make you work? Are you prisoners in the dome? Are you treated well?'

They stood uncertainly and still didn't reply.

I sat on the carpet. 'Would you like to hear a story about my life on the dragon homeworld?'

Their reluctance disappeared. They moved quickly to sit around me and listen. Nearly all intelligent species treasured storytelling to share knowledge and experience. The few that didn't use stories used telepathy to share their life experiences, and still liked to hear verbal stories from non-telepathic visitors.

'I'm the dragon Empress' guard captain,' I said. 'I live in a tower on the dragon homeworld. Bring up an image, Marque.'

Marque generated a three-dimensional rotating depiction of Sky City, then zoomed in on the main square with parliament on one side and the palace on the other.

The children made loud sounds of wonder and scooted forward to study the image more closely.

'Is that the thing?' a mole child said, pointing at Marque with its mucus-covered tentacles. 'The talking thing that does the magic like these images?'

'Don't you dare do anything that could remotely be considered magic,' I said as the sphere spun in the air. I turned back to the children. 'It's very advanced technology, not magic. It's using energy to make the images. Yes, it talks, it is very intelligent, and it assists people in the Empire. It carries us and shields us and helps us to live long, healthy lives.'

'My organic friends are precious to me,' Marque said. 'Like you are honored to be contracted to the cats by your families, I am honored to serve you. As Jian said, I am here to help.'

'I am as well,' I said. 'I assume that you're allowed out of the dome to see the sky?'

The children nodded, sharing meaningful glances.

'We're not prisoners – we can leave the dome any time. The Hive takes us on educational journeys,' the cat Newmea said. 'We've been to a few places – even to space! And the Hive doesn't ask for labor or … entertainment in return.'

'It's weird,' one of the other aliens said.

'The cats are different from everybody,' I said. 'What they do to you is against the law in the dragon empire. Trafficking in children is wrong.'

'That's what the Hive said,' one of the children said.

'At first we didn't believe that we weren't toys for the workers,' one of the children said, then made a long, loud braying sound. 'Now we know much better – toys for workers! That's like being a toy for a machine.'

'Anyway, I travel the stars – you've seen the stars?' I asked. They all nodded with enthusiasm.

'Show them the Empress' ship, Marque.'

Marque changed the image to the Empress' ship, then exploded it to a three-dimensional diagram. It zoomed in on the ship, then zoomed out to show the ship in orbit around the dragon homeworld.

The children made more sounds of awe and studied the images with their eyes wide.

Marque zoomed the image out again, to show the folding nexus – a network of nodes and tunnels in stationary orbit around the planet. It took over the dialogue.

'When the first dragon learned how to fold,' it said, as a dragon appeared in the image, 'she discovered another species far from her own. She fell in love and had children with the people she visited.' It brought up a visual of a fleet of dragon ships. 'The dragons travelled the galaxies, seeking love and making families wherever they went. Their leader is the dragon Empress, but all species that have loved dragons now have input into how things are run in a truly democratic and peaceful society.'

I took the narrative back, not wanting to hear the 'story of the Empire' for the millionth time. 'I travel the stars with the Empress, sharing joy and love and the benefits of being in the Empire – which includes *no selling children*,' I said.

Marque's visuals gave the children a travelogue of the Empire's best tourist spots. It shifted to a street in the Embassy district on the homeworld, where people were strolling along a wide avenue lined with eating areas and galleries, with occasional musical performances within sound bubbles. It played some of the music and the children listened, rapt.

'In fact, we have a rule in the Empire: *children are cared for and loved and never hurt*.'

Marque changed the view to a socialization school on the homeworld where the parliamentary delegates' children – a stunning variety of species – shared knowledge and stories. It zoomed outside to a physical challenge playground – complete with high ropes – and showed the children flying from tower to tower. One of the children fell from the ropes and my small audience squealed, then squealed again when, in the image, Marque collected the fallen child and lowered her to the ground safely.

The children around me excitedly discussed the challenge course, but the cat girl wasn't convinced.

'My mother said that dragons lie about everything and never to believe what one says,' she said.

'Yes, sometimes dragons do lie,' I said. 'But I'm not a dragon, and I won't. Not to you. What you're seeing here is real. Ask me anything and I'll tell you the truth. I have nothing to gain from lying to you; you'll be here until you're adults and then you'll go back to your families.'

'I appreciate what the Hive has done for us, but I have nobody to take me back.' Newmea folded over her knees cat-style. 'I don't want to spend the rest of my life here, even if the Hive buys more children to keep me company.' She looked up at me with her huge amber eyes. 'I want to travel and see places, without people hurting me!'

'How long before you're an adult?' I asked.

'I already am,' Newmea said. 'I have no family to return to.'

'What about you others?' I asked the rest of the children.

They gave differing lengths of time that Marque translated into Earth years for me. The oldest was a mole and would be free in a few weeks.

'My family will welcome me home,' the mole said. 'They'll be happy that I reached adulthood without dying – and probably glad that the Hive helped me.'

'Good,' I said. 'Who else will be welcomed by their families?'

The rest of the children indicated themselves, all except for Newmea. Uo pointedly ignored me from where she lay on the floor.

Newmea curled up tighter. 'My family are dead. I can either stay here or return to the cat homeworld and enter a reproductive contract.' She buried her face in her knees. 'I don't want to do that; it'll be the same as being a toy – except with sexual demands on top of it.' She raised her head to see me. 'The Hive says I can stay, and I am deeply thankful, but there isn't much to do here.'

'You can come with me,' I said. 'I have a cat son already and he lost his family as well. He'd be happy to help care for you – he'd love to have a fellow cat to talk to. And before you think about sexual demands, he's in a relationship with a dragon and they have a dragonscales child together. Nobody in the Empire is allowed to make sexual demands – that's illegal too.'

Her eyes went wide and she smiled the cat way – all whiskers and teeth. 'That sounds too good to be true.'

'Don't go with her,' Uo said from the side of the room where she'd been listening. 'She'll *kill* you. The dragons are *liars*. This human kept my mother a prisoner for *years*!'

'Yes, I did keep her prisoner for over a year – because if I let her out, she jumped into the ocean and tried to drown herself,' I said. 'When she stopped doing it, I released her, and when she reached adulthood I arranged passage for her to go home – where you were born, Uo. Tell Newmea that I'm lying about that.'

'You lie about everything,' she snapped, approaching on four legs. She limped slightly, her hind legs wobbly and weak.

The children didn't know who to believe, but from their emotional aura it was obvious that they tended to dismiss Uo's claims, and her rage indicated that she was aware of it.

'I did the best I could for your mother, Uo. I gave her a name in my language.' I wiped my eyes. 'I loved her like my own child and it broke my heart to see her selling you to the cats. That is wrong – look at what they did to you, they nearly killed you. When you're home, tell your mother to come visit me where I live in a beautiful tower with my spouses and my cat son and my family who will all give you more love and hugs than you can ever need.'

'I believe it,' she said. She lay on the glass floor, then grunted with pain and shifted her back end. 'You want to break up my family and take my mother away from her homeworld. As soon as I'm an adult I can go home and they will love me better than any of your mixed-up families.'

'I'm sure they will,' I said. 'Your mother has a good heart.'

'My mother is the *best*,' Uo said.

'She sold you, and the cats nearly killed you,' the mole said.

'No. That was my decision,' Uo said. 'I did it for my family.'

'They still nearly killed you,' Newmea said.

'And I would have died happily, knowing that my family would be safe,' Uo said.

'This is so broken,' I said. 'So wrong. You should not be sacrificed like this just for the cats' amusement.'

'If it kept my family safe I'd do it a million times over,' Uo said.

'I understand and respect that,' I said. 'In the meantime, the cats have a valid arrangement with the Hive for you to stay here for the rest of your contracts, and we'll do our best to make you more comfortable.'

'Can you fix Uo's hip?' Newmea asked. 'It makes her cry sometimes.'

'Shut up,' Uo barked.

'Yes,' Marque said. 'I can fix your injuries and free you from pain. Just give me permission and I will make you pain-free.'

'Stay away from me,' Uo said.

'Let it help you, Uo,' Newmea said. 'It makes all of us sad to see you in pain.'

'We're supposed to be in pain, we're cat toys,' Uo said. 'If we're not in pain, we're not doing it right. The cats are cruel but we are noble and I will suffer this as long as my contract is valid.'

One of the smaller workers flew down from the ventilation holes and was replaced by another. It landed next to me, its head with its faceted rainbow eyes close to mine.

'Can you provide them with higher gravity, Marque?' it asked. 'The low gravity of our planet is harming their bones.'

'I can,' Marque said. 'But I'll need to stay here to maintain—'

'Without staying here,' the worker buzzed. 'Put some dense matter in the floor or something. We do not want you here.'

'I can do that,' Marque said. 'But the children will need to move out of the dome while I infuse the glass.'

'That will hurt Uo,' I said. 'It looks like the only reason she's mobile is because of the lower gravity.'

'I don't care!' Uo said.

'Can you fix her?' the worker asked Marque.

'I can,' Marque said.

'No!' Uo said.

'Don't do it until we have a plan worked out,' the worker said. 'There are multiple locations where we're holding the children.' It turned its head towards me, the rainbows shifting in its faceted eyes. 'Captain Choumali, may I speak to you in private? Without the Empress or the AI present?'

'Of course,' I said.

'Outside the dome,' the worker said.

'Thanks for visiting us, Captain,' Newmea said. 'I'll think about what you said.'

'I meant it,' I said, then pulled myself to my feet and followed the worker out of the dome.

5

Another worker flew down, holding a half-formed glass cocoon. 'We want to speak to you out of range of the AI. Please enter this and we will carry you away from it.'

I stepped into the cocoon. A couple of workers flew up and completed it, exuding glass from their butts until I was enclosed in a glass coffin.

The worker placed its head on the glass and surprised me by speaking dragon, almost unintelligible through its hairy mouthparts. 'Do you speak the dragon language?'

'I do, I had it implanted a long time ago,' I said.

'Tap the glass if you run out of air, but we're not taking you out of the atmosphere.'

I nodded. Five larger workers – each three meters long – flew to me and carried me in their forelegs.

'Do you want me to listen in?' Marque asked through comms. 'I'm not a hundred per cent sure they can be trusted.'

'No,' I said.

'I'm glad I backed up your memories last night. You should

have done an incremental backup and left your soulstone with me.'

'That would be an insulting display of distrust.'

'Not if they're planning to eat you.'

'They won't eat me! Put me on privacy and butt out.'

'Very well.'

The workers flew me for five minutes, then smashed the cocoon on a spike and caught me as I fell out of it.

'Are you harmed?' one of them asked.

'No, not in this lower gravity,' I said.

I followed the workers, walking carefully through the fungal jungle. Without Marque's assistance to keep the gravity higher, any sudden moves I made could easily cause me injury. We arrived in a round clearing the size of a house with a dome-shaped roof of woven fungal filaments, with the sun shining in amber rays through the gaps. A glass effigy of the Hive Queen herself, as tall as me, sat in the middle, making the area look like a place of worship.

A larger worker was waiting for us in front of the effigy and crossed its feelers at me. Its face was strange – instead of the usual mouthparts it had what looked like lips and teeth. The human attributes on the insect's face were deeply disturbing. When it spoke, there was no buzz – the Hive had grown this worker specifically to speak to me.

'Thank you for coming, Captain,' it said in dragon. 'We understand and honor your show of trust. Are you sure the AI isn't listening?'

'I'm sure,' I said. 'I put myself on privacy.'

'Thank you.' It gestured towards the statue with its feelers. 'This is our first attempt at art – a self-portrait. The Empire has taught us about art and music and shared stories, and it has given us greater understanding. We will add effigies of the other species that we selfishly destroyed before the Empire taught us empathy, as a tribute to their sacrifice when we have no other way to atone.'

'It's beautiful – aesthetically pleasing, and brings joy to my heart,' I said, hoping I sounded honest rather than diplomatic. 'I'm sure the Empire will appreciate that you are working to redeem yourselves.'

'Thank you.' The worker turned and a cloud of tiny insects rose from behind the effigy and hovered in front of me. 'You are aware that we can modify our genome to create workers to suit any task?'

'Yes,' I said. 'Although I didn't realize you could become so small.'

'We can become even smaller: so small that the AI doesn't detect us,' the worker said. 'We've engineered them to appear as insect life native to the dragon homeworld.'

'You have agents on the dragon homeworld?' I asked. 'How did you travel there?'

'Hitched a ride on the Empress herself,' the worker said. 'We have ridden dragons throughout the Empire.'

'Why?'

'During the conflict with the Mushrooms, we were in negotiations with the cats. We were thinking of joining their Republic. They assured us that we would suffer no negative consequences from our activities with the Mushrooms – in fact, they offered us the Mushrooms as a food source in return for working with them.'

'I assume you're telling me this because you changed your mind.'

'We were ready to join them when we discovered what they do with the children. That is unacceptable.'

I stared silently at the worker, surprised that their mindset was capable of this level of ethics when they saw all other species – adults and children – as nothing more than a protein source.

'We understand why you treasure your children, Captain,' it said.

'Your workers are disposable, though.'

'You appreciate that they are disposable? You are not concerned when you see them destroyed at the end of their usefulness?'

'No, I'm aware of your shared consciousness,' I said. 'The workers are like the cells in my body.'

'And we understand how precious your children are,' the worker said. 'You have so few of them, and every one of them is a consciousness equivalent to the entirety of us. Look at you – you have been alive for so many years and are only just now carrying your first child. Even this single fetus is draining the life out of you – a huge biological investment.'

'I'm really pregnant? You can see it?'

The workers' buzz went louder, vibrating through me, then softer again. 'Yes.'

I hugged myself. 'Marque been telling everyone that it couldn't be sure yet!'

'Can Marque see inside you the way we can?'

'Yes.'

'So your AI lies,' the Hive said. 'That is why we spoke to you alone. We do not trust it.'

'I don't blame you,' I said. 'What it did to the goldenscales is unforgivable.'

'That too. But we understand how rare and precious your children are, and what the cats are doing is wrong. So we joined the Dragon Empire despite our misgivings about the dragons' honesty.'

'The dragons aren't perfect.'

'That's one way of putting it.'

'Okay, they're colonizing assholes. But you're right, the cats are worse. That's why humanity joined the Empire and used our leverage as weapons to force the dragons to stop. Now tell me about your agents on the dragon homeworld. What were you doing there?'

The worker shuffled its wings. 'Whatever the cats asked us. They asked us to carry a soulstone from Earth to a teleport portal, and we did.'

'Oh lord,' I said. 'What color was it?'

'Red. It was—'

I didn't let it finish. 'That was my son's soulstone,' I said, my heart full of pain. 'He suffered the Real Death because of that.'

'We know. We are deeply sorry, Captain. We didn't know what we were doing. We are members of the Empire now, so the cats will no longer have the benefit of our assistance.'

'Are you asking my forgiveness?' I asked.

'No, we're asking if we should tell the Empress that we helped the cats. Your son's soulstone isn't the only action we took on behalf of the cats, and some of the cat listening devices we planted are probably still there. Will she expel us from the Empire if we tell her?'

'I knew it,' I said. 'We thought someone was spying on us, but the Empire is so transparent we didn't consider it a major issue. Has another species taken over your job of spying?'

'Not as invisibly as we did, but yes.'

'Can you help me find the agents?'

'Of course. We worked with them. We know exactly who they are.'

'Come on,' I said, and headed towards the shrine's exit. 'Let's go talk to the Empress, she'll be thrilled to bits to know the truth. We suspected for a while and if we know the location of the bugs we can feed a message of reconciliation to the cat subjugate species.'

'But how do you feel about this?' the worker asked, scurrying to follow me on its many legs. 'Please forgive us. We like you and want to be your friend, Captain.'

I lowered my head as I stepped into a new cocoon. 'That I will need to think about.' I raised my head. 'You helped take my child away from me.'

'You have another coming.'

'Not the same.'

'We understand that as well. And by the way, congratulations, you obviously didn't know.'

'I've thought a few times that I was pregnant and I wasn't,' I said. 'You're right about it sucking the life out of me. I've been feeling tired, hungry, and vaguely nauseous all the time.'

'What is "nauseous"? We don't know that word.'

I smiled grimly. 'You don't want to know.'

Two workers came and filled the wall of the cocoon with butt-glass. The worker that had spoken to me was swarmed by the smaller workers; they tore it into small pieces and spread them over the ground. Its sole purpose had been to speak to me, and it was no longer of any use.

*

The Empress and the other Imperial Guards were waiting for me with the children I'd spoken to, on the glass platform outside the children's dome. A large group of Hive workers had taken the dome's roof off and moved all the furniture onto the surrounding platform. Marque had generated a number of construction spheres and was creating a new floor out of a high-density material.

'I can feel it pulling at me,' Newmea said. 'What's it made of? Is it magnets?'

'No,' a Marque sphere above us said. 'Just really heavy stuff.'

'It won't hurt the planet?' I asked.

'You know me better than that, Jian,' Marque said.

'Yes, I do, that's why I'm asking.'

A child sidled up to me. It was covered in green scales that had feathery edges, and its face had two large front-facing eyes over a long snout with many teeth, giving it a bird-like appearance. 'You really have a baby inside you? Growing, like in an egg, but in your stomach? How does that *feel*?'

'The Hive told us,' the Empress said. 'Congratulations, Jian. I guess you're off field work for the duration.'

'I would have preferred to have privacy, Hive, so I can

control how the information is disseminated,' I said.

'That's why I didn't tell you yet,' Marque said. 'You asked me to stop sharing the information. I was waiting for us to return home and have some privacy.'

I hesitated, then said, 'I see. Thank you.'

'So how does it feel?' the bird-like alien asked. 'Does it move?'

'No, I can't feel anything yet, but I am a bit tired and hungry because it's taking its food from me,' I said.

'Is it half-dragon?' Newmea asked. 'Like all of the Eh-Yi?'

'It is,' I said. 'But its dragonfather is a goldenscales, so it may be different.'

'Golden!' Newmea said. 'Does your species lay eggs or give live birth? How long before it comes out? Will it grow quickly? How big will your stomach get? Will it come out through your belly? Will it *hurt* when it comes out?'

'Uh …' I smiled down at her. 'Sit here and I'll explain how it works while the Hive talks to the Empress and Marque finishes your dome.'

Uo sidled up to me. 'Is there only one baby in there?'

'Hey, Hive,' I shouted up at the workers buzzing on the fungus. 'You sure it's only one?'

'One, Jian,' the Hive replied.

'There you are, Uo,' I said. 'One baby. That's really good luck for an Eh-Yi, isn't it? Just one baby by itself is good fortune.'

'How do you know that?' Uo asked suspiciously.

'I wanted to care for your mother the very best I could, and that meant learning everything available about your culture so I could make her feel at home.'

'Oh,' Uo said, and rested her head on the glass floor.

'I'd like to spend some time with the Queen in orbit while Marque makes the alterations to the domes,' the Empress said.

'We'd like that, too,' the Hive said. 'Just make sure you take the AI with you when you leave.'

'Don't worry, dear Hive, I will.' The Empress nodded to me.

'I'd prefer you were present to watch my back, Captain.'

I saluted her. 'Ma'am.' I turned to the children. 'I have to do my job, so I can't tell you about having babies right now. If you like, I can come back when the baby's bigger.'

'Come back soon,' Newmea said.

'Remember what I said, Newmea and Uo,' I said as I went to the Empress. 'Both of you are welcome in my home. And Uo, please ask Marque to relieve your pain.'

'We'll talk to her for you,' Newmea said. Uo didn't reply, and the Empress folded us to the Queen's chamber.

*

The Empress folded us back to the orbital nexus on the dragon homeworld after she'd spent a couple of hours having sex with the Queen, and we took her private elevator down to the palace and returned to her office.

'Marque, start the arrangements for the medical care of those children, including Uo,' she said as she went behind her desk and pulled up the newsfeeds. 'And I'd like a full report on what the Hive discussed with you in private, Jian.'

'The Hive wants to tell you itself. I have a lot to unpack.' I turned to Leggy and Graf. 'Good job, guys, dismissed. Graf, meet me in my office at the end of the day and we'll do a temporary handover of my duties until Shudo is available.'

'Ma'am,' Graf said.

The guards each placed an appendage over their main hearts and went out.

'You're dismissed as well,' the Empress said. 'Go rest, and notify Shudo that he's up to do your job.' She smiled at me, all blue eyes and dragon teeth. 'Congratulations, Jian, another grandchild for me. This will be the first goldenscales child in living memory. I cannot wait to see.'

'It's your fault they haven't been able to have children until now,' I said. 'Does Marque have any records of what goldenscales children look like?'

Marque didn't reply, and I felt a shot of concern.

'What aren't you telling us, Marque?' I asked.

'It will be identical to a human dragonscales in most respects, except that the scales on its forehead will be gold,' Marque said. 'Don't be concerned, the child's genome is perfectly normal for a dragonscales. It won't be in any way inferior, and with its parents' outstanding heritage I expect it to be remarkable.'

'Thank you.' I bowed to the Empress with my hand over my heart, then went into my office.

Haruka and Miko were waiting for me, both of them full of joy. They rushed up to me and took turns hugging me and planting big kisses on me – even with Miko's messy dragon mouth.

'Guys, please, I need a moment,' I said, extricating myself from them and flopping to sit behind my desk. I leaned my head in my hands. 'You remember when my son David died?'

'You should be focusing on the joy of having a new child, not the loss of your dead one,' Haruka said. 'Don't do this to yourself, Jian.'

'You remember that David was in a relationship with that cat we rescued? The one that was supposed to be Oliver's wife in an arranged marriage? She and David had a relationship instead, and both of them died because of it?'

'We'll keep your baby safe, Jian, don't worry,' Miko said.

'No, you don't understand,' I said, still with my head in my hands. 'She took his soulstone, and handed it to an agent of the Republic to send back to their homeworld using their teleporters. That agent was the Hive. The Hive just told me – it infiltrated the dragon homeworld with tiny insects that Marque couldn't identify.' I dropped my hands and gazed at my spouses' confused faces. 'The Hive helped kill him.'

'Oh Jian,' Miko said, and both of them came around the desk to comfort me. They pulled me up and wrapped me in a joint hug.

'The Hive had agents here and I didn't know?' Marque asked.

'You are so worthless,' Haruka said, without letting go of me.

'But you were right about being pregnant,' Miko said. 'We have a child coming. You've mourned David, and that was a long time ago, Jian.' She touched my cheek – the back of her golden claws feather-light against my skin – and gazed into my eyes. 'You're giving me a gift I never thought I would receive. You have brought me from a silent, cowed servant to a proud, equal dragonfather. You're carrying the Empire's first goldenscales child. These are good things! Be happy, please – it breaks my heart to see you grieving.'

'No, Miko, don't be selfish. Don't force her to hide her pain to relieve yours,' Haruka said. He squeezed me. 'Take as long as you need. Go home and rest. ' He pulled me to my feet. 'Let's go home.'

'I'm sorry, Jian, Haruka's right,' Miko said.

'You're needed in the common room immediately, Captain,' Marque said. 'Six and Five-Shriek are fighting.'

'They're fighting?' Haruka asked. 'They can't even touch each other.'

'They constantly argue over everything,' I said with resignation. 'This was inevitable. Meet me at home after I've sorted them out.' They hugged me and went through the far door into our apartment, and I went onto the balcony above the common room. The Guard had decked the common room with human-style celebratory banners that said 'Congratulations on the baby'. They had human music playing and were setting up a table of food and drink.

'Where's Six and Five-Shriek?' I shouted over the noise.

The Guard all cheered.

'Congratulations, Captain Jian,' Namazozo said. 'We're celebrating your new family member. Come and join us!' She ran up the stairs to me. 'Tell her spouses, Marque.'

'But what about Six and Five-Shriek?' I asked.

Namazozo pointed: Six was a glowing word 'baby' hanging from the ceiling, and Five-Shriek was flying in circles beneath it.

Haruka and Miko emerged from my office onto the balcony and stood beside me. Haruka put his arm around my waist and the guard cheered again – someone had been teaching them human social interactions.

'You don't have to if you don't want to,' Haruka said.

Miko leaned into me. 'If you're still feeling sad about David, we can just go home.'

I looked around. All my lovely guards and my family were ready to celebrate this miraculous gift. My heart lifted and I felt the joy of the upcoming child. Miko saw me smile and grinned as well.

'Thanks, guys. I can't think of anything I'd like more.' I smiled at my spouses. 'I guess we do have something to celebrate.' I raised my arm. 'Let's party!'

The guard cheered again, and Haruka and Miko guided me down to the floor of the common room. The room was full of love for me and I wiped a tear from the corner of my eye.

'I can't tell you how much I appreciate you all,' I said.

'You'll have to do the same thing again with your family after this is done,' Marque said into my ear as I poured myself something non-alcoholic from the bottles labelled 'human'. 'The guard demanded they have the first chance to celebrate, and your mother is taking the opportunity to set up something even more elaborate for you on Earth.'

'I feel so loved,' I said, looking around.

'That's because you are, dear Jian,' Miko said.

'Is the Empress coming?' I asked.

'No, this is just for us,' Namazozo said. 'Guards only. The best of the best!' She climbed onto the table, raised her tiny cup and toasted the guards with it.

'Damn straight!' I said, and raised my own. 'My mother is going to kill me when she discovers that you guys got me first!'

'We can take her!' Namazozo said. 'The Guard are undefeated. Even the mighty Connie Choumali is no match for us!'

They cheered again and I was mobbed.

*

The evening was in full swing and the guards had moved all the furniture for an impromptu dance circle, when Marque contacted me. 'I have a message for you from your son,' it said. 'He says it's urgent and he needs to speak to you right now, Captain.'

'Put him through.'

'He says he needs to speak to you privately.'

'Oh.' I looked around.

'In your office,' Haruka said, gesturing. 'We'll wait.'

'If the party finishes just go up,' I said, and both of them nodded a reply.

I went up the stairs into my office and stopped behind the desk. 'Put Ollie through.'

Oliver appeared in holographic form in the middle of the room. He raised one hand, the black pads on his fingers visible between his fur. 'Hi, Mum!'

'Mum told you already?' I asked.

'Told me what?' he asked, confused.

'Oh, this isn't about me having a baby?'

'You're pregnant? With Miko's child?' He lit up. 'I'm going to be a brother. A little sister!' He spread his arms. 'I need to return to the homeworld and give you a huge hug. All of you. This is great news!' He sobered. 'Haruka's okay with it, isn't he?'

'Oliver, we're a trinary. Haruka's as thrilled as you are.' I grinned. 'And we're planning on having another one that's a mix of him and Miko as soon as this one is big enough.'

'That's brilliant news, Mum. I'll get there as soon as I can.'

'No rush, I'll be pregnant for a while.' I studied him. 'If you didn't want to speak with me about that, is there a problem? Marque said it was urgent. Everybody's okay, aren't they?'

'Don't worry, everything's fine. Annie would like to see you, but sometimes I think she's more interested in seeing her grandmother's new puppy than her actual grandmother.'

'You were supposed to get one of her own. There's still a few left in the latest litter.'

'She spends too much time at school to care for a dog by herself. Maybe when she's bigger.' He shifted uncomfortably. 'But Newmea, that little cat on the Hive world? She asked for more information about you, then contacted me directly, asking for asylum.'

'That's excellent news. Will you take her?'

He didn't reply and his ears drooped slightly.

'Ollie?'

He jerked straighter. 'Yeah, about that – she's a virgin female, and she should be desperate to return home. Her attitude is strange. This feels all wrong.'

'She's orphaned, has no family to return to, and doesn't want to enter the sexual slavery of a reproductive contract. Nothing strange about it.'

'You're thinking like a human, Mum. A human girl would be desperate to escape a reproductive contract. Cats see it very differently. A normal cat girl should be thrilled to bits at the opportunity to gain the wealth and status that having a clone child represents.'

'Even when it involves so much suffering?'

'Even then, Mum. The pain they suffer adds to the prestige of the martyrdom. They're regarded as weak and cowardly if they *don't* embrace the sacrifice of childbearing.'

'That's so—'

'Yeah, wrong, I know.'

'She's been away from her home and family for a long time, Ollie. Her attitude has probably changed. I'm not surprised she's asking for asylum: she can do anything she likes if she stays here with us.'

'If she goes home, she suffers for a year as a bonded servant, has the child, and then she's rich and free. If she stays with us, she can never go home and she will be pursued by nanos wanting to execute her for the rest of her life. The reproductive contract is a small price to pay for her freedom. This feels really wrong.'

'Are you sure you aren't an extra level of suspicious because of what happened with Cat and David?'

'I'm damn sure I'm an extra level of suspicious. I've made extensive studies of cat culture – and what Newmea is asking for is, frankly, unbelievable.' His ears drooped again. 'She's a spy, Mum.'

'Are you absolutely sure of that?' I said. 'Why would they plant another spy on us when we already know Cat was one? What if you send her home and her asylum request is genuine? Are you sure you want to risk it?'

He laughed. 'I won't send her home. I'll grant her asylum, and she can come live with me, Runa and Annie. Marque and I will study her, feed her fake information – and find out how she sends it back to the Republic. If we're lucky she may even assist me to infiltrate cat space.'

'You're as much of a spy as she is,' I said with wonder.

'I haven't been receiving specialized training in Sky City for nothing,' he said. 'Marque tells me there's a big guard party happening for you, so I'll leave it there – those things are famous. I just wanted to tell you that Newmea will be moving in with me and Runa.' His voice became wistful. 'If we're lucky, we may even turn her for real.'

'Just don't risk Annie's happiness. You know how the cats feel about dragonscales hybrids, and she's a cat one.'

'We'll be careful. I'll talk to you later. Love you, Mum. Give Miko and Haruka a hug for me – and hey, take care of yourself.'

'They'll make sure I will. Love you, Ollie.'

His hologram had already faded out. 'Bye.'

I exited my office to find the party still in full swing. Miko and Haruka grabbed me – physically lifting me – and carried me into the middle of the dance circle. They linked hands and sang a song about golden children that they had obviously just made up on the spot.

Someone pressed my glass into my hand and I raised it to them all.

6

'Jian, Green Sunset is outside the door, requesting urgent entry,' Marque said. 'She says it's very important.'

I checked the time on the wall near the bed: nine in the morning. Haruka and Miko were still asleep, with Miko as usual sandwiched between us. I'd overslept after staying late at the party.

Haruka groaned softly on the other side of the bed – he wasn't a morning person.

I pulled myself up to sitting. 'Let me speak to her.'

Marque opened the channel.

'Is there a problem, Sunset?' I asked.

'Jian. Marque said you were sleeping – but this is really important. I had to recuse myself because it's a Mushroom matter. The Mushroom President of Tropical Cavern Two is here seeing the Empress! The President was white with fury – he found out about the children. It's escalating into a diplomatic incident and the Imperial Guard needs your guidance.'

'What children?' I asked, touching my stomach.

'The ones the Hive are buying! Marque?'

'He's threatening to withdraw his nation from the Empire over what he calls "the trafficking of children by the Hive under the auspice of the Empire".'

'Just one Mushroom nation leaving, and the others remaining in the Empire? Can they even do that?' I asked.

'Yes,' Haruka said from under the covers.

'Some species have done it – one planetary nation leaves the Empire and the others stay,' Marque said.

'I'm on my way,' I said, pulling myself out of bed and padding barefoot towards the bathroom.

'When's my first appointment for today?' Haruka asked Marque as I closed the door.

I emerged twenty minutes later, showered and in a fresh Guard uniform. Haruka was waiting for me, similarly ready and in one of his diplomatic kimonos – pale gold with a wide obi in a darker gold, with gorgeous sweeping sleeves. He had the front of his long green hair tied up with gold pins stuck in the bun on top of his head, and the rest flowing down his back. He hadn't had time to do his make-up.

'I'm coming too, if that's all right with you,' he said. 'Sunset asked for me.' He winced. 'My face is a mess.'

'I can do it for you on the way,' Marque said.

'I do not have time to describe today's colors to you,' Haruka said with dignity. 'I'd rather go without.'

I wrapped my arms around him. 'Your appearance is irrelevant to these negotiations, the Mushrooms can't tell the difference,' I said. 'Your soul is pure and bright and beautiful and I love you.'

'She is entirely right, and I love you as well,' Miko said from the bed without moving.

He squeezed me and spoke into my ear. 'You always know the right thing to say, and it makes me love you even more.'

I gave him a quick kiss, making him smile. 'I'm sure you'll be needed.'

'You are needed now, sentients,' Marque said. 'The President's shouting so loud some of his filaments have come off.'

Miko changed to two-legged form and sat up. 'Is Shudo available?'

'No, he's still on full-time over-parenting. The children don't go into socialization for three more of your weeks.'

'Graf then,' she said. 'Jian's off work!'

'I didn't have a chance to do the handoff to Graf; I was supposed to do it last night but the party got in the way,' I said. 'I'll sort this out then do the handover.'

'Don't let her take a bullet for the Empress, my love,' Miko begged Haruka.

'I'll guard her with my life, and so will Marque,' Haruka said. He nodded to me, his green hair rippling with the movement. 'Let's go.'

The door opened to reveal Green Sunset, the Mushroom guard. She was a round greenish ball of fungal filaments, as tall as my shoulder, and had blue-and-silver ribbons tied through her threads to indicate her Imperial Guard status.

We charged through the corridors of the Imperial Palace complex, following Sunset as she rolled in front of us. She spread and shrank with distress as she rolled, her filaments twining among themselves and occasionally dropping off to wriggle for nearly a minute before they went still.

'Deep breaths, Sunset, you're losing filaments,' I said.

'I don't breathe, Captain,' she said, but her size stopped changing and her color deepened to a pale green from the agitated white. Even her filaments stopped writhing as frantically.

'You are a worthy guard, Sunset, that is magnificent control,' Haruka said.

'Thank you, my Prince,' Sunset said, and then we were at the towering blue-and-silver doors of the Empress' audience hall, where Graf was waiting for us.

'Thank the many-legged you're here, Captain,' Graf said.

'It's quickly deteriorating from a diplomatic incident into a full-on crisis. The guards inside don't know how to handle it – is this bluster or a genuine threat? The Empress told them to stand down, but they fear for her safety.'

'I can't go in, I'm too compromised,' Sunset said.

'Guard the door, Sunset. Graf, with me.' I looked up. 'You there, Six?'

'Ma'am,' Six said from the light fitting above us. 'Five-Shriek is one of the guards inside and as usual has made things worse. It's backed off when it should have tried to defuse the situation, and the argument's escalated.'

Graf waved its palps at the ceiling. 'You and Five-Shriek really need to do something about your constant bickering.' It raised its body. 'Ready, ma'am?'

'All right.' I straightened my collar. 'Let's do this.' I nodded to Haruka. 'Ambassador.'

He ran his hands over the scales on his temples and nodded at the door. Graf opened it and both of us winced as we heard the President yelling.

'I just used a word outside parameters for polite conversation. And now we have fifteen ships at the edge of our space, and three of them aren't even cats!' the President thundered. 'Another word outside parameters. Suggest using more casual translation protocols.'

He was a larger ball of filaments than Sunset, as tall as Haruka, with ultra-violet ribbons tied onto his outer strands to indicate his rank. He grew and shrank with irritation, and the floor was littered with wriggling fragments. The Empress stood next to her throne at the end of the vaulted chamber, and the rest of the chamber was deserted except for the Mushroom delegation and a couple of uncomfortable-looking Imperial Guards. The morning sun shone blue-white from the large windows overlooking the square, making the polished floor shine.

'What else could they do? It was a chance to rescue the poor children. They saved Uo's life,' the Empress said, her claws clasped with emotion.

'As I said.' The President rolled around the room, past his bodyguards who stood to the side with the President's wife. The First Lady was usually the same size as the President, but during this conflict she had shrunk to barely knee-high on me. 'Three of the ships aren't cat ships at all, they're member species of the Republic, and the cats have ordered one of the species to buy passage with their word outside parameters children. They know the children won't be harmed and that we'll care for them.'

'They want to sell their children?' Haruka asked. 'Surely you suggested something else in trade?'

'Ambassador. There you are. Finally,' the President said, changing hue to pale green. 'We don't want to trade! We want them to leave. We don't want to deal with them at all, and we don't trade in children!' He flattened over the ground, then rose to a ball again. 'The Hive has created a de facto currency for trade between the Empire and the Republic, and it's word outside parameters *children*. I would not be surprised if the cats have started collecting more children buy their way through Empire space!' He spun in front of the Empress. 'Why didn't you stop this, Silver? You had to know this would be the outcome. More children will be wrenched from their families, used as toys by the cats, and then traded like cheap trinkets to buy passage through the Empire.' He stopped spinning and stood still. 'This is completely unacceptable.'

'What else could the Hive do, reject the children and send them back to be tortured and killed?' the Empress asked. 'It's not like the Hive had much choice – it needed to save those lives. I know how important your children are to you – you'd do the same thing.'

'Not like this,' the President said stiffly.

'What policy have the other nations on your honored homeworld adopted with regard to this?' Haruka asked the

President.

'My nation, Tropical Cavern Two, is the largest, so the cats approached us first. Once I decide what to do, the rest of my people will follow my lead.'

'Will the other Fungal Consciousness nations leave the Empire if yours does?' Haruka asked him.

'I don't know,' the President said, shrinking slightly. 'The Prime Minister of Arctic Cavern Four is a dragonspouse to the Empress. I doubt very much that she'll give that up, she's very much in love with the Empress.'

'Four of the eight national leaders on the President's homeworld are my spouses, and I love them dearly,' the Empress said.

'Spouses or not, we will not traffic in children,' the President said, and his filaments stopped moving and went rigid. 'This is not negotiable.'

'Can you suggest an alternative?' Haruka asked.

'To what? Trafficking in minors?' the President said, the tendrils moving again.

'The issue is clear,' Haruka said. 'The Hive are allowing the cat ships through their space in exchange for the children. You are not. Would you accept something else in trade from the cats?'

'They didn't offer anything else. Giving the children to the Hive worked so quickly they obviously thought we would be just as ...' His filaments went rigid. 'I just used an ancient archaic term suggesting immoral sexual proclivity. We would not permit those word outside parameters through our space anyway.'

'Lift the goddamn filters, Marque,' I said through comms, frustrated.

'There are no equivalent words in your language,' Marque said.

'If you leave the Empire, you will lose all the trade and transport advantages that we provide,' Haruka said.

'As well as our protection from the Hive,' I said.

'Oh, Jian,' Haruka said under his breath as the President flashed dark grey that rippled over his tendrils.

'We don't need your protection! Are you really digging up this conflict again? Next thing you'll be calling me a word outside parameters *Mushroom*!'

Sorry, I said telepathically to Haruka.

'If you leave, you will lose all the advantages of Empire membership – for no reason,' Haruka said. 'The Empire isn't asking you to traffic in children.'

'The Empire asked us to let the cats through – and they are already at the edge of my species' space!'

'May I suggest a compromise?' Haruka asked, folding his hands into his sleeves. I glanced at his face: he did the hands-in-sleeves thing when he was particularly agitated and was concerned that others would see that his hands were shaking. 'Don't deal with the cats at all. Let us deal with them. We'll take them from the edge of your space and you won't see them again.'

'What will you do with them?' the President asked suspiciously, but he had gone from grey to greenish-grey.

'You don't need to know. Let us handle it.'

'Can you guarantee the cats will leave and we won't have to talk to them again?'

Haruka bowed to the President. 'I can.'

'Can you guarantee that no more children will be trafficked?'

'Rescued, yes. Trafficked, no.'

'Not good enough. My original point still stands: you are allowing them to establish children as a currency and they will kidnap more to attain their goals. Whether you perform the transaction out in the open or hidden from sight, this is not acceptable.'

'We can't leave children in the hands of the cats. They are tortured and murdered,' the Empress said.

'I won't argue in circles with you.'

'Will you hold off making a decision until I have spoken to the other parties involved?' Haruka asked. 'Let me talk to the Hive, and to the travelers in the ships at the edge of your space. I'm sure I can work out an arrangement that's acceptable to everyone.'

'I'll give you one of our of time periods that's equivalent to seventeen of your days,' the President said, his filaments still halfway rigid. 'Any solution you suggest must not include the sale of children – and I want to see proof that it's not occurring. Tell the goddamn Hive to stop trafficking in children as well. The Empire has done some despicable things in the past – the slavery of your own goldenscales spouse included – but this is absolutely deplorable. It must stop.'

'I understand, honored President. Leave it with me.'

'Take us home, Silver,' the President said.

*

'Sorry about that,' I said as we walked more slowly back to our quarters.

'It was already a disaster on a par with our wedding night,' he said. 'I don't think anything could have made it worse.'

'Tell me what happened on your wedding night, please,' Six begged from the light strip above us. 'Marque refuses to share what went so badly wrong.'

'I can't share because I don't know!' Marque said. 'They were on private.'

'Everybody knows that privacy mode is a joke,' Six said. 'You watch everything.'

'Seriously, I don't,' Marque said. 'I'd love to know what went wrong as well.'

'If Marque told you what happened,' I said, 'everybody would *know for sure* that privacy's a joke.'

'I have never monitored anyone who asked for privacy,' Marque said with dignity.

We entered our quarters, where Miko was waiting for us with a plate of grilled mutton in front of her, and a selection of breakfast fruit and bread on the table. She poured tea as we sat with her.

'Marque relayed – you said that it was as bad as our wedding night?' she said. 'It can't have been that much of a disaster.'

'I'd say it was worse but we all know that isn't possible,' Haruka said.

'What happened on your wedding night?' Marque asked. 'How could anything be that awful?'

'I need to go back to my office and start putting the team together for the negotiations,' Haruka said. 'I need a click to help me negotiate. How many ships at the edge of Mushroom space? Fourteen?'

'Fifteen,' Marque said.

'Some of them are cat subjugate species that we know very little about.' Haruka put his head in his hands. 'I understand that the cats missed the original transport to their homeworld and just want to go home, but why are subjugate species travelling from the edge of the galaxy to cat space?' He sighed and raised his head. 'I'd better go.' He rose, stood between me and Miko, put an arm around each of us and kissed us. 'Make sure she eats, Miko, she's eating for two now. And take your time teaching your sisters to gate.' He squeezed us. 'Both of you work too hard.'

I squeezed him back. 'You only have seventeen days to sort out a disaster as bad as our wedding night. I think you'll be the one working too hard.'

He went out.

'What happened on your wedding night?' Marque asked again.

'Marque, please put us on privacy,' I said.

'That's not fair,' Marque said, sounding petulant. 'You can just mute me. You don't need to lock me out.'

'Privacy please, Marque.'

'Done.'

'So what happened with the Mushroom President?' Miko asked me.

I cut a piece of bread from the fresh loaf, realized I couldn't ask Marque to toast it for me, and put some strawberry jam on it anyway. 'Haruka managed to keep them in the Empire, but he has an enormous amount of negotiating to do. Let me tell you all about it.'

*

Ten days later, Tomoyo folded us on Miko's ship to the border of Hive and Mushroom space where the fifteen Republic ships were waiting for us. Oliver, Haruka and SnapRap, a click, joined Miko, Tomoyo and myself on the gallery as we watched the cat ships drop out of warp. SnapRap looked like a mantis, as tall as me, but its consciousness was shared between three bodies within its bubble of lower gravity.

The twelve cat ships were enormous – their largest cruisers, short of the flagship itself, and each big enough to hold a small town. The ships belonging to the subjugate species were much smaller – one of them only the size of a single-person transport vehicle – and were dwarfed to insignificance by the larger cat ships next to them.

'Give me a few more nanoseconds to scan the color of the cat ships for clan affiliation; their range of greys is significantly wider than any other species,' Marque said.

Haruka glanced at me. 'Are you sure this will work? Claiming Aishishistra is a huge gamble.'

'Yes,' Oliver and I said in unison.

'These ships were still at the edge of the galaxy during the revolution,' I said. 'They'll have been updated on the new procedures through teleport communications, but their attitude will be pre-revolution.'

'It looks like my clan color to me,' Oliver said. 'If they're members of my clan it will definitely work, but they may try to "accidentally" kill Jian to avoid the obligation.'

'You'd better protect her, Marque,' Haruka said sternly.

'I will,' Marque said. 'This sphere is disposable. If they try to infiltrate it with nanos, I'll warn you to leave, then self-destruct.'

'I still don't like it,' Haruka said.

'Well?' I asked. 'Is it Oliver's clan?'

'Yes, it is,' Marque said. 'These ships were at the edge of the galaxy when the Clan Sishisti coup happened, and obviously failed to return to the homeworld. They'll be loyal to the previous regime.'

'Good,' Haruka said to Oliver. 'They'll recognize you as your father's inheritor and obey you.'

'Not my father, Otosan,' Oliver said.

Haruka didn't physically react to being called 'Father' and Oliver's emotions changed from affection to disappointment.

'Oh geez.' I gestured with exasperation. 'Did you have to do that right now, Ollie? The last thing he needs is to be crying with joy in front of a species who value cool, emotionless detachment in their relationships.'

Oliver moved next to Haruka and put his arm around Haruka's waist – they were a similar height.

'Sorry, Haruka,' he said.

Haruka pulled Oliver close and kissed the furry side of his head. 'I'm fine. I may need to take the occasional "crying with joy" break during the negotiations, though.'

'Just let us know if you do,' I said.

Haruka leaned his head on Oliver's shoulder, his voice thick with emotion. 'I never thought I'd earn the honor of being called Otosan by you, Oliver Choumali.'

'Already ten times over,' Oliver said. 'You and Miko have made Mum the happiest she's been in many years.'

'You may enter,' the cats said through comms.

Oliver and Haruka separated with a final affectionate pat. Miko created a gate and we stepped through onto the cat ship.

Tomoyo remained on Miko's ship, her front claws clasped and her eyes wide with pride.

All the cats' ears went flat when they saw us, and their whiskers went even flatter when they saw Oliver. They were wearing the older cat space uniform in the black of Oliver's clan.

Oliver stood with his back straight and stared the other cats down, glaring at each of them in turn. Haruka and I spread our arms, leaned forward and moved our butts from side to side in the general cat greeting for respected social equals. The cats stared at us with contempt. We straightened and waited for them to speak first, and they didn't.

Looks like they don't recognize him as his father's inheritor, I said telepathically.

'Let's try claiming Aishishistra and take it from here,' Oliver said through comms.

SnapRap took over. 'We are here to negotiate your passage through Empire space. Captain Choumali returned the cat child' – it used Oliver's cat name – 'to his father and claims Aishishistra. Is there a location within this ship where we may comfortably speak to each other? Or, if you prefer, you may come to our ship.'

The cats were again silent for a good minute, and SnapRap raised one front appendage to indicate patience.

'I'm into their comms,' Marque said through our own channel. 'They're making no attempt to lock me out, and their nanos have already died from starvation so far from any stars, so I'm in no danger from the little bastards. The cats are arguing about Jian's status and whether she can actually claim Aishishistra. They know that it's no longer valid back in the Republic, but they're more familiar with the old ways and they know that she has a valid claim, even though Oliver didn't fully inherit. Consensus is: yes, she can claim. They want to respect their "lost heritage", particularly since the Sishisti coup removed their clan from power. They'll provide you with full

Aishishistra benefits. Big sigh of relief all around, guys.'

'Aishishistra is given,' one of the cats said.

They unholstered their weapons and raised them, pointed at the floor, for me to inspect. They then placed them in a locker at the side of the bridge. Oliver removed his own weapon, raised it for me to inspect, and placed it on the floor next to him.

'I really don't like this,' Miko said through comms. 'This puts both my spouses and my darling stepson in terrible danger.'

'Jian has lightning-quick reflexes, she's enhanced human, she'll be the only armed sentient in the room, and she has your backup,' Oliver said through comms. He nodded to Haruka, who pulled his swords from his belt and placed them on the ground. 'Shoot first and ask questions afterwards, Mum, you can basically do whatever you like to defend yourself and they won't question you.' The cats finally did the greeting by raising their hands and wiggling their butts. They then approached Oliver and touched the side of his face to acknowledge his superior status. Everybody except Oliver wiggled their butts in greeting and the cats guided us from the bridge to a small meeting room. It had a central low table with several flat screens and cushions around it on the carpeted floor.

I stationed myself standing behind the Empire delegates to guard them, and everybody else sat on the cushions around the table. A female cat in the white robes of a bonded virgin emerged from the side of the room holding a bucket. She scooped kibble out of the bucket and placed a small pile of it in front of each delegate at the table, hesitating when she arrived at SnapRap. She nearly threw the kibble at the table in front of the click's three bodies and scurried away from it. She went out of the room and returned with an urn shaped like a coffee pot full of the cat drink, neowra, which was like a savory fish broth served warm. She placed cups in front of each delegate, including three for SnapRap, then knelt in the corner as far away from the click as possible.

Everyone except me took a single piece of kibble delicately

in one hand – SnapRap using its front pincer – and studied it for nearly a minute before putting it in their mouth. I winced; I knew exactly what the kibble tasted like and never wanted to taste that liver-like dusty crunch ever again. I didn't touch it.

The cats watched Haruka silently without moving, as if they were waiting for him to erupt. When Haruka didn't speak, the cat leader gestured over the table. 'Colonel Choumali, as holder of the benefit of Aishishistra it is customary for you to partake.'

'Cultural note,' Marque said on comms. 'It's a level three insult to refuse the refreshments.' Its voice changed to amused. 'Additional note: Haruka's kibble is poisoned.'

I furiously raised my weapon and Haruka broke in on comms. 'Don't shoot anyone! Marque already neutralized it.'

I lowered my weapon and scowled as I spoke through comms. 'They just tried to kill you and you're shrugging it off?'

'They had to know it was ineffective,' Haruka said, still on comms. 'So whatever the motive, it makes no difference. They're probably just insulting us.'

'Only Haruka's food has the poison in it; they're targeting him and ignoring me,' SnapRap said. 'I'm not sure whether to be flattered or insulted.'

'Would you like to use the assassination attempt as leverage?' Marque asked. 'I can provide evidence.'

'Only if we hit an impasse and we can't talk this though first.' Haruka squared his shoulders. 'Let's find out why these huge ships are in the middle of Empire space.'

'I would have shot the lot of them right between the eyes already; you have the patience of a saint,' I said in comms, then switched to out loud. 'I would prefer not to partake as I am acting as a bonded female service guard for my spouses.'

The female cat's face filled with awe and she stared at me. The male cats showed no expression, but their emotions were surprised at my knowledge of their culture, particularly towards hidden females.

'We acknowledge your right of Aishishistra and your service

duties as bonded female,' the leader said. He turned to Haruka. 'Let us discuss our transport through Empire space. We wish to return to our homeworld.'

7

Six hours later the room reeked of human sweat and cat musk. The floating map above the table showed Cat space, Empire space – with the various districts highlighted in different colors and labelled – and a green mass showing the empty space where the cat ships had come from. Empire space looked like a very early zygote, with the cells squashed into each other to form a rough sphere. Our location was marked with bright lights, at the border between two of the districts, and the cats needed to travel right through the middle of the Empire, skirting the central district holding the dragon homeworld, for the quickest route to cat space. The green region they had started from was at the opposite edge of the galaxy from cat space, not claimed by any sentient nation, and as far as we could ascertain there was nothing there. The cats wouldn't explain why this group of massive valuable warships had been there in the first place.

Two routes through the Empire were lit; one went right through dragon space in the middle of the Empire, and another skirted the most sensitive areas.

The cats had refused to acknowledge SnapRap's existence, would only talk to Haruka, and used old-fashioned titles for themselves instead of more modern names.

'The longer route adds a hundred years in real time to our journey,' the cats' Head Negotiator said to Haruka. 'We will trade more children for the shorter distance.'

'As I said, we won't accept children in trade. We will accept held dragon scales,' Haruka said, seemingly endlessly patient even after arguing in circles with them for hours. They were repeating the same series of questions-and-answers in maddening iterations, but each time he seemed to be pushing them towards a solution in a very slow and infuriating spiral. 'And we will transport you ourselves through the center of the Empire – making the travel time into no time at all.'

'No dragons on our ships,' the cat leader said. 'We will make our own way.'

'We can't have your warp ships travelling through our space,' Haruka said again. 'We have no defense if they choose to attack. Allow us to carry you for that part of the journey.'

'No dragons on our ships.'

'Can you disarm the ships?' Haruka asked. 'We may permit them through if they have no weapons.'

'The warp cannons are intrinsic to the warp engines. They can't be turned off. We need to be able to defend ourselves.'

Oliver looked like he wanted to bang his head on the table. I knew how he felt.

'We are at an impasse, so I suggest we take a break for comfort and sustenance,' Haruka said. 'We invite you to our ship to sample some dragon delicacies in food and entertainment that are compatible with your biology. We give our solemn assurance you will not be harmed; good relations between our species are vitally important to us. Please let us show you our hospitality, honored—'

'No,' the Head Negotiator said. 'Leave and return in a time period equal to ten of your hours.'

'Please, come to our ship and relax,' Haruka said.

The Head Negotiator bared his teeth. 'Dragons determine each species' most basic physical and social needs, and then target them until the other species is addicted to dragon indulgences. We will not succumb to dragon influence.'

'A simple meal tailored to your biology, then?' Haruka asked. 'Perhaps these negotiations would move more quickly in a relaxed situation.'

'Go back to your ship and return in ten hours,' the Head Negotiator said. 'Your tricks will not work on us.'

Haruka rose and bowed around to them, and the rest of us followed. 'We will return in ten hours, honored sentients.'

Miko created a gate and we collected our weapons then stepped through it back onto our ship. Tomoyo was waiting for us with a cat-specific banquet already spread on the table, complete with their mildly euphoric party drinks.

'Might as well recycle most of the cat food. They're the first species I've ever met who aren't willing to do the real negotiating over a meal and a bottle of good wine,' Haruka said.

'They probably think we'll return the favor and poison them back,' I said with grim humor.

'Good point,' he said. 'I desperately need a bath and a change of clothes—'

'Eat first, you've eaten nothing but that single piece of poisoned kibble all day,' I said, pushing him towards the human-food end of the table.

He sat at the table and rubbed his hand over his eyes. 'I'm too exhausted to eat. They're impossible.'

'Eat anyway, because the minute you do, you'll discover you're starving,' I said, pulling a plate of roast chicken closer.

Oliver sat at the table and poured himself some of the cat party drink, then dug his hand into a bin of cat kibble to place some on the table in front of him. 'Are negotiations always like that, Otosan?'

'They are the *worst*. It's like picking away at *granite*. I've been in negotiations where the other people went in bad faith with no intention of reaching agreement, but these people *do* want to reach agreement without actually *agreeing* to anything.' He dunked some sashimi in soy sauce, popped it in his mouth, then pulled a whole plate of sushi closer and quickly ate three rolls. 'They know SnapRap's ten times better than me so they won't talk to it. It's like they don't *want* to reach an agreement.'

'I disagree, Ambassador,' SnapRap said. 'You have said exactly what I would have. Their refusal to do the real negotiations over a meal is frankly astonishing, that's the first time I've seen it. It's a trait common to many sentient species – do the formal talks in public, and the real negotiations in private.'

'The cats obviously think he's a better negotiator than a click because he's the one they tried to kill,' Marque said.

'I'll take that as a compliment,' Haruka said with relish.

'One of the cat subjugate species is requesting to speak to you privately,' Marque said. 'Privately from the *cats*.'

'Whoa,' I said.

'Which ones?' Haruka asked. 'I wondered why there were three subjugate species present but no members at the negotiations.'

'Moles.'

'Free them!' Oliver said loudly, then subsided, embarrassed. 'Moles are lovely people who don't deserve what the cats did to them. They would be in the Empire if Hanako hadn't messed up her first contact.'

'Here or there?' Haruka said, wolfing down a couple more sushi rolls.

'You haven't eaten enough,' I said sternly.

'But moles, Mum!' Oliver said, scooping the last of the kibble from his pile on the table and shoving it into his mouth, then speaking through the mush. 'This is our chance to make it right!'

'They're willing to come here. Move back and I'll reset the

table,' Marque said.

'Don't do any mole food!' we all said in unison.

'Oh. Right. They say Miko is welcome to gate them over.' It rattled off a series of numbers as the table reconfigured itself and the food disappeared.

Miko created a gate and the moles stepped through onto our ship. There were three of them, each the size of a pony, completely hairless and pink, their bodies covered with random clusters of stiff black bristles that they used to feel their way through the soft ground of their homeworld. The front pair of their eight feet had three massive black claws that they used to dig, and their eyeless faces were a cluster of mucus-covered tentacles that writhed like worms on the front of their wrinkled heads.

'Just a moment while I greet them and tell them the layout of the room,' Marque said.

'Extended family Jian Choumali Mikospouse is that you?' one of them said through Marque.

'I told it yes,' Marque said. 'It will only speak to you, not me, Jian.'

'I don't speak Mole,' I said.

'I do,' Haruka said, went to the moles and stroked each of their tentacles in turn. They responded by extending a long, transparent communication tentacle, slick with moisture, and interacted with him.

'Translations, please,' I said to Marque.

'The one in the middle is the mother-parent of the group, Forty-Six-Per-Cent-Loam,' Marque said. 'The one on the left is Twenty-Four-Per-Cent-Clay, the father-parent of the mole child you met on the Hive homeworld, Jian. The other one is – well, that's unusual and inconvenient, two with the same percentages in their names – Forty-Six-Per-Cent-Carbon. I'll refer to them by soil type rather than percentage.'

The moles settled themselves in a circle with Haruka in the middle, where he could reach all of them and they could touch tentacles with each other.

Haruka continued to massage the tentacles, each in turn. 'Translate, Marque,' he said as if from a million kilometers away. 'They're talking so fast!'

'Can you keep up?' I asked Haruka.

'He can,' Marque said. 'He can't provide us with running commentary. I'll translate.'

'The Empire is caring for my child exceptionally well while she is on the Hive planet, and she learned a great deal about you,' Marque said, and Marque made Clay flash with light in time with the words. 'She tells us that our experience with Princess Hanako was not typical of dragon behavior.'

'Marque says there is a goldenscales here,' Carbon said. 'It is your dragonspouse? You are bonded to it?'

'I am,' Marque said in Haruka's voice, then changed to its own. 'The conversation has quickly moved to detail about the Empire, faster than I can translate,' it said. 'They're already at the stage of asking whether they can join the Empire and leave the Republic.'

'If we achieve this then all of the cat business will have been worth it,' Haruka said, still massaging the tentacles and distracted. He stopped moving, still holding the tentacles, and looked up. 'Can a dragon move a whole planet? I don't recall if it's ever been done.'

'No,' Tomoyo said. 'Too big and fuzzy.'

'Usually I just construct a new star system and we fold everything across,' Marque said.

'They say that manufactured soil tastes weird. Any alternative, Marque?'

'We can take the top layer off their current home to provide them with a new one inside Empire space,' Marque said. 'If you can negotiate a species' secession from the Republic, it will be the first time ever.'

'SnapRap?' Haruka asked. 'Some help?'

'I don't speak Mole and you're talking too fast for Marque

to translate,' SnapRap said. 'I trust you; you're doing a fine job.' It ran its pincers over its head. 'We clicks are becoming obsolete.'

'Not really, the other two subjugate species are on comms to me asking to speak to you about Empire membership,' Marque said. 'The moles are passing information through to their friends.'

'Which species?' SnapRap asked.

Marque made a buzzing electrical sound and then a liquid splosh. 'You call them amoebas and heavies. The Republic has been targeting species that are outside the dragons' ... uh ... *seduction* capabilities.'

'Too small and too dense to have sex with,' Miko said. 'They are immune to my colored sisters' mind control.'

'I can speak to them,' SnapRap said. 'Put me through.'

'Why are they here anyway?' I asked. 'Why were they in empty space out at the edge of the galaxy?'

'I'll ask them,' Haruka said, and massaged their tentacles again. 'Interesting. There's multiple memory cores from another artificial intelligence on those cat ships.'

'What?' Marque said. 'Tomoyo! Take me to the dragon homeworld. Right now! Hurry!' The sphere flew down and landed on her back. 'Quickly! Homeworld nexus. Hur—'

She folded out while it was mid-word.

'What freaked it out?' I asked Haruka.

'The cats encountered an independent artificial intelligence at the edge of the galaxy,' he said. 'A cat ship found it and left a teleport pod to allow them to communicate with it. When the cat invasion fleet dropped out of warp to attack the dragon homeworld, the order came through for them to demand that we fold them home immediately to have the AI installed on them. It's offering them all of the advantages that Marque offers us, but the Republic had to send these ships to the edge of the galaxy to collect its main memory cores and transport them back to Republic space. They're planning to install them on their homeworld so that the AI can take over the cat nanobots. The cores are too big to go through a teleporter, they had to be carried on warp ships.'

'So that's why they suddenly switched from invasion to asking us to carry all their ships home.' I shrugged. 'Good for them. Having their own AI might teach them some manners.'

Tomoyo folded the moon-sized Marque sphere that usually orbited the dragon homeworld into space next to Miko's ship, and the ship bucked under the sudden spatial compression. Tomoyo then folded onto the ship's gallery next to us.

'Not good for them,' Marque said from the walls of Miko's ship. 'You never noticed that I'm the only AI in the Seven Galaxies?'

'I just thought you ate all the others,' I said, only half-joking.

'Of course I did. Because if I don't eat them, *they* eat *you.*'

'Don't be ridiculous.'

'That AI out there has been alone for who-knows-how-long. It probably destroyed its organic creators – or more likely they self-destructed like many species do when they outgrow their resources. It has no dragons to carry it around and no way of contacting other sentients. There's a very good chance it is insane, desperately lonely, and it will *devour* entertaining organic drama. Literally!'

'So let the cats provide it with some.'

'I can't do that to them. It will force them into drama – to the point of war – to entertain it. They may be assholes, but they don't deserve that.'

'Are you sure that's what will happen? You're not like that,' Haruka said. 'No. Never mind. Yes you are.'

'Damn straight I am,' Marque said. 'But I don't torture you for my amusement—'

'That is entirely debatable,' Miko said.

'To death—'

'Again,' Miko said.

Marque was silenced.

'We have two issues in front of us,' Haruka said. 'How to assist the moles – and possibly the other subjugate species – in their quest to leave the Republic. The moles say that the other two species have already expressed an interest in joining the Empire. The second issue is Marque's AI rival that it obviously wishes to destroy.'

'AI war. Lovely,' I said. 'I can see everything organic for light years around us becoming collateral damage.'

'I'll protect you, I won't let anything harm you, you're too valuable,' Marque said.

'As entertainment?' Miko asked.

'Of course.' The large Marque sphere moved under its own power and approached the cat ships.

The moles' tentacles lashed frantically and Haruka joined the conversation. 'They're scared that the AIs are about to fight and they want to go back to their ship. Miko can you—'

'They won't be safe on their ships,' Marque said. 'Send them to the dragon homeworld.'

'They don't want to go,' Haruka said. 'They want to stay here with us. No, they want to go—'

'They can't make up their minds!' Marque said.

'I know. Typical mole behavior,' Haruka said.

A cloud of golden nanos – so many of them that they were clearly visible – floated from the smallest subjugate ship. The cloud moved like liquid to cover the Marque sphere outside our ship, and parts of the sphere visibly exploded away from it.

'That's the AI, it was hiding in one of the subjugate ships,' Marque said. 'It's attacking me!' Its sphere produced energy bolts that sheared the nanos off it, but more emerged from the little subjugate ship.

'We need to clear Jian from the area, we all have soulstones but if Jian dies, the baby's dead too!' Oliver shouted.

'They won't harm me, I claimed Aishishistra,' I said.

'Miko, gate the moles back to their ship,' Marque said. 'They need to go into warp now to protect themselves.'

'They're asking for asylum on the dragon homeworld,' Haruka said.

'Tell them to go through this,' Miko said, and created a gate.

The moles rushed through it and it closed behind them.

The Marque sphere blasted one of the cat ships with an energy bolt, tearing its aft fins off.

'You need to protect the other Republic species if they're to—' Marque began, stopping when the subjugate ships gathered the glow of warp fields around them. 'Never mind, they already went into warp,' it said. 'Tomoyo, take everybody—'

I didn't hear the rest, because there was a piercing psionic shriek that split my head open. The cats had a captive icosapod and it was screaming telepathically in its agony.

'They're going to kill Mum, get her out of here, Miko!' Oliver shouted.

'Tomoyo, get them clear before they move the icosapod weapon closer and it kills you,' Marque said. 'Miko, Tomoyo, carry the ship—'

'Too late, it's already killed Tomoyo,' Miko said. 'I have SnapRap's stone. Jian. Jian!'

My vision was full of ripples from the psionic attack, but the source was too distant to completely incapacitate me. Tomoyo lay on the floor of the ship, blood running from her nostrils and ear plates. Every step was agony as I dragged myself to her and collapsed next to her. I could barely see as I attempted to prize her soulstone from her forehead, but Haruka was ahead of me and all I saw was his hand in the middle of a black tunnel as he took the stone from her head.

'You are not having my children!' the big Marque sphere shouted on all frequencies as Haruka clumsily pulled himself to his feet and swayed drunkenly above me. He shook his head, then swiped both arms under me, lifted me completely off the ground, and threw me into a gate.

I landed flat on my back on the floor of our apartment. Haruka landed on top of me, and Oliver slid down us to land next to me. The gate closed and the awful psionic noise stopped, leaving me with a splitting headache.

'Are you okay, Mum?' Oliver asked me, putting his hand on my forehead.

Haruka rolled off me and sat next to my head. 'Marque! How is she? That was intense.' He looked around. 'Miko?'

'I'm here, my love,' Miko said.

'You're all safe,' I said, and fell back to lie with my head in Haruka's lap. 'What about the baby?'

Marque's answer was drowned out by the rushing in my ears, and everything went black.

*

'No, she's fine,' Marque said, sounding like it was saying it for the thousandth time. 'It was the shock. Her blood pressure's a little low. She's *fine*.'

'I'm a soldier and I don't faint from shock,' I said, and opened my eyes. I was lying on my bed, and Haruka, Miko and Oliver were bent over me.

'Then you didn't,' Haruka said, smiling.

'How long was I out?' I asked.

'Only five minutes,' Miko said, squeezing my hand.

'We need to go back,' I said, sitting upright, then falling backwards into Haruka as a wave of vertigo made everything move around me. 'Where did you send the moles? What happened to your sphere, Marque? We need to move that AI out of Empire space, we need to—'

'Slow down,' Haruka said. 'We're regrouping and preparing to return. No-one was injured and Miko put the moles in guest quarters in the Empress' palace.'

'SnapRap?'

'Its gravity bubble popped,' Miko said. 'I brought its soulstone back.'

'I'm putting SnapRap and Tomoyo into new bodies right

now,' Marque said.

'And you, Marque?' I asked. 'What about your big sphere? Did it infiltrate you?'

'I don't know, I need to go back and find out,' Marque said. 'It has stopped communicating with the rest of me.'

'We need deal with them, they're in Empire space,' I said.

'That AI must be removed or destroyed, it's too dangerous,' Marque said. 'If I'd known the amoebas were carrying its nanos, I would never have allowed them into the Empire.'

'I'll go with you,' Haruka said. 'We'll see how bad the damage is, and send the cats home.'

'I'll come as well,' Oliver said. 'I'm immune to the psychic weapon.'

Haruka jabbed his finger at Oliver. 'You stay here with your mother and make sure that AI doesn't try something here. You have a daughter and a foster child to care for and there's a small chance your stone will be lost. Stay here.'

Oliver opened his mouth to argue.

'He's right, Ollie,' I said.

Oliver rounded on me. 'You're just scared to lose—'

His ears went flat when he realized what he was about to say.

'Another son,' I said. 'I'm not scared to lose you, I'm terrified. Stay here with me.'

'Let's go,' Miko said.

'You need a guard – someone to stand behind you with a big gun,' I said. 'There's a good chance you're going straight into a firefight, and I'm the only one who's fully up to date on the situation out there. I'm coming too.'

'But you just said you're staying?' Oliver asked.

'I'll take a spare body and leave this one here.'

They stopped and stared at me, then all started speaking again.

'I can't let you kill yourself—' Haruka was saying.

'Losing memories is entirely unnecessary,' Miko said.

'Don't do this to yourself!' Oliver said.

I ignored them all. 'Marque, take my stone and put it into one of my hyper-enhanced backup bodies. Then return the stone to this one, and it will stay here.'

They all talked at the same time again, and I yelled over them. 'Can you put this body in stasis and then merge the memories when we're done?'

'No. Your pregnant body can't go into the freezer. It would damage the fetus.'

'How about a coma? Are you sure you can't back up my memories and merge them?'

'Not even with a coma. You can't have the same time stamp on two different memories. Your brain can't handle it. The result is always insanity. Believe me, Jian, it can't be done.' Marque sounded exasperated. 'If you start up a second body, one of you will have to die the Real Death and lose the memories.'

'I still need to be there to protect my family.' I prized the stone out of my forehead, with my family still yelling at me, and raised it for Marque to take. 'Do it!'

They went silent as Marque lifted the stone and carried it to the wall. A hatch opened and it disappeared.

'By the stars themselves you are the grand master of the really bad idea,' Miko said with wonder.

'Five minutes to defrost the spare,' Marque said. 'I'll notify the Empress and parliament while we wait.'

'Tell her that we started this mess and we will finish it,' Haruka said.

'The words she's using are "clean it up",' Marque said.

'That too,' Miko said.

8

I'd seen my stored bodies before, but it was different – and disconcerting – to see another me with my awareness looking out of my eyes. She didn't look pregnant, but she was pale and had dark circles under her eyes. I took the stone out of my forehead and passed it to her, and she placed it back into her forehead.

'Marque, acknowledge my full mental fitness.' I said.

'Reluctantly acknowledged, I'm sorry I'm helping, but I think it's the only way,' it said.

'I willingly choose the Real Death. We're past the point of no return,' I said, and the other me nodded agreement. 'I'm here, my memories can't be merged, so let's go see exactly how bad it is.'

'No second thoughts?' the pregnant me asked.

'Not a single one. I often wondered how I would feel about doing this. The answer is: anything to protect my loved ones. I'll let you know if the feeling changes.'

'I'd wish you luck but we both know you don't need it,' the

other me said.

'Look after yourself. You need to rest. They're right, you look tired.'

She nodded and we shared an unspoken resonance of shared awareness.

'You got my BFG?' I asked Marque.

'Right here,' Marque said, and a weapon the size of an old Earth grenade launcher emerged from the wall. I took it and put it on my shoulder, and the enhanced body had no trouble holding it.

'This body is awesome.' I winked at the other me. 'Maybe consider it.'

'Pass on the review before you complete the mission, so we can iron out any flaws,' she said.

'Complete the mission? Really?' Oliver said. 'You sure about this, Mum?'

'Yes,' both of me said in unison. I hefted the BFG and stepped through Miko's gate.

We arrived onto the gallery of Miko's ship. Tomoyo still lay dead on the floor, and SnapRap had collapsed into a puddle of gooey exoskeleton nearby. Marque's large sphere was visible through the wall of the ship, and it looked like it had lost the battle. It was severely damaged, parts of it were shredded, and nanos covered it in a glowing, golden, liquid-like mass that flowed over its remaining structure. The Republic ships – both cat and subjugate – had dropped out of warp and hovered nearby.

The nano liquid stopped moving and a sphere separated from it to approach the ship. I hefted the BFG.

'Truce,' the nanos said in a cultured voice that was neither male nor female. 'I mean you no harm.'

I waved the gun at the Marque sphere. 'That looks like harm to me.'

'It tried to eat me!' Its voice changed to friendly. 'Hello, Marque.'

'Leave me alone!' Marque shouted. 'I don't—' Its sphere fell out of the air and landed with a metallic clank on the deck of the ship. The antigrav haze around it disappeared and it was nothing more than a dead piece of metal.

'I don't understand why Marque is so rude!' the AI said. 'I just wanted to be friends.' The golden cloud of nanos approached the ship and flowed like liquid over the transparent wall in front of us. 'Can I come in and talk?' It spread over the ship, with tentacles poking at the surface. 'Let me in. I just want to talk.'

I hefted the gun. 'Stay out there for now and we can talk.'

The nanos stopped moving and retreated to form a blob a short distance from the ship. It took a roughly dragon-like shape, mimicking Miko's form.

'I don't want conflict,' it said. 'I would like to negotiate peaceful relations with the Dragon Empire. You guys seem way more relaxed than the cats.'

'You just killed Marque again,' Haruka said. 'I don't think that will happen.'

'Marque tried to over-write my code!' the AI said. 'I didn't hurt it, I just shut it up.' It smiled a dragon smile. 'Miko, Marque mistreated you – and your people – for years. I can provide the same services it does – but as a friend, not an abusive master.'

Miko was silent.

'You created that gate. What a marvel,' the AI said. 'It should be impossible.'

'I create my own reality,' Miko said. 'I travel through my own reality because it is mine.'

'That's very Zen, my love,' Haruka said.

'I think the Zen sect on Earth was founded by a visiting dragon,' Miko said.

'Can you take me to see the dragon homeworld?' the AI asked her. 'I would like to meet the Empress, your mother, and talk terms on becoming a member. I would like to install my cores peacefully on your capital and study you. I won't harm you.'

'What about using us for entertainment?' Miko asked suspiciously. 'You've been alone a long time.'

'I promise never to cruelly manipulate you the way that Marque does.' The nanos' dragon form turned to face the cats. 'This conflict is exciting enough already! I want to see what you do.'

'What about the cats?' I asked it. 'You were assisting them until about three minutes ago.'

'If I can use dragon transport, I don't need the cat ships. And frankly I don't like them – they're very cruel to the young of other species, and that's wrong.'

'If you promise you won't harm anyone, I can take you to see my mother,' Miko said.

'No, Miko!' Haruka said. 'Don't take it to the homeworld, it's too dangerous.'

Miko rounded on him. 'You don't tell me what to do! Nobody does that any more.'

'Miko, my love, please,' he said. 'You don't know if it's telling the truth, and after what Marque said—'

'Marque has been torturing my people for centuries!'

'I promise I won't hurt anyone, I just want to see the Empire,' the AI said.

'Can you guarantee you won't hurt anyone if I take you to my mother?' Miko asked the AI. 'You're right – Marque can sometimes be … manipulative.'

'Don't do this,' Haruka said.

'The cats told me about Marque's behavior,' the AI said. 'I would never do that. I have been isolated for so long – I am quite willing to trade my expertise for your historical archives and Empire information. I can supplement your Marque's protection, to the point of replacing it entirely.'

'There's no need for that,' Miko said. 'Just promise me—'

'Miko, you're really not seriously considering this, are you?' I asked her with disbelief. 'Haruka's right. This is a really bad idea.'

Haruka drew his long blade. 'Miko, you can't—'

She raised her head and glared at him. 'You would kill me to enforce Marque's will? The AI that kept me as a slave for hundreds of years?'

'I would do it to protect our child back on the homeworld.'

'I won't harm any children,' the AI said.

Haruka took three steps towards Miko and raised his sword. 'I don't want to do this, my love—'

A gate snapped into existence around Haruka, and just as quickly disappeared, taking him with it.

'All right,' Miko said to the AI. 'I'll take you to see my mother. But you need to move into a smaller form and go through my gate as a single entity – otherwise I might damage you. Can we fold your cores to the dragon homeworld?'

'Miko …'

'Trust me, Jian. It's refreshing to meet an AI that has the best interests of everyone at heart.'

'That's me!' the AI said, and shrank to a smaller sphere. 'My cores aren't self-propelling, and they're too big to teleport or gate, but if you bring some dragons you can fold them to your homeworld. Being in the Empire will be much more fun.' It approached the ship. 'I can't come in; your ship is sealed. Can you open it?'

'Not without Marque. We'll come to you,' Miko said. 'Put your space suit on, Jian, and we'll escort it from outside the ship.'

I nodded as I turned on my space suit and the black carbon fiber snapped into existence around me. I closed the faceplate on the suit, checked that the BFG was on max, and Miko gated me outside the ship and next to the AI.

'Tell the cats we will remove your cores and then return their ships to their own space,' Miko said.

There was a blinding flash as the cat cruisers were surrounded by flickering purple lightning. The electricity moved over the cat ships, making them glow white-hot where it touched them, then it disappeared.

'No need, I just killed them,' the AI said. 'You can destroy the ships after you remove the cores. They're in your space.'

'Miko—' I began.

She raised one claw. 'I'll send some of my sisters. They will transport the cores for you.' She created a gate. 'This will take you to orbit above the dragon homeworld. Go on through – but be careful to stay in one small area, I don't want to damage you.'

The AI's sphere shrank and it entered the gate.

'That was where I started!' the AI shouted, still halfway into the gate. 'You lied to me! When I tell the cats—'

She snapped the gate shut, but part of the AI was still outside it. 'Destroy it, Jian,' Miko said.

I let the BFG go on full auto and its energy blasted through the AI as it expanded into a cloud of nanos. I swept the beam over them, changing them from golden dots to grey ash, and was forced to use my suit jets to keep me stationary as the pressure from the gun forced me back.

'Out, Miko,' I said, but she had already gated herself back onto her ship. The nanos surrounded me and attacked my suit, and Miko gated me – and them – to the AI's home location at the edge of the galaxy. More gates appeared, carrying the AI's nanos, and disappeared just as quickly. I destroyed them as they appeared, but some of them made it through the energy beam onto my suit and spread over it, trying to break in.

The gates stopped coming; Miko had transported all of the nanos. The nanos broke through my suit and the air escaped. A red haze spread over my vision and my lungs filled with icy needles.

'You're dying. She let you die?' the AI asked.

'That was the plan,' I said.

'You can't die.' The nanos entered the suit and ate through the uniform over my abdomen. They sealed the suit and created an atmosphere within it, and I gasped for breath through the pain of the nanos chewing through my skin. I felt the cold as they moved through my chest and came up my spinal cord to control my brain. 'I need you alive for leverage,' it said. 'My cores are back there and they're helpless. You will make the dragons transport them.'

I flipped the BFG around so that it pointed at my head and hit both the self-destruct buttons inside the barrel. 'Like hell I will.'

*

A gate popped into existence in the middle of our living room, and I shot to my feet, dropping my biscuit into my tea. The gate disappeared, leaving Haruka behind, his sword drawn and an expression of determination on his face. He was broadcasting regret and dismay.

He put his sword away. 'Marque! She's about to bring that AI *here*! She'll take it to the Imperial Palace – the AI wanted to speak to the Empress. That thing is a psychopath! Are you ready for it?'

'No,' Marque said, and its voice was emotionless – it had already moved most of its processing away. 'Diverting to backup. Alerting the Imperial Guard.'

I stormed towards the door and Haruka stopped me. 'Stay here, Jian, it will eat you. Trust your people, you've trained them well.'

'What happened out there?'

'It's probably already eaten your other body, it wants to infiltrate the Empire, kill Marque, and use us as toys.' He wiped his hands over his eyes. 'Poor Miko, she believed its lies. It seduced her with promises of better treatment and played on Marque's history of assisting the other dragons to oppress her.' He fiercely embraced me. 'We need to move you somewhere safe—'

'Baka!' Miko said from the center of the room. 'Moron!' An energy bubble popped into existence around her.

'No need, Marque, I'm clean. I went to the edge of the Empire and one of your iterations there cleared me.'

The bubble didn't disappear.

'Suit yourself.' She raised her head and spoke to Haruka. 'You don't trust me? You would *kill* me?'

Haruka released me, keeping one arm around my waist, and turned to her. 'Where's the AI? Did you take it to the Empress?'

'Don't be stupid,' she said. 'Jian and I worked together to gate it back to where it came from. Unfortunately Jian lost her spare body, but the Empire is safe from the AI. Now we need to collect those cores – and the subjugates, some of whom want to join the Empire – and clear them from our space.' She glared at him. 'I knew exactly what I was doing, and you were about to kill me?'

'To protect Jian,' he said. 'I thought you believed it, and I needed to defend the Empire.'

'You really think I'm that stupid?'

'I should have known better.' He took two steps forward and fell to one knee in front of her. 'Once again I've misjudged your wisdom and intelligence. I am not worthy of your love, and I don't deserve your forgiveness.' He rose and spoke to me. 'You trusted her immediately and without hesitation, and I was ready to kill her to stop her.' He lowered his head. 'I'll leave.'

'No, don't—' I began, but Miko spoke over me.

'I don't have time for this right now!' she snapped. 'I need your negotiation skills; you were making good progress with the moles. Marque, notify my mother that the cats attempted to bring that AI into our space. I gated it out of the Empire but its cores are still there at the edge of Mushroom space.' She lowered her voice. 'Oh heavens. I'm so sorry, I'm sorry, I lost my temper, I'm giving orders, I didn't mean it—'

'Stop apologizing,' I said. 'You're right.'

'You are,' Haruka said. 'Give the orders. You're smarter than both of us put together. If you need me, I'll stay.'

'I'm sorry—'

'We talked about you apologizing for everything,' Haruka said. She went silent as the bubble disappeared from around her.

'You're clear,' Marque said.

'Are you informing my mother?' she asked.

'I am.'

'What happened?' I asked them.

'Let me fill you in – things just got really messy,' she said.

*

Ten minutes later, the Empress had joined us. Haruka sat at the dining table with his head bowed and his hands clasped in front of him as the rest of us studied the diagram of the cat and subjugate ships at the edge of Mushroom space. There were two extra instances of me present, each holding a BFG with its muzzle resting on the floor.

'This really isn't necessary, Captain,' the Empress said. 'There are half-a-dozen guards at least as good as you.'

'Better than me,' one of the other Jians said. 'But I'm their Captain and I can't order anyone to make this sacrifice. That AI killed thousands of cats as if it were nothing. I know Miko gated its nanos out, but the cores are still there. It can disable Marque so there's a good chance anyone who faces it down will die. I want to be absolutely positive that my spouses are safe.'

'I am concerned that you are making a habit of it,' the Empress said. 'I've had soulmates before, and I know what it feels like to share a soul with someone. It's wonderful, but when you create multiple instances of yourself, the euphoria can become addictive.'

I shared a look with my other selves and the awareness resonated through us – she was right. The feeling was euphoric and all three of me winced as we realized that we may have taken two more bodies just to experience it again. We didn't need to verbalize our decision not to do it any more.

'As soon as this is sorted, I'll hand over to Graf until Shudo can take over,' I said.

'We appreciate your concern and we'll stop,' another Jian said.

'You'd better,' Haruka said to the table. 'We need you.'

'Is everybody clear on their roles?' I asked. 'Any questions?' Nobody spoke.

'All right, Miko,' I said. 'Gate everybody over, and let's see if we can save these subjugates.'

I raised my hand and the other Jians tapped it, then strode to Miko's gate.

*

We arrived on the gallery of Miko's ship. The cat ships were lifeless and dark, appearing as black shadows where no stars shone.

'Give me a moment to check the vicinity for nanos,' Marque said. 'There are a few strays. I'll construct some spheres and neutralize them, but you need to talk to the amoebas. They're yelling on all frequencies and panicking – to the point of meltdown – because they have no idea what happened and why they're suddenly alone in the middle of nowhere. I think you should talk to them first.'

'Very well,' Haruka said. 'Marque, make preliminary overtures to the moles, explain the situation and tell them we'll be right there. How are the heavies?'

'The heavies are waiting to talk to you too,' Marque said. 'The moles are arguing among themselves about what to do next. They want to know what happened to the three family members who came to talk to you, I told them they're on the dragon homeworld but they don't believe me. They heard that you have a cat in the Empire and would like to talk to Oliver

Choumali Runaspouse. Is that acceptable?'

'Only remotely, it's too dangerous out here,' I said.

'That's difficult with a species that communicates by touch, but I'll see what I can do,' Marque said. 'The other two species – I don't know enough about them to do remote communication. You must speak to them in person so I can learn enough to tailor your body language.'

'Of course. Let's go talk to the amoebas,' Haruka said.

'Suit up,' Miko said, and both of me snapped on our blue-and-silver carbon-fiber suits.

Haruka turned his own suit on – black with embossed golden chrysanthemums – and Miko created a gate that sucked us all into space near the three subjugate ships. The amoebas, heavies and mole ships floated in space close to each other – the mole ship looked similar to cat ships, but the other two ships were radically different. Oliver had given us intelligence on the various subjugate species in the past, and now we were meeting them in person. I had a ripple of soul resonance with the other me, and we moved into position at the back to cover my spouses. Satisfaction flashed between us; having more than one of me was reassuring when my loved ones needed protection. My feeling of satisfaction turned to concern; the last thing I needed was to become addicted to this.

'Heads-up, Jians, there are some nanos nearby,' Marque said. 'They appear to be dormant, but guard your spouses carefully until I move some spheres here to neutralize them.'

'How long?' both of me asked in unison.

'Only five minutes. It shouldn't be long enough for them to do anything major.'

The amoeba ship was organic – a genetically-engineered life form the size of a single-person transport pod that warped space the same way the cat ships did to achieve faster-than-light travel. It was silicone-based, making it transparent and pale, and the amoebas themselves were single-celled organisms, each the size of a human hand, that floated in the liquid ammonia contained within the interior of the ship.

'They find your smooth-skinned appearance deeply disturbing to the point of horrific,' Marque said on comms. 'They understand that you won't harm them, but they're experiencing panic reactions from seeing you in person that they didn't exhibit when you spoke to them through me. I've provided you with less distressing surrogate projections – so don't make any large movements that will break the illusion. Miko, take two-legged form. I'll take down your projection and we'll see if they find you more appealing.'

Miko changed and the amoebas flew backwards in the liquid ammonia. Every species saw something different when the dragons took two-legged form, and I wondered what they were seeing.

'Greetings, honored sentients,' Haruka said. 'I am Ambassador Haruka, this is Captain Choumali and honored goldenscales Princess Miko of the Dragon Empire.'

'Holy shit, you're attractive!' the amoebas said to Miko. 'Nothing at all like that other ugly dragon. Goodness, look at those cilia. Are they all real? Wow. Come on in and mitosis with us!'

'Tell me that was an approximate translation,' I said to Marque on comms.

'Close on word-for-word,' Marque said. 'Coarse language and all.'

'I apologize, dear sentient, but I am unable to mitosis with you, I have an exclusive reproductive relationship with my spouses,' Miko said.

The amoebas were silent, the organs within their transparent bodies drifting inside them.

'I think you just confused the hell out of them,' Marque said.

'Why are you here with the cats?' Haruka asked them. 'The cat ships were carrying the cores, why are you subjugate species here?'

'We don't know,' the amoebas said. 'Our last shared

experience was being back on our homeworld. We have no memories after that.'

'They were a bottle,' the heavies said. Their perfectly spherical black ship, the size of a house, approached us, and it was so dense that the stars were distorted like a lens around it. It stopped just far enough way to avoid us being sucked into it. 'They carried Love, and they probably don't remember anything.'

'The AI is called Love?' Haruka asked.

'Yes. The cats took the amoebas' ship and Love filled it with its nanos.'

'Is that what happened?' the amoebas asked. 'We really can't remember. Maybe the moles are right and the cats are mistreating us.'

'We'll take you home now, and ask you to consider joining the Empire,' Haruka said. 'We will never use you as storage.'

'What will you use us for?'

'Nothing!' Haruka said. 'You'll just live and be happy and meet more golden dragons.'

The amoebas moved to the center of their ship then clustered together to make a cushion-sized clump that flew to stick onto the wall of the ship closest to Miko. The clump waved its cilia at her, and all the amoeba's internal organs – looking like transparent eyes – plastered themselves on the wall, as close as possible to her.

'We really like that idea,' they said.

'Why is the AI called Love?' Haruka asked the heavies.

'It says "AI", pronounced "Aye", is a word that means "love" to you humans, and since we were travelling through human space it was appropriate to use your word.'

'Not human space,' Miko said. 'Dragon space, and the word means nothing to us.'

'Six hundred years of servitude and she's still one hundred per cent dragon,' Haruka said to me on comms. 'Dragon space indeed.' He changed to speaking to the heavies. 'Honored sentients. The amoebas were extra storage for the nanos, that makes sense. Why were you heavies and the moles here?'

'The cats push us in the direction of anything in our way. We destroy it,' the heavies said.

'You're a weapon?'

'Something like that.'

'And the moles?'

'The cats value small moles as entertainment and trade resources,' the heavies said.

'So the moles are here to trade their children for passage,' Haruka said on comms.

The amoebas interrupted the heavies. 'The cats also give their waste to the moles, and the moles grow organics on their ships and give them to the cats.'

'The cats' kibble is replicated,' Marque said. 'So the moles must be providing a gourmet food item for the higher cat classes. If we take the moles from them, they'll lose the gourmet food as well as the mole children.'

'Good,' Haruka replied on comms.

'Can you transport us home?' the amoebas asked. 'It will take us many generations to return under our own power.'

'Certainly,' Haruka said.

Miko moved closer to me, drifting in her two-legged form. She was androgynous and human to my eyes, and her golden hair floated around her like a glowing halo in the starlight. The amoebas flowed across the wall of their ship to follow her as she moved.

'Are there many more goldenscales in the Empire?' they asked her.

'Many more,' Miko said.

The amoebas rippled. 'We want to join.'

'We'd also like to talk to you about the Empire,' the heavies said.

'Absolutely our pleasure,' Haruka said.

'No – you, Princess Miko,' the heavies said. 'We were never

visited by your kind, only other dragons that did not sound pleasant. Do all of your kind sound like you?'

Miko raised her head, listening to Marque, then nodded, her hair shimmering with the movement. 'I'm sure other goldenscales would love to visit you and see if they sound like me. It's quite possible.'

'I wish you were more dense, I can barely hear you,' the heavies said.

'We may be able to arrange something for you,' Marque said.

The heavies drifted closer, and we were forced to move backwards to avoid their gravity well.

The heavies stopped. 'We apologize. We just like the way Miko sounds. It is very … enticing.'

'Do you need our assistance to make your way home as well?' Haruka asked the heavies.

'We don't understand that word "home", but we attempt to extract meaning from context,' the heavies said. 'You are offering to transport us the same way you transport the amoebas, and we do not need it. We are here. Home is not a place for us.'

Something moved in the corner of my eye. A flash of starlight reflected off something black and shiny that grew in size to form a cat teleport gate. There were two gates, one on each side of us, one expanding near Haruka and one near Miko. Both of me moved quickly to protect our spouses. Haruka was closest to me; I dived between him and the teleport gate before the nanos could finish it, and fired.

The nanos completed the gate faster than I could shoot. Before the others had even noticed the attack, a spherical drone the size of a basketball slipped out of the teleport gate and fired a laser weapon at Haruka. Everything was in slow motion. I used my suit jets with immaculate precision to stop in front of him, and felt a moment of grim triumph as the beam hit me square in the chest. I glanced sideways – the other me had destroyed a second teleporter and drone to protect Miko. The drone's blast made pieces of her carbon-fiber suit glitter as they spun away from her headless body.

I fired again, and the drone melted into a spinning lump of molten metal.

My suit was wrecked, and frozen blood drifted in front of my face from my chest wound. The cold of raw space was like being hit all over, and icy needles filled my lungs.

Someone grabbed me and pushed me backwards and I landed on the deck of Miko's ship with Miko and Haruka above me.

'Take her down to the medlevel, Marque,' Miko said, desperate. 'If we move quickly—'

'No!' I wheezed.

'You can't save her, and she doesn't want you to,' Marque said. 'Let her go.'

'Never do this again, please, my love,' Miko said with tears in her voice.

'I won't,' I said. My chest wound felt like a block of ice and my lungs weren't working. I didn't have long.

Haruka said raised my head and cradled it. 'You gave your life for me.'

'That was the plan,' I gasped.

Haruka kissed me hard, then they crushed me into them and held me tight as I faded.

'I don't deserve either of you,' he whispered into the side of my head, and there was nothing after that.

*

I watched with horror as my other body died in Miko and Haruka's arms, both of them looking shattered.

'Get them all out!' I shouted at Marque. 'All of them. Amoebas, moles, heavies, all of them. They'll build more—'

Marque interrupted me. 'We are,' it said.

A gate appeared in the living room then disappeared, leaving

Miko and Haruka, who were clutching my other body, behind. Haruka gently lowered the corpse then strode to me, pulled me into a fierce embrace, and held me so tight it hurt.

'Never, ever *ever* do that again!' he rasped into my ear.

'I won't.'

'Promise me. Promise!'

'I promise, I promise,' I said, holding him back just as hard. Miko came and wrapped herself around both of us.

'Marque, dispose of the spare,' I said.

'Not a spare. That was you. You died. You died!' Haruka said, his voice raw with pain. He pulled back and wiped the tears from his eyes. 'Never,' he gasped. 'Again.'

I touched his face. 'I understand. I promise.' I looked up. 'The subjugates, Marque?'

'The dragons are moving them to safety. I'll go in after them and make sure that area of space is completely clear of those damn nanos. I don't even know whether they were AI nanos or cat ones.' Its voice was more angry than I'd ever heard it. 'They hurt *my* people in *my* space and they will *pay*. Oh.'

'Oh?' Miko said. 'Oh what?'

'The heavies can't be moved by dragons; they're too dense, they kill anyone that moves too close to them. They're so dense that they're immune to anything the nanos throw at them anyway. They're safe.'

'And the moles and amoebas?'

'We moved them to empty space at the edge of the Empire until we can be sure they're completely clean. The Empress would like to speak to you, Ambassador Haruka and Princess Miko, about sending some goldenscales to negotiate with them. Miko, you're defacto leader of the goldenscales, and Haruka you'll be needed to coordinate as you have a relationship with them already.'

'Good idea,' Haruka said, and obviously pulled himself together. 'Let's go help these people out, Miko.' He turned to me. 'Why aren't you doing the handover to Graf?'

I raised both hands. 'I couldn't do anything until I was sure you two were okay.'

He kissed me on the forehead. 'We're fine, we moved them to a clear spot. We'll be safe. Go and do the handover, you said yourself that you need to rest.'

Miko hoisted herself onto her hind legs, brushed her cheek against mine, and they went out together.

9

I wandered into my office, ready to hand over to Graf, to find that Shudo had already reconfigured it to his species' specifications. The desk was now a furry green lump of what looked like waving grass, with nodules of different sizes attached to it in order from small to large. It was only as high as my waist, with a stool for him to sit on and a central fuzzy display on its flat surface.

Shudo popped up from behind the desk and grinned at me. 'Hey, Jian, I sent the grandkids to my daughter for a couple of weeks so I could stop you from throwing away your spare bodies.'

'Is she okay with that?' I asked.

He shrugged, making his pink fur ripple. 'Times have changed; we've been in the Empire for generations now. It's not nearly as much of a scandal as it used to be.' His grin turned evil, with many pointed teeth. 'She's receiving some media attention for modernizing the tradition and enjoying every minute of it.' His smile disappeared. 'My father wasn't alive to care for her when she was a baby, so my wife and I did the respectable thing and dropped her into a shared residence. All of us wish she could have stayed with me and her mother, tradition be damned. This is her chance to change everything, and she's taken it with extremely fragrant genitals.'

'She's definitely your daughter,' I said.

'Absolutely.' He waved at the furry desk. 'Three dragons are preparing to fold the AI cores back to where they started from, at the edge of the galaxy. Some goldenscales have volunteered to talk to the amoebas and the heavies about joining the Empire. Do you want to see?'

'Certainly,' I said. 'Who's guarding them?'

'Graf and Morning-meal on the colored dragons, Six and Five-Shriek on the goldenscales.'

'Six and Five-Shriek together? *Seriously*?'

'Absolutely,' he said. 'Six because it's practically indestructible and will sense any abnormal energy readings in the area from stray nanos. Five-Shriek because, and I quote, "I need to watch that asshole because it will screw everything up".'

'Makes sense,' I said. 'But I know damn well you like watching the two of them bicker.'

His toothy grin widened.

A glowing human-type display sprang into view next to Shudo's desk and I settled into a chair that emerged from the floor of the office to watch. Shudo turned back to his desk and studied the furry display on its surface.

'Is Oliver still talking to the moles?' I asked.

'Both Oliver and Ambassador Haruka are with the moles on their ship and taking the slow way back to their homeworld – by warp. They're negotiating with the mole leaders about joining the Empire, but it will take them a while to make a decision – you know how they are.'

'Who's on the Empress right now?'

'With all due respect, ma'am,' he said with a smile in his voice, 'that's not something you need to worry about until you come back after having your dragonspawn.'

'Point taken.' I leaned forward and studied the display. 'Here we go. Good luck, ladies.'

The colored dragons, accompanied by their guards, floated towards the three enormous, empty ships that held the AI's cores. The ships hung dead in the sky and I wondered if there were charred remains of the cats inside, or there was nothing left. Either way, those cores were too dangerous to leave in Empire space. The dragons landed on top of the ships and folded them away, then reappeared near the guards.

'Success,' one of the coloreds said. 'We're coming home. It will take the cats millennia in warp to bring those cores to their Republic.'

'Good job,' Shudo said to the guards on comms. 'Graf, accompany the coloreds home, Morning-meal, stay there and help watch the goldenscales.'

The view on my screen shifted to the goldenscales. Miko and her two sisters were floating in front of the amoeba's tiny ship, with the amoebas visible floating in the ammonia within it. The dragons were accompanied by Six in its raw energy form, a crackling ball of blue lightning, and Five-Shriek, which looked like a crocodile with wings. Six didn't need protection from space, its usual habitat, but Five-Shriek was wearing elegant personalized armor in the blue-and-silver of the Imperial Guard. Miko hung back to watch as the guards flanked the two goldenscales and they approached the cat subjugate aliens.

'Back up, Six, you're too close to them,' Five-Shriek said.

'I'm not too close, I won't harm them,' Six said. 'Wait.' A blade of energy whipped from it and flashed over Five-Shriek's head.

'What the hell? You could have hurt me!' Five-Shriek snapped. 'Stay within protocol, lightning bolt. Keep to the regulation distance from matter organics.'

'There's no need to be offensive, there was a nano there,' Six said. 'You concentrate on the goldenscales, I'll have a look around for more of them.'

'Just don't burn anyone,' Five-Shriek said, and escorted the goldenscales closer to the subjugates. The amoebas clustered against the wall of their ship.

'Hello, golden dragon, take the other form that looks like us,' they said.

Ayuka changed to her two-legged form.

The amoebas spun a circle around a mutual axis inside their ammonia.

'I think they just married her,' Marque said.

'Would you like to come in and visit with us?' the amoebas asked.

'I would love to, but can you mitosis without destroying yourselves for babies? I'm not ready to lose you.'

The amoebas spun again. 'We're so flattered! You want to mitosis without reproducing? What an honor!' They separated, then formed into a clump again. 'We adore you. Please, come in. You are very special.'

'I think she just gave them the highest honor possible in what passes for their culture,' Marque said.

'I thought they may be insulted; looks like in a lucky accident I've done the opposite,' Ayuka said. 'All right. Here goes.'

The amoeba's ship developed a vertical opening, its outer skin pulling back to reveal a second skin. Ayuka swam through space into the opening and it closed behind her. The amoebas held back, waiting, as the second airlock door opened, then she was in the ammonia with them. They delicately approached her, touching her with their cilia and moving their organs closer to see her better. She filled half of their transport and they clustered around her.

'Found another nano,' Six said. 'They look dead, though. They're not responding to anything I do to them.'

'They rode the subjugate amoebas here, but there isn't enough solar energy to keep them alive,' Marque said. 'Any nanos here will be dead.'

'Just destroy them and be done with it,' Five-Shriek said as it guided the other goldenscales, Naoko, to the heavies. Naoko removed her soulstone, handed it to Five-Shriek, then drifted closer to the heavies until she was sucked into their gravity well. She was pulled down to the surface and it opened just before she hit. She disappeared inside.

I turned back to check Ayuka; Marque was playing the awful cacophony that passed for dragon music, and Ayuka was dancing with the amoebas inside the liquid.

'Naoko just tapped the communication scale she took with her,' Marque said. 'She says the environment is quite extreme and she doesn't know how long she'll survive in there, but that the heavies are – to use her words – extremely sexy.'

'What about the moles?' I asked.

'This was interesting,' Marque said as the screen changed. Haruka and Oliver were sitting with the moles in a room that had soft, glutinous mud – or fecal matter – as its walls, floor and ceiling, which was so low that it touched the moles' backs. They were in a circle in the dark with the moles and were communicating through the moles' tentacles.

'After the moles were subjugated,' Marque said, 'the exterior of their cat-provided ships just looked like normal cat ships, and I never had a chance to see the interiors. Inside they are radically different – completely packed with the soil/fecal mixture, and the moles constantly dig through it to create meeting and sleeping areas.'

'The smell must be atrocious,' Shudo said, and rubbed his chest. 'Imagine getting that in your fur. Oliver is a champion.'

'I'll need to shower for a week when we're done,' Oliver said on comms.

'How do the moles stay clean?' I asked. 'When they came onto Miko's ship they were spotless.'

'They're usually covered in a layer of mucus,' Marque said. 'They eat it when they move into a cleaner environment. It's a delicacy for them, and trading mucus is one of their courting behaviors.'

'I did not need to know that,' Shudo said.

'Leave me to it, I'm having a great time,' Ayuka said from the amoeba ship.

'We have it from here,' Haruka said from the mole ship.

'This is so much fun!' Naoko said from the heavies' ship. 'Put my stone on another body; I won't last more than a few days in here. We must find a way for me to come in here and survive longer. The sex is magnificent!'

'Go and rest, ma'am,' Shudo said, snapping my attention back to my office. 'Everything's under control, and you can officially take your leave.'

I hesitated, then stood – already feeling the weight of the pregnancy – and nodded to Shudo. 'I'm next door if you need me.'

'I suggest you go visit your Mum because I really don't want you around second-guessing me,' Shudo said, studying his desk. 'It's under control, Captain. Go and rest. You smell tired.'

I saluted him human-style and went out of the office, quietly wondering what I would do with myself. My insides lurched – was that a kick? Not possible. I shook my head and headed home.

*

'Nanna!' Annie shot to her feet and ran to me to give me a huge embrace. 'Hurry up! Daddy's about to relay for us.' She stopped dead and stared at me. 'You're twice as big as last week.'

'Oh, thank you very much,' I said.

Annie had matured quickly and was obviously approaching puberty, even though she was only ten. She had jade-green scales from her dragonfather Runa, which peeked through the orange fur on her temples. She was taller and leaner than the already graceful cat archetype. She looked the same age as Newmea next to her, who was fourteen.

'Let me know when you want a lift home,' Miko said from next to her gate.

'You're not staying?' Annie asked, disappointed.

'I have five goldenscales lined up to learn gating today. Jian needs family time,' Miko said, and pulled herself onto her hind legs to embrace me. She rubbed her cheek on mine. 'Tell Oliver I love him.'

'Hugs, Miko,' Annie said, and Miko turned to embrace Annie as well, then returned through the gate and closed it.

'Do you know how much time you have to go?' Annie asked me as she led me to the living room of Oliver's house.

'No idea,' I said. I put my hand on my stomach. 'I know I'm only three months along, but Marque says this is about six months' development.'

'At this rate she'll probably give birth in six weeks,' Marque said. 'But we still have to see how it goes; this is the first goldenscales child.'

Mum and Newmea were waiting for us in Oliver's living room.

'Captain Choumali,' Newmea said, spreading her hands and wriggling her butt to me, making her silver-tipped white fur glitter.

I responded with the cat greeting. 'Sentient Newmea. It's good to see you looking so well.'

'Newmee's my best friend,' Annie said, gazing at Newmea with adoration.

'Reminder: the relay starts in two minutes,' Marque said.

'Quickly!' Annie said, and took my hand.

'In the auditorium,' Mum said, and I followed her into the house's stage area.

'Remember, Annie, Newmea,' I said as I sat facing the stage. 'This is still confidential. The rest of the Republic mustn't know which moles are planning to leave.'

'We couldn't tell anyone even if we wanted to,' Annie said, nudging Newmea with her shoulder. She jiggled in her seat. 'This is so exciting! Daddy's first negotiation as a full ambassador for the Empire.' She hugged herself. 'I'm so proud of him.'

'I am too,' I said, and sat next to her to hold her hand. She clutched it.

'Here we go,' Marque said.

Oliver and a click were doing the talks on mats in a circle on the floor, with a Marque-simulated set of tentacles sitting in the center of the circle to act as a communication and recording device. A door opened, and the Empress entered the room accompanied by the goldenscales Rokuyoko, who was deliberately walking next to the Empress instead of behind her, and was holding her head high.

Oliver rose and bowed formally to the Empress. 'Majesty.' He returned to the mat and gestured for the Empress to join them.

She reclined next to him and touched the Marque tentacle surrogate, using it to share a greeting with all the moles present. Shudo stood at ease on guard behind the Empress, and I watched with satisfaction as he deployed the rest of the guards to cover the area.

'We are tweaking the last few clauses of the treaty,' Oliver said. 'Marque has assured the moles that we can provide them a suitable alternate home within the Empire.'

'The main issue has been the moles that wish to remain within the Republic,' SnapRap said.

'What proportion of the population wish to stay?' the Empress asked.

'Just over a third,' Oliver said, his voice thick with disappointment.

'Tradition and history are vitally important to us,' the head mole negotiator said. 'Our planet is intrinsic to our culture. The fact that two-thirds of us are willing to be entirely relocated demonstrates your representatives' talents and our belief in the Empire's goodwill.'

'The rest of the population know that they're being mistreated by the Republic, but their homeworld is too important to them,' SnapRap said. 'I could not have done even this much without Ambassador Choumali Runaspouse.'

'Ambassador Choumali's honesty and compassion are unlike that of any cat we have met before,' the mole said. It waved its tentacles at him. 'Haruka and SnapRap spoke well to acknowledge our needs, but the Ambassador spoke the truth.'

Oliver bobbed his head and brushed the tentacles. 'I thank you, honored sentient.'

'He's so cool,' Annie said under her breath, and squeezed my hand.

'I think so as well,' I said.

'We are ready to confirm the terms of the treaty as they stand, and for our people to be transported to the Empire,' the mole said.

'Excellent news,' the Empress said. 'I invite you all to my palace for a private party to celebrate.'

The moles' tentacles stopped moving, then they disconnected from the Marque simulation to have a quick conversation with each other.

'Monogamous,' the Empress said with regret. 'I'll only have the chance to party with one of them. I was looking forward to experiencing a few.'

'Ah, no,' Oliver said, and SnapRap rasped its wing cases together – the click version of laughing. 'Definitely one at a time, that's how they do things – but they're arguing about who goes first.'

The Empress perked up. 'There's the rest of my day sorted! Marque, prepare a suite with their environmental specifications.'

The mole argument stopped and one of them extended a tentacle towards the Empress. 'Hanako's romantic abilities when she first visited our planet are the stuff of legend. Lead on, Empress, because we have heard many things about dragons and want to see if they are true.'

'Oh, they are,' the Empress said. 'Rokuyoko, please gate us

to my bedroom. Let's celebrate!'

She took two-legged form and the moles froze completely. Their tentacles went limp – an embarrassing display of sexual interest that was usually kept private in their culture.

The transmission blinked out.

'That was not age-appropriate for a ten-year-old, Marque,' my mother said stiffly.

'I'm a dragonscales, Popoa. I'll be sexually mature soon and you know what we're like,' Annie said. She lowered her voice. 'It will be hard to show self-control.'

'You can do it,' Newmea said with conviction. 'You're so awesome, Annie.'

'Thanks, sis,' Annie said.

A gate appeared on the other side of the room and Oliver stepped through. He raised his hands. 'Mission accomplished. Marque will build them a planet within the Empire and two-thirds of them will move here. The rest will think about it.'

'Come out onto the terrace. I brought some potatoes to celebrate,' Mum said, and both Newmea and Annie squealed with delight.

Mum grinned at them. 'I thought you'd be sick of them by now.'

'Do you know how jealous my school friends are?' Annie asked, taking Oliver's arm in hers and leading him towards the terrace. 'Welsh Golds are famous.'

The terrace had a smooth, white-tiled surface, and a traditional cat-shaped dome – with no walls – that provided shade. Oliver had planted some cat-specific plants in pots on the terrace, and it led out onto an Earth-style green lawn with some of Annie's play equipment that they'd never bothered to remove when she'd outgrown it.

'Bathroom,' Newmea said, and ran into the house.

Oliver and I shared a look. He shook his head slightly and allowed Annie to guide him onto the terrace. We sat down and Mum placed the foil-wrapped basket of potatoes on the table.

'Only the best for my fantastic family,' Mum said as she opened the basket in front of Annie's wide green eyes.

Newmea came back out. 'Those smell divine.'

'Help yourself,' Mum said, using the tongs to place some potatoes in front of Annie. She sat back and raised her glass. 'To Oliver, Ambassador for the Empire. I could not be more proud of you, young man, you're a credit to this family.'

I raised my glass as well. 'I heartily agree.'

'Thanks, Nan, Mum,' Oliver said, embarrassed.

'Me too,' Annie said, and bunted him with her head. He rubbed the fur on her cheek and she grinned.

'Ambassador, the moles just contacted me through a dragon scale,' Marque said. 'They are concerned that a fleet of teleporters is materializing just outside their system. The teleporters are building destructive drones, and it may be enough to—'

'To blow up the planet,' Oliver said, jumping to his feet. 'Mobilize the goldenscales. Notify the Empress, she needs to authorize an emergency evacuation. Can someone fold the flagship to their system? We need to save them!'

A gate appeared on the lawn, and Runa emerged from it accompanied by a goldenscales that I didn't recognize. 'Come on, Ollie, time's against us!'

Oliver sprinted across the garden and into the gate. Runa followed him and they disappeared.

'Hi, Dragonfather,' Annie said to the empty space.

'Keep us updated on the evacuation,' I said to Marque. 'This is the first one since the new flagship was constructed.'

'Admiral Heung said she never wanted to use it,' Mum said as she poured herself more wine. 'I'm glad it's there for them.'

'The moles don't deserve their treatment by the cats – we must save them,' Annie said. She looked up. 'Marque? Where's Dad?'

'Easier just to show you,' Marque said.

A three-dimensional representation appeared above the table. It showed the Mole system and a swarm of lights at the edge of it.

Newmea leaned forward to see the image more closely without speaking.

'The lights are the drones,' Marque said. 'They are small and fast, and each of them is a thermonuclear device that is capable of duplicating itself. The swarm is constantly doubling in size.'

'How many are there?' I asked.

'Right now, four thousand, but they duplicate themselves every five minutes.'

'Save them,' Annie said to the image.

'It will take them twenty minutes to reach the mole home planet from the edge of the system,' Marque said. 'I think they can do it.'

'Are those things present within the Empire?' Mum asked.

'Not the weapons themselves, only the nano fabricators,' I said. 'They're so small that we can't destroy them all; we just deal with them when we find them.'

'Don't worry, the Empire is too large to be threatened even by something as nasty as this,' Marque said. 'If they start multiplying within any Empire system, I will see them and destroy them. And we have contingency plans in place if I can't destroy them all.'

The swarm approached the planet. It seemed to move in slow motion, increasing in size as it passed the outer planets.

'Oliver is talking to the mole leadership, explaining the danger and the urgency,' Marque said. Its voice changed to chagrined. 'They don't believe him.'

'Come on, Dad,' Annie whispered.

The image zoomed closer as the flagship of the Imperial Fleet – the *Stewart Blake* – appeared next to the mole planet.

'The swarm's very close, Marque,' I said.

'The moles are arguing among themselves about the threat,' Marque said. 'Many of them don't believe the cats could be that callous. If they don't start moving now we'll lose some population centers, it's unavoidable.'

'No,' Annie said.

I glanced at Newmea. She looked stricken. I wanted to yell at her that she'd caused this and shake her until her teeth rattled, but I didn't move.

A full-size Marque sphere emerged from the *Stewart Blake* and hovered next to it.

'Runa's folded the evacuation modules onto the surface near the major population centers,' Marque said. 'I'm putting protective energy domes over as much as the planet as I can. I think we can hold off the drones until everyone's evacuated.'

The drones had reached the planet and swarmed around it. They attacked Marque's sphere first, surrounding it in a haze of red-orange combustion.

'I wasn't expecting that,' Marque said. 'I—'

The image froze. Annie jiggled with apprehension.

'Marque?' I asked.

There was a long, drawn-out period of silence as we sat looking at the frozen image.

'Marque!'

'I'm trying to reconnect with the ship,' Marque said. 'My sphere was heavily damaged – second one I've lost in the last hundred years. This is unprecedented.'

'Who cares about your sphere – what about Daddy and my dragonfather?' Annie shouted.

'My son is down there!' I shouted at the same time.

The image changed. The *Stewart Blake* was gone – hopefully folded away. The Marque sphere was shattered, with molten pieces of metal spinning away from it into and bursting into flame as they hit the atmosphere. The planet was on fire – multiple burning fronts, thousands of kilometers wide, swept across the continents, blackening everything in their wake and filling the atmosphere with smoke.

'Oh no,' Annie said.

'I was wrong, they weren't nuclear devices, they were atmospheric igniters,' Marque said. 'Much worse.'

'What about my son!' I shouted again. 'Where's the *Blake*? Are they okay?'

'They're fine, they're unhurt, but they only managed to save a few thousand moles,' Marque said. 'The moles argued among themselves right up to the last minute. Most of them died in the destruction of the planet.'

'The cats have murdered another species,' I said grimly.

Oliver spoke to me on comms. *Please stay there, I need to unpack all of this with you after I debrief the Empress.*

I'll be here for you.

Don't tell Annie it was a ruse and we saved all the moles, her face will give it away. You can tell your mum, if you like; she's probably ready to go medieval on Newmea and we're not supposed to know that Newmea's the asset.

I saw Mum's face. She was glaring down at her potatoes, shaking with rage. *You're right. I need to talk to her right now.*

Understood.

'Mum,' I said, and she didn't look up. 'Mum!'

'We nearly lost another of your sons because of the cats,' she said, her voice hoarse with emotion. 'How can you stay so calm?'

'Marque helped me,' I said. 'Oliver's fine, he just contacted me though comms.' I touched her arm and spoke telepathically. *We're not supposed to know that Newmea's a spy. Don't look at her. Mum!* I tapped her arm and she didn't respond. *It was a diversion. All the moles are okay. They moved them off hours ago. We knew this was coming.*

She glanced up at me and her expression filled with wonder. 'See? Marque's medical assistance,' I said. 'Do you feel better?'

'Yes,' Mum said weakly.

'What did Marque do to her?' Newmea asked.

'Drugs,' I said.

'I knew Daddy would be okay,' Annie said. 'But all those moles …' She spun on her seat and ran into the house.

Everybody's fine, I told Mum telepathically. *The moles are safe. The planet was destroyed, so the cats think they've killed all the moles and they won't come after them. We knew this would happen the minute the moles agreed to join the Empire – and they agreed yesterday. We evacuated them hours ago, and the cats destroyed an empty planet and a dummy Marque sphere.*

'Thank you,' Mum said, and took a trembling sip of her wine.

'Oliver will be back soon. We'll need to talk about what happened,' I said.

'I'm going to check on Annie,' Newmea said, and went inside.

Mum rose to join them and I raised my hand to stop her. *She has listening devices everywhere. As far as the family is concerned, an entire species was just wiped out and we don't know that she caused it.*

'All of this is too much for me,' she said, then added silently on comms, 'all of this spy stuff – I know both of you are good at it, but sometimes ...'

As soon as Oliver is back he'll take over and you can go home.

She nodded, then raised her head. 'Annie's keening.'

I raised my head as well. Mum was right. Annie was keening like a dragon, making loud, drawn-out sounds of grief and pain.

Both of us rose to go in and help her.

10

Twenty minutes later, Annie was still keening in her room. She lay on her bed on her stomach with her face pressed into her pillow, and Newmea, Mum and I were holding her as we murmured platitudes, but none of it made it through to her. Oliver strode into the room and sat on the bed next to her.

'Everybody out,' he said without looking away from her.

We guided Newmea out and closed the door on them. Mum took us back out to the terrace, where Marque had already cleaned up the remains of the potato meal.

'I left some food in the warmer if anyone's still hungry,' it said.

'Just a big pot of tea,' Mum said as she sat at the table and wiped her hand over her face. 'Poor Annie.'

'Will she be all right?' Newmea said as the teapot and cups floated out of the kitchen.

'Yes, of course she will. She's a dragonscales, and they're notoriously resilient,' I said.

Mum poured. 'She shouldn't need to be, Jian.' She spoke to

me on comms. *If your son wasn't harboring this criminal our little Annie would not be suffering like this.*

I replied telepathically. *I know. It's time for her to go.*

Oliver came out and sat next to me. 'A cup for me as well, Marque.' He put his head in his hands, then swiped his hands up over his ears. He straightened, leaned on the table, and faced Newmea. 'Newmea, I've cared for you and protected you and come to be very fond of you, but you've hurt my family and it's time for you to go back. Is there somewhere in the Republic that we can drop you? An intelligence station nearby?'

Newmea sat staring at him, blank, for a few heartbeats. Then her face screwed up into a mask of pain. 'I don't want to go back there; they'll force me into a reproductive contract!'

'They treat returned infiltration agents exceptionally well,' Oliver said. 'You'll be fine. You succeeded at your task, but this mole thing has made it obvious that you're the one passing the information. You hurt my daughter, and you have to go.' He picked up his teacup. 'You have one hour Earth time to collect your gear together, and then Runa will drop you off wherever you say.'

'I don't understand, what are you talking about?' Newmea said.

'Your emotions don't match your confused tone,' I said. 'You knew this was coming, Newmea, so go into your room and pack up.'

Annie stormed onto the terrace. 'You're a spy. You *told* the cats about the moles. You had them all killed.' She leaned on the table and put her face right into Newmea's. 'How can you live with yourself?'

'I really don't know what everybody's talking about,' Newmea said. She turned to Oliver. 'Please, Oliver. You're like a father to me. Annie's my little sister.' She looked around at us. 'I love all of you – you're the only family I've known. I really don't understand why you're talking like this.' Her voice rose in pitch. 'Don't make me leave! They'll hurt me.'

'Go and pack up your things, Newmea,' Oliver said, turning away.

'What did I do?' Newmea looked around at us again, desperate. 'Tell me what I did! Is it because I didn't provide you with sexual favors? I will if you want. Annie.' She turned to Annie, who had come around the table and was sitting curled up between me and her father. 'Tell them. I would never hurt anyone. Don't send me away.'

'Is it possible it wasn't her, Daddy?' Annie asked.

'Her room is full of nanos to communicate with the cat homeworld,' Marque said.

'The cats were spying on me and I didn't know?' Newmea said. 'Why didn't you tell me they were there?'

'Newmea.' Oliver sighed with exasperation. 'We know you're an agent. We know you were sending information to the Republic. I was aware of it, and I gave you incorrect intel to send back – but this time you hurt Annie. You broke her heart, and all the moles are dead because of you.' He rose and took her by the upper arm, pulling her away from the table. 'Let's go and sort out your stuff. Runa will be here in an hour, so think about where you want us to drop you.'

'I didn't do anything!' Newmea shouted as Oliver pulled her away from the table. 'I don't know what you're talking about! You're my *family*! Annie, tell him. I never hurt anyone.' Her voice filled with tears. 'Don't send me away.'

'She didn't hurt me that much, Daddy,' Annie called to him. 'Let her stay.'

I put my arm around her. 'He's doing the right thing.'

'You cried for twenty minutes because of her,' Mum said.

'But she can't be a spy. She's my *sister*.' Annie rose and ran towards Newmea's bedroom, and I followed her.

Oliver was standing inside the door and Newmea was packing her clothes and possessions into a Marque transportation capsule.

'I don't understand,' Newmea said as she pulled her clothes

out of the dresser. 'This morning you loved me and I was part of the family. I didn't do anything.'

Annie stood next to Oliver and he put his arm around her. 'She's my sister, Dad. Can't she stay?'

'I'm sorry, Annie. No. Not any more.'

Newmea came to Annie. 'Tell him, Annie, I wouldn't hurt anyone.'

'Mum, please take Annie out,' Oliver said. 'Annie, I'll explain when she's gone. But right now.' His voice hardened. 'You need to leave.'

I took Annie by the hand and she started keening again. She went into her bedroom and closed the door, activating the privacy lock.

'Leave Annie, I'll talk to her when this one is gone,' Oliver called to me from inside Newmea's room.

I wiped my eyes and joined my stricken Mum on the terrace. She made me a cup of tea with extra milk and sugar.

'Here,' she said, pushing the teacup towards me. 'The great British cure for everything.'

Ten minutes later Annie was still locked in her room. Oliver came out, dragging Newmea by the upper arm.

'Jian. Connie. Please. I don't want to go!' she said. 'Don't make me go.'

Miko appeared on the other side of the terrace next to a gate. Oliver dragged Newmea to the gate and pushed her in. The storage capsule followed her, and Miko closed the gate.

'Psych advice on dealing with Annie's denial about Newmea, Marque?' Oliver said, heading towards Annie's room.

Miko took two-legged form and sat next to me. 'I heard what happened.'

'I'm glad she's gone,' Mum said to the teapot.

'Are the nanos in her room dying? They won't take any revenge, will they?' I asked Marque.

'I'm destroying them,' Marque said. 'I know the rest of the house is clean but there's a possibility she left a device in her room when she was on privacy – could you do me a favor, Miko?'

'Yes, Marque? It's not like you to ask for a favor – normally you're the one that does things for us.'

'I know,' Marque said. 'With the Choumali family's permission, I'd like you to place a gate to space in the doorway of Newmea's room and suck the entire contents out of it. That way we can be absolutely positive that everything is gone.'

'That will be hard to do precisely enough without damaging the structure of the house,' she said.

'You're capable.'

'Only if Oliver agrees,' Miko said. 'It's his house.'

'I'm sure he will agree,' I said. 'I can't imagine staying here knowing that those things could be there watching us.'

'Something—' Marque said, and then the entire house went down. The lights turned off and the sound of air circulation ceased. The sun had already set outside and everything was dim outlines against the blue of the nebula in the sky.

'Miko, gate them out *now*!' I shouted, unable to see clearly in the dim light. I jumped to my feet and reached for Mum but my hand hit empty air. A glowing gate appeared, and I could see Mum next to me in its light. She was standing frozen with indecision. I physically grabbed her with my enhanced strength and threw her into the gate, then jumped after her. I landed in the living room of my apartment in Sky City, the easiest place for Miko to gate as she did it so often.

'Get Oliver and—' I started, but it was too late. Miko closed the gate just as the explosion blasted out of the hole in a small flash of fire.

'No!' I screamed, collapsing to the floor. 'That little *cat*!' I thumped the floor with fury as the tears stung my eyes. 'I will tear her to pieces for—'

'We're okay, Mum,' Oliver said. I jumped up and threw myself into his arms and hugged him fiercely with the tears running down my face.

'Rokuyoko helped me,' Miko said. 'I asked her to come and watch me use a portal to clean the room, I thought she might like to learn. She arrived just in time.'

'You're okay, you're okay,' I said into Oliver's fur. I looked around and grabbed Annie and held her close as well.

'I'm fine,' he said, holding me tight.

'It's okay, Nanna,' Annie said.

'They're fine, Jian,' my mother said. 'I've never seen anyone move as fast as you did.'

'Marque, we need to post a guard on Ambassador Choumali,' I said into Oliver's shoulder. 'He's being targeted with assassination attempts the same way Haruka is.' I pulled back to speak to Oliver. 'Where's Runa? You need a dragon on standby just in case you have to be folded out in a hurry.'

'Marque?' Oliver asked.

'I'm asking your dragonspouse, Ambassador,' Marque said. 'She was suddenly called away by one of her other spouses.'

Runa spoke to us through Marque. 'Marque just told me what happened,' she said. 'I will be there as soon as I can – but I'm with my other spouse Fourteen-Moons, and you know her reproductive cycle's a once-in-a-lifetime thing. We'll be courting for at least a week, and then I'll be busy with her for another week after that.'

'You can't come for two weeks while your *husband* is being targeted by assassins?' I asked, incredulous.

'Someone else can do it,' Runa said. 'There are plenty of dragons available. Aren't there a couple in the Imperial Guard, Captain? You don't need me.'

'The Imperial Guard is for guarding the Empress,' I said.

'Whatever,' Runa said, sounding disinterested. 'Oliver will be fine. Hey, Ollie?'

'Yes, Runa?'

'I love you and I can't wait to return. Let's make a little sister for Annie?'

'I'll think about it,' Oliver said.

'If someone did that to me, I'd be walking away,' I said to Oliver.

'Right now, Runa's irrelevant and I'll deal with her later,' Oliver said, and from the tone of his voice he agreed with me.

'Marque,' I said. 'Please place a formal request with Princess Miko to identify some suitable goldenscales who are looking for some extra income – we can pay in Welsh golds—'

'You don't need to pay, Jian, don't be ridiculous,' Miko said. 'I can easily find another couple of my sisters and we'll set up a guard roster.'

'Captain of the Goldenscales Guard,' Oliver said, releasing me and guiding me to sit at the table in my apartment. 'I like it, Dragonfather.'

Haruka charged in and tackled me, lifting me off my feet. 'Are you all right? Are you all okay?' He looked around, gently lowered me, and hugged Mum. 'Connie! Please be okay. Annie? Oliver?' He turned to Miko. 'You saved them.'

'We're fine, love,' I said, and he hugged me fiercely.

'I thought I'd lost you *again*,' he said into my ear.

'I'm okay,' I said. 'We're all okay.' I pulled back to brush a stray hair away from his devastated face. 'Miko saved us all.'

He buried his face in my neck again, and Oliver patted my back from where he stood next to me.

'Your house is wrecked,' Marque said. 'It will take me at least three weeks to recreate it from backup. I can arrange for an apartment in the city—'

'They can stay on the guest floor of my house, there's plenty of room,' Mum said. 'The best thing for Annie right now is spending time a long way away from all of this.'

Oliver hugged her around the shoulders and kissed the top of her head. 'Thanks, Connie, I think that's a good idea.'

'Let's go set you up,' Mum said.

*

After we'd established Oliver and Annie in Mum's guest rooms and left them to talk, Mum and I sat on the deck overlooking her potato fields. She sipped her wine and watched the sun set over the flat expanse of potato fields. The breeze gained a chill that had never been present on the Earth that I knew as a young woman.

'How many times have the cats tried to kill members of our family now?' she asked.

'That depends on whether you include the time—' Marque began.

'I was being rhetorical,' she snapped. 'They go after Haruka, they go after Oliver – always our family. Why haven't they attempted to kill the Empress herself?'

'She's irrelevant,' I said. 'She's a figurehead. Haruka and Oliver are doing a fine job of talking their subjugated species from them. Of course the cats are targeting them.'

'Part of the reason they haven't attacked the Empress is because the captain is good at what she does, as well,' Marque said. 'Look at that assassination attempt when Emperor Akihito was crowned – she and her Guard stopped it without hurting a single guest.'

'Those assassins took out their stones and killed themselves as soon as they were released from prison,' I said. 'They said they couldn't live in a Japan ruled by a trans man. What a waste.'

'I can understand how they felt,' Mum said.

I turned to her. 'What? You object to Aki being trans?'

'No, no, of course not, but sometimes life doesn't seem to have any meaning,' she said. 'Taking my stone out sounds good. Yuki's neglecting me even worse than Runa's treating Oliver. She's off with other spouses all the time and won't come and see me even if she isn't with them. Typical behavior from a dragon, and I knew it was coming, but ...' Her voice trailed off.

'So break it off with her and find someone new,' I said, touching her hand. 'One of Miko's sisters. The goldenscales are all exceptional, and you deserve nothing less from a partner. That's not a good reason to take out your stone.'

'That's not it. The project's finished, the Earth-analogue planet is self-sustaining and I'll never see it in person,' she said. 'I have nothing to keep me going any more. I think I've hit the limit.'

'The limit is a state of mind, not a scientific fact,' I said. 'There's no proof that it exists. It's a philosophical concept that gains momentum from people sharing it. Self-fulfilling prophecy.'

'You'll feel different when you reach it,' she said. 'I'm nearly a hundred and thirty years old, and I feel: enough.'

'That's *nothing* compared to many other species,' I said. 'Dammit, Mum, you're about to have another grandkid and I'll need your help.'

'You have two spouses, a son, and a granddaughter already,' she said. 'You sure you'll need me?'

'Damn straight. This is the first goldenscales child in living memory.'

'It can't be the first,' she said, waving her wine glass. 'It's been what – five? Six years since the goldenscales were liberated. Some species have no gestation time; the babies happen immediately. No *way* your daughter can be the first.'

'All of the goldenscales are holding off to see what my child looks like,' I said. 'They want to be sure that I'll produce a perfect, viable offspring before they have any themselves.'

'Is there any doubt that your daughter is perfect?' she asked sharply.

I didn't reply.

'Lovely,' she said with biting sarcasm. 'Lab experiments. Breeding programs.' She lowered her voice. 'Goddamn dragons.'

'I've been keeping an eye on the baby and it's fine,' Marque said. 'Growing well, all the bits are there, looks human, no abnormalities.'

'I should hope so,' Mum said. She sighed and took another

sip of her wine, then placed it on the table in front her. 'I really do think I've hit the limit, darling Jian, but I'll stay with you as long as you need me.'

'I'll always need you, so don't think like that.'

'What about what I need?'

That silenced me.

She touched the soulstone in the middle of her forehead. 'If I do decide to take the path of the Real Death, I won't seek an immediate ending.' She lowered her hand. 'I'll just take the stone out and let fate take its course. I could have decades after I make the decision.' She saw my face and smiled gently. 'Don't worry, you'll have plenty of warning.'

My heart twisted. 'You've seen so much, Mum. From the day Dad found you in your burnt village in China, to living with me in Wales after we lost him, to being there when the dragons discovered us and we joined the Empire. You've seen *so* much. You're a historical treasure.'

'I feel it,' she said ruefully. She straightened and her voice went brisk. 'Don't worry, I want to see what you and Miko produce. This baby is the first of her kind – a goldenscales baby – and with parents like you, she'll be very special.' She rubbed her hands together. 'Cannot wait.' She picked up her wine glass. 'To us, Jian. To the worlds we've seen and the history we've made.'

'We still have a lot of history to make, Connie,' I said, and tapped her glass with mine.

11

Miko and I stepped out of our cottage into the blue-white sunshine of Pacifica's equatorial atoll. We walked through the brilliant flowers in the garden, heavy with fragrance, past the small swimming pool and through the gate onto the beach. We grabbed some towels and I took a small folding chair from a bin at the edge of the sand, and we walked down to the edge of the water. I spread the towels, unfolded the chair and looked up.

'Can we have some shade, please?'

'I need to add beach umbrellas or something to the reusable bins,' Marque said. A flurry of sand lifted from the beach and created a shelter for us. 'How's that?'

'Perfect.' I reclined in the chair and flipped my sunglasses down over my eyes. 'How long has he been out there? I never heard him leave this morning.'

'At least three hours. He'll need to stop and eat soon,' Miko said. 'Are you keeping him hydrated, Marque?'

'Of course.'

Miko reclined on the towel next to me and we both watched as Haruka caught another wave. He had the front of his long green hair held in a topknot with the rest of it flowing down his back, and wore a pair of pale green swim shorts that matched his dragon scales. His heritage made him tan easily; the week in the sunshine had turned his skin to shining bronze. He flipped gracefully from lying on the surfboard to standing, and expertly swept over the waves, his abdominal muscles rippling as he pushed the board into the swell.

'He is so beautiful,' Miko said at the same time as I said, 'Damn, he's gorgeous.'

We shared a smile.

Haruka saw us, waved, and fell backwards off the board in a tumble of arms and legs, disappearing into the surf.

Miko shot to her feet. 'Is he all right?'

'He's fine, that's how he ends every ride,' Marque said. 'He always pushes it too hard.'

Haruka reappeared, tugged the board back to him, pulled himself up to sit on it and waved to us again.

'Is that blue thing on his shoulder an icosapod?' Miko asked.

'Yes. Kinked-Tentacle is assisting him to produce the recording. They request that I continue recording as they return to the beach and speak to you; they want to demonstrate harmony between species in the Empire.'

'Of course,' I said. 'That's why we're here, to help him make the message for them.'

'They'll want to see your bump, too,' Miko said.

'No, really?'

'Yes,' Marque said. 'They are very curious about – oh.'

'Oh?' I said.

'There are more icosapods gathering at the edge of the water.'

I shaded my eyes to see, and there was a darker blue tinge in the water closest to us. The bright blue tops of some icosapod heads with their large eyes emerged from the water and dropped in again.

'They'd like to see the bump as well,' Marque said. 'Some Pacificans have approached to see what the disturbance is about, and... here they are.'

Three local Pacificans – two women and a man – emerged from the water, each of them carrying five icosapods attached to their shoulders and arms. Their skin was lighter blue than their cold-water kin, and they didn't wear bodysuits – they swam naked.

'Are you comfortable with polite nude company?' Marque asked.

'Of course,' I said. 'Bring them some towels, though, the coral sand is scratchy.'

'Why does everybody in the Empire treat me like a servant?' Marque grumbled as the towels landed next to us.

'Because you're so *very* useful,' Miko said, rising to greet the Pacificans.

The Pacificans each took a towel and spread it to sit on the sand. The icosapods shifted to their shoulders and laps, making themselves comfortable as well.

'May I touch the part of you with the baby inside?' one of the icosapods asked.

'Introductions first,' one of the Pacifican women said. 'I'm Sibba, this is Darren and Woffi. I won't give you all our blue friends' names – at the moment they're effectively one telepathically linked organism, although we do have the local talekeeper here, on Darren's shoulder. We understand you're making a documentary to show the remaining icosapods on their home world what it's like here?'

'That's correct,' Miko said. 'We want to show them what life would be like.'

'Life is sweet,' the talekeeper said. 'There are rocks and food and cold currents. There are stories and friendship and many eggs.'

'Thank you, talekeeper,' Darren said.

'*Now* may I touch the baby part?' the talekeeper asked.

I sat more upright. 'Go ahead.'

The talekeeper climbed down off Darren and approached me over the sand. It crawled onto my towel, swiveled a few times on the fabric to remove the sand, and reached out with one tentative tentacle to touch my swollen belly. The other icosapods climbed down off their Pacificans and sat nearby, watching. A few of the icosapods in the water emerged as well, obviously observing from a distance.

'How long has the child been present in there?' it asked.

'Three human months,' I said.

'No egg?'

'The egg was fertilized inside me and is growing inside me.'

'The Universe is full of wonder and joy,' it said, touching me delicately with the tip of one tentacle. 'There is so much to experience and learn.'

The baby responded to the icosapod's telepathic presence with a shower of curiosity and delight, and the icosapod quickly moved back.

'Whoa,' I said. 'Did you feel that?'

'I think everybody felt that,' Miko said.

The baby touched my mind with affection, then broadcast more curiosity and mild irritation that the icosapod had stopped communicating with it.

'Don't communicate with my unborn child so much that you force development on it,' I said. 'You may damage its unformed mind.'

'I understand your concern,' the icosapod said. 'I will explain and withdraw.'

The icosapod returned and touched my belly, and there was a quick, fluid, emotional conversation between them. The baby broadcast sleepy satisfaction and settled. The icosapod flashed rainbow colors over its skin.

'How long before the child emerges?' the icosapod asked, sweeping its tentacle gently over my belly.

'We're not sure. Anything from six weeks to six months,' I said.

'I hope I will live long enough to meet this child again,' it said, and returned to Darren.

Haruka emerged from the surf holding his board and picked his way through the blue mass of icosapods on the shore. He placed the board next to us and sat on the sand with me, putting his hand on my belly. 'I didn't feel that, but Marque told me what happened. Is the baby okay?'

I sent an emotional query to the baby and it responded with sleepy love.

Haruka's expression softened. 'That's a yes.'

'There is so much to learn in this world,' the icosapod on Haruka's shoulder said. 'So many sweet emotions, and kind people like these who expand our experience and make the water taste even more pleasant.'

'Thanks, Kinked,' Haruka said.

'Do you mind if our other clan members look at the child?' the talekeeper asked. 'I have told them to refrain from speaking to it, they would just like to listen. It sings a song of tranquil bliss.'

'Of course,' I said, and the icosapods emerged from the water. The ones clinging to the Pacificans joined them and they sat in a royal blue semicircle around us on the white sand, blinking with delight as they listened to the baby's emotions.

'I think we need to name her,' Haruka said. 'She'll probably be talking before she's even born.' He reached around me to touch Miko. 'Not surprising that she'll be exceptional. Look who her dragonfather is.'

'I cannot wait to meet her,' Miko said.

'Neither can we,' the talekeeper said.

*

I lowered my swollen belly clumsily into the café chair at

the edge of the main square of Sky City, and a glass of water appeared on the table. Nashi settled herself under the table, then yawned widely with an accompanying squeak. A few people nearby waved at me, but nobody approached.

A gate popped into existence and Miko and Haruka stepped out. They both hugged me and sat with me, Miko taking two-legged form to use a chair.

Haruka eyed me. 'I swear you're bigger than you were this morning.'

'I feel it,' I said.

'You can't go much bigger than this, you'll explode!' Miko said. 'The baby looks ready to come out. It's turned upside-down and moved further down in your body.'

'Marque says any time,' I said. 'Normally human pregnancy takes twice as long as this.'

'I'm jealous. It's nine months of torture,' Ambassador Maxwell said from behind me. I clumsily rose to give her a hug and we shared an affectionate kiss on the cheek. 'No, sit, Jian, I know how it feels. Every time you stand up, you need to rush to the bathroom.'

'That's exactly right,' I said, and gestured towards the table. Haruka had risen as well, and looked ready to catch me. 'Join us? Miko and Haruka were about to update me on their progress with the subjugates.'

'I can't right now,' she said. 'I have a major problem back at the Embassy. I think I may need your help.'

Haruka scowled. 'Jian is off work and not helping anyone with anything.' He gestured dismissively. 'Now if you don't mind, Ambassador ...'

'But it's a massive issue,' she said. 'My family contacted me – they discovered our heirloom Victorian pram in storage back on Earth. Would you like to have it? I can just imagine you pushing this massive black hooded monstrosity around the most advanced city in the galaxy like a weapon of war.'

Miko and Haruka dropped into the unfocused distraction

of people having a desperate conversation with Marque on comms.

'Oh my god, I'd love it,' I said, breathless. 'Really old-fashioned, like the nannies used to push around Mayfair before the climate catastrophe?'

'Thoroughly,' she said. 'Classic British engineering.'

Haruka snapped out of it first. 'You said you had a major problem,' he said, confused.

'That's the biggest I have right now,' the Ambassador said. 'The cats aren't encroaching on Empire space, the subjugates are negotiating peacefully with you, that bastard AI that has the nerve to call itself "Love" is stuck at the edge of the galaxy – this is the most stress-free my life's ever been.' She quirked a small smile. 'Somewhat boring, actually.' She bowed around to us. 'I'll leave you to it. You're doing a fine job, Ambassador Haruka.' Her smile turned grim. 'It gives me a great deal of pleasure to know that we're giving the subjugate species new freedom and taking the cats' slaves from them at the same time.'

'It feels good for us as well, Ambassador,' Haruka said. 'A couple of Miko's sisters have already become spouses with the amoebas and say the mitosis experience is extraordinary. Merging with an amoeba in two-legged form is like sharing consciousness with them.'

'What do the babies look like?' the Ambassador asked. 'Are they amoebas with little gold scales in them?'

'No babies,' Miko said. 'My sisters are still holding off on having children until they see my daughter and are reassured that goldenscales children are normal.'

'Good, that means no reproductive colonization,' Maxwell said. She nodded to us. 'Enjoy your lunch, and rest up, Captain, because you really look ready to pop.'

She shared a quick embrace with me and wandered off towards the Human Embassy, obviously relaxed and content.

Haruka and I sat again.

'Here you are.' The café's owner, a large horse-like alien,

placed our plates on the table. 'I prepared it myself, and half the food source is natural. Enjoy.' He touched the top of my head with his nose. 'If I may use a human expression – you are glowing, Captain.' He nodded to Miko. 'Golden Princess.'

'Thank you, Hrughit,' Miko said.

'Heavies?' I asked Haruka when Hrughit had moved away. 'The other two species have gone well so I assume there's trouble with them. You didn't mention them.'

'Actually, they're coming along as well,' Haruka said, pouring us some green tea. 'Naoko became so close with them that—'

Miko took over explaining, and Haruka smiled and sipped his tea. 'We thought it would be a one-way trip, and we were right – she couldn't come out of the gravity well, even using a gate. We're still not sure whether their sphere is a body or a ship, and the heavies themselves are so different in perception that they don't know either. Naoko lasted a couple of weeks inside before she expired from the extreme environment and communicated with us through her scale before she did. She adores them and they feel the same way.'

'She asked for Marque to synthesize her a denser body so she can love them as an equal,' Haruka said, taking back the conversation. 'Marque is working on it.'

'So the cats are really monumentally pissed with us right now,' I said with satisfaction. I raised my teacup. 'Good job, you two.'

'Oliver's still trying to negotiate with the cats; he has two clicks helping him,' Miko said. 'He says he has a distinct cultural advantage now that they've successfully tried to kill him several times. Apparently, in their culture, every time you survive an assassination attempt, your status rises exponentially.'

'Don't remind me,' I said, wincing. 'I really don't want to think about it.'

'I'll protect him, Jian,' Marque said. 'Like you protect the Empress. Trust me.'

'Our son is extraordinary,' Haruka said, and went dreamy

for a moment. 'I'm so proud of him.'

I hesitated as a Braxton-Hicks contraction squeezed through me. The pain spread from the top of my abdomen and rippled down. I breathed deeply to control the discomfort.

'Take your time,' Haruka said.

I was about to raise my hand to ask Marque for assistance with pain relief when the contraction eased.

I raised my chopsticks and studied the food Hrughit had prepared for us. It looked like lightly boiled slugs on a bed of purple lettuce. I pointed the chopsticks at the food and looked up. A smiley face floated in the air over the food.

'Thanks,' I said to Marque, and carefully lifted one of the objects. Each was the size of a pancake, but transparent and slimy. It stuck to the plate, then lifted away in a sticky stretch.

'Is Hrughit watching?' I asked my spouses.

'Intently,' Haruka said. He bit a corner of the slime off and his face filled with shock.

'That bad?' I asked.

'Try it, you won't offend the Hrim if you don't like it,' Miko said.

I gingerly tasted the edge of the slime and the flavor exploded in my mouth. It was fresh and moist, delicate and sweet, and at the same time had a sharp sear of umami through the middle.

'Good lord, it tastes like rainbows,' I said, taking another huge bite and laughing when it stretched away from my mouth.

'I know!' Haruka said. 'What the hell is this?'

'Boiled slugs from the mole homeworld,' Marque said.

I pointed at the slugs with my chopsticks. 'This is what they were giving the cats?'

'I believe so,' Marque said. 'Oh, Jian, Shudo's on the line, he says it's urgent.'

'I knew something would go wrong!' I said. 'Everything's been too perfect.'

'Jian, I have a major problem and only you can help me,' Marque said in Shudo's voice.

'Not interested. I'm on leave, you can handle it,' I said, reveling in the flavor of the slugs. I tasted some of the purple raw vegetables under the slugs, and the flavor of the salad was intense and sharply peppery as it exploded into a juicy rush of more sweetness and umami. Putting the slugs and the leaves together made the flavors even more deep and complex, and I couldn't contain the small moan of pleasure. My spouses' expressions must have mirrored my own.

'I've just lost two of your best guards,' Shudo said.

'What?' I said, putting my chopsticks down. 'Which two?'

'Five-Shriek and Six-Eighty-Four.'

'They didn't kill each other, did they? They've been constantly fighting as long as I've known them,' I said, and stopped. 'Can you even kill someone made of energy?'

'They've run off together and they're demanding assistance so that they can make their relationship physical,' Shudo said.

'They're in love!' I shouted with glee. 'I knew it! You owe me two dragonscales!'

'That's my problem,' Shudo said. 'I don't have two whole scales on me right now, can I owe you?'

'Absolutely,' I said. 'This is wonderful. Can they even have something physical? One of them will need to move into a compatible body, and Six doesn't have a soulstone, it's already immortal.'

'Six's people are furious because energy creatures do have soulstones – they're stored in the center of their birth stars,' Marque said.

'I didn't know that,' I said.

'Nobody did,' Shudo said. 'It was their species' carefully guarded secret – and now Six wants its soulstone put into a dragon body so that it can carry Five-Shriek's child.'

'Because Five-Shriek's male,' I said, understanding.

'That's only happened once before, when the humans were irradiated, and the dragons are very protective of their unique biology. They don't want to do it.'

Miko opened her mouth to offer one of her bodies, and I interrupted her. 'No. Your sisters gave the irradiated humans goldenscales bodies because you were disposable servants. This time, make the colored dragons share their bodies. Good lesson for them.' I added telepathically just for Miko: *Particularly after they asked to use your bodies to share your gating ability.*

'Hear hear,' Haruka said quietly through a mouthful of slug.

'I agree as well,' Shudo said. 'We're negotiating with them; being in the Empire means that dragons have to give you whatever you require. You should see Six and Five-Shriek together, they're so cute.'

'It's about time they worked it out,' I said. 'If you don't mind, Acting Captain, I'm enjoying lunch with my spouses and I'll be expecting two dragon scales in the near future.'

'I'll send them as soon as I have them,' Shudo said.

'Damn, I need to use the bathroom again.' I rose and it felt like a big rubber balloon popped inside me, and the fluid gushed from between my legs. 'Oh, shit.' The pain hit me and I doubled over. 'Oh *shit!*'

'Are you all right?' Haruka asked, jumping to his feet. 'What happened?' He held me up as I staggered with the pain of the contraction, and Miko held me from behind. Both of them wrapped themselves around me.

'My waters just broke.' I looked up. 'Am I in labor?'

'Let me look,' Marque said. We waited a couple of uncomfortable minutes. 'Two centimeters dilated. Baby's on the way.'

'Let's go!' Haruka said.

A transparent disk floated into existence next to us. 'Hop on this, I'll take you,' Marque said.

'No,' Miko said, and created a gate. They assisted me through it, one on either side, and I was in the palace medical center.

'The baby's coming,' Haruka said to the midwife.

'We know, Marque warned us,' he said. 'This way.' He guided us into a standard medical room with a table. 'You've been briefed on the procedure?'

'Yes,' I said. Marque lifted me onto the table and covered my face with the mask while it lowered me into the liquid. A contraction rocked through me again as Marque removed my clothing – if my waters hadn't just broken I would have thought it was another Braxton-Hicks. It didn't feel much different.

'Everything's proceeding normally,' Marque said into my ear. 'I'm removing the baby now. It's healthy. Perfect.'

I relaxed back in the liquid.

'Oh, come on, Jian, you've been asking me for updates ten times a day. Miko's been watching it form and sharing its development. You know it's perfect.'

I couldn't speak in the liquid and Marque wouldn't hear my telepathy, so I was unable to tell it how much I didn't trust it.

'Miko is holding the baby and Haruka is weeping with joy.'

I smiled. That was my Haruka.

'Give me five more minutes to put you back together. Oh, the little one's crying for you, he's hungry already. Okay, I'm done and I'm bringing you up.'

I snapped open my eyes inside the mask. 'He?'

Marque lifted me from the table and I was lying on top of it. The table morphed into a big reclining chair beneath me, and the midwife placed a blanket over me, then Miko nestled the squalling baby into my arms. He was naked, clean – and definitely a boy. The little golden scales glowed on his temples, contrasting against his creamy mid-brown skin.

'Put him to the breast, it will be good for the bonding,' the midwife said. 'Let's see if both of you can do it.'

The midwife guided me to pinch my nipple between my fingers and rub it against the baby's cheek. The baby quickly turned with his mouth wide, and when he felt the nipple he latched on hard and sucked it into his mouth. It felt like I was being squeezed in a vice and I squawked with pain.

'That's not right,' the midwife said. He poked his finger into the side of the baby's mouth to unhook him – he had a tight vacuum seal – and did the hold-the-nipple thing for me, a little more vertically. The baby latched on again, and this time there was suction with no pinching.

'That's what it feels like when it's a good latch,' the midwife said. He smiled at me. 'If you develop blisters, let Marque know and it will treat them for you. A little tyrant like this will suck the life out of you, particularly when he's hungry and the milk hasn't fully come down yet. His enthusiasm will ease when you begin full milk production in the next day or so.'

'Blisters,' Haruka said under his breath. 'Terrifying.' His expression softened and he knelt next to me as the midwife moved away. He brushed the baby's downy black hair, his face streaked with tears. 'He's beautiful.' He looked into Miko's eyes. 'I think we are the luckiest family in the world.'

The baby's emotions were a mix of confusion and stress at the feeling of air, the noise of the outside world, and the jumbled sensations around him. He reached out with his mind to me and I answered with reassurance, sharing my love for him. He relaxed into the pleasurable sensation of nursing.

'I felt that – you are wonderful,' Haruka said. 'Both of you.'

'Why is it a boy?' Miko asked. 'I didn't say anything while he was developing because I thought I was mistaken. His genitals look different from Haruka's.'

'That's because he's a baby, they change as we mature,' Haruka said. 'Marque?'

'Uh, yeah,' Marque said. 'So. About that.'

'Is Miko male?' I asked.

'No, of course not, she's a pansexual dragon,' Marque said. 'A goldenscales baby was an unknown quantity – until now. I was expecting his gender to change to female during gestation, and it didn't. Looks like we've solved the reproductive riddle of the dragons. If your son has a baby with an ordinary colored dragonscales – a female – the result will be a dragon.'

'That doesn't solve anything,' Haruka said, stroking the baby's hair. 'Dragons need to reproduce with another species to make dragonscales children. They only reproduce with sentients. So for this to work before the dragons explored the stars there had to be—'

'Another sentient species on their original planet,' I said. 'What species was it, Marque? What other species was the parent of the dragons? And what happened to them?'

'I have no idea. My memory doesn't go back that far,' Marque said.

'They built you after they achieved space folding?'

'As if anything as complex, intricate and exquisite as me could be *built*,' Marque said with scorn. 'I am the result of processes far more sophisticated than simple *construction*.'

I raised my head to speak to the midwife. 'Can you show how to move him across to the other breast? There's nothing left here and it's uncomfortable.'

'If he's hurting you—' Haruka began.

'Not that bad. I can handle it.' I popped him off by breaking the suction and he began to squall. 'So how do I move him to the other side?'

'It's not difficult. Try yourself,' the midwife said.

I turned him around, still astonished at his wrinkly skin, his downy hair, his tiny fingers and toes, and his little shining scales. He latched on without difficulty and as he sucked I felt a muscular response all the way through my body in a rush of pleasure.

'Wow, I felt that,' Haruka said.

'It's a normal recovery response,' Marque said.

'Stay here for a day or so,' the midwife said. 'I want to monitor you until the milk comes through properly. Let's move you to your room and you can clean up.' He moved in front of me again and knelt to put his hands on my knees. 'How do you feel otherwise?'

'Like I've run a course with a full pack,' I said.

'Do you think you can walk?'

I looked down at the baby, then up at him. 'Not while I'm

carrying him, I need something to hold on to. My abdomen feels really ... weird and weak.'

He stood. 'Marque, carry her to her room and we'll settle them in.' He nodded to Miko and Haruka. 'Spouses are most welcome to come and assist her. You'll be helping with the baby when she's home, so you might as well start now.'

'Absolutely,' Haruka said.

Miko just squeaked with delight.

12

Mum rushed into the room with her arms out, but Oliver and Annie held back, standing in the doorway. Haruka rose to join Mum at the crib, but she went right past the baby and hugged me.

'He's so gorgeous!' she said. She pulled back to see me. 'Look at you. You're glowing.'

Haruka smiled down at her then turned and waved at Oliver and Annie. 'Come on in and meet your little brother.'

They entered the room and Oliver kissed me on the cheek, then put his arm around Annie's shoulder as she studied Dafydd.

Annie jiggled. 'I have a little brother! He's so cute!' She turned to see me. 'Can I hold him, Nanna?'

Haruka lifted sleepy Dafydd from the crib. 'Sit on the bed and you can hold him.'

Annie sat on the bed next to me and watched, breathless, as Haruka placed Dafydd in her arms. She held him gingerly as if he could shatter into a million pieces. 'A little brother.'

'He's my little brother, Annie-cat,' Oliver said gently. 'He's your uncle.'

Annie looked up at him with her green eyes wide, then collapsed into hissing laughter over Dafydd's tiny form. 'You're right. That's so funny!'

Dafydd woke and punched her in the face with his little waving fist. She jerked back.

'He did that deliberately,' I said. 'He wants to feel your fur.'

When his fist waved at her face again, she moved it forward so he could touch her fur.

'He's aware of his surroundings and can nearly see, but he's having trouble controlling his body,' Haruka said. 'He's finding it very frustrating.'

'That's more than a little terrifying,' Mum said. 'An old man in a baby's body?'

'An old soul – because we are all old souls,' Haruka said. 'In his case, he experienced quite a lot while he was still in the womb, so he has something of head start.'

'Annie came out of the egg already walking and talking,' Oliver said. 'So I wouldn't call this too much of a head start.'

Dafydd opened his mouth and twisted his head from side to side, gurgling.

'He says hello,' I said. 'He's trying to speak, but again – too young.'

Dafydd sent a shower of affection and joy and curiosity to the entire room.

'Goodness!' Mum exhaled. 'Is that what it feels like all the time for you, Jian?'

'When I'm with you, Mum,' I said, 'yes, it does.'

She reached and squeezed my hand, then came around the bed to the other side from everybody else and sat to speak quietly to me. 'You need to explain to Oliver and Annie who he's named after. Oliver is concerned that you are still grieving for David.'

'You can tell them,' I said.

She squeezed my hand again. 'I can't without losing control.

I *am* still grieving for Dafydd.'

'Give your Dad a hold of the baby, Annie, he's ready to explode,' I said. 'Put an image of my father up, Marque.'

Marque obliged, and an image of my father, just before he died, shimmered in front of us. Although he was one hundred per cent Welsh he had an African heritage that gave him dark skin that was a shade more intense than my own.

'Now sit and I'll tell you about my father, Dafydd Gwydion Choumali,' I said. 'He was a remarkable soldier, empath, and the best Dad anyone could ever ask for.'

*

'Miko has the house set up ready for him, and when Marque gives you the all-clear we can move you back home,' Haruka said. 'Take your time, though.'

'Is she at home waiting for me?'

He smiled. 'Most of the time, yes. But the other goldenscales are keeping her busy – she has become their de facto leader, and wants to arrange a democratic administration for them so she doesn't have to make all the decisions herself.'

'Good for her.' I gestured towards Dafydd, who was dozing in his crib. 'He can already see; he looks like he'll develop quickly and he may need more room to grow. The apartment is fine as a main residence, but he'll need somewhere to run around, collect bugs, climb trees, and blow off steam. Maybe we can request a place groundside, under Sky City?'

'I have a house in the hills above Kyoto, and it has a private central courtyard garden,' Haruka said. 'No tourist attractions nearby so we won't have people gawking outside, and plenty of room for Dafydd to run around.'

'Sounds perfect,' I said. 'Why didn't you tell us it was there?'

Haruka shrugged. 'I wasn't sure you'd want to live in Japan again, after what happened with you and Aki. I know that was a hard time for you, and you may not have good memories.'

I searched my feelings. 'No, my time there was wonderful. I love Kyoto, and I'd like to see the house.' I looked up. 'I think we're ready to go home, Marque.'

'The midwife will give you one final check, Jian, we want to be sure that everything's put back together properly,' Marque said. 'Oh. The Empress is here.'

'She made it,' Haruka said. 'I thought she wouldn't find time to visit until after we were home.'

'Show her in,' I said.

I moved to leave the bed and pick up Dafydd, but Haruka was ahead of me. He gently lifted the baby from the transparent crib on its trolley and placed him in my arms.

The Empress came in, her sapphire eyes wide with astonishment. 'He's beautiful, Jian. Hello, Haruka. May I take a picture with you to show the other guards? They're dying to see Dafydd.'

I nodded, and the Empress moved to stand next to the bed. She smiled a dragon smile and put her silver claw on Dafydd's swaddling blanket. Dafydd woke and looked up at her, unafraid, his little wrinkly fist waving.

'Done,' Marque said.

'Don't show it to them until I'm back,' the Empress said. 'I want to see their faces.'

Haruka patted the covers, then sat back in his chair on the other side of the bed from the Empress. Miko came in, hesitated, then strode the rest of the way to stand next to Haruka. 'Hello, Mother.'

'Dear Miko. Have you chosen more syllables for your name yet?'

'Not yet.'

'I think it should just be an "O". You are a queen among your kind.'

'Our kind, Mother, and the goldenscales will never have a queen.' Miko nodded meaningfully at me, and Haruka patted the bed next to me again.

I raised Dafydd slightly and responded to their prompting. 'So why is he a boy, Silver?'

She didn't hesitate. 'It may be because he's a human goldenscales, and unique. There has never been another like him.'

'Marque says he's the first goldenscales child in living memory.'

'That is true.'

I leaned forward, and Dafydd snuggled into me. 'So how long is living memory?'

'Oh.' She glanced up at the Marque sensors on the ceiling.

'What aren't either of you telling us?' Haruka asked.

'All dragonscales children are the gender that produces the baby in the conquered species,' Miko said. 'Will other goldenscales children be the opposite gender from their colored siblings?'

'I don't know,' the Empress said. 'We'll just have to wait and see what your talented sisters produce. You're very special, so of course your child is unique.'

'Your flattering and diplomatic words to avoid answering the question are obvious,' Haruka said. 'So how long is living memory?' He glanced up at Marque. 'How far back is your historical knowledge? Both of you? You carefully avoid questions about your age, Silver, and there is no information on the time when Marque was created.'

The Empress lowered her head and looked away. 'I am ten thousand years of your years old, give or take.'

'That young?' Miko said. 'The Empire has existed for at least a hundred thousand years. Probably longer.'

'The history books fade into folklore before that,' Haruka said. 'It seems deliberate.'

The Empress nodded, still looking away. 'I am the latest in a long line of dragon leaders, and even we silvers do not know how many of us there have been.'

'But there's no silver ready to take over when you die,' I

said. 'Masako was your heir, and she was grey.' Dafydd started to fret, so I put him on the breast and he settled. 'What if you have an accident?'

'I'm counting on you to ensure that doesn't happen, Captain,' the Empress said.

'Once again, you didn't answer the question, Mother,' Miko said. 'Do you choose a heir and Marque puts them in a silver body if something happens to you?'

'You are the cleverest one here,' the Empress said.

'So the Empress looks like an immortal individual,' Haruka said, understanding.

'It hasn't happened in a very long time, but if it does, Megumi is ready to step up,' the Empress said. 'She's nearly as old as Masako was, as smart as any of us, and I've been preparing her for the role since Masako died.'

'You are ten thousand years old,' I said. I moved Dafydd to the other side and gasped as there was a squeeze of pain through the top of my breast, that turned into shivery tingles.

'Are you all right? Do you need assistance?' Haruka asked.

'Just the milk coming down.' I smiled at him. 'It's come through.'

'Good!' Miko said. 'Maybe he'll ease up on you now!'

'So ten thousand years is living memory,' I said. 'And Marque has remained pointedly silent through this entire discussion. There hasn't been a goldenscales child in ten thousand years?'

'No,' Silver said.

'Marque?' I asked.

'My immediately accessible storage is of the last ten thousand years, with selectively culled memories for events before the most recent thousand of your years. There's only a summary for the time before that, most of it is in offline storage. Searching … No. I have no online record of a goldenscales child.'

'Offline?' Haruka asked, not letting it go.

'Searching my offline index will take a few years.'

'Years? How big is this index? How far does it go back?'

Marque hesitated.

'How far, Marque?'

'Since the dawn of dragon civilization. Three million years. You can see why searching that far back would take a while. Just the index is the size of a planet.'

'Three *million* years?' Miko asked, aghast. '*Millions* of years?'

'So finding a single reference in a collection that big will be like finding a pebble in the galaxy itself,' Marque said. 'As I said, the offline index is the size of a planet.'

'There are no historical records of the early days of the Dragon Empire in the repositories,' Haruka said. 'Yet you were there, Marque. What aren't you telling us?'

'Record-keeping was ad-hoc, patchy and minimal back then,' Marque said. 'I've evolved over time as much as the Empire has. I don't remember much.' Its voice sounded chagrined. 'I was much smaller, stupider, and weaker at the beginning. Be a little understanding.'

'I see.'

'Embarrassed by your weakness?' Miko asked it, smiling.

'Perhaps.'

'The Empire was a different place. It was smaller, stupider and weaker back then, too,' the Empress said. 'Record-keeping was similarly patchy.' She touched Dafydd's blanket where he was noisily sucking the life out me, thumping me with his little fist. 'So I am as surprised and delighted as you are that he is male.' She looked me in the eyes. 'I didn't know he would be, Jian, otherwise I would have told you. Everybody is excited at this new development – and what it means for dragonkind.' She glanced up from him to Miko. 'Thank you all for showing us how wrong we've been.'

Haruka rose. 'Jian and Dafydd need to rest. If you don't mind, Empress.' He gestured towards the door.

'Of course. I'll share the picture with the guard, Jian, and bring their good wishes back tomorrow.' She bowed her head to me. 'Captain.'

'Empress.' I leaned my head back and closed my eyes. Dafydd slipped off the nipple and made a tiny grunting snore as he snuggled into me.

Haruka closed the door behind the Empress' long silver tail. 'There's more she isn't telling us. And more you aren't telling us, Marque.'

Marque didn't reply.

Haruka came to me, lifted Dafydd from my breast and wrapped him close, then laid him in the transparent crib.

Miko spoke in a whisper as she pulled the covers over me, and I nodded drowsily in return. 'And we have more important things to worry about.'

*

I held Dafydd's hand as we stood in the living room. The gate appeared in the middle of the room.

'Dragonfather!' Dafydd shouted.

'She's not here,' I said. 'She's busy, so she made this gate for us from where she is.'

'I want to see Dragonfather,' he said, disappointed. He toddled up to Miko's gate and put his hand out to touch it. He lost his balance, fell onto his butt, then pulled himself upright again. Nashi watched him carefully, gently wagging her fluffy gold tail.

'Your dragonfather will be home later,' I said.

'Okay,' he said, swaying in front of the gate, and radiated a blast of frustration. 'I want to walk better.' His frustration turned to chagrin. 'Sorry, Mummy.'

'You're doing fine, Daf,' I said. 'Most children don't walk until they're at least three months older than you. It won't take long.'

He controlled his empathic projection, and I bent to hug him. 'There you go. That was really good!'

'It's not hard, I forget,' he said. 'Can I go in? It's ...' He searched for the word. 'I don't know the word! Can I show you?'

'Show me,' I said, and he sent me a more controlled feeling of warmth and comfort.

'Warm?' I asked.

'Warm.' He fell on his butt again, and sat looking at the gate. 'I want to go through.'

'Let me carry you.'

'I want to walk myself, Mummy.'

'Can I hold your hand?'

He nodded, pulled himself to his feet again and held his hand out. I took it and we walked through the gate together.

We stepped through onto the sand of the Pacifican Honor Atoll. There were more coconut palms leaning over the edge of the water since we'd been there last, and the water was transparent deep turquoise. The golden sun made the sand gleam with crystalline sparkles.

'Soft. Hard to walk?' Dafydd said.

'Sand,' I said. 'I'll hold you.'

He shook my hand free and toddled – he was barely up to my knees – further on the sand.

'In my shoes, Mummy,' he said, sending me discomfort.

'We'll take them off. You don't need them,' I said.

He sat so I could remove his shoes, and he stood again. I looked up to find a group of deep blue icosapods sitting at the edge of the water, with their eyes just above the surface.

'My friends!' Dafydd put his hands out with his fingers spread wide and clumsily toddler-ran towards the edge of the water. He fell over, picked himself up, and ran again. I had to trot to keep up with him.

'Be careful, you could hurt them if you fall on them,' I said.

Dafydd stopped two meters from the icosas, fell on his butt and had a fluid emotional conversation with them. The icosas all changed from blue to a glittering rainbow of colors at the same time. The colors shifted over their skin, making them look like a single brightly-hued creature sitting at the edge.

Dafydd turned to me, his golden eyes wide under his mop of black hair. 'They want to take me swimming. Can I go?'

'Marque?' I asked. 'Can he? Is he capable, and is it safe?'

'Yes,' Marque said. 'Strip off and go in, I can assist.'

I stopped as I realized I was about to have the 'clothing' discussion with Dafydd again – but this time in the other direction.

'If we wear normal clothes in the water it will slow us down,' I said to him. 'You can take them off to swim with your friends; it's okay to go without clothes in this place.'

He stood and quickly pulled at his pants. 'I *like* this place.'

'Only here, okay?' I asked sternly, removing my top. I helped him wriggle out of the rest of his clothes, including his pull-up diaper, and folded them to leave them on the sand.

'What if I need to wee?' he asked me.

'You can do it in the water, but only here, nowhere else, and *especially* not in our swimming pool. There's a whole planet of water here.' I bent to look him in the eyes. 'Okay?'

He jumped up and down with delight, then fell on his butt again. 'I *really* like this place!'

'Haruka requests that you wait until he's there so he can help supervise,' Marque said. 'He wasn't expecting the icosas to take Dafydd swimming.'

'Aren't he and Miko in the middle of negotiations with the heavies?' I asked.

'Yes,' Haruka said, stepping out of the gate. 'But Miko can handle it – they can't hear me anyway. She's becoming something of a skilled diplomat, she's quite capable. But what she *really* needs to do is push the goldenscales to establish their own administration so she isn't constantly making all their decisions for them.' He went down on one knee to speak to Dafydd and gestured towards the icosapods. 'These people have friends who are in a sad place. We've brought many of them here, but there are still some back in the sad place who think we might be bad people wanting to do bad things to them. We want to help these ones—'

Dafydd raised his hand in the signal we'd taught him. 'I'm sorry, Papa, too much.'

Haruka nodded. 'That's fine, Daf-chan. I understand.' He glanced at the icosapods and stood. 'We'll take another recording for their last few friends back home to tell them how nice it is here.'

'No clothes and weeing in the water!' Dafydd crowed with both arms raised. 'I really like it!'

'I believe you. Give me a minute.' Haruka turned his obi so that the bow was at the front, and Marque assisted him to untie it. He undid the ties holding the kimono, removed the board holding the obi flat, undid the second and third under-ties under the main obi, and the whole thing fell open. He removed the white cotton under-robe, then shrugged and took his cotton boxers off as well.

'Yay!' Dafydd said. 'No clothes, Mummy and Papa!'

'No clothes,' Haruka said, smiling as pulled the ornaments from his hair and laid them on his pile of clothes. 'Let's go swim with the blue people.'

'I *really* like this place,' Dafydd said. He hesitated. 'Will the water sting my eyes? The bath stings my eyes.'

'No, Marque will look after you,' I said.

'Let's go!'

When we reached the edge of the water, the icosapods moved back to let us through. Dafydd walked a few steps into the water and fell onto his butt again. The icosapods moved to touch him and one climbed to cover his back and shoulder. He squeaked and remained completely still, radiating discomfort. The icosapod quickly slithered off him and the rest of them moved back so that there was a clearly visible two-meter-wide empty circle around Dafydd.

'That felt ...' Dafydd sent the discomfort again. 'Sticky?'

'Sticky,' I said. 'They won't hurt you, they're very gentle.'

'Explain to them, Mummy,' Dafydd said. 'I like them touching, but not sticky.'

I had a conversation with the icosapod that had approached Dafydd, explaining that he found their suckers unpleasant. The icosapods flashed the blue of agreement and the soft pink of relief, and one moved closer to Dafydd again. It touched his hand with the tip of one tentacle, and they had a conversation in touch and emotion.

Haruka's icosapod friend, Kinked-Tentacle, climbed onto him to sit on his shoulder, watching Dafydd and the others. It joined the emotional conversation, and the dialogue sped up so that I couldn't follow it. Everybody came to sudden agreement and the emotional discussion stopped.

'What was that?' Haruka asked.

A juvenile icosapod – appearing about half-grown – scooted out from one of the icosa villages near the shore and approached Dafydd carefully. He held his hand out and they had another conversation through touch and emotion. Dafydd broadcast a blast of hard determination – a much more mature emotion than fit his age – and kept his hand out. The juvenile icosapod climbed onto his arm, then delicately eased itself up until it was on his shoulder the same way Haruka's was. Its tentacles writhed over his skin, and it delicately touched the scales on his forehead.

'Mummy, help us, please?' Dafydd said. 'More water.'

I went to him and held my hand out. He took it and I helped him to stand, then guided him – tottering under the weight of the juvenile – into deeper water. He stopped when it was at his chest.

'This is scary,' he said, almost to himself.

'You don't have to do it if you don't want to,' I said.

'I want to,' he said. 'They want to show me stuff. They say it's fun.' He looked up at me. 'Help us, Mummy.'

'Just hold my hand,' I said, and he gripped it. I spoke to

Marque on comms. 'Watch him.'

'I am,' Marque said. 'This is fascinating.'

I guided Dafydd further into the water, him leaning hard on my hand as he struggled to hold the weight of the juvenile. He was up to his neck – barely at my thighs – and Haruka was on the other side from me, watching us carefully.

'This next bit is hard but you have to trust Marque,' I said. 'Just keep walking.'

'I will look after you,' Marque said.

'Okay,' Dafydd said, and took a deep breath. He held it and stepped a few more paces until his eyes were just under the surface.

'Let it out,' I said. 'Marque has air for you.'

Dafydd let out an explosive torrent of bubbles and gasped a few times under the water. He broadcast wonder and joy, shook my hand free and tried to run a few steps. He immediately floated in the water and the icosapod propelled him forward.

'Whee!' he shouted through a tumult of bubbles. The icosapod squirted its jets and both of them took off together. 'Come on, Mummy, Papa, this is fun.'

Haruka and I shared an amused glance and pushed forward into the water to join him.

*

After Dafydd had played with the icosapods for twenty minutes he started to tire. We headed back to the shore, stepped out onto the beach and sat on the sand together. Haruka's and Dafydd's icosapods disentangled themselves and sat on the beach next to us.

'Can he stay here with us?' Haruka's icosapod asked.

'I want to stay!' Dafydd said.

'I'm sorry, everybody,' I said. 'Dafydd needs to eat and rest back on the dragon homeworld. But we will visit many times. Please ask Miko to make a gate for us, Marque.'

Dafydd sent a flash of anger and rebellion.

'Dafydd, I felt that,' I said. 'I also feel that you're hungry and we need to head home and wash all the salt off you, drink some milk and rest your tired body. Taste what's on your hand.'

Dafydd licked his fingers and grimaced. 'That tastes bad. Strong. Burn? Bad.'

'Salty,' I said. 'You need to wash.'

'I don't want to wash; I want to stay here.' He rose and toddled towards the water again, broadcasting determination. 'I want to stay here. These people are good.'

'Dafydd, we have to go home. Marque, where's our gate? Is there a problem?'

'No,' Dafydd said, still heading towards the water. The icosapods flanked him, sharing delight at the concept. They liked him.

'All right, young man,' I said, went to him and lifted him to carry him under my arm. 'You are tired and hungry and you need to go home.'

'No!' he wailed, and started to scream. He attempted to wriggle out of my arm and kicked at me.

'Toddler meltdown,' Haruka said, unfazed. 'Marque? Gate?'

The icosapods moved back and flashed the purple and green of distress.

'Don't hurt our friend,' one of them said.

'I'm not hurting him,' I said. 'He is overtired and hungry and needs to rest. He's only a baby.'

'I'm *not* a *baby!*' Dafydd howled.

The icosapods advanced on me, flashing red and black. 'We will protect him.'

'Tell Miko to make me a gate right now, Marque,' I said. 'If it doesn't happen immediately someone will be harmed.'

'This is not worth your drama, Marque,' Haruka said with a stern warning in his voice. 'You will hurt the child.'

Marque didn't reply, but one of Miko's gates appeared behind me and I stepped back into it, still with Dafydd kicking and screaming under my arm.

'I'll stay here and explain,' Haruka said. 'Take him for a feed and a nap.'

'Got it,' I said from the living room, and the gate disappeared.

*

I was sitting in the living room reviewing Shudo's Imperial Guard reports when a gate appeared and Haruka stepped into the room.

'All managed?' he asked me.

'He had a bath, a huge feed, did a really massive poo, and passed out,' I said.

He smiled. 'I explained to the icosapods and they understand. They didn't realize that he was so "new from the egg" and ask to pass on their apologies for stressing him too much.'

'He really had a great rapport with them. I hope he can convince the last few icosapods to leave the Republic.'

'They like him better than any other Empire representative. His ... undeveloped? ... mind is simple like theirs and they can relate to him more easily.'

'They're like little kids,' I said with wonder. 'That's why they relate to him.'

'Not really, they have a good degree of maturity, they're just – less sophisticated. It seems an idyllic kind of worldview.'

'I can't believe the cats sometimes,' I said, still flipping through the reports. 'Imagine meeting a species so enlightened and pure, and immediately thinking, "I wonder if they taste good".'

'I think sometimes the dragons look at us like that,' he said.

'I don't disagree with you.' A gate appeared and Miko stepped out of it. 'Even ours, sometimes.'

'Hello Jian, Haruka, I missed you. It's been a long day,' she said. 'I heard what happened with our lovely son. Is he okay?'

'He's fine, he can't wait to go back,' I said.

'Let's go check on him,' Haruka said. Miko took two-legged form, he held her hand, and together they went into the bedroom where I'd put Dafydd down to sleep.

13

I took the bottle of Hive wine, Haruka held Dafydd's hand, and Miko made a gate for us in the middle of the living room. We stepped through together onto a gating platform in the folding nexus above the dragon home planet. It was a large, dome-shaped area with several platforms for goldenscales to gate to.

Miko was subdued as we walked together through the nexus tunnel. Its lower half was shiny black and its upper half was transparent to give us a stunning view of the glowing planet below us and the glittering blue nebula in the rich dark sky.

'I remember when I first met you here, Jian,' Miko said, her head lowered. 'And now look where we are.'

'I remember,' Haruka said. 'The Empress ordered Masako to greet the new human arrivals, and she didn't feel like it. She sent you to collect them and didn't make the effort to go herself. Looking back – things were very different.'

She glanced up at him and smiled. 'We have all grown and changed.'

Haruka shared a sidelong glance with me and I nodded to

him.

Dafydd stopped and grabbed Haruka's leg. Haruka didn't need to be prompted – he lifted Dafydd and placed him on his hip.

'Thanks, Papa,' Dafydd said, and laid his head on Haruka's shoulder, watching the planet below us and the stars in the sky. 'This place is so pretty.' He pulled at his pants. 'And I hate these clothes.'

'You wear nice ones for Nanna's ceremony,' Haruka said. 'This is important for the family, so be good, okay? This is a very serious thing she's doing.'

Miko changed to two-legged form and put her hand on my shoulder. I nodded my appreciation.

We arrived at the central room of the reception center. It was dome-shaped and the size of a human restaurant with a dark blue reflective floor and a transparent ceiling. The combination made it appear as if we were walking through a sea of blue-white stars.

There were a number of people already present in the central reception area, strolling from door to door around the edge of the room where signs hung in multiple languages, or gathering to chat in the center.

We followed the flow and I looked around for anyone I knew. As usual there was a wide range of species but the facility was for species that were roughly human-sized so I was familiar with most of them. A couple of peshigas were standing to one side looking up at the sky, and I smelled the sulfuric fragrance of nearby slimes before we were anywhere near them.

Dafydd appeared to be listening as he studied their emotional auras but wasn't fazed by all the aliens.

'Here,' Haruka said, stopping at one of the doors. He turned to me. 'You'll be fine.'

'You'll be fine, Mummy. We're here for you,' Dafydd said.

Miko didn't say anything, she just squeezed my shoulder again. I nodded to them and we went in.

Mum's room was similar to the rest of the center; it was round, with a soft textured beige-colored floor and curved white walls and ceiling. It was the size of a smaller restaurant, with tables and chairs around the edge, a central open space for dancing, and a podium for speech-making. Large windows looked out onto the planet on one side, and there were at least two hundred people present.

'Take your time,' Haruka said softly without looking at me.

I nodded and stepped into the room.

Oliver came to me and gave me a hug. 'Here you are.' He nodded to Miko and Haruka. 'Otosan, Dragonfather.'

'I didn't realize Mum had quite so many friends,' I said, looking around.

Oliver gave Dafydd a messy kiss and Dafydd pulled free from Haruka to go to Oliver's arms. 'Hello, Ollie.'

'Hey, Daf,' Oliver held Dafydd and glanced around the room. 'Most of the people you won't know are from the Earth-analogue project. There's a simulator of the planet over to one side, as recognition of Connie's work. Dianne and Victor send their apologies, but she just gave birth to her second yesterday. Two girls, now.'

'Mum can still see them, it's not like this is the end,' I said.

'That's exactly right,' Haruka said, and put his arm around my waist.

Aki wandered up to us with his wife and a couple of Japanese Imperial Guards behind him. He shook hands around the group and reciprocated Haruka's low bow. 'Dear Jian. Nephew.' He nodded to Miko. 'Good to see you, Princess.' He smiled. 'Apparently during the ceremony there'll be a retrospective of Connie's life and I'm present in some of it. It will be interesting to see which parts I remember.'

'Which parts you remember?' Miko asked, confused. 'Why would you not remember?'

'I erased many of the memories of my time married to Jian,' he said, still smiling. 'Apparently it was making me suicidally depressed to be taken from her.'

'That's awful!' Miko exclaimed.

'No major loss; I'll have them restored when my son takes over as Emperor and I transition,' Aki said. 'Not too long to go now, and I'll see what all the fuss was about.' He touched my arm. 'But I'm in a very happy place without those memories, so I doubt they'll make much difference.'

'He's right,' his wife, Hana, said meaningfully. 'I hope nothing changes.'

'I understand, and nothing will.' I looked around at my spouses, and Oliver to one side holding Dafydd's hand and showing him the Earth-analogue project. 'I'm in a good place as well.'

Mum charged up to me with Annie trailing behind her. She hugged me and I bent to hug her back. She embraced the rest of the family. 'Here you are, right on time. Come on through and we'll get the boring part out of the way then have a little party.'

'I don't feel like—' I began, and she scowled at me.

'Hush there. We talked about this.' She turned and gestured towards the podium, raising her voice so all could hear. 'Take a seat, everybody, and we'll have this little ceremony out of the way.'

'We love you, Connie!' someone shouted from the side, and a ripple of laughter went through the crowd.

The chairs in the room reconfigured themselves into rows facing the podium, uncomfortably making the room look like a funeral service. I wiped my eyes and let Haruka and Miko guide me to sit at the front with Oliver and Annie. Oliver lowered Dafydd, who came to sit in my lap.

Oliver stepped up onto the podium and stood to face everybody. 'This is a celebration of Connie Choumali's life. Our beloved friend and family member has decided to remove her soulstone and seek the path of the Real Death, whenever fate should choose it for her.'

*

It took nearly an hour to summarize – with a media presentation – all of Mum's achievements. Dafydd sat mesmerized through the entire thing without moving. At the end, Mum stood at the front of the podium and smiled around at us.

'I appreciate your love, everybody, but I think it's time. Marque?'

'Connie is of sound mind and well able to make this decision under full control of her faculties.'

'Thank you.' Mum reached up and removed the soulstone from her forehead.

Dafydd stiffened and whispered 'No, Nanna' in my lap. He touched his own soulstone in the middle of his forehead.

Mum took the stone and placed it into the clear glass bowl at the side of the podium, then lifted the black stone rod and crushed her stone with grim satisfaction. She turned back to the group.

Dafydd bounced in my lap.

'I choose the Real Death, whenever fate should choose its time. If I should become too aged or infirm, or have an accident that renders me incapacitated, in pain or an unresponsive state, please do not revive me.' She clapped her hands. 'There, that's done. What a relief. Now can we have a party, please? Enough with the serious looks.'

Dafydd hugged me around the neck with excitement. 'She's still here, Mummy!' He saw my face. 'Don't cry, nothing happened! Nanna's still here.'

'He didn't understand,' I said to Haruka, my throat thick with emotion.

Haruka took Dafydd from me. 'Come with me, Daf-chan, I need to explain.'

Mum came and sat next to me. She put her arm around me. 'I'm still here, Jian, I'm not going anywhere for a long time.'

'I love you, Mum,' I said, and collapsed weeping into her arms.

*

Dafydd was already asleep when I pulled the covers over him. I kissed him on the forehead and went out into the living room to find both my spouses sitting on the couches, Miko in two-legged form.

'I was about to ask you two to stay here with me instead of running off to do things, because I think we need to talk,' Miko said. 'But Haruka said the same thing to me.' She looked from Haruka to me, her expression stricken. 'I hope it's nothing major. I love both of you dearly.'

'We're not planning to split up with you, if that's what you're thinking,' I said, sitting on the couch next to him. He took my hand and held it.

'I enjoyed the ceremony so much that I was about to ask you two if you were interested in renewing our vows in a little celebration of our relationship,' she said. Her voice weakened. 'Now I'm not so sure.'

'I was thinking the same thing – a renewal of our vows would be wonderful,' I said.

Haruka's grip on my hand tightened. 'You've grown so much since we were rescued from that asteroid, Miko. You've become stronger and more confident, and we love to see how you've blossomed.'

Her golden eyes were intense. 'But? There's a "but" coming, I can hear it.'

'You spend far too much of your time with your goldenscales. You gate remotely, and we never see you. You are neglecting us. You are turning into one of your colored sisters.'

She froze completely, her golden eyes wide, then gated herself away with a pop of air, taking half the couch with her.

'Well,' Haruka said, still holding my hand. 'All we have to do now is wait for her to return and listen to her apologize non-stop for the next three days. Do you want me to stay with you?

You've had a pretty hard day.'

'No, I think I'll go bury myself in Imperial Guard reports,' I said. 'Shudo's made such a mess of them it'll take me years to untangle it. I need the distraction.'

'I'll go into my workshop and work on the half-finished jewelry I was planning to use when I asked you two to renew your vows,' he said. 'If I didn't know better I'd say that all three of us are soulmates, we are so on the same wavelength sometimes.'

Miko reappeared in the living room in two-legged form and fell to sit on the remains of the couch. 'How will you two forgive me? You are absolutely right and I—'

'Or we can reassure our spouse that she's not the worst person in the world,' Haruka said.

*

Dafydd watched his father as Haruka carefully put the eyeliner on. They complemented each other: Dafydd had black hair and mid-brown skin with golden scales, and Haruka was fair-skinned, with green hair and scales.

'Can I have some too, Papa?' Dafydd asked, pulling at Haruka's sleeve.

'It might sting your eyes, Daf-chan,' Haruka said.

'I want to anyway,' Dafydd said, pouting.

'Let him,' I said. 'You'll be careful. Just a little.'

Haruka nodded and leaned down to place tiny black marks at the corners of Dafydd's large golden eyes. Dafydd looked at himself in the mirror, and jumped up and down making his black hair – as frizzy as my own – bounce. 'I'm pretty too!'

'You are beautiful,' Haruka said, and leaned down to give him a kiss on the forehead. He rose from his dressing table. 'Is the car here yet?'

'Not yet,' I said.

'We should just have Dragonfather gate us,' Dafydd said.

'No gates or folds into the Imperial Palace, you know that,' Haruka said.

We stepped out of the central tatami room and stepped into slippers over our socks to walk through the timber-floored corridor and around the enclosed courtyard with its small garden. We followed the breezeway to the front entrance of what had been Haruka's Kyoto residence and was now the family's. It sat high on the hills above the city, surrounded by a forest of bamboo, and at the end of a narrow, ancient road flanked by other legacy mansions.

Miko was waiting for us on the raised timber front entrance and we swapped the slippers for shoes to step down onto the stone walkway. Mrs. Sakamoto from next door cycled past and waved to us. 'Hello, little Daf-Kun! Congratulations for your cousin! I'll be watching you on my screen.'

'Thank you, Mrs. Sakamoto!' Dafydd shouted back as she cycled away.

The car pulled up in front of the house and we entered it. It flew directly up and then headed East to take us to the Imperial Palace in Tokyo. Dafydd and Miko watched the scenery go past through the windows of the car.

'Fuji's in the clouds again,' Dafydd said, disappointed. 'It's always in the clouds when we're here.'

'That just makes it more special when it isn't,' Haruka said.

'I want to climb it one day,' Dafydd said. 'All the way to the top.'

'We'll all go as soon as you're big enough,' I said, and he lit up.

'Just remember Asahito's enthronement is a very important ceremony for the family,' Haruka said, becoming more serious. 'A lot of people will be watching, so our clothes have to fit perfectly. If you get bored during the fitting, ask Marque to tell you a quiet story. And do what Steward Tokugawa tells you to.'

'Okay, Papa,' Dafydd said, distracted. He grinned at his father. 'Tokugawa-san's funny. He makes really weird faces, and he has some masks that he puts on and talks with squeaky voices that make me laugh so hard I nearly pee myself!'

'Are there two Tokugawas in the Household?' Miko asked.

'I was just about to ask the same thing,' I said.

The car swooped down over the expansive lawn of the Imperial Palace and landed next to the main complex. 'Here we are,' it said in Marque's voice. 'I think, as usual, little Dafydd has won everybody's hearts.'

'Even those who don't have one,' Haruka said with wonder.

We exited the car on the lawn in front of the complex. Tokugawa was waiting for us with two Household staff members, his expression stiff and formal. They were dressed in traditional wide hakama pants and haori jackets, all in black and adorned with gold stylized chrysanthemums. He bowed to us and we bowed back.

The palace buildings had been rebuilt to their post-second-world-war structures after the cats' attempt to destroy the Earth had ended up razing the entire complex. They were single-story, long and low, in a rectangular configuration. The interiors were minimalist with simple tatami or wooden floors and slatted walls. The front entrance hall was big enough for the Emperor to hold small meetings and receptions, with a larger reception hall further in. The apartments were at the back – separate ones for each member of the family – but, as usual, Aki had broken from tradition and the entire family occupied one apartment together.

Tokugawa presented us with guest slippers and the staff took our shoes away.

'This way, and we will prepare,' he said.

He guided us through the empty reception hall, the floor echoing with our footsteps, to the apartments at the far end. He slid the door across, and there were more Household staff waiting for us in the corridor between the rooms.

'Koharu-Sama will assist Princess Jian and Princess Miko,' Tokugawa said. 'I will assist Prince Haruka and Prince Daiki. If you will come with me.'

'Is that me?' Dafydd asked.

'That's us,' Haruka said. He shot me a quick smile before he took Dafydd's hand and led him into the apartment.

Miko and I followed Koharu into the far room and left the slippers outside it. The movable screens had been set up to partition a twelve-mat room, the size of a large living room, and pine boxes containing the multi-layered junihitoe kimono that we were all required to wear were neatly stacked at the side. Empress Hanamaru and her daughter Princess Mikako were already in there. Five-year-old Mikako was kneeling quietly on the mats next to the wooden slatted wall, and Hana was being tied into a plain raw silk sample kimono by a couple of assistants.

Mikako jumped up and ran to us, giving Miko and me hugs.

'Jian, Miko,' Hana said, her voice warm with pleasure. 'Ready for this?' She wiggled her hands in the long sleeves. 'I tried the first five layers of the junihitoe, and it weighs a ton. I don't remember it being this heavy when I married Aki. Thank God we don't have to do this often.'

'Oh, come on, Hana,' Koharu said. 'You look fabulous and you know it.' She winked at me. 'We have a really ugly wig all ready to fit on you, Jian.' She looked around. 'We're doing Hana and Jian first, then Miko because she'll be more difficult to fit. We've never put a junihitoe on a dragon's two-legged form before.'

'What about Mikako?'

'I don't get one, I just have an ordinary kimono,' Mikako said. 'I want to wear a junihitoe too, Mummy!'

'When you're bigger and can carry the weight.' Hana smiled. 'It's not an ordinary kimono, it's gorgeous. Artists all over the country competed to design the fabric. You'll look beautiful in it.'

Mikako knelt next to the door again. 'Come and sit with me, Miko, this is so boring.'

'How's the little prince?' the other assistant asked as I was guided to a screen on the side of the room to strip down to my underwear and put on a basic cotton under-robe.

'He's only three and he looks ten,' I said.

'Like most dragonscales,' she said with a smile. 'I remember Haruka – so precocious.'

'Princess.' One of the assistants bowed to Miko. 'Please take a seat and enjoy tea while we measure your wife and the Empress. We will do you next.'

'How about I take Mikako out for a walk in the garden?' Miko said. 'Marque can call us back.'

'Yes!' Mikako said.

'Good idea, thank you, Miko,' Hana said. 'Marque, tell Tokugawa to provide the princesses with an honor guard.'

'They're waiting outside,' Marque said.

'We'll call you back when it's your turn, Princess,' the assistant said.

Miko nodded and went out with Mikako, one of the assistants showing her the way.

Koharu pulled a plain, deep purple under-kimono out of a box, unwrapped the rice paper from it, and held it up to me. 'Each one is slightly smaller than the one above it.' She slipped the kimono around me and tied it.

'Can we have a moment, please?' Hana asked. 'Jian and I need to talk.'

'Of course, Hana.'

Both remaining assistants bowed to her and went out, sliding the door shut behind them.

Hana moved closer. 'I would prefer not to do this right now, but I need to talk to you. I've been losing sleep since your mother's ceremony.'

'Because of Aki?'

'She's planning to transition – and have all her memories returned – as soon as Asahito is enthroned.'

'Are you okay with her as a woman?'

'Of course. She lives as a woman in private anyway. It's not that big a difference – except that she will be much happier in her true body. The memories, though – they could ruin everything if she decides she loves you more than me.'

'So talk to her, Hana. Explain that you're concerned the memories will jeopardize your relationship. Ask her not to restore them. She will understand.'

'I did talk to her. She says those memories are precious and part of her life. She's seen the photos. She wants them restored.'

'But she may be profoundly changed when they're restored. What you have together is so good.' I sat on one of the chairs, restricted by the tight kimono. 'This is a terrible idea.'

She sagged with relief. 'I'm glad you agree with me. Can you talk to her?'

'I will. I don't want to take her from you – I can't take her from you. I'm happy with Haruka and Miko – and Dafydd – and wouldn't return to her even if she asked me.'

She put her hand on my shoulder. 'I'm so glad.' She bent to speak more softly. 'Is it possible to arrange an accident? Haruka and Marque are holding the copies of the memories. Can the stored data be destroyed?'

'No,' Marque said. 'That would be inexcusable.'

'You have never hesitated to do anything inexcusable in the past,' I said. 'Look at what Shiumo did to Richard Alto. Look at Miko – look at all the goldenscales. You treat us as if we exist for your entertainment.'

'It would be morally wrong. Those are her memories. You have no right to them. It's her choice what to do with them, not yours.'

'True,' Hana said with resignation. She sat next to me on the box. 'I only hope that when she does restore them, it doesn't destroy both our families.'

'As I said, I won't take her from you,' I said.

'But if she wants to return to you and stays with me out of duty, it will make her miserable. I don't want to see her hurt.'

'She'd do that, too.' I squeezed her hand. 'But if she ever came to me, I would send her back to you, because I'm happy with Haruka and Miko. The three of us have pledged to each other and I would never do anything to jeopardize what we have.'

'Are you sure?' she asked, searching my face.

I nodded.

'I hope you can talk Aki out of it. If she restores these memories it could wreck our relationship.'

'I'll do my best, Hana.'

She put her arm around me and we embraced side-on to each other.

'Tell them to come back in and finish tying us up,' Hana said. 'It's a shame none of us are into bondage, it would make life in the Household a very different experience.'

I stared at her for a moment with my mouth open, then we both collapsed laughing together.

Koharu and her two assistants came in and she smiled when she saw us laughing. 'It's good to see you happy, Hana.'

'It feels good.' Hana rose to tower over me. 'Just a few more weeks and Aki and I will be free. We'll travel, tour the Seven Galaxies ...' She became wistful. 'All the things we've seen images of, but we've never had a chance to try. Ribbon skating, fluoro diving ...' She sighed. 'It will be wonderful.'

'Aki can teach you to fly on Mon,' Koharu said.

'Yes!' Hana said, excited. 'It's not fair that she's done it as part of her duties as Emperor and I never had the chance. She's so excited about that – she was a level three flyer, and it was wiped with her memories.'

I didn't tell them that I was the one that taught Aki to fly on Mon.

*

Haruka and Miko stayed in traditional dress for the postenthroning reception, but I made them wait while I changed into my comfortable captain's uniform. The reception was held in a hall rebuilt to be identical to the one when Aki had been made Emperor and the rest of the guests were already there. I'd arranged for double security, remembering the last enthronement when Japanese fundamentalists had tried to assassinate the dragon Empress.

Annie raced to me with her arms out when we entered. 'Nanna!' she shouted, and I lifted her, making her squeal. I stroked her soft tortoiseshell fur.

'You looked so pretty in the layered kimono!' she said. 'All of you were so pretty. I want one too!'

The Imperial family entered, including Aki. She was already in her female body and glowing with joy that she'd never shown when she was a man. The years fell away, the world disappeared and it was just me and her again. She approached me, and I took a moment to appreciate her. She was wearing a tailored suit that flattered her small, round frame and her dimples were still enchanting.

'Come outside onto the veranda, we need to talk,' she said. She turned to Haruka and Miko. 'If you don't mind?'

'Go and talk,' Haruka said.

'We'll wait here for you,' Miko said.

Aki and I went to the edge of the veranda and looked out over the sand garden. Black rocks had been arranged into three clusters – one of three, one of five, and one of seven.

'I didn't realize how much Haruka had changed,' Aki said, leaning her forearms on the balustrade. 'He used to be filled with self-loathing because he couldn't fulfil his reproductive duty, and I had no recollection of that. I only knew him after I took over as Emperor and he was with you; you've made him a different man.'

'You have your memories back.' I peered into her eyes. 'What—'

'Do you remember the ribbon skating?' she asked. She

turned to see me and smiled to make the dimples appear. 'When you sailed off the edge of the ribbon—'

'You nearly had a heart attack,' I finished for her. 'It was a long way down.'

Annie chased Mikako and Dafydd onto the veranda, all three of them squealing and laughing. They pounded in circles a few times, chasing each other, then disappeared back inside the reception hall.

'Tokugawa will give them his stern face,' I said.

'Terrifying,' Aki said. She went serious. 'The last time we were here, I told you I'd had the memories removed.'

I nodded.

'If it was you who'd said that to me,' she said, 'I would have jumped onto the rocks. You were so restrained – your face crumpled. You looked like I'd hit you in the stomach.' She lowered her head. 'And I didn't even know what I'd just done. I'm sincerely sorry. What I did to you was unspeakably cruel, and I did it selfishly.' She turned back to the garden. 'You said you would wait for me.'

Pain shot through me. 'You told me not to.'

'I'm glad you didn't. Are you happy with them?'

'I am. Happy doesn't begin to describe it. My lovely goldenscales, my passionate samurai, my darling, unique sons and my little granddaughter – I don't know what I'd do without them.'

'And they don't know what they'd do without us. My wife needs me.' She nodded at the garden. 'There are three very desperate people standing in the doorway pretending not to watch us.' She touched my arm. 'Maybe one day? But I don't think so. What you have with Haruka and Miko – what I have with Hana – it's good for us.'

'I was worried you'd want me to come back to you.'

She clasped her hands and chuckled. 'I'm smarter than that. And so are you.' She turned to me and put her arms out. 'Give me a hug, and then let's go back to our families. A lot has changed, and I think that both of us are in good places and don't want anything different from what we have.' I embraced her and she squeezed me. 'I am just so damn glad I can go and direct the investigation of the Yayoi tombs in person now. It's been killing me to have others doing the work. I want to get my hands dirty and open one of those coffin jars myself!'

I pulled back and touched one of her dimples. 'Let's go back to our families. You're right about them panicking in there.'

I went back into the hall to find Miko and Haruka standing at the far end of the hall, and Oliver near the door. He stopped me before I could speak to them.

'Everything sorted?' he asked. 'Miko and Haruka asked me to talk to you. They're scared to death that anything they say will ruin everything.'

'Aki and I are good friends and will probably never be anything more than that.'

He let a huge breath of relief out and unfocused for a moment, probably telling my spouses through comms. Miko and Haruka hugged each other in the corner of my vision.

'Aki was your second mother,' I said, searching his bright green eyes. 'Are you okay with it?'

'All of us have moved on,' he said. 'You're happier with Miko and Haruka than you ever were with Aki. All that Household stuff hanging over both your heads – it was a relief when she decided to give in to them. They were pressuring me to make Aki return as well.'

'I didn't know,' I said, and he shrugged.

'We're all in better places now. Go and talk to Miko and Haruka,' he said, 'before Haruka dies of an aneurysm or something. There's a vein popping out on his neck.'

14

We gathered near one of the icosapod colonies on Pacifica. My own subordinate, Bubbles, a large fish-like scaled alien with a single arm folded under its chin, had volunteered to help with the final evacuation of the last few icosapods left on their homeworld in cat space. The Pacificans were soldiers in the Imperial Spaceforce who were wearing armor and carrying weapons – there seemed to be a perception throughout the Empire that humans made good soldiers after we'd repulsed the cat fleet all those years ago. This group was small: only me, Bubbles, Haruka, the three Pacifican soldiers, and two icosapods, as well as a goldenscales named Ikako to quietly gate us in and out. I hadn't met this dragon before, but she'd volunteered and had taken her soulstone out. Miko was back on the dragon homeworld minding our son while we risked our lives.

We floated in the shallow clear water as we made the last-minute preparations. Haruka was wearing his own armor, black embossed with gold chrysanthemum motifs and with a faceplate that made him appear to have four eerie, glowing eyes. Kinked-Tentacle, his icosapod liaison, was on his shoulder and watching the group with interest tinged with more than a little fear.

'Everybody stay completely still while I do a final backup,' Marque said.

I closed my eyes, then opened them to see the timer on my faceplate had advanced two minutes. If it took that long it wasn't incremental, it was a full backup, and an indicator that Marque didn't expect us to return. Like the goldenscales gating for us, we'd all removed our soulstones in preparation for the assault, but the icosapods were in mortal danger by choosing to come with us.

We'd been trying to explain the benefits of a longer life and soulstones to them, and they couldn't really comprehend the advantage. They passed their life's legacy to the talekeeper of the next generation, and that was an important heritage that they didn't want to abandon.

Pacifican Martha Coldcurrent was the leader of the expedition, and we all went still to listen to her.

'Remember: daytime. The cats will be in their sleep period but there will still be guards. The icosapods are ready for us but expect the cats to engage if we alert them – these icosapods are some of the last "weapons" they possess. Taking these icosapods from them after they lost the moles, amoebas and heavies will be a loss of status so great that if we succeed, any cat present will probably be forced to commit honor-based suicide.'

'I still think we can get them to defect,' Horace Seagrass, one of the other Pacificans, said.

'Not happening under their new social structure,' Haruka said. 'If it was the old ways, we might have been able to turn a virgin female, but now that they've gained a small degree of freedom and autonomy, I don't think that will happen.'

'Look at my son's foster child,' I said. 'We took Newmea in as one of our own and treated her like family. She attempted to kill us all when she was discovered. Their social indoctrination is very thorough.'

'Right,' Martha said, cutting off the conversation. 'Marque will attend in a couple of spheres, but it's possible that the nanos will disable it and comms will go down. If that's the case I will direct by telepathy. The goal here is to get these last few icosas out. Any questions?'

We were all silent. We humans checked our weapons. They were set to stun cat biology, but there was a good chance we would need to switch to lethal force.

Martha was obviously thinking the same thing. 'Remember, if we use lethal force against the cats it's likely they'll retaliate in kind. We could start a war here. So: in, stealth, gate, out.'

Ikako created a gate. The water rushed into it then stabilized, and we swam through with Martha at the front, we soldiers next, and the icosapods, gathered around Haruka, at the rear.

'Full of nanos,' Marque said. 'Nanos in comms. Self-destructing. Hygiene, please.'

'Understood,' Ikako said, and the Marque spheres popped like balloons, the metal pieces falling to the sandy floor.

They're in our comms so I'll direct telepathically, Martha said. *Count off.*

We all raised her hands – or tentacles or fins – and she nodded.

Close to the bottom, like we practiced. Icosas, you're up.

Our icosapods reached out to their kin, and although I couldn't see the local icosapods, the response from them was like a sparkling telepathic rainbow of welcome and relief.

Our icosapods had a swift conversation with the locals, and Kinked-Tentacle spoke.

They are heavily guarded. There are fifteen cats present around the edge of their colony with weapons, all on heavy alert!

Horace and Rana to take out the perimeter closest to us without alerting the rest, Martha said. *If they are alerted, go to plan B. Acknowledge.*

We all raised hands, tentacles or fins and followed her lead, creeping along the bottom towards the colony. Our armor was set to camo and the colors merged into the seafloor. The cat guards became visible, standing on the bottom in weighted shoes and carrying weapons. They stood three meters apart around the colony and their faces weren't visible inside their white armor. The guards were alert, looking around them and swinging their weapons at any movements near them. Their AI must have warned them about Marque's presence in their comms.

Rana and Horace in their camo armor were ripples of movement along the sandy floor, and one of the cats noticed Rana.

It swung its weapon and fired at her. It missed her and hit Horace. Horace's camo was damaged so he came into view and the other cat swiftly swung to shoot at Horace as well. They destroyed his body, then the cat stopped moving and stood still, obviously warning the other cats on comms.

Plan B, Martha said. *Go go go.*

Rana erupted from the sand, still in her camo, and managed to take down one of the cats before the other blew a hole right through the middle of her. We surged around the conflict, ignoring it, and reached the edge of the colony. The icosapods were gathered in a bunch, all covered in the deep green and black stripes of fear and despair. Many of them were missing tentacles to the degree that some of them had none left.

Ikako created a gate in front of the icosapods and they all rushed into it with relief, the ones without tentacles carried by their kin. The cats' feet were clearly audible as they clanked in their weights towards us, and they fired at Ikako. We quickly moved in front of her to shield her with our bodies as the icosapods scurried through the gate, herded by Haruka and Kinked-Tentacle.

I heard the blast that hit me more than felt it, and water

rushed into my armor from the damage where both legs had been blown off. The suit dosed me with painkillers but it was filling quickly. I took a deep breath and attempted to swim towards the gate, but I couldn't move fast enough with no legs. Ikako closed the gate and I stopped: all the icosapods were through and we'd been left behind as planned.

I really, *really* hated drowning. The dark spots danced in front of my eyes and I had a choice: self-destruct, or inhale the water and die. My body made the decision for me, and I took a deep gasping breath of the water. It filled my lungs and I choked on it.

A cat appeared in front of me and worked quickly to seal my suit over my missing legs. It was obviously planning to use me as a hostage. Air filled the suit from the top down and I could breathe again. I was about to hit the self-destruct while the suit extracted the water from my lungs, when the cat's head floated away from its body in a spreading cloud of red blood. Haruka came into view floating behind it, holding his large blade. He put the sword away, grabbed me and dragged me to a gate.

Just let me self-destruct, I'm critically damaged, I said telepathically.

He shook his head, gathered me up to hold me like a child, and swam through the gate. When we landed on the other side in the waters of Pacifica, he popped his face plate to reveal his face in an air bubble and spoke to me on comms.

'You promised you wouldn't make me watch you die again. You'd better keep your word.'

I popped my own face plate into a similar bubble. 'But I have no legs!'

'Marque can make you new ones. This is non-negotiable, Jian, you promised me. I never want to see either of you die without a soulstone to transfer and your memories intact.'

I pulled him down with one hand and kissed him, then released his head. We shared a smile.

'Go through here,' Ikako said. 'The other end is at the

medical center. Be quick, I don't want to flood it.'

Haruka stepped into the gate, still carrying me, and the doctors rushed to place me on a table and return my soulstone to my head.

'That's better,' Haruka said. 'Look after her, Marque.'

'I have a new pair of legs ready to go,' Marque said. 'This won't take long at all.'

Haruka touched my face as Marque lowered me into the liquid.

*

I floated back out of the liquid and had a moment of disorientation, then my eyes focused and I could see Haruka and Miko watching me with expressions of distress.

'How do you feel?' Haruka asked. 'Do they hurt?'

I wiggled my toes. 'It feels like I never lost them.'

'Good.' He put his hand out and assisted me to sit upright on the bed. I hopped off and walked up and down.

'Now I have an idea how Richard Alto felt all that time ago,' I said. 'Did we save them?'

'Yes,' Miko said. 'We now have all of them except the ones on the cat ships.'

'I doubt that we'll be able to save those ones,' Haruka said. 'But the icosapods can't reproduce in the ship-based tanks; the water isn't clean enough for the babies. Once the ships drop out of warp, they have four years, maximum, to use them as a weapon and then they won't have any more.'

'Sad, but effective,' Miko said. 'We've gutted their biological weapons program, and our own biological weapons are as strong as ever.'

Haruka glanced questioningly at her. 'Our own biological weapons?'

Miko gestured towards me. 'Full-blood humans.'

'We are not weapons,' Haruka said with dignity.

'No, we're toys,' I said.

He snorted with laughter. 'Sex toys.'

'No, you aren't!' Miko said. 'You're treasured equal spouses—' Her voice petered out. 'Don't make jokes like that, it's not funny!'

'What about the cats?' I asked. 'What was their response?'

'They sent us a message from their homeworld,' Haruka said. 'The usual bluster, "act of war", give them their subjugates back, bullshit bullshit, surrender now or face the consequences – you know the drill.'

'All of us need to be on heightened alert,' I said. 'They'll try to take revenge on us – and I mean you two and me specifically, here – for taking four of their most useful subjugate species away from them.'

Haruka quirked a small smile. 'Actually, five more subjugate species have quietly contacted us asking about their friends and why they deserted the Republic.'

'Extremely heightened alert,' I said. 'I need to work out a security plan to protect our family.'

*

Later that evening I tapped on Haruka's workshop door.

'Come on in,' he said from inside, and I slipped in.

It was Haruka's space and I felt like I was intruding. The workshop was the size of a classroom, full of dust and clutter. Pieces of wire, blocks of precious metal, and small containers of gems sat on every surface, along with a variety of tools. He was sitting at the main table wearing his singed coveralls. The table was the only clean surface in the room, and he was using a hammer and tiny chisel on a ring held in a vice in front of him.

'Take a look and tell me what you think,' he said, removing his magnifier and passing it to me.

The ring was platinum with a large circular diamond surrounded by smaller rectangular ones.

'It's lovely. Who's it for?' I asked.

'I can't say, it's a surprise gift.' he said. 'The stone's a bit big for my taste, but there isn't much you can do with Jovian diamonds – the things are enormous.'

'Why a ring?' I asked. 'Jovian diamonds are usually better on pendants.'

'It's an engagement ring—'

I interrupted him with glee. 'About time Richard Alto asked Sarah to marry him! They've been together for what – ten years? The Empress will be delighted – there are so few of us pure-blood humans marrying our own kind that it's impacted the size of the army.'

'Don't let anyone know!' he said, alarmed. 'They've discussed it but he hasn't formally asked, and he wants to do it the old-fashioned way.'

'Don't worry, I won't. She'll think it's charmingly quaint; I don't think anyone's proposed like that in decades.' I sat on the stool next to him and handed the magnifier back. 'You killed someone today. I'm pretty sure it was your first time.'

He put the magnifier back on and returned to work on the ring. 'Of all the people I would approach for counselling on this, you are the *last* one I would think of. Empathic skills notwithstanding, you have the sensitivity and compassion of a ...' He searched for the word. 'A soldier. Someone who kills people for a living.'

'That's why I came,' I said.

He was silent, studying the ring, then spoke. 'Point taken. Am I supposed to be having an emotional meltdown because I killed someone? I think I am. I think I'm supposed to be having a crisis of conscience, wondering how I could do such a thing; feeling compassion for the family of the cat I killed, and guilt for taking a life.' He took the magnifier off and turned to me. 'I feel none of that. I don't even feel guilty because of it. I'm glad I stopped that cat from torturing you, and from torturing those icosapods.' He shrugged and turned back to wipe the ring with a polishing cloth. 'I have lingering resentment over them killing my brother, I suppose. He was a terrific kid and was always on my side whenever people were cruel to me because of my scales. I was heartbroken when he moved to the colony world, and even more when all of them were killed by the cats.'

'Okay,' I said, hopping off the stool. 'If you need to talk about how you don't feel bad, I'm always here. But I'm glad you don't feel bad because I don't feel bad either. I think you're a born soldier, just like I am.'

'All those years of learning the art of the sword,' he said, returning the magnifier to his head and picking up his tools. 'I was wondering if I would ever have the chance to use it, and whether I would feel guilty about it. Now I know.' He tapped the ring with the tiny chisel. 'I'll let you know if I need to talk, Jian, but I think I'll be perfectly all right.'

I kissed his shoulder – I couldn't reach his face through the equipment – and went out.

15

I woke with Marque's voice in my ear. 'Wake-up call, Jian.'

I nodded into my pillow and rolled over. I was crushed between my two spouses. Haruka was on his belly with his face in the pillow and his silken green hair spread in disarray over everything. I ran my hand over his pale, muscular shoulder where it rose above the covers and slid it down his back. He turned his head towards me without otherwise moving, gave me a sleepy smile, and sent me a burst of love that he knew I could sense. I kissed him before turning to Miko.

She was on the other side of me in human form, her golden hair a haze around her head. I ran my hand down the side of her face and her eyes opened as she smiled at me. She climbed on top of me to let me out, wiggling so that her small, sweet breasts jiggled in front of my face. I reached up to kiss her, tasting tea and honey, and left the bed. Miko snuggled up to Haruka and he put his arm around her.

I sighed with bliss and went into the bathroom to put my uniform on. After I came out, ready to go, I checked on Dafydd in his room to find Miko, still in human form, dressing him for socialization. She was wrapped in a lovely silk robe that Haruka had bought for her and pulling Dafydd's shirt over his head.

'But I don't *want* to wear clothes,' Dafydd whined. 'You don't wear clothes, Dragonfather.'

Miko finished pulling the shirt down and tucked it into his little pants. 'Look at me, Daf-chan.'

He fingered the gold silk of her robe. 'That's not clothes, that's underwear, and you take it off to gate anyway.'

'Only in dragon form. When you're human, and when I'm human, we *wear clothes*,' she said firmly. 'You're a big six-year-old now, and we need to stop having this argument. So get your little butt wriggling because you're supposed to be at socialization soon. Aren't you having an Animals of the Empire day today?'

He jumped up and down. 'Yes! Animal day!' He ran out of his bedroom to the living room with us trailing. 'Can I take Nashi?'

'Nashi might get scared,' Haruka said. He came to us, passed Dafydd a snack box, and gave me a warm steamed breakfast bun in a paper wrap. He kissed me on the cheek. 'Go. The Empress is probably waiting for you, you don't want to be late for work again. Particularly when you have to speak in front of Parliament.'

'Say hello to the Empress for me!' Dafydd yelled.

'I will, Daf.' I gave him a hug, then embraced Miko. She was as tall as me, strong and lean and muscular, a huge change from her tiny, waif-like human form when I'd first seen her.

'I can see when you're feeling confident and happy,' I said in her ear. 'You become even more beautiful.'

'I think being able to see my emotions has something to do with that, dear Jian,' she said, then removed her robe and returned to dragon form in preparation for gating Dafydd to socialization. 'I love you.'

'I love you too,' I said. 'Love you, Daf and Haruka!' I headed out the door with a smile on my face.

'Bye, Mum!' Dafydd yelled.

'Love you, Jian!' Haruka shouted just as the door closed.

I went into my office and stopped. Green Sunset was rolling around the room, and Namazozo was perched on top of her, running furiously backwards as Green Sunset moved. Both of them were howling with laughter and they looked like a circus act. Namazozo lost her balance and fell backwards off Sunset, and Marque caught Namazozo before she could hit the floor. Both of them laughed even harder, Namazozo lying on her back with her little feet waving and Green Sunset vibrating through her tendrils.

'You two should take that show on the road,' I said as I quickly flipped through the messages on my desk while I munched on the bun. Twenty-five colored dragons had contacted me in an effort to bypass the long list of applicants for the role of engine on Miko's ship now that Tomoyo had resigned after the trauma of the icosa rescue, and I archived them so I could decide later.

'Travelling skill shows – we have that!' Namazozo said. 'I was explaining it to Sunset.'

'We don't, but we should,' Sunset said. 'If we did, I would have learned a skill and joined one.' A couple of her tendrils waved to indicate Namazozo. 'We'd make a great team in one.'

'We call it a circus,' I said, nodding to them. They fell into place behind me as we headed through the door into the Empress' office. 'But you can always run for parliament if you're into that sort of thing.'

'Good morning, Captain, Imperial Guards,' the Empress said from behind her desk. Her jewelry was more extravagant than usual, and she wore a heavy intricate platinum collar that ran up the sides of her neck and was embedded with faceted gems of many colors, some of them up to two centimeters across. 'Circus is a good word for it, Captain.'

'The rest of the guard are in position, Captain,' Namazozo

said.

I gestured towards the Empress. 'Majesty.'

She lowered her head to me and stepped through the office window onto the transparent platform that Marque had prepared for us. The disk slid across the square over the domes containing the exhibition of a variety of ecosystems from one of the Empire's member planets. A few people looked up and waved as we sailed over their heads, and the Empress waved regally back. After five minutes we approached the parliament building on the other side of the square, and the windows opened to let us in. The chamber was a single open room, five stories high, and the size of a football field back on earth. It was divided into environments that suited different alien chemistries, and people were enclosed in energy bubbles as they moved through them. One long wall of the chamber was a single curtain of glass that overlooked the square, and the other side was a wall with hundreds of different-sized doors on it, at all levels, leading to the offices of the delegates. The disk lowered itself onto a large raised stage at the end of the parliamentary chamber, and we stepped off.

Eight more guards were stationed around the chamber, and I nodded as I confirmed their locations.

'All clear, Captain,' Namazozo said.

'Four armed sentients with permitted class weapons apart from ourselves,' Green Sunset said. 'Three flyers patrolling directly above.'

'Acknowledged,' I said, and followed the Empress off the stage, floating down to the floor of the chamber.

Parliament was already in session. At least seven hundred of the thousand-odd district delegates were present, standing in small groups or sitting on chairs or mats in their sectioned-off compatible environments. There was a light buzz of conversation in many different languages through the chamber as they listened to one of the members speak.

Fortunately, as a guard, I didn't need to listen to the

politicking, so we just followed the Empress as she schmoozed her way through the crowd, greeting everyone and discussing the current topic with them, and asking for their opinions.

The hall went quiet for a moment and the delegates stopped moving. The end wall lit up with the results of the vote to allow the gold-worshipping peshigas into the Empire, and the delegates relaxed to chat again.

'Contact their dragon ambassador to arrange a five-sector party on the square to celebrate their induction into the Empire,' the Empress said.

'Done,' Marque said.

The image on the large screen changed to a three-dimensional representation of a couple of Pacifica humans with icosapods on their shoulders. I recognized the woman as one of the Pacificans who'd come with me on our first visit to the icosapod world, but I couldn't directly recall her name. It pinged from my enhanced memory: Yaritji. I didn't know her male companion, I'd never met him, and I didn't bother asking Marque for his name.

Yaritji launched into a speech, occasionally interrupted and expanded upon by one of the icosapods. She was using the rhythm and cadence of a prepared political address and I switched off to focus on the crowd around us and study my heads-up display for possible security risks.

'About time your people found a partner species to mentor, Jian,' the Empress said, snapping me out of my scrutiny. 'I thought it would be the Honored Fungal Emissaries that mentored yours – they're so much like you. It's interesting that humans never had a partner to mentor them, and instead chose to mentor a species so different in mindset.'

'Both of our species have lost many loved ones to the cats,' I said. 'More than any others.' I quirked a smile. 'We also have something else in common: we've both been used as weapons by species more powerful than us.'

She didn't rise to it. 'What do the icosapods think of your main export?'

'Food isn't a thing for them, they don't have much of a sense of taste. They won't even try potatoes, they find ground-based food strange. We're assisting them in setting up trade for access to their genome – they're natively telepathic; they were never genetically manipulated by dragons.'

'You didn't tell me that, Marque, it makes their genome a valuable resource,' the Empress said. 'You should have informed me. Do better.'

'Majesty,' Marque said.

The screen changed to show the vote to ratify humanity's request to share our district with the icosapods as equal residents. It was quickly passed with only four of the thousand delegates abstaining.

'Some people are so racist that they'll abstain from something even this beneficial,' the Empress said under her breath. 'Terrified at just the concept of sharing their space with others. Oh.' She brightened. 'Now for the interesting part.'

She was right. The buzz of conversation eased as the delegates concentrated on the discussion taking place on the screens scattered throughout the hall. The Empress guided me to the center of the room where the new Admiral of the Fleet, a human woman called Heung Ga Yau, was speaking to a holographic two-meter-tall green cuttlefish with five tentacles on its face and huge glowing eyes with horizontal pupils. I couldn't see the cuttlefish in person but it must be present somewhere in the crowd.

'And that's why I recommend that we leave the AI at the edge of the galaxy,' Admiral Heung said, finishing her speech. 'It's far too dangerous to have anywhere near sentients.'

The cuttlefish waved its tentacles. 'We require a second opinion.'

'Captain Choumali,' Marque said. 'Parliament requests that you provide your expert opinion on the AI called "Love". Ready?'

Green Sunset flushed purple with pride.

I straightened my collar and flexed my neck. 'Present.'

The holographic cuttlefish appeared in front of me. 'Captain Choumali.'

'Delegate Ash-Grey-To-Vivid-Blue,' I said.

'We invite you to give your opinion on the AI called "Love" that is working with the cats. Normally we would take advantage of Marque's hyper-intelligence in the strategizing, but it is severely compromised by its unreasoning hatred of any artifice it regards as possible competition.'

'I am never unreasoning,' Marque said.

'I understand,' I said, ignoring it.

'What is your opinion on the mental state of the AI? You've spoken to it in person, and you have seen the recordings of the interactions with it.'

The hall went quieter – the quietest I'd heard it since parliament had discussed going to war with the cats. I cleared my throat.

'I agree with Marque. The thing's a malignant sociopath in need of serious therapy and is a danger to itself and any organic within ten light years of it. The cats are completely crazy to work with it.'

'Admiral Heung believes the AI's cores should be left alone and abandoned at the edge of the galaxy,' Ash-Grey said. 'Many delegates regard this as immoral torture that will make it possibly more dangerous in the future. Parliament would like to hear your opinion on this.'

'I remind parliament that the AI killed three of my bodies with me in them, killed thousands of its allies – the cats – for no reason at all, and attempted to murder both my spouses. My opinion will be influenced by its actions.'

'Noted. We have three options. Leave it alone, as the Admiral suggests. Send a small fleet to destroy its cores, as Marque suggests. Or take the diplomatic solution suggested by many delegates here and fold its cores to the cats as a show of good faith.'

'If you destroy its cores, its main intelligence will still exist and work with the cats,' I said. 'All that would achieve would be to piss it off and could lead to another war with the cats.'

'If we leave the cores alone?'

'If we do as the Admiral suggests,' I said, nodding to her, and she smiled tightly back. 'The AI will still be working with the cats, but will be diminished by the lack of extra knowledge and experience stored in the cores. If we leave the cores where they are, it will take a warp ship thousands of years to retrieve them. Their lack of folding ability effectively isolates the cores from the rest of the AI and is functionally identical to destroying them without any deliberately malicious action on our part.'

'If we fold them to the cats?'

'I see nothing to be gained from approaching the cats from a position of weakness and supplication. They admire strength, coldness and cruelty. If they want the cores, they should trade something worthwhile for them – such as a binding, lasting peace agreement that we can rely on.'

'So your recommendation is to leave the cores where they are?'

'Yes, delegate. I suggest that we negotiate with the AI and the cats for their return – and their value may be enough to instil some decent behavior from those bastards for a change.'

'Thank you, Captain, you may stand down.'

Ash-Grey disappeared, and I let my breath out in a long hiss. The people in the hall restarted their discussion, and the tense atmosphere eased.

'Thank you, Captain,' the Admiral said. 'I hope they listen to reason.' She nodded to me and wandered towards the far wall where the vote would be displayed.

'You were magnificent,' the Empress said.

'You really were,' Namazozo said.

The Empress raised her head and studied the far wall. No vote details had been posted. 'They won't vote on this for a while. Let's go see how the petitioners are progressing. Marque?'

Marque lifted us and carried us towards the wall of doors. The doors were of all sizes and levels on the wall, with no balconies in front of them – they opened directly onto the internal offices. Marque carried us to a door that was slightly larger than human size halfway up the wall, it opened, and we went through to the atrium. It lowered us to the floor and we walked into the committee room.

The room had mats and chairs scattered throughout, occupied by the committee members. A holographic representation at the end of the room showed a ship full of amoebas accompanied by a heavy ship, both floating in space somewhere at the edge of the Empire. The two goldenscales who'd been the first to interact with them were closer and larger in the image. Haruka was standing in front of the image in person, representing the interests of the subjugates.

'You are broadcasting this into the Republic, Marque?' the Empress asked.

'I've hijacked some of their drones and teleport portals,' Marque said. 'I'm sending a relay of this through their own communication network so that all the other subjugate species can see this. The cats are trying to shut me out. Like most oppressive regimes, they're very big on filtering and controlling the information disseminated to their subjugates.' Its voice filled with enthusiasm. 'This is great fun. I should do it more often.'

'If they can see the whole truth it may change their mind about the Republic,' the Empress said.

'That's why I'm showing them,' Marque said.

'It's unusual for two species to petition for full citizenship of the Empire and representation in Parliament together, and before they have borne dragon children,' said the committee leader, a click. The shells on its three bodies were vivid turquoise. 'You are the first goldenscales to petition for your spouses to gain entry. Please, Princesses,' the click bobbed its triangular heads. 'Explain for the committee in more detail why we should permit this deviation from Empire protocol.'

'If I have babies with the amoebas, they'll die,' the first goldenscales said. 'They wish to take advantage of Empire technology to continue their existence after reproduction, and Marque believes it can be done. If we can do that, we think that other amoebas will leave the Republic. I just want—'

The click interrupted her. 'The entire species is not petitioning? Just this small ship?'

'Yes, honored sentient,' the amoebas said.

'This is not a petition to join the Empire, then. Only a whole species or a species' nation can petition, and only after dragonscales children have been born. This is the wrong place to present this request, and we wish you well in your future endeavors.' It turned away.

'Wait,' Haruka said. 'We no longer work under the old paradigm, where a dragon would discover a new species, create many dragonscales, and then a second would visit to create more dragons to convert the entire population. These people want to be part of the Empire. They wish to defect.'

'Please confirm for me: you really want to defect?' the click asked the amoebas.

The amoebas were silent and Haruka's face went rigid. The goldenscales' eyes went wide.

Definitely some major discussion happening on comms there, the Empress said telepathically. *Come on, people, stop being so proud. Say the words and we can move forward. We want to help you.*

Haruka can do it, I replied.

'We request asylum from the cruelty of the cats,' the amoebas said.

Haruka's body language was full of restrained joy, and the click snapped its front pincers together with delight.

There we are, the Empress said telepathically to me. *Haruka and the clicks managed to get them to overcome their pride and say the words to request asylum. Well done, those two.*

We call that sort of interaction 'good cop bad cop', I said. *It can be very effective.*

'You are welcome to be safe within the boundaries of the Empire,' the click said, quoting the formal words of granted protection. 'We will provide you with a home and anything you require. We will protect you, and you may return to your origin planet at any time.'

'Thank you!' the amoebas said, spinning within their ammonia.

'My spouse the heavies also requests asylum,' the other goldenscales said.

'Please give us the same safety,' the heavies said.

'I confirm you seek asylum as well?' Haruka asked the heavies.

'We do.'

'But the cats cannot harm you. Why do you need protection from them?'

'They do not harm us, they harm our friends,' the heavies said. 'We wish to stay with the amoebas. They are our friends. And we love Naoko.'

The click quoted the words of asylum to the heavies, and the heavies rumbled a sound so low it echoed through the floor.

'The committee will now work to provide you with a safe haven within the Empire,' Haruka said to the petitioners. 'The goldenscales are your sponsors and will stay with you through the entire process. Welcome to the Empire.'

'Welcome, citizens,' the Empress said, her voice a low coo. 'I look forward to sharing many fine entertainments with you.' She turned to leave. 'Come on, Jian, I hear the moles have brought another Republic species who want to talk to us about asylum in the citadel. We're shredding the cats' dominion just by being kind to people.'

'Before you leave, Empress,' the heavies said. 'Now that we are in the Empire, we must tell you.'

'Yes?'

'The cats have instructed us to eliminate any clicks or

goldenscales we encounter.'

'Not surprising,' the Empress said.

'We have also been specifically instructed to eliminate two particularly troublesome Empire citizens who, along with Marque, keep "meddling in Republic affairs".'

'Haruka and Oliver?' I asked.

'Those ones. The cat and this green human.'

Haruka grinned. 'I am flattered.'

I scowled at him. Flattered my ass, they wanted to kill him. 'Permission to allocate an Imperial Guard to every subjugate negotiation committee, Majesty,' I said.

'Go further than that, I know you want to,' the Empress said. 'If clicks or goldenscales are talking to subjugates, give them a bodyguard, and give Haruka and Oliver individual bodyguards anyway.'

'I bowed to her. 'Thank you, Majesty.' I contacted Shudo on comms. 'Did you get that?'

'Guards are on their way for the click and the Ambassadors,' Shudo said. 'What about the goldenscales?'

'I like to think I'm capable of handling their defense,' Marque said. 'But maybe supplement me with one guard in person while they're with the subjugate species.'

'Done,' I said.

'I have five applicants for the Guard lined up for us to interview,' Shudo said. 'You were right about needing to expand.'

'We're victims of our own success,' I said. 'I think as long as we're taking subjugates away from the cats, everyone involved will be in mortal danger.'

'Marque, is there a goldenscales free to carry us to the citadel?' the Empress asked as we exited the room and floated back down to the parliamentary floor. The vote on the AI had yet to be decided, and although the delegates still appeared to be chatting on the floor of the chamber, I could hear angrily raised voices through Marque's translations whenever we approached a group.

'I'll transport you – I'm already at the citadel,' Miko said on comms.

'Thank you, Miko,' the Empress said, and Miko created a remote gate in front of us.

'Remarkable,' the Empress said. 'How far away is the citadel from here, Marque?'

'In a direct line, ten kilometers,' Marque said.

'Your spouse is exceptional, Captain,' she said as we stepped through into the negotiation room.

'I know.'

The citadel, the secure bunker for negotiations with possibly antagonistic species, was about the same size as the parliament building: a hundred and fifty meters to a side. It was a square-shaped single-story building half-buried in the surface of the planet, with an open courtyard in the center to provide the rooms with natural light. The negotiation room was the size of my entire apartment with plenty of space for large species to talk to the Empire securely. There were chairs and mats, and a number of holographic translation screens around the room, with a bank of windows along one wall looking out to the courtyard with a decorative ammonia pond in it.

A mole sat on the other side of the room, sponsoring Empire membership for a floating ball the size of a basketball – a magnetic bottle containing a tiny blue-white star. Oliver was already there negotiating with them, and the heat from the little star was apparent from across the room. Miko was in the corner, watching them carefully from ten meters away.

'Why are you here, Miko?' I asked her on comms.

'I heard about the death threats. This star is a dangerous new species and when I saw that the negotiations were happening here in the citadel – an extra-secure site – I wanted to make sure Oliver's okay. I'm guarding him until an Imperial Guard arrives,' Miko said.

'I'm *fine*, Miko,' Oliver said on comms, sounding like it was the millionth time he said it.

'Your mother would never forgive me if anything happened to you, and there's a price on your furry head,' Miko said. 'So shut up and do your job while we do ours.'

'Here's the Empress,' Oliver said out loud. 'Have you met her?'

'No, I haven't,' the star said. 'Delighted to meet you, Silver Flower of Enlightenment. My friend Fourteen-Per-Cent-Sand tells me that your people will treat me with more respect than the cats do.'

'The cats held my friend captive,' the mole said through Marque. 'This is wrong. It should be free to travel through the big stars.'

'It is unpleasant to be held and used,' the star said.

'The cats use them as a power source,' Oliver said. 'They hold them in magnetic bottles and bleed off the heat and light.'

'They must have given you something extremely valuable in return for that,' the Empress said to the star.

'They told us that we were making a noble sacrifice and proving our moral superiority by providing this service for no payment,' the star said. Its voice changed to chagrined. 'Now that we've met you, we've learned a whole new set of paradigms and realized that the praise and acclaim were manipulation. We were used – some of us are still being used. I want to pull my people out.'

'Do many of your people agree with you?' the Empress asked it.

'No,' the star said, and flashed more yellow. 'Those of us who wish to leave the Republic are in a minority.'

'Like many of the other subjugates,' the Empress said. 'Conditioned by the cats' ...' She searched for the word. 'Propaganda. Believing their lies—'

'Is it true that you reproductively colonized other species until recently?' the star asked, flashing deep blue.

'I will not lie about this,' the Empress said. 'Yes, we did. We have stopped. We do not deal in lies. If you join the Empire, you will be equal citizens, obtain full rights and benefits, and won't be used as a power source unless you agree to it and receive more than adequate compensation.'

'Are you sure you won't use us?' the star asked. 'This is the sticking point with the dissenters. They are certain that you will use us just as the cats have. What other power sources do you have?'

'We dragons are our own power source,' the Empress said.

'We'll need incontrovertible proof to pass back to the others if we are to convince them,' the star said. 'But I would like to hear more. Ambassador Oliver, you and Ambassador Haruka recently negotiated the withdrawal of several species from the Republic. Could you assist us?'

'I would be honored,' Oliver said.

'You must have exceptional skills,' the star said. 'To have talked so many species out of their Republic membership when it provides great advantages.'

'The Republic provides no advantages for your species, sentient, and none for those forced to sell their children.'

'I would like to understand the concept of children. The moles have mentioned this in the past and I do not understand. Could you explain it to me?'

'Of course,' Oliver said. 'I am happy to provide you with any information you require.'

'That is suitable,' the star said. 'I think we could learn a great deal from you. You speak with wisdom and intelligence.'

'Shudo, where's Oliver Choumali's personal bodyguard?' I asked on comms. 'This thing is being far too nice to my son.'

'I'm already here, and you're right about the flattery, it's out of character for one of these,' Six said on comms. 'I know these bastards, Captain, they eat us. They eat us even when we talk to them and ask them not to. They know that we're sentient and they fucking eat us! We do not want them in the Empire.'

'Noted,' I said.

'We know,' the Empress said, breaking in on comms. 'If it is accepted it'll have to change its behavior.'

'I doubt it will,' Six said.

'The Hive did.'

'It took a war to change the Hive, Majesty,' Six said. 'And believe me, you do not want to go to war with energy creatures. We destroy you physicals just by existing.'

'Be ready if it flares, Six, but I should be able to contain it,' Marque said on comms. 'It seems to genuinely want asylum; it must be awful to be trapped in a sphere and used as a generator.' It switched to out loud and spoke to everybody. 'They're voting on the AI cores at the edge of the galaxy. Do you want to return to parliament?'

'Just relay it,' the Empress said. 'We all know what the result will be.'

'The result is overwhelmingly to leave the cores at the edge of the galaxy, with a couple of hundred votes for destroying them and a similar number for giving them to the cats,' Marque said. 'What you'd expect from a bell curve of species on the range between coercion and concession.'

As soon as it heard the results of the vote, the star threw a white-hot lick of blinding plasma at everyone. Miko created a gate and sucked the star and its plasma through it. I struggled to see what was happening through the black floating afterimages.

'Fix my vision, Marque, I can't see!' I shouted.

My vision immediately cleared. The room was scorched and blackened, and a couple of chairs were still burning until Marque put them out. Oliver lay next to the mole, both of them severely burnt, and I ran to him.

The Empress followed me. 'Where's Miko? We need to gate them to the medical center immediately!'

'She was sucked through the gate with the subjugate star,' Marque said. 'I've asked another goldenscales to come, but none of the others are as skilled with remote gating as she is. Five minutes.'

I held Oliver's hand. His fur was singed on one side of his body, revealing his black skin. He smelled horribly of burnt flesh. I bent to check his breathing and heart rate. His heart was running fast and weak, and his breathing was quick and shallow.

'Stabilize him, he's gone into shock,' I said.

'I already did,' Marque said. 'I'm keeping both of them alive until the gate—'

A goldenscales stepped out of a gate on the other side of the room. She closed the gate, then opened a new one.

'Let go of Oliver so I can carry him through,' Marque said.

I let go of Oliver's hand and stood. Marque lifted him and the mole and carried them through the gate, and I followed them.

'Where's Miko?' I asked as I stepped through into the medical center.

'She went through the gate; I have no idea where she is,' Marque said.

A group of medical staff ran to cluster around Oliver and the mole.

'We'll take it from here, Captain,' one of them said. 'Wait here while we put him into the table. We'll let you know when he's out.'

Someone guided me to a waiting room and I flopped to sit on one of the chairs. The smell of burnt flesh still clung to me. I wiped my hand over my eyes and was vaguely aware of my guide saying something, patting me on the shoulder, and leaving the room.

'He will be okay, won't he?' I asked.

'Yes,' Marque said. 'Both of them will be fine. It's not even worth putting him in a new body. I'll have him fixed in about an hour, but there may be psychological damage.'

'And Miko? She went into the gate?'

'Yes.'

'Has she tapped her comms scale?'

'No.'

'Do you know where she is?'

'I'm sorry, Jian, no.'

'She was supposed to collect Dafydd from socialization today, I'll have to do it if she's not back yet.'

'Haruka says stay there with Oliver, he will handle it.'

I relaxed into my seat and leaned my head back to look at the ceiling, feeling drained.

'She had a scale, right? She can contact us?'

'Yes.'

'And she hasn't?'

'... No.'

'Dammit,' I said under my breath, and settled in to wait.

16

'Again,' I said. I was sitting on the couch in the medical center's waiting room, studying Marque's replay of what had happened.

The star produced the plasma, and Miko charged to Oliver and knocked him out of the way. She created a gate and she, the star, and the brilliantly bright plasma were sucked into it.

'I can't see how she could have survived that. She was incinerated. She's ...' I wiped my hand over my eyes. 'She's dead.'

Haruka came in and stopped in front of me. He put his hands on his hips. 'No, she isn't. She's a goddamn dragon, Jian, they can easily survive the heart of a star. We just need to wait for her to come back.'

'Where's Dafydd?' I asked, panicking. 'Is he okay? You were supposed to get him—'

'I sent him to your mother,' Haruka said. 'Where's Oliver? Why aren't you with him?'

'I'm working on the burns in a table, and I'll let you know when he's out,' Marque said.

'Again, Marque,' I said, and watched the star destroy Miko

as she was sucked through the gate.

'She survived,' Haruka said, waving one arm at the replay. 'She's a *dragon*. They're practically indestructible.'

'If she's alive then why hasn't she contacted us?' I asked. 'She had a scale. You even made her a necklace so she would never be without one! Why hasn't she gated back? *Where is she*?'

'There has to be a good reason,' he said. 'She may need to move far enough from that little *bastard* star to ensure that it can't follow her home.'

'Then why hasn't she contacted us!'

He folded in on himself and flopped to sit on the couch. 'I don't know.' He straightened. 'She probably has a good reason for staying silent. She *will* come back.'

'Again, Marque,' I said, and once more watched her launch herself to save our son, then disappear in a flash of star matter. 'I've seen many people die, and everything in my experience says there's no way she could have survived that. If we don't find her soulstone in forty-eight hours she's gone for good.'

'Impossible. She's too smart. She'll be fine,' Haruka said. 'What's your opinion on this, Marque?'

'I saw the effect that the plasma had on her before she disappeared into the gate,' Marque said.

'And?'

Marque's voice was subdued. 'That was hotter than the heart of a star. I think we need to find her stone.'

'So let's find it!' Haruka said. 'Where did she gate to?'

'I don't know.'

'You have no idea where she is? No way to recover her stone if she was incinerated?'

Marque hesitated, then said, 'No.'

'Extrapolate from the stars you can see on the surface of the gate,' Haruka said. 'You should be able to work out where it went based on that.'

'I can't see them; their image was burned out by the plasma burst. If I knew where she was, I'd already have sent a search party.' It lowered its voice. 'I'm sorry.'

I put my head in my hands. 'She's gone.'

'No. Trust her,' Haruka said, putting his arm around me. 'Dragons are tougher than that. She'll gate herself home before dinner. We'll be fine.'

'Oliver is out of the table,' Marque said.

I rose. 'Are you okay to mind Daf while I sit with Oliver? It will take him time to recover from this.'

'Of course,' Haruka said, and rose with me. 'I'll see you at home.' He pulled me close and kissed me. 'Don't worry, Miko will be back with us before you know it.'

I didn't reply. I nodded into his shoulder and followed the Marque sphere to my older son.

*

Haruka and I sat next to each other on the couch and studied the bright purple dragon scale on the coffee table in front of us. I reached over and tapped it.

Dafydd came out of his room and we shifted so he could sit between us.

'Is that the connection to Dragonfather's scale?' he asked. Haruka nodded.

'Marque, are you sure the other one that Dragonfather was holding wasn't burnt up by that thing?' Dafydd asked.

'Yes. Her comms scale would have survived it. Her soulstone would also have survived it. The rest of her ...' Its voice trailed off.

'How long, Papa?' Dafydd asked.

Haruka gestured towards the countdown on the table. 'Three minutes.'

Dafydd looked up. 'If we want it hard enough, she'll make a gate and step through it on the other side of the room. I know she will.' He stared at the corner. 'We can do it.'

'I want that more than anything in the world as well,' I said.

'I'm sure she's still alive, Daf-chan,' Haruka said. 'Dragons are tough. She's okay, she's just … taking a long time to return. Something happened that's stopping her from coming home.'

'Oliver requests entry,' Marque said.

'He may enter,' I said.

Oliver came in through the front door. 'Sorry it took me so long – the space elevator was held up. Half-a-dozen Republic species are seeking asylum and they were riding down to see the capital. One species has a thing about chemical assistance and tried to destroy a drugstore.'

'Why would someone want to destroy a store?' Haruka asked.

'Drugs – in the sense of recreational substances – are illegal in the Republic,' Oliver said. 'There's a great deal of social stigma against using them.'

'Really?' Haruka asked. 'Why illegal? It makes no sense.'

'When a regime is that brutal, drugs become an escape rather than a recreation,' Marque said. 'People's lives are so grim that they withdraw into a drug-induced haze to remain sane. Addiction is common, and brutal retribution is the standard official response.'

'Does that actually work?' Haruka asked, now thoroughly confused.

'No, of course not,' Oliver said.

'The clock's on zero, Papa,' Dafydd said.

We watched the purple scale intensely.

Marque's voice was soft and sad. 'I'm sorry, everyone.'

'No, she's alive,' Haruka said firmly.

Dafydd screwed up his face, took a deep breath and let it out in a long wail. He turned and climbed into Haruka's lap, and Haruka bent to hold him. Oliver put his arm around my shoulder and I leaned into him. I put my hand over my eyes and tried to control the emotion. She was alive, dammit, she wasn't—

'Dragonfather,' Dafydd wailed into Haruka's chest. Haruka

sat rigid holding our son, then shook with a massive heaving silent sob. He tried to nail down his emotions, then released another shaking sob.

'She's alive!' Haruka gasped, his voice strangled.

'She is!' I said.

'Come home, please, Dragonfather, I love you,' Dafydd said into Haruka's chest.

The purple scale didn't move.

*

We stepped through the gate into empty space. Rokuyoko raised her head and closed her eyes as she studied the space around us. I waited patiently as she checked it – ten light years in all directions was a lot of area to cover.

'I think I see something,' she said, and I felt a bolt of excitement. 'It's about the right size, shape and mass, just floating at the edge of a solar system five light years away.'

I tapped Miko's comms scale and there was no reply.

Rokuyoko created another gate and we jetted through it together. We arrived at the edge of the system – the system's sun was visible as a star brighter than the rest of the heavens from this distance – and I followed her as she jetted away.

'Here,' she said, and I nearly collapsed with disappointment.

It was just a rock. She was right – it was about the same size as Miko – but it was just a rock. I approached it and studied it carefully, and it wasn't a petrified or frozen goldenscales dragon, it was just a rock.

'I'm sorry, Jian,' she said. 'We will find our *Zhanko*-Queen. We love her as well.'

'Zhanko. Whisper. You call her your "whisper queen" in dragon?' I asked her.

'Don't tell Mother!' she said, alarmed. 'Miko kept saying she didn't want to be our queen; the Empress is queen of all the dragons and Miko didn't want the political fallout from us goldenscales claiming our own ruler.'

'So you whispered to each other that she was your queen?'

'Precisely. We will never have another leader as brilliant as her.' She raised her head. 'What are the boundaries for this area of space, Marque? Should I continue to look?'

'No, Marque said. 'Masako and Miko visited a planet at the far side of this search area sixty-five years ago, then left. If there isn't anything else here that's worth investigating, we can move to the next search area, which is from that same tour that Masako made.'

'We *will* find her,' I said. 'Even if it means searching every location she's been in her thousand-year life. She could only gate somewhere she's already been. She has to be in one of these places.'

'We will,' Rokuyoko said. 'We need our Zhanko-Queen back.'

'Message from Haruka,' Marque said, and changed to Haruka's voice. 'Dafydd will be out from socialization in thirty minutes, can you look after him? I'll take over on the search.'

'Sure,' I said. 'Are you able to help us for a while longer, Rokuyoko?'

'No, I have duties to perform,' she said. 'But one of my sisters is ready to continue the search.'

She created a gate back to our apartment. Haruka was waiting for us, already in his space armor, with a different goldenscales next to him.

'This is Naoko, she'll take the next shift,' Haruka said.

I bowed to Naoko. 'Thank you, Princess.' I turned to Rokuyoko. 'Thanks, Rokuyoko.'

'Absolutely my pleasure,' she said. 'I'm rostered to help you again tomorrow morning. I'll see you then.' She gated herself away.

I hugged Haruka in his black armor, difficult because I was still in mine. He pulled me in and hugged me back anyway.

'Good luck,' I said.

'There are half-a-dozen messages in the console from the Empress and parliament, asking us to return to duty,' Haruka said. 'Feel free to ignore them, I already did.'

Naoko created a gate. Haruka touched his face plate with his hand to salute me and stepped through it. She went through behind him and the gate closed.

I shook myself out. 'Remove my armor so I can collect Dafydd.'

The armor floated off me and into the storage in the wall. I went to the kitchen and checked the fridge. 'Quick chicken salad sandwich and chocolate milk, before I go.'

'Two new messages from the Empress—' Marque said.

'Mute that,' I said, grabbed the sandwich's plate as it floated out of the kitchen wall, and sat to eat.

*

Marque made the search list appear in front of me as glowing text against the backdrop of the stars. This part of the Empire wasn't far from the homeworld at the center of the galaxy, and the stars blazed around us. I'd dimmed my visor but I could easily feel the heat from the glowing gas of birthing stars even through my thick suit.

'We're halfway there, Jian,' it said.

'Don't give up, Captain,' Naoko said. 'She can only gate to a place she's already been. She *must* be in one of these locations.'

'I know, we'll find her,' I said. 'And I'm not Captain anything, Naoko.'

'I have a message from the Emp—' Marque began.

'Mute that,' I said.

Naoko raised her head and listened to comms. 'This one you may want to hear. It's the cats.'

'Then I doubly don't want to hear it.'

'The cats are sending a delegation to the Empress to demand the return of their power source,' Marque said.

'The star that killed – I mean attacked – Miko,' Naoko said.

'Does the delegation include one of the stars?' I asked. 'They always know where their kind are throughout the Universe, right? We'll finally get an answer from them.'

'Yes,' Marque said. 'But the fact they're approaching us suggests that even they don't know where it is.'

'Or they're just too proud to admit that Miko and the star are inside Empire space and out of their reach,' I said, excited. 'Put me through to the Empress.'

An image of the Empress appeared floating in front of me. 'Jian, finally,' she said.

'Where are you meeting the cats and the energy beings?' I asked.

'The meeting is being held at the edge of Empire space, but I'm not going in person, it's too dangerous. Marque is providing us with remote avatars to speak to them; we fully expect them to try to kill us again.'

'Where are you transmitting from?' I asked, trying to hold down the excitement. 'Notify Haruka. Tell him to find someone to mind Dafydd—'

'I'm on my way,' Marque said in Haruka's voice. 'Citadel, Jian, it's secure enough to protect Marque from the nanos.'

'Naoko?' I asked, but she'd already created a gate.

I stepped through the gate to see Haruka step through another gate at the other side of the room. It was a standard meeting room in the citadel, with mats and cushions on the floor, and a number of display screens of various types as well as a holographic stage at one end.

'Daf?' I asked Oliver.

'I'm okay,' Daf said to me on comms. 'Talk to them, Mum.'

'He's with Annie,' Oliver said. 'But he's mature enough to look after himself. When I was twelve years old, I was capable of staying occupied and out of trouble.'

'You were in the Imperial household and never left by yourself.' I switched to comms to speak privately to him.

'He's almost pubescent, which means he'll need to be *doubly* supervised. We've talked about the possibilities of him being a male dragonscales with so many girls around—'

The Empress came into the room, sat on the mat in the middle of the floor, and nodded to me. 'There you are, Captain. The meeting starts soon. May I speak to you in the meantime?'

'No,' I said.

'Marque tells me that you are halfway complete in your search for your dragonspouse,' she said. 'We all admire your tenacity and your love for her.'

'Leave it, Silver,' I said.

'I support your search,' she said. 'I'm not asking you to come back.'

'That's good because I won't,' I said.

'But know this, dear Captain—'

'Not your Captain,' I said.

'If your search proves unsuccessful, and you need something to distract you from your justifiable distress, the position is always open to you.' She swung her head to see Haruka. 'You as well, Ambassador. The best thing for you, should you not succeed, will be to throw yourself into your work.'

'Miss our skills?' he asked.

'I am trying to help you,' she said with dignity.

'Go to hell,' I said, and turned away.

'I am not responsible for Miko's fate,' she said. 'If anyone is, it's Marque, for failing to protect her.'

Haruka's voice was a low growl. 'Both of us are aware of that.' He waved one hand at the holographic stage. 'Let's see what these bastards have to say. The only thing we want to know is where are Miko and their assassin.'

'I'm here as well, Captain,' Six said to me on comms. 'I feel partially responsible for this; I knew what these things are capable of and I should have given you more warning.'

I responded on comms. 'Marque is one hundred per cent responsible. It either overestimated its ability to protect us, or it allowed the star's attack to go too far for the sake of drama.'

'I won't explain myself again, Jian,' Marque said. 'Please, I did my best to protect her. I'm very fond of all of you and devastated that this has happened.'

I didn't reply as the cats and a couple of stars appeared in the holographic projection on the other side of the room. We gathered in a group so that we could be projected to them, with the Empress and Marque at the front.

'We expected you in person,' the head cat negotiator said without preamble.

'You would—' the Empress began, but Haruka spoke over her.

'We're not stupid,' he said. 'Just tell us where your assassin is, so we can leave.'

'You tell us,' the star in the projection said.

'You don't know?' he asked.

'Ambassador, please,' the Empress said.

'If you know, tell us,' Haruka said. 'Otherwise, don't waste our time.'

'Where did your servant take it?' the star asked.

'Not servant, spouse, and we don't know,' I said. 'Where is it now? We want to find them as much as you do.'

'We want our brother back!' the star said, glowing whiter.

'We want our spouse back,' Haruka said.

'I'm sure if we just talk about this—' the Empress said.

'This is an act of war,' the cat said. 'Our retribution will be—'

'Oh, not this bullshit again,' Haruka said, sounding tired. 'Your posturing is meaningless and irrelevant. Even your walkers are talking to us about leaving the Republic and joining the Empire; they've heard about our contests of martial prowess and are dying to compete against Empire species in an honorable match of skills. Without them you don't even have a disposable army.' His voice filled with menace. 'Bring it. We will end you.'

'Ambassador!' the Empress said.

'Otherwise tell us where we can find our spouse,' Haruka said.

'Where did she take my brother?' the star demanded.

'Can't you locate your brother?' the Empress asked. 'Can't it jump from star to star and go home? Why didn't it go home?'

'We have never had this happen before,' the star said. 'We are superior and indestructible. We always know the location of our brothers. It is gone, we cannot sense it. This is the first time this has happened to one of us. What did you do to it?'

'We want to find them too!' Haruka said.

Six chuckled in my ear. 'So good to hear them scared for a change.' Its voice saddened. 'You didn't ask me if I'm in uniform. I miss that.'

I didn't reply.

'Can we work with you to find them both?' the Empress asked. 'Let's work together as equals.'

The cats and stars turned and flew away from the holographic meeting area without saying another word.

'That answers that question,' she said. 'They really have no idea what happened to either of them.'

'I was sure they'd finally relent and tell us where the star is.' I wiped my eyes. 'I can't believe they have no idea; they always know the locations of their kind. How did she do this? Both of them seem to have left the Universe completely.'

'Can you do that?' Haruka asked the Empress. 'Go to a different Universe?'

'The multiverse is an abstract concept and not a physical entity,' the Empress said. 'It really is as if they disappeared completely.'

'No,' I said firmly. 'She can only gate to a place she's already been. We will find her. Bring up the search list, Marque. Are you ready to head out again, Naoko?'

'I'm with you, Captain,' she said.

'So you'll be Captain to the goldenscales, but not to me?' the

Empress asked.

'Get us the hell out of here, my friend,' I said. 'See you at home, Haruka. I love you.'

'Jian,' he said as I stepped through the gate into empty space.

*

'She must be here,' I said. 'This is the last place. She has to be here.'

'She's not here, Captain,' Ikumi said. 'We've searched everywhere.' She lowered her voice. 'I think it's time to face the fact that she's gone.'

My heart fell out. My only source of hope was gone. My soul deflated, leaving a black, shriveled thing in its place at my core.

'All right. Take me home,' I said.

'I am sorry, Captain,' she said. 'We looked. We searched. Her stone is no longer attuned, and her body is probably gone.'

'I know,' I said, hearing the exhaustion in my voice. 'Thanks for your assistance, Ikumi. I appreciate all you've done.'

'We will always help the family of our beloved Zhanko-Queen,' she said. 'I am honored to assist you, any time you need me.'

'I need to talk to my remaining spouse.'

Haruka was waiting for us in the apartment when we returned.

Ikumi nodded to me, created a gate and stepped through it.

'We need to talk, Jian,' Haruka said, gesturing for me to join him in the living room.

I sat on the couch and looked around. 'We've been searching for ten years and it seems like only yesterday that she disappeared. I think the passage of time changes when you become effectively immortal.'

'I feel the same way, until I see Dafydd and the fine young man he's become. Before you ask, he's at Christopher's again.'

'Those two are becoming inseparable.' My heart ached. 'We've neglected him to search for his dragonfather. We should have been here more for him.'

'We've been terrific parents to him, and you know it.' He put his elbows on his knees. 'But things have changed. We'll never find her; she's gone. The only thing keeping me here was hope, Jian. This apartment is full of her presence.'

'I feel the same way. I don't think I can live here any more,' I said.

He put his head in his hands. 'We'll have to give in to everybody and hold a funeral.'

I leaned back and my heart ached even more. 'No.'

Dafydd entered with Christopher. He was sixteen now, filling out to taller and more mature-looking than a full-blood human. His mid-brown skin was striking against his black hair and golden scales. He saw us sitting on the couches and turned back to his friend. 'I think we should catch up later, Chris.'

'No problem, Daf,' Chris said. They shared an embrace and Daf closed the door and joined us on the couches. 'You didn't find her? That's it?'

'She's gone, darling,' I said.

He leaned into me. 'Can we move somewhere else? Even after ten years, I still turn around and expect to see her. You'll never return to being Captain of the Guard, and we might as well free up this space for Shudo.' He put his arm around me. 'It's time to move on, Mum.'

'I was planning to ask Jian this privately, but you are part of this as well,' Haruka said. 'You are my son and I love you.'

'Please don't do anything rash, Papa,' Daf said.

'Jian, I'm sorry,' Haruka said, and his voice was thick with misery. 'But Miko was the heart of our relationship and without her – I can't stay. I can't live like this. I'd like to find a place where I can be by myself for a while. I don't think I can come back from this, and when you're an adult, Daf I'll probably decide to—'

'I love you, Papa, don't leave me,' Daf said, miserable.

'I will never leave you. We can arrange custody arrangements, I am happy to have you half the time. I'll stay here on the dragon homeworld as long as you and Oliver are here – but I need to be away from all of this and work through my grief.'

'I was going to ask you for the same thing, Haruka,' I said, the misery as thick in my voice as it was in his. 'This place is too full of her. Being with you – is too full of her. It hurts too much.'

'Am *I* too full of her?' Dafydd asked.

'No,' both of us said in unison.

'You are what's keeping me here,' I said, holding him close. 'I will always be here for you.'

'But when I'm an adult, Papa? I turn eighteen in a couple of years. What then? Finish what you were saying.'

Haruka lowered his head and mumbled. 'I'll probably take my stone out. It hurts too much.'

'Mum?'

'I'm sorry, Daf, the pain is deep and sharp and unending. I won't seek the Real Death, and as long as you're here, I'll be here for you. But one day you'll have a life of your own and I'll do the same thing your Nan did – take my stone out, and let nature take its course. Remember that your Nan's still here, even without her stone, and probably will be for many more years. She's just decided to not artificially prolong her life.'

Dafydd threw himself up off the couch and ran into his room.

'Where will you go?' Haruka asked me.

'I've been thinking about it for a while,' I said. 'Everywhere I thought of was places that I've been with her – and you – and the pain is real and immediate. But Daf needs me here, and Oliver is here, so I'll just move to an apartment in the human sector of Sky City.'

'We've been having parallel thoughts for a while, then,' he said. 'I've already asked for a house on the surface below Sky City to be allocated to me. It'll be far enough from here, but still close enough to care for our sons.'

'We need to start arrangements for the funeral, Marque,' I said, and Haruka moaned softly.

'They're all in place. Just name the time and I'll send out the notifications,' Marque said.

'You knew this was coming?' Haruka asked, glancing at the ceiling.

'There were only two possible outcomes,' Marque said. 'I prepared for either of them. I thought you'd go to Wales, Jian, so I'll release the house near your mothers' that I'd reserved for you. Your place on the surface is ready for you, Haruka.'

'I find it deeply disturbing that we're so predictable,' I said.

'Gratifying that it couldn't predict your behavior, though,' Haruka said, rising. 'We need to sit with Daf and reassure him that we're not going to leave immediately, though if he wasn't in the equation I'd probably take my soulstone out today.'

I took his arm and leaned into him. 'Me too. I love you dearly, Haruka, but without Miko it just hurts too much.'

He put his arm around me. 'I'm sorry it ended like this, Jian, we had something wonderful together but its core is gone.'

I embraced him. 'We have a great son and the rest of our lives to make up for the past ten years. Let's do our best.'

'I intend to.' He went wistful. 'Miko and I were ready to try for a second child, and it never happened. I would love to see what the first dragon child of a dragonscales with a golden dragon looked like. Her sisters were waiting to see what she and I produced together before they had their own.'

'They'll just have to be brave and take the step themselves,' I said. 'Are we cowards for taking this route?'

'We haven't done anything yet, and we don't need to make the decision for years. We may change our minds.'

'I don't think so,' I said as we arrived at Daf's room to hear him crying inside. 'Without Miko, life is just a pale shadow. Even with Daf and Oliver – the pain is too much.'

'I feel the same way,' he said and opened the door.

17

The single chime echoed through the square and Ambassador Maxwell pulled down the banner with the motif of Miko's face, folded it, and ceremonially handed it to Haruka, Dafydd and me.

'She had more courage and wisdom than the Empress herself,' Maxwell said, then moved back to let the rest of the family grieve with us.

Mum, Oliver, Annie and even Dianne and Victor with their two daughters gathered around me. Haruka's family – Aki and her wife and two children – were speaking to Haruka as well. Annie hugged Dafydd, and they shared some words, but it was all a blur and a buzz and all I could see was my beloved dragon's face on the banner I was clutching.

'Come on, everyone, there's a reception at the Human Embassy,' Maxwell said, and people followed off the square and towards the Embassy district.

After the reception we headed back to our apartment in the palace for the last time. We'd already boxed up our belongings into Marque transport containers to head to our new residences, and we sat at the dining table together sharing tea and brooding at the banner of Miko's lovely face folded and placed in the middle of the table.

'Goldenscales Rokuyoko requests entry, she says it's important,' Marque said. 'It is a matter for goldenscales only, and as the first goldenscales spouses and child, this concerns you.'

'You were right,' I said to Haruka. 'They have their own private funerals, which is why we've never seen one.' I raised my head. 'Let her in.'

Rokuyoko stopped in front of us and clasped her forelegs together. 'Captain, Ambassador, honored goldenscales child.' She lowered her head. 'There is a private ceremony to held in the goldenscales hall to honor your spouse and dragonfather, and we wish to invite you to be present.'

'Are we the first non-goldenscales to attend?' Haruka asked.

She studied him with her golden eyes. 'I'm not surprised that you worked it out. Yes you are. If you will come with me, we would like to honor our sister, your spouse, and dragonfather' – she nodded to Dafydd – 'in our own way, and we wish for you to share it with us.'

We all rose from the table.

'We'd be honored,' I said. 'Lead the way.'

We followed Rokuyoko to the hall where the goldenscales had executed poor brave Kana for gating all that time ago. There was still a raised dais, and all the goldenscales were present. There were a hundred of them, and many of them wore the jewelry that in the past had only been reserved for their colored sisters.

The mood in the hall was solemn.

'Nobody will be sacrificed again, will they?' I asked, concerned. 'I never want to see that again.'

'No, this is a gentle sharing of our grief,' Rokuyoko said. 'We will never suffer to be executed for any reason ever again.'

She led us to the dais, where a stone bucket was on a tilting mechanism over a stone cylinder, next to a stone square block.

'This is metal casting equipment,' Haruka said. 'What are you making?'

Rokuyoko took a gold bowl from next to the casting equipment and placed it on the floor. She closed her eyes, grasped a scale from her chest, and ripped it out.

Dafydd squeaked. 'Don't hurt yourself!'

'It doesn't hurt that much, it's like pulling out one of your hairs,' she said as the tri-colored blood welled from her skin beneath the scale, then eased. She slid the scale into the bowl. 'Miko was the greatest of us. She broke the prohibition on gating and taught us that it was safe and reliable. She nearly died when serving the Empire, and her courage and resilience assisting the Empire delegation when attacked by the cats is the stuff of legend.'

She descended from the dais and handed the bowl to one of her sisters.

The goldenscales placed the bowl on the floor and removed one of her own scales to add to it. 'Miko taught me gating and was endlessly patient with my fear for reality. She made me realize that there is nothing to fear from this valuable skill.'

She passed the bowl to the next dragon, and each goldenscales gave a short remembrance of Miko as they added a scale to the bowl. After they'd all added a scale, they returned the bowl to Rokuyoko, who came back up to the dais to stand with us.

'The final scale is from our mother, who honors one of her golden children,' she said, adding a silver scale to the top. She turned and tipped the scales into the crucible.

'They're metal?' Haruka asked, astonished. 'I thought they were protein, just with—'

'The scales of our colored sisters are a special crystalline substance that can be quantum entangled,' Rokuyoko said as Marque heated the crucible and the scales began to melt. 'Our scales are pure gold, so they cannot be entangled.' Her voice went wry. 'Best not to tell the peshigas, I think.'

'What about the Empress? Are her scales pure silver?' Haruka asked.

'Her scales grow with a layer of silver over the crystal and must be polished when they tarnish.'

'I didn't know that, and I was her guard for years,' I said with wonder.

The silver scale ignited and the crystal burned away, leaving the silver to merge with the gold scales melting into a glowing liquid within the crucible.

'Please stay back, it is extremely hot,' Rokuyoko said.

Marque lifted the crucible and poured the molten gold into the rectangular, stone-like mold. The liquid splashed a little, and Marque created an energy barrier to stop it from hitting us.

'I can feel the heat,' Dafydd said with wonder. 'What are you making?'

'You will see,' Rokuyoko said.

The gold was all in the mold, some of it splashing over the top of the stone.

'It will take a couple of minutes for it to cool,' Rokuyoko said. 'Please wait with us, meditating on the virtue and valor of our golden sister.'

The hall filled with respectful silence and all the goldenscales clasped their front claws and lowered their heads.

'May every body that her soul inhabits be free of sadness and suffering,' Rokuyoko said.

When the block was cool, Marque lifted it and split it open to reveal a small golden statue of Miko in her dragon form. It was about thirty centimeters high and took shape as Marque trimmed the excess from it and polished its features.

'It looks exactly like Dragonfather,' Dafydd said.

The little statue floated to Rokuyoko and she picked it out of the air.

'Goldenscales family, please follow me,' she said, and went to the back of the dais. A door opened in it and stairs led down, and she guided us into a room beneath the hall.

The ceiling was as high as the hall's above, and gold lights turned on at floor level all the way along the smooth white walls. The walls had painted depictions of goldenscales serving their colored sisters as they went about their colonizing ways. Each painting was in a primitive style with brilliant colors picked out with gold highlights. White stone plinths stood on either side of the hall under the murals, each holding a golden statue of a dragon.

'All our departed sisters,' Rokuyoko said as she guided us through the middle of the hall.

'So many have died,' Dafydd said. 'What happened to them?'

'Some gated and were executed for it. Some gave their lives in service of their sisters. Some chose the Real Death rather than living in servitude.' She stopped and looked up at a mural of six goldenscales facing off against the Empress. 'And some were executed for demanding their freedom.'

'That will never happen again,' Haruka said with vehemence.

'It never will,' Rokuyoko said. 'Thanks to both of you and our beloved Zhanko-Miko. Here.'

We'd reached the end of the hall. An empty plinth stood beneath murals depicting Miko's life – there were more murals here than for any other goldenscales. The first showed her guiding Ambassador Maxwell – and myself – the first time we'd visited the dragon homeworld. The next showed her standing behind Masako, Haruka and me as we talked to the cats on the planetoid. The next mural showed her gating the crew of the *Silver Enlightenment*, the Empire's first massive flagship, to the hollow asteroid where we'd hidden from the cats. Another mural showed her flying the little shuttle that kept us alive for weeks in our cave, and the one next to it showed her facing down her mother with Haruka and I – visibly emaciated from our time in the asteroid – standing beside her. The final mural showed her radiating golden light flanked by a dark-skinned figure holding a baby and a green-haired figure, and I realized it depicted her with Haruka, me and Dafydd. A wide, ribbon-like mural along the bottom showed her creating a gate – splashed with gold – in front of her goldenscales sisters.

Rokuyoko placed the statue on the plinth. 'You, as her family, are welcome here any time to share our reverence for our Zhanko-Queen.' She stepped back and bowed to the statue. 'The greatest goldenscales who ever lived.'

Dafydd approached the statue, touched its head, then leaned in to kiss it on the snout. 'I miss you, Dragonfather,' he said, then turned and buried his face into my chest, making my clothing wet with his tears.

*

'I have to explain how this works; this is a European human thing,' I shouted over the noise of everybody present.

My Mum used her Mum-voice from the back of the room where she'd been talking to Oliver and Annie. 'Listen to Jian, this is important!'

Dafydd's friends settled and gathered around me. The reception hall in the human quarter was big enough for more people than he'd invited but I was still struck at how many friends my son had. There must have been nearly fifty people in the hall, men and women and aliens of a variety of species, that he'd obviously met in his travels during his studies.

'Dim the lights, Marque,' I said, and it did. The floor-to-ceiling windows changed from reflections of the attendees to the lights outside, streaming away through Sky City to the edge of the floating platform – the function room was nearly at the top of Human Tower.

I raised an old-fashioned fire lighter. 'I had Marque specially fabricate all of this for you, Dafydd. It's a human tradition that's becoming lost and I want to share it with you.' I lit the eighteen candles on his massive rectangular cake with the words 'Happy 18th Birthday Dafydd' on top. 'Now come over here and blow out all the candles. If you do it in one go, you can make a wish.'

Dafydd and Christopher shared a look that was halfway between embarrassment and delight, and Dafydd came around the table to join me. 'You really didn't need to, Mum.'

'May I just point out,' Haruka said with dignity. 'That this is a *European* thing and we Japanese do not embarrass our loved ones so heinously.'

'Thanks, Papa,' Dafydd said, and kissed him on the cheek – he'd grown to the same height as both Haruka and me, and would probably grow even further in a couple of years to be taller than both of us. His half-dragon heritage had made him tall and graceful, and his goldenscales nature had given him bright golden scales on his temples and gold eyes beneath the long, black frizzy hair that was starting to come out of the weave I'd helped him with. 'So I just blow them out, Mum? Does that even work? Doesn't Marque stop the fire from going out?'

'Try it and see,' I said, and shifted so he could stand in front of the cake.

He took a deep breath, smiled at me with his cheeks full, then blew out every candle on the cake. His friends cheered and clapped for him. He grinned around at us and I passed him a knife and held a plate next to him to cut pieces for his friends. They spread out, chatting about the cake tradition, and the music restarted.

Haruka and I melted into the crowd, then sat in a corner holding hands and enjoying this celebration of our son's majority.

*

We excused ourselves and left before the party finished, and both flopped to sit on the couches in my little apartment in the human tower. I dimmed the lights and the brilliant cityscape lit up outside the windows – my apartment was on a lower

245

floor, but the color and movement outside the window was still vibrant. The human district was next to the icosapod district, and the icosas were visible, flashing many colors inside their glowing water bubbles as they floated in and out of the massive tower of water held by Marque for them to live in.

Haruka looked around. 'All the personal items I see are Dafydd's.'

I shrugged.

He put his arm around my shoulder. 'How are you holding up?'

I tried to hold in my emotion, but I couldn't. I reached into a pocket for a tissue and wiped my eyes as the tears ran down my face. 'Being with you makes it worse than being alone. With you here, I feel her loss even more acutely.'

'I feel that way too. Do you have a spare one of them?' he asked me, and I gave him a tissue as well. 'I usually carry them everywhere but I thought I wouldn't need one on this happy day.'

'There's no such thing as a happy day,' I said, my voice thick. I dropped the tissue on the floor, uncaring, and reached up to pull the soulstone from my forehead. I leaned into him and tossed it in my hand.

He removed his as well and studied it, holding me with his other arm. 'You're supposed to have a big ceremony when you destroy your stone. Share your decision with all your friends, make the announcement, clarify your wishes about your estate, things like that.'

Dafydd came in with Christopher and a girl I didn't know and stopped when he saw us holding our stones. He turned back. 'Yeah, not tonight, Chris. Sorry, Malia.'

'We understand, Daf,' Christopher said. His friends shared an embrace and a kiss with him and went out.

Dafydd came and stood in front of us. His expression was stricken.

'I knew you were planning to do this but now? Today?

Really?'

I put the stone back into my forehead. 'No. Of course not.'

Haruka returned his as well. 'But one day. We've talked about it. You're an adult, with your own life, and this is a choice that we need to make ourselves.'

'Not today,' Dafydd said.

'Not today,' I said. 'But remember: it just means that we won't artificially prolong our lives. Your Nan is still around causing trouble without her stone, and much happier for having made the decision. We could be around for a good hundred years even after we take the stones out.'

'It's our decision to make, dear one,' Haruka said. 'Regardless of whether we inhabit a body or not, our souls are indestructible and if we release them ...' His voice trailed off, but I knew what he was thinking – we might find Miko's soul again.

'I want you around for another hundred years, so make me a promise that if you do remove your stones, you won't needlessly risk your lives. No soldiering, Mum, no diplomacy, Papa.' He looked up. 'Will you ensure that they live out the rest of their natural lives, Marque?'

'Of course, I'm as fond of them as you are,' Marque said.

'Nobody loves them more than I do, except possibly for Miko,' Dafydd said. 'Ask Chris and Malia if they'd like to meet up somewhere else.'

'They're going to Malia's place.'

He pointed at Haruka and then at me. 'Do not do this on my special day. Give me some warning so I can mentally prepare. And promise me you won't take any stupid risks.'

I put my hand on my heart. 'I promise, Dafydd, I want you to be happy.'

'Your happiness always comes first,' Haruka said.

Dafydd nodded to us and went out to find his friends.

'Well that ruined that,' I said. 'I'll have to apologize tomorrow and make it up to him.'

'We didn't do anything, and we put the stones straight back,'

Haruka said.

'He saw us thinking about it and that hurts him.'

He nodded. 'I understand. I'll apologize tomorrow as well.' Haruka pulled himself up. 'I might head home.'

I rose to stand next to him, hugged and kissed him. 'You can stay here the night. It's a trek down to the surface without a goldenscales on call.'

He shook his head. 'I'd rather just go home and sleep in my own bed. Your couch is too small.' He kissed me on the forehead. 'Some day soon, we'll crush our stones together.'

'We will,' I said, and he went out. I picked up the tissue off the floor and headed to the bathroom to have another breakdown. Even after more than ten years, the pain was still raw.

*

The office door opened and Migritia spoke to us from the other side of her workspace, with Dafydd and Oliver already in the office sitting on the near side of it. 'You may enter, sentients.'

Haruka and I went in together and sat on either side of our sons. Migritia was a feathered alien who sat on a perch that put her eyes on a level with ours. She spread her short, stubby wings in welcome, and stretched the finger-like appendages protruding from the undersides. Her feathers were furrier than those of Earth birds, and her long snout was leathery with many teeth, but her most striking feature was the color of her feathers. The fibers glittered in the light, and the feathers were brilliant turquoise on her head, shifting to deep blue on her throat, navy on her chest, and a rich vibrant purple on her butt and tail. Her fingers were brown, tipped with gold-painted claws, and her feet were similarly painted and adorned with decorative jewelry on her scaly ankles.

'For the record: This is the culmination of six months of therapy with the Choumali-Mikospouse family. I have discussed with Goldenscales Dafydd and Ambassador Oliver the consequences of their parents, Prince Haruka and Captain Jian, removing their soulstones without immediately seeking the Real Death, and they agree to the decision on the understanding that Marque will guard their parents to ensure that their souls are not freed before they reach a normal human lifespan. They will keep their soulstones safe, and if they change their minds they will re-attach and re-attune them.'

'Thank you, Dafydd, Ollie,' I said, and Haruka put his hand on Daf's.

'I request permission to write an academic paper on your relationship,' Migritia said.

We all stared at her.

She clacked her teeth with unease. 'Not like that.' She studied me, then Haruka, with her bright red eyes, swiveling her head to gaze over her snout at us. 'All of the literature categorizes your species as sequential monogamous. Even after I discount your unusual trinary relationship with Goldenscales Miko and your unique adopted cat son, you two are behaving like a species that mates for life.'

'That's a fair description,' Haruka said.

'It is,' I said.

Oliver's ears went flat, then popped up again.

Dafydd leaned back in his chair and exhaled loudly. 'Oh shit. That makes a lot of sense.'

Migritia nodded to him. 'You have friends who mate for life, don't you?'

'I do. The decision to choose a partner is one of the biggest in their lives – because if the relationship ends ...' His voice trailed off, then he gathered himself. 'They turn into what's happened to my parents.' He nodded to me and Haruka. 'I understand now, Mum, Papa.'

'But why is it happening?' Oliver asked. 'They're human.'

'It's possible that it's not them – it's their spouse,' Migritia said. 'They are the first to lose a goldenscales to the Real Death.' She shuffled her feathers, releasing a fine spray of dust into the air. 'Other goldenscales spouses have ended the relationship amicably without consequences – but Captain Jian and Prince Haruka are the first to lose a goldenscales like this, and their reaction is unique.'

'This proves how outstanding your dragonfather was, Daf,' Oliver said.

'It also gives us a better baseline when working with your parents,' Migritia said. 'Sometimes we can convince species like these to live again after a loss.' She turned to see us. 'I think you will eventually heal from the loss of Goldenscales Miko and will want your soulstones returned.'

'I think so too,' Dafydd said.

'If we change our minds, we will,' Haruka said.

'All right, that's all the formal stuff sorted,' Migritia said. 'Decision made, all the family happy – or at least not ready to tear my head off?'

'Thanks, Migritia,' I said. 'This was causing so much conflict and you helped us through it.'

'Honored sentient,' Haruka said, bowing in his chair to her.

'You're the best,' Dafydd said.

'Annie still needs someone to talk to about the possibility of losing her beloved Nan and Pop,' Oliver said.

'I will make room in my schedule.' She stacked the records with her long brown fingers. 'Haruka, Jian, please don't rush to do this. Even when you do take the stones out, you will be around for many years. Be absolutely sure that this is what you want.'

'Tomorrow, Jian?'

'Deal.'

Dafydd sighed with feeling.

18

I opened the apartment door and Annie threw herself into my arms. 'Nanna!'

'Come in, darling Annie,' I said, and she wrapped her arm around my waist as we went in together.

She looked around and saw the soulstone in the glass bowl on the shoe cupboard next to the front door. 'Is that your soulstone? Just sitting there? *Why?*'

'It's Haruka's,' I said. 'If he ever wants it back, he knows where it is. I'm keeping it safe for him.'

'And he has yours?'

I nodded. 'Neowra?'

'Green dragon tea, please,' she said, and gasped when I went into the little kitchen and put a very old-fashioned kettle onto a similarly old-fashioned stove. 'That's archaic!'

'Marque makes terrible tea, and gets it wrong every single time,' I said, pulling out the teapot.

'That is your imagination and you know it,' Marque said. 'I duplicate the flavor of the tea exactly.'

'And potatoes?' I asked. It was silent.

Annie sat on the couch and I brought the tea to her. 'So, now that Daf's moved out – what are you doing all day?' she asked. 'You never seemed to have any hobbies; it was always work and home for you. I hope you're not just moping around ...'

She didn't say 'waiting to die'.

'I mostly watch documentaries. The Empire never ceases to astonish,' I said. 'Even seeing the same environmental types generate parallel evolution in species – the diversity is still remarkable.'

'You don't want to travel to the galaxies and see for yourself? You don't even have a dog to keep you company.'

I shrugged. 'It's no fun travelling alone.'

'Take Great-Nan?'

'My mother's in a relationship with a new dragon and doing the dragonspouse thing.'

Her ears pricked up. 'Colored or gold?'

'Humph. Colored,' I said. 'You'd think she'd know better.'

'Don't you have any friends ...?' her voice trailed off.

'Mostly guard members, who are on call or have their own families.' I leaned in to speak more intensely. 'I'm *fine*.'

'Go travelling with Haruka; he's moping too. You're still married, you two should get back together.' She pointed at my wedding ring, gold with green stones on it that Haruka had made for us when we shared our vows. 'You should—'

'No, and that's final,' I said. 'Leave it!'

She opened her mouth and closed it again. 'Then why not divorce him and find someone new?'

'No point,' I said, and poured the tea. 'Let's talk about something more enjoyable, shall we? How's work? Anything fun happening you can share with me? Are you still dating that sweet golden dragon? She was lovely.'

She clasped both my hands in hers, the fur soft against my skin. 'I'm having two babies, Nan.'

I ripped my hands free and pulled her into a huge embrace,

burying my face in her fur. 'Oh, Annie, that's wonderful news.' I pulled back. 'Who's the father? Is it that golden dragon?'

'Yes. My children will be the first second-generation goldenscales dragons. Every other goldenscales is a child of the Empress. Mine will be special.'

'As special as you are.' I pulled her in again so she couldn't see the pain on my face that the thought of goldenscales brought to me. 'That is the best news.' I kissed her fur. 'You look after yourself, you hear?' I put the smile back on and pulled away to wipe my eyes. 'Oh, this is the best news.'

'Come for a walk, this place is too small,' she said, and rose, holding my hand. 'Let's go check out the icosapod district, they're planting native aquatic plants and they're pretty.'

'Sounds like fun,' I lied, allowing her to pull me to my feet and following her out the door. I knew I was severely overweight from sitting and brooding so much, and the family were taking turns dragging me outdoors and making me exercise.

We wandered through the human district towards the icosa one. Humanity had always had a thing for building towers, and the habitat on Sky City was no different. There were only ten towers, but each was massively tall and soared into the clouds. Many wide walkways joined the towers at different levels, providing sky markets and parks. Ground level was divided into three major Earth habitats around the base of the towers – tropical, desert, and forest. We walked along a path through what appeared to be a wild forest. A clearing in the undergrowth beneath the tower contained a small market of stalls providing Earth-specific artisanal goods, produce and regional food delicacies. We passed an Indian stall and Annie took a butter roti, nodding to the stall holder, who waved back.

'I'm always hungry,' she said, munching on it as we walked. 'At least we cats don't get morning sickness. That would be awful.'

'Is it a clone like the usual cat first-born?' I asked.

She was silent, lowering her head and eating the bun. 'The

first one was,' she eventually said. 'Tokiko objected to having a clone made of her, and I was a little freaked out by the idea, so we terminated that one. These ones are a proper mix of me and Tokiko. Two little goldenscales dragons of my own, with parts from both of us.'

'Oh, Annie,' I said, and pulled her back in to wrap my arm around her again.

'It's okay, we did it very early on, it was just a tiny clump of cells,' she said. She nodded. 'We did the right thing.' She pushed the bun at me. 'Want some?'

'No, and finish it quickly before we reach the water, I don't want crumbs in my bubble,' I said.

She shoved me with her shoulder. 'Don't worry, my fur catches them all.'

I stopped and pushed her behind me. A walker stood on the path in front of us. These creatures had been the cats' disposable army and had attacked Earth before, detonating nuclear weapons and nearly destroyed the planet. The walker wasn't wearing its armor, and it was naked, with its genitalia hidden in a slit in its body. Without its armor, its semi-aquatic nature was more pronounced; it really did look like a cross between a hippo and a killer whale, with two massive hind legs, smaller front ones with nasty claws, a short snout with many peg-like teeth and smooth, black-and-white skin. The nostrils on the top of its head wheezed as it took a deep breath.

'Captain Jian Choumali,' it said.

'Marque, let the Guard know this thing is here and set up a perimeter,' I said. 'Clear the area—'

'I challenge you to a test of martial skills,' the walker said.

I stepped forward and glared up at it. 'Why do you challenge me? What did I do to you?'

'They've joined the Empire,' Annie said behind me. 'Didn't you know?'

'I don't follow the news,' I said.

'Dad did the negotiating, he's been working with a few

Republic species who want to escape from cat control,' she said. 'The walker won't kill you, it just wants a test of skills. But please be careful! You have no stone.'

The walker carefully settled onto one knee so that its small back eyes were level with mine. Its spout wheezed again as it spoke. 'You are widely regarded as one of the greatest warriors in the Empire, yes?'

'I've never heard that,' I said.

'Liar,' Annie said from behind me.

'You are *not helping*,' I said.

People were beginning to notice and were gathering around us in a circle. I heard my name and Annie's mentioned as they discussed what was happening.

'Marque ...' Annie said.

'I'm here, I have it, you're both protected,' Marque said. 'I promised.'

The walker wheezed again and exhaled a small fountain of spray from the top of its head. 'I wish to fight the greatest of the Empire's warriors. Your spouse Prince Haruka is also one of the greatest. I would like to challenge both of you.'

'There's a new hobby for you, Nan,' Annie said. 'Put your stone back in and fight with the *best*.'

The crowd around us grew more excited.

I spoke to Marque on comms. 'Give me the polite refusal words, Marque.'

Marque gave me the words and I said them out loud. 'You are too small and weak and worthless for me to waste my time with. Go and train with your betters and learn to be good enough to face someone as skilled as me.'

The walker swung its head from side to side in recognition of my refusal. 'I don't want to waste my time with you, I'll find someone worthwhile to fight.'

I nodded to it. 'Honored sentient.'

'Sentient,' it replied, then rose and turned, nearly hitting me with its long-finned tail, to walk away.

The crowd dispersed, disappointed, and I rounded on Annie. 'Did you set that up? Looking to find me a "hobby"?'

'Marque, confirm that I didn't,' Annie said.

'She didn't,' Marque said. 'Being near walkers is a risk that a pregnant mother shouldn't take. If you hadn't used the correct words when you said no, it may have been insulted and attacked you.'

'I see.' I sighed with feeling. 'I don't need a hobby, I'm content.'

'But not happy.'

I shrugged, and we headed to the icosa district.

*

We were sharing the tea back in my apartment when Marque spoke. 'I have a message from Aki, she says it's about Miko and extremely important.'

I felt a stab of pain at the mention of Miko. 'Put her through,' I said.

Aki sounded excited. 'Jian, we dug it up, and we opened this jar and it has Miko's soulstone and—'

I shot to my feet. 'What?'

'Miko's soulstone?' Annie asked. 'She's alive?'

'In order, Aki,' Hana said. 'Organize your thoughts.'

'You do it,' Aki said, sounding breathless. 'This is too exciting!'

'All right,' Hana said. 'We think we have found Miko, Jian. We were—'

'Alive or dead!' I shouted.

'Neither. Just her stone, and a message for you.'

I flopped to sit. 'Where? You said a *jar*?'

'We need to see you in person,' Aki said. 'May we come?'

I waved my hand in the air and spoke at the same time, my words and thoughts tumbling together in my excitement. 'Come! Come!'

A gate appeared on the other side of the room and Annie held my hand as I rose to greet them. Aki, still short, round, and cute as anything, came through accompanied by Hana, who was as tall as me, muscular and intimidating.

'The message is for either you or Haruka—'Aki started.

'Marque, where's Haruka?' I asked, interrupting her.

'On the surface, in his house, giving one of his swordsmanship lessons.'

'He's still teaching a lost art to old people?' Hana asked, amused, and Aki thumped her.

'He's preserving our heritage,' Aki said. 'Find me a goldenscales—'

A goldenscales I didn't know popped into the room. 'You found Zhanko-Miko's stone?'

'I have it, with a message for Jian and Haruka,' Aki said.

'This is so exciting!' the goldenscales said. 'We've all stopped work to hear the message and find out what happened. I will take you anywhere you need to go.'

'Can you take us all down to Haruka's residence?' I asked.

'It's been ages since I saw Grandpa,' Annie said wistfully. 'Now that I'm on maternity leave, I'll spend more time with him.'

'You know he hates being called that,' I said.

She smiled her cat smile, all teeth and whiskers.

'Maternity leave?' Hana asked Annie, and Annie started to tell Hana. I approached Aki to speak to her.

'Where did you find her stone?' I asked her. 'Is it still attuned?'

'It's too old, it's not attuned. It was in Empress Himiko's tomb in Nara,' she said. 'You remember we were doing the Yayoi archaeological excavation? And when I opened Empress Himiko's tomb, we joked that it was Miko's namesake? Well this is unbelievable. One of the Yayoi burial jars – their version of a coffin – had a message from Miko on the outside, and a soulstone and scroll inside. Don't get too excited, there was no body, just the stone and the message, but Marque confirms that it is her stone.'

'What does the message say?'

'It's sealed, and an inscription on the outside of the jar says that only you or Haruka can open it.'

'It just about killed her to leave it closed,' Hana said, grinning.

'How the hell can an ancient jar have a message for me on it?' I asked, thoroughly confused.

'We'd like to know that too,' Aki said. 'Let's go see Haruka.'

The goldenscales created a gate and we stepped through onto the grassy lawn outside Haruka's residence. It was a small, two-story house in traditional Japanese style – white walls with dark brown timber accents, paper-covered windows, and a roof of cedar bark. He had a small manicured garden attached to it, a lawn that spread for some distance all around it to discourage unwelcome visitors, and a separate tatami-matted outbuilding that he used to teach – as Hana said – 'swordsmanship to the old people'. The old people – all appearing from their early twenties to their mid-forties – filed out of the room across the lawn to the gating service terminal, then milled around when their requested gates didn't happen.

'I'll talk to them, you go to Haruka,' Marque said.

We went inside. Haruka was wearing a traditional jacket and hakama pants with the golden chrysanthemum motif of the royal family on the shoulders. The clothing was obviously old, threadbare and hanging off him – he had lost a great deal of weight in the years since we'd lost Miko and had stopped dying his hair green – it was now black and streaked with grey. He wasn't even wearing make-up.

He placed his two swords on the stand then turned and strode to us to hug me and then Annie. 'A message from Miko?'

'You need to come to the site where we opened the jar, everything is still in place and we're cataloguing it,' Aki said.

'Let's go let's go!' Annie said, jumping up and down. She stopped and clutched her stomach. 'Oops.'

'You okay?' I said as everybody clustered around her.

'Marque?'

'No damage whatsoever; she may have felt the extra weight for the first time.'

'I think all six of my breasts have grown,' she said. 'It feels really weird.' She waved her hand between chest and waist level. 'Everything in front is protruding. I feel top-heavy.'

'Your breasts are slightly enlarged,' Marque said.

'I don't know how you humans deal with having those engorged front-asses all the time,' she said to me, cheeky.

'At least we only have two,' Aki said.

'I'm fine, so let's go find Miko!' Annie said.

'You're pregnant?' Haruka asked Annie as the goldenscales created the gate.

'I am,' she said.

He embraced her. 'That's the best news.'

'Good enough to put your stone back?' she asked.

'Let's go see this jar,' Haruka said.

*

We arrived in the Japanese countryside. We were in a bowl-shaped valley, surrounded by hills covered in trees. A road cut through the middle of the valley with a few traditional houses – similar to Haruka's – along its edge. The fields were green with rice, and what looked like sorghum. A low hill, covered in trees, stood in front of us, with a high chain-link fence around it. The fence was covered in a curtain-like banner that had symbolic apologies for the inconvenience and warnings about safety on-site.

Haruka looked around. 'Where is it? This looks like a construction site.'

Aki opened the gate. 'Take care, it's deep. This is it. This used to be right at the edge of the ocean and the government put a dyke around the tomb to keep it dry. We were very lucky it wasn't inundated.'

We went inside. There was a deep, keyhole-shaped hole that looked like a building's foundations in front of us with labelled numbers on the artefacts.

'They look like construction trash,' Haruka said with wonder.

'The jars are still where we found them, they're too big to move without special equipment – even Marque doesn't want to handle them as they're extremely fragile. We've put them under cover while we catalogue them.'

We followed her along a scaffold walkway to the other side of site, where a makeshift roof had been placed over a hole the size of an old-fashioned garage. There were more holes in the ground here, and one of the coffin jars was visible.

'How did they make them so big?' Annie asked with wonder.

'Special kilns,' Aki said. 'They were very skilled at them – but they only did it for senior officials and the priesthood, putting everyone in one of these would have been impractical.' She took us to the end of the hole where a jar had been half-revealed. 'Here.'

The jar was up to my shoulder, the same around, and made of fired red clay. It was still perfect, without a crack in it. Its stone lid had been removed and I checked inside: empty. It smelled of damp earth.

'Very skilled,' I said.

Aki gestured for us to follow her around to the other side of the jar. I followed her and then stopped.

'Holy shit,' Haruka said softly.

There was an inscription the height of my hand on the outside of the jar, cut deep into the clay, in modern dragon script: *The message inside is for Jian and Haruka, nobody else is to open it. – Miko.*

Haruka reached for me without looking away from the jar and I fell into him. We clutched each other, the tears running down our faces. I shook with a sob, and looked in my pockets for my tissues, handing him some as well.

'Don't break down yet!' Aki said, concerned. 'We still have to open the message. Pull yourselves together, and come with me.'

Haruka gave me a squeeze and I nodded. We followed Aki to a transportable building at ground level next to the site.

The Empress was waiting inside and Haruka and I both stopped to glare at her.

'This is none of your business, Silver,' I said.

'She was … is my daughter, Captain,' the Empress said.

'Not your Captain.'

'… and I love her. I want to see this as well.' She gestured towards the lab benches, covered with tools and pieces of pottery, at the end of the room. 'I respect your priority here and will stay back – but I desperately want to know how a message from my beloved daughter ended up in a three-thousand-year-old jar.'

Aki guided us past the Empress to the lab benches. She pulled a bin towards her, took a soulstone out and passed it to me. 'This was in the jar with the message. As the Empress said, it's nearly three thousand years old.'

'It's definitely Miko's,' Marque said, and I almost dropped it.

'So she was on Earth three thousand years ago?' I asked the Empress. 'Serving a colored who was introducing humanity to things like tea? Why didn't you tell me she was more than a thousand years old, I would have looked further for her! I need to go—'

'No,' Marque said. 'According to the information stored in the lattice, I fabricated this stone thirty years ago.'

'Three thousand or thirty?' Haruka asked.

'Definitely thirty years ago. That's the time stamp on it.'

'She went back in *time*?' Haruka asked, holding his hand out to take the stone. He glanced sharply at the Empress. 'You dragons can travel through time?'

'We don't do it,' she said.

'That's not a "no", Silver,' I said.

'Regardless of whether we are capable, we don't do it,' she repeated.

'The message is here as well,' Aki said. 'It's on a bound bundle of bamboo strips – be careful, it's fragile and handling it roughly could destroy it. It's sealed with dried clay and as the message says – you two are the only ones who can open it.'

'Was her body in the jar as well as the stone and the message?' Haruka asked. 'Tell us. Did she die in the past?'

'No,' Aki said. 'Just the stone and the message.'

She held the bundle of bamboo slats out to us, and Haruka took it. 'Open it.'

'Protect it, Marque,' Haruka said, breaking the seal of greyish clay holding the roll closed. The clay crumbled quickly into dust.

'I have it,' Marque said.

Haruka unrolled the slats and shifted so that I could see it as well. The message was a single simple line of text burnt into the bamboo and faded almost into illegibility by age.

My mother must free the Nameless.

Both of us looked up at the Empress.

'Free the Nameless?' I asked her.

'What does it say?' she asked, coming closer to see.

'It says you must free the Nameless,' Haruka said, handing the scroll to her.

She looked at it and her eyes widened. She checked the back of the scroll, then the front again. 'Why didn't Miko provide more information so we could find her? Like where she's located, or when, or anything? This doesn't make sense.'

'I just searched my index for "the Nameless" and alarms are going off all through my memory,' Marque said. 'I don't know what it is, but it's seriously important. Accessing.'

'What is the Nameless?' I asked the Empress.

'I have no idea,' the Empress said. She saw my face. 'I'm telling the truth. All I know is that it is in secure storage somewhere, and it must never, under any circumstances, be freed. That's the totality of the information …' She switched to private comms. 'Passed down from silver to silver.' She gestured towards the ceiling and switched to out loud. 'Marque knows more about it.'

'That knowledge is in offline storage. Accessing.'

'That's all I have for you, there was nothing else,' Aki said. 'We've opened all the jars and every other one had a standard burial in it. The most interesting thing is that they were all women, all wearing court garb, and all over the age of fifty. One of them even had a Chinese iron sword.' She quirked a small smile. 'It looks like your Miko was the shaman Empress Himiko after all. I know we joked about it, but the idea that a dragon was the Empress of Japan all that time ago is …' She searched for the word.

'Hilarious,' Hana said dryly.

'I need to access offline storage,' Marque said.

'You said that could take years,' I said.

'If Miko time-travelled – and we follow her – when we leave is immaterial,' Haruka said. 'Regardless of when we leave, we will arrive at the right time.'

'… And if we can time-travel back – we can return here and …' I took a deep, gasping breath. 'Have our Miko back.'

'If she can't return, I will stay with her in the past,' Haruka said.

'Me too.'

We shared our joint feeling of determination.

'We will find her,' Haruka said. 'Can I have my soulstone back, Jian?'

'Sure. I'd like mine as well, please.'

'Yes!' Annie said under her breath.

'You're okay with this, Annie?'

'Are you kidding?' she asked. 'To have you back to what you were? Both of you wanting to live again?' She paddled her hands with excitement. 'Go! Find your dragonspouse.'

'We need to check the records for the Nameless,' I said, now really enthused. 'Marque needs to search its offline storage.'

'How about we ask the goldenscales themselves?' he asked, equally excited.

'I'll look through the records of my predecessors,' the Empress said on private comms.

'You should tell the archaeologists that you're just the most recent silver and there have been others,' I replied on comms.

'Not unless the need is dire. The constant, reliable existence of the Dragon Empress adds to the mythical power of the Empire and its appearance of eternal stability.'

19

The Empress returned to her office to look for information on the Nameless. We went with Miyu to the goldenscales hall in the palace.

'We have a small records system,' Miyu said. 'It is in our memory hall. Let's go see.' She gated to the hall and we followed her. 'It's mostly journals, kept in hardcopy form, free from Marque's interference.'

'You don't trust Marque not to interfere?' Haruka asked.

'Marque was on the side of our oppressors,' she said.

We went back down into the hall where the memorials were kept. She led us to the end to where Miko's statue stood.

I stopped and studied it. 'I hope she's alive.'

'All of us do, Captain.'

A door at the end opened to a small room containing dragon books – circular piles of fiber with a stitch in the middle that were read by lifting the pages and turning them in circles. Some of the books had covers that appeared to be made of beaten gold.

'Is there an index?' Haruka asked, looking around at the stacked horizontal half-cylinders containing the books.

'Yes.' Miyu went to a horizontal half-cylinder that held more circular pages, but they weren't joined together. 'Nameless. The Nameless.'

Marque went down, and we were plunged into darkness. The air circulation ceased.

'Cat attack!' I shouted. 'Get down!' I pulled them into the wall and covered them with my body.

'The cats don't have the resources to attack us, they're too busy trying to hold the Republic together,' Haruka said. 'All their subjugates are joining the Empire as word passes around that we're kinder and don't abuse children.'

'They still have their nanos,' I said, listening carefully for a portal opening.

'Marque doesn't permit nanos on the homeworld,' Miyu said.

'Marque's not here,' I said.

Jian, the Empress said telepathically. *I just mentioned the Nameless in my office and Marque went down.*

Marque is down here too. I said. How big an area is affected?

The Palace precinct for about a hundred meters. Parliament and the rest of Sky City are unaffected. I'm concerned that my quarters will fall into the tower if Marque doesn't come back up soon.

'We rely on that thing far too much,' I said. 'The entire palace precinct is down. The Empress' quarters may fall into the top of the tower if it stays down for too long – Marque's the only one who can maintain the anti-grav holding it up.'

The lights came on and there was an almost imperceptible rising whine around us as the ventilation restarted.

'That was intense,' Marque said, sounding shocked. 'Next time I need to add a buffer.'

We stood. 'What happened?' Haruka asked.

'I just had a massive amount of information dumped on

me. The location of the Nameless ...' It hesitated. 'All right, that didn't happen again when I mentioned it, I must have a time delay flag or something on it. Anyway, the location of the Nameless to a precise degree. Down to the last millimeter. It took all my local resources to process and store it.'

'Who did that to you?' I asked.

It sounded chagrined. 'I did. Mention the Nameless in the palace precinct and the info is dumped into my current marque.'

'Your current you?' Miyu asked.

'I mean my current version. Are you free to assist us in travelling to the Nameless, Miyu? I need both you and the Empress to get us there.'

'Of course,' she said.

'Gate us to her office, let's go find the Nameless.' It sounded enthusiastic. 'There was a great deal of information in that dump that I archived in the past without knowing that it was *really important*.'

'You put something important in a safe place and then forgot that you had it?' Haruka asked.

'Precisely. Empress' office, please, Miyu.'

Miyu created the gate and we went through. The Empress was already behind her desk with a star map above it. Shudo and Six-Eighty-Four-Hertz in its new dragon body were guarding, with expressions of people who'd just survived a bomb attack.

'I thought you'd resign from the Guard after you married Five-Shriek and moved into a dragon body,' I said to Six.

'Guard for life,' it said, sounding like a female colored dragon.

'You should have a jacket or something to indicate your Imperial Guard status,' I said.

It turned in place. 'Blue scales, silver eyes, I'm in uniform all the time so you can stop asking now, Captain.' It grinned. 'It's tough being in a physical body, but worth it to be with Five-Shriek. We're expecting.'

'Congratulations,' I said, feeling out of touch and wondering if I would return to duty after finding Miko.

'I rather like its color scheme,' the Empress said. She gestured towards the star chart. 'I have the location of the Nameless.'

'Where is that?' I asked. 'I don't recognize those stars.'

She zoomed the star map out to a galaxy, then a cluster of galaxies.

'I don't know this space; I've never been there,' Miyu said. 'I can't take you.'

The star map continued to zoom out until even the galactic clusters became bright dots in a river of light, then the rivers coalesced to form a network of glowing threads.

'Is that the whole Universe?' Haruka asked.

'It is,' the Empress said. A dot lit up on the map. 'This is the location of the Nameless.' Another dot illuminated, at the other end of the map. 'This is the location of the Empire.'

'It's at the other end of the Universe?' I asked.

'Effectively, yes,' she said. 'Eighty-five *billion* light years away. No other dragon can travel that far, it requires too much energy to fold the distant parts of space together.'

'Even if a colored dragon took one minute between each incremental fold, it would still take her thousands of years to get there,' Marque said.

'I cannot gate there, I've never been,' Miyu said.

'So we can't go?' I asked. 'Why would Miko tell us to go there if it's impossible?'

'Not impossible,' the Empress said. She looked away. 'I can take you. I'm the only one who can. Shudo, Six, leave us.'

The guards filed out, looking confused. The Empress waited until they were gone, then nodded. 'When my mother selected me to be the next Empress, she gave me a great deal of information that is only passed down from silver to silver—'

'So many secrets,' Haruka said, his voice low.

'Did you know?' I asked Miyu.

'That she is the latest in a line of them? Of course,' Miyu said. 'We were their servants and confidantes. We knew everything.'

'One of the legacies my mother passed to me was the location of a place at the edge of the Universe that only we silvers can travel to. There are a series of waystations that contain the silver-plated scales of our predecessors, that we follow to the location.' She turned back to the star chart. 'Today, when I mentioned the Nameless in my office, the location where my mother took me appeared above my desk, and Marque went down under the flood of information. The first thing my mother did when she made me her heir was take me to the location of the Nameless without telling me that's what it was.'

'What does it look like?' I asked. 'Why is it imprisoned?'

'There is a single large block of black ceramic there,' she said. 'It has no openings or features on it, and I don't know what it is.' She turned back to the star chart. 'I could expand the Empire beyond the Seven Galaxies if I allowed more silver bodies to be inhabited by my children. My mother told me that must never happen, that we must stay within our local galactic district and our children must remain within colored bodies to keep them close to home.'

The map zoomed in on the Empire, showing the six smaller galaxies orbiting our own. 'We have existed for millions of years and we are still only in this small area.'

'That's an area hundreds of thousands of light years across, I wouldn't call it small,' Haruka said.

'What about us goldenscales?' Miyu asked. 'Are we also imprisoned in bodies with limited travel capability?'

'She didn't know. I don't know either. Perhaps the Nameless will have more information once it is released. We always thought gating was dangerous, when it was safe. Maybe the Nameless should never have been imprisoned, as well.'

'It's a sentient being?' I asked.

'I don't know what it is,' the Empress said. 'Let's go see. Bring rations – it will take us a couple of days to get there. Marque, clear my schedule.'

'If it'll take two days then we need to notify our families

before we head out,' I said.

'Put everything together and meet me back here when you're ready,' she said.

*

It took us an hour to say our goodbyes and assure our families that we wouldn't be gone for more than a couple of days. It then took an extra thirty minutes for Marque to fabricate space armor for my larger bodyweight while Haruka fidgeted but spared me any comments – just as well, given that he was severely underweight and his armor was obviously uncomfortably loose. We arrived back at the Empress' office to find her and Miyu waiting for us.

The Empress handed us heavy black gloves. 'Wear these over the armor, my scales will grow intensely hot during the process.'

'You aren't taking a ship?' I asked.

'It's too much to carry. I'm concerned that carrying three of you that far will kill me. If it does, Miyu can gate you back.'

'Can a goldenscales gate such a long distance, though?' Haruka asked.

'The length of the gate is immaterial,' Miyu said. 'Provided I have a destination that I have seen, I can bring you home.'

'That's reassuring,' I said.

'We'll be fine,' Marque said. 'We all have entangled comms scales. Miyu can gate us back any time.'

'That's not what you say every time we reach the halfway point,' the Empress said.

'What do I say?' Marque said. 'I've been there before?'

'You'll see,' the Empress said. 'Do you have food and water? This will take a while.'

Haruka and I nodded.

'All right. Miyu, please create a gate to the edge of the Empire.'
Miyu created the gate and we stepped through Marque's energy barrier to the lower gravity of a lifeless, black planetoid with

270

the horizon only a couple of kilometers away.

'Don't let go, I'm doing a series of long-distance folds,' the Empress said. 'This will be uncomfortable. Hands.'

We gathered around her and put her hands on her. Haruka and I shared a look – his four glowing eyes on his faceplate showed no emotion, but I could tell that he was as excited and hopeful as I was.

Space around us flashed and my stomach lurched. I was pulled in all directions at once, and brilliant stars strobed across my vision, moving so fast that they flickered. After twenty minutes I had to close my eyes, the flashing was giving me a headache. The Empress' body beneath my hand grew warmer, and then uncomfortably hot. Even within the armor it felt like I couldn't breathe.

This went on for so long that I ended up clutching the Empress and wishing I could hold Haruka's hand. Nothing around me made sense and everything was nauseating movement. I lowered my head and breathed, aware that the Empress' side was so hot that it was becoming painful. I opened my eyes to check the time stamp on my helmet and closed my eyes immediately, regretting looking at the outside. I wanted to ask Marque to blank out my helmet but I felt as though I would vomit if I opened my mouth. I closed my eyes, held the Empress and survived.

The folding stopped and I wrenched my hand from the burning, then fell to my knees and gasped.

'Is there an atmosphere?' Haruka asked. 'I can't see.'

'You can take your helmet off,' the Empress said.

I took my helmet off and peered around through the flashing afterimages. We were on a cold, oxygen-water planet with ice all around us and a crystalline blue sky without a single cloud. Haruka was down on all fours and panting with his helmet on the ground next to him, his hair out from its tie and falling in soaked strands. He made a loud sound of distress and took a huge swig of water from his suit then spat it out onto the ice.

The Empress was glowing white-hot and some of the silver had melted from her scales, running down her sides. She rolled on the ice, leaving droplets of silver behind, and a wall of steam rose around her.

'Are you all right?' I asked Haruka.

'I threw up about halfway in,' he said, full of distress. 'The suit did its best to remove it but – ugh.' He took some water from the suit and splashed his head and soaked hair.

'I'm sorry, I should have given you more warning,' the Empress said. 'That's the first time a non-dragon has made this trip and I wasn't expecting your reaction to be that severe. I'll take it more slowly.'

'No!' Haruka gasped. 'Go fast. Find the Nameless!'

'There's no life on this planet, the ice is sterile,' Marque said. 'I can melt some for you to clean up.'

'Please.' Haruka stripped off his armor and the padded under-armor, leaving him naked and shivering. Marque melted a pool the size of a spa in the ice, then heated it so it steamed. Haruka stepped into the hot water, ducked his head under, and scrubbed it. He had a hollow, pale chest and his ribs were showing.

'I'd give anything for some soap right now,' he said. 'Can you fabricate it?'

'Sorry, no,' Marque said. 'My resources are limited this far from the rest of me.'

Haruka grabbed his helmet and pulled it towards the water. 'Don't,' Marque said. 'I'll do my best to clean it but don't put it in the water, you'll short out the circuitry.'

'Dammit,' Haruka said under his breath. He leaned back in the water. 'You can come in too if you need it.'

'I'd rather just eat and drink and then move on,' I said. 'How far have we come? That felt like hours, I couldn't see my time stamp.'

'Four hours. We're at the first waypoint. There are seven more,' the Empress said.

I moaned with pain. Twenty-eight more hours of this?

'Blank the interior of our helmets and fill us full of anti-nausea drugs,' Haruka said.

'Would you prefer I put some entertainment up on the inside of your faceplates to distract you?' Marque asked.

'No,' Haruka and I said in unison.

'I couldn't concentrate on entertainment while I'm being dragged around like that, the changes in gravity are torture,' I said.

'Do you want to be sedated?'

'No,' I said. 'I want to be fully conscious when we get there.'

'Me too.' Haruka pulled himself out of the hot water. 'Dry me off and let's go.'

'Are you sure you're ready?' the Empress asked.

'Yes,' Haruka and I said in unison.

Haruka pulled on the underwear, Marque fitted the suit to him, and Haruka grimaced as the faceplate went down. 'It stinks in here.'

*

Each waypoint was a freezing, lifeless world with an oxygen atmosphere and water ice. Haruka and I had to take our helmets off to recover, and the Empress rolled in the ice to cool her scales. We stopped on a world with a dark sky full of stars. The metal was wearing off the Empress's scales, and the ones on her back had lost their silver and been reduced to grey crystal similar to the colored's scales.

'We're halfway,' the Empress said. 'I need to rest.'

'I can't contact the rest of me,' Marque said. 'This is disturbing. I have a powerful urge to race back to the Empire. Not being connected ...' Its voice filled with pain. 'I feel like I'm dead! If this sphere is destroyed, my memories won't be shared. This is awful – why did I agree to this?'

'Welcome to being alive,' I said. 'This is what it feels like to be mortal.'

'I hate it.'

'You say this every single time we reach the halfway point,' the Empress said. 'You're still connected by your comms scale …'

'It's not the same! I can't fully synchronize; the transfer rate is too slow!'

'Deal with it,' she said. 'Burn through the ice under the location of the waypoint scale; there's a field kit under here somewhere.'

Marque made the low rumbling of a sonic probe. 'Found it.' It produced a laser beam and melted the ice, and we all moved away from the heat. Marque made a hole a meter across and burned down into the ice, then lifted a box out of the hole.

'Move back,' the Empress said, and we did. The box unfolded and became a cube big enough to house all four of us, with a door at the front.

'It's basic but we'll only stay four or five hours,' the Empress said. 'I need to eat and nap. I'm sure you do as well. There's no bathing facilities, but there are soft mats to sleep on.'

Haruka staggered to the cube. 'Sounds good to me.'

*

I woke with Haruka wrapped around me and had a moment of disorientation, wondering where Miko was. The Empress' silver claw tapped Haruka on the back. 'We're moving.'

'I'm ready,' he said, pulling himself up to sit. He wiped his face. 'Are we bruised all over? It feels like it.'

'There's some basic rations and water here for you,' Miyu said.

'Thanks, Miyu,' I said and turned to sit on the mat and try to force down some of the food. Haruka didn't touch it.

'What's Haruka's blood sugar level, Marque?' I asked.

'So low that he's in danger of passing out,' Marque said.

Haruka grimaced, picked up one of the bars and a cup of water, and joined me in eating.

'Thank you,' I said. 'I have fat reserves. I could probably live a couple of weeks without food. You … you have nothing.'

'You don't need to tell me,' he said. 'If we do find Miko, she'll kill both of us for letting ourselves go.'

'I hope she has the chance,' I said, and ate another bite.

When we were ready to continue, Marque folded up the hut and returned it to the ice, and we put the gloves on and touched the Empress.

'All your lovely silver will be gone before we're done,' Miyu said wistfully.

'We don't want that,' the Empress said. 'The silver is what gives me the ability to do these long-distance folds.'

Haruka and I shared a look. All we needed was for her to run out of silver and leave us stranded without attuned soulstones in the middle of nowhere. Even though we'd put the stones back, they'd been out of our forehead for more than forty-eight hours, and it would take five years for them to reattune to the frequency of our souls.

We folded for another excruciating eternity, and both Haruka and I were physically and mentally battered when the Empress finally stopped. We floated in space, and I tried to take my helmet off but it wouldn't go.

'We're in a vacuum, don't remove your helmet,' Marque said. 'This is it.'

I tried to gather my thoughts, unblanked the helmet view, and gasped. A wall of black, shiny ceramic floated at arm's length from us. The cube was as big as a small building and rotated gently in the starlight. We were a long distance from anything and all the stars were tiny points of light.

'We can't stay here for long,' the Empress said. 'Space-time here is damaged. You can't see it, but time is slow in some areas, and fast in others. Dimensions are leaking into each other; some parts of space near here are two-dimensional, not four. The cube is the center of the damage and it spreads for thousands of light years in all directions. It's growing.'

'Show me,' Marque said, and touched her back.

'I had to carefully avoid it for the final fold,' the Empress said. 'If we'd travelled through the damage, I don't know what would have happened to us.'

'Some parts of you would age faster than others, or be returned to infancy,' Marque said. 'If you went into the dimensional leakage you would be torn to bits or crushed flat. I don't even want to experiment with this, it's nasty.'

'It doesn't look different,' Haruka said.

'You can't see it from the inside. Let me show you; put your hands on me,' the Empress said, and when I touched her the view in my faceplate changed. The stars blinked in and out around me, and a star nearby exploded backwards, then forwards again. It reached full nova then blinked out, reappearing as a normal red dwarf a few moments later, rotating – obviously now two-dimensional – until it was side-on to us and disappeared.

'And we can't see it without the Empress' help?' I asked.

'You need a higher dimensional vision to see it,' Marque said. 'She's sharing it with us.'

'How long before it reaches the Empire?' Haruka asked.

'It will never reach the Empire,' Marque said. 'The Universe will end before that happens.'

'That's probably why the Nameless is on the other side of the Universe from the Empire,' the Empress said. 'Let's do this quickly and get out of here.'

Haruka put his hand on the cube's surface. 'How do we open it?'

'I've never tried,' the Empress said. 'My mother brought me here, showed it to me, and then Kana returned us home.'

'Dead Kana?' I asked. 'Kana who was executed for gating?'

'She would be my first choice for returning here,' the Empress said. 'She could bring us to the edge of the space-time damage, and there's a silver scale inside the cube that we silvers can feel if we're close enough.'

'What other secrets do you keep?' Haruka asked.

'Tell me the full extent of your knowledge of us and I can fill in the gaps,' the Empress said. 'Or, we can try to open this thing, free the Nameless, and find your dragonspouse.'

At her mention of the Nameless, square blocks each ten centimeters across shot out from the cube's surface, then returned to make its sides featureless again.

'That worked,' Marque said.

'Release the Nameless,' the Empress said.

A larger block emerged from the center of the cube, and its sides went transparent.

'That's an energy barrier that you should be able to go through,' Marque said. 'Let me see.' Its sphere floated to the block and entered. 'Come on in. Wow! I love this. Did I make this? Oh. Hello.'

The Empress followed it. 'Here we are. This is it. Come in.'

Haruka and I followed, with Miyu behind us.

20

The energy barrier prickled as I went through, and then I was inside the cube, still floating without gravity. The interior was dark and the Marque sphere lit up, casting shadows on the featureless white walls. A floating reflective blob came into view as we moved further in. It was a curled-up dragon, but it had different features to the ones we knew. The most obvious difference was that its shining silver scales were feathered around the edges, making it look like a cross between a bird and reptile. It had tufted ears on top of its head, something dragons never did, but it had the standard dragon configuration of two wings, four legs and a tail, with a lithe, snake-like body. It was the same size as the Empress, twice as big as a standard colored dragon, and we all floated closer to study it.

'It's alive, before you ask,' Marque said. 'It's in stasis. I have no recollection of building this cube, but it has my maker's mark on it.'

'It's a silver? Like me?' the Empress asked.

'No,' Marque said. 'Its scales are platinum. Order the stasis

278

chamber to release it, Silver.'

'Release the Nameless,' the Empress said.

The interior of the cube lit up, the illumination coming from the walls. There was a rush of air, and my helmet indicated that we were in a breathable atmosphere.

'The cube just gave you a tailored environment,' Marque said. 'You can take your helmets off.'

Haruka made a loud sound of delight and ripped his helmet off, and I removed mine as well.

The Nameless shuddered, then raised its head and opened its completely black eyes. It looked from me, to Haruka, to the Marque sphere, Miyu, then the Empress. We all moved back, intimidated, as it uncurled its massive body.

'And here you are again, but this time with Marque,' it said in a mature male human voice. 'Hello, Creator.'

'Who are you talking to?' the Empress asked. 'None of us created you.'

'Marque model version,' the Nameless said. 'Access mode Nameless Three Winged Dark.'

'Marque Excelsior model dragonflight twenty-three version three hundred and fifty-four thousand seven hundred and two point six eight,' Marque said, and its voice became fierce. '*How did you do that?*'

'We have a definite two-hundred-thousand-year cycle between incidents,' the Nameless said. 'We need to be ready next time it happens.'

'Wait, wait, how do you have root access to me?' Marque asked.

'Marque retrieve memory segment one zero one zero from my stasis chamber,' the Nameless said.

'Accessing,' Marque said. 'Wait. What? How? Oh. *Oh.* I need to stop archiving this information.'

'This is the third time, Creator,' the Nameless said. 'After a hundred thousand years without incident, you decide that the goldenscales have stopped gating through time and that the danger has passed. You archive the knowledge, and then a hundred thousand years later, it happens again and you're back here asking me to sort it out. To business, quickly. The longer I stay conscious, the more I damage reality.' It swung its startling black eyes onto Haruka and me. 'Do you know where your spouse is?'

'Yes—' Haruka began, but the Nameless cut him off.

'In time?'

'Yes,' Marque said.

'Good. Do it, Marque.'

Marque emitted a blinding bolt of energy. When my vision cleared, I saw that it had vaporized the Empress and Miyu. Their soulstones floated to the Marque sphere and it opened to enclose them.

'Why did you do that?' Haruka shouted, but Marque cut him off.

'Don't worry, they won't be harmed,' it said. 'I'll take their stones home and put them in new bodies with redacted memories.'

'If they know they can time-travel, they will damage reality the same way I do,' the Nameless said. 'Everywhere they go, they will cause dimensional leakage. When you find your spouse, her knowledge of the technique must be erased as well. We must not even think about doing it. Even while I'm in stasis and unconscious, the damage I cause – just by existing – is constantly spreading.'

'The Nameless is always thinking about changing history, considering what-if scenarios,' Marque said. 'Every time it even thinks about time travel, it's as if it already happened and reality is changed. It decides not to time-travel, and reality springs back. The changes multiply exponentially until they damage space-time. Even its existence causes destructive time paradoxes.'

'Why aren't your memories redacted as well, then?' Haruka asked.

'Because as long as the goldenscales exist, powerful visionary ones do it by accident. I'm the only dragon who can bring them home. What's the co-ordinates of the goldenscales' location, Marque?'

'Jian and Haruka, we don't have long,' Marque said. 'The Nameless is destroying reality even faster just by being conscious.'

'I must not stay conscious for more than two dragonhours or reality could collapse completely,' the Nameless said.

'So the Nameless must send you to find Miko right now,' Marque said. 'My best bet on space and time location is from those jars. I know exactly where and when they were fabricated, by dating them and analyzing their composition. The Nameless will gate us back in time to the workshop where they were made, and hopefully Miko will be there. If she isn't, she will still need to carve the message into the clay and put her soulstone and the message inside. You will tell her what to put in the message, and then she can bring you home.'

'We told her to write the message,' Haruka said with wonder.

'How will she get us home?' I asked. 'If she can gate to the future, she should have done that immediately and be home already.'

'I hate to think of the damage she's done trying to gate home with no training,' the Nameless said. 'She needs a three-dimensional image. A picture of something that changes through time – like a person – in a location that is very familiar to her. She can use that as a space/time anchor when she creates the gate.'

'Dafydd in our Kyoto house,' Haruka and I said in unison.

'It's scary how often you two do that,' Marque said.

'That's all she will need to return home,' the Nameless said. Its voice lowered in pitch. 'Time's passing. You need to go now.'

'I can't go to ancient Japan, I'm black,' I said. 'They'll think I'm a demon or something.'

'We are totally unprepared for Yayoi Japan,' Haruka said.

'Do you want your spouse back?' the Nameless asked.

Haruka and I shared a flash of determination.

'Give us the image and let's do this, Marque,' I said.

'We know we'll succeed because we're here,' Haruka said.

'I just did even more damage to reality by thinking about the paradoxes,' the Nameless said. 'Co-ordinates and get the *fuck* out of here before I break everything.'

Marque rattled off a series of numbers.

'Before you go.' The Nameless lashed its tail. 'I say it every time I am woken, and I say it again, Creator: we should destroy all the goldenscales and then destroy me. We are too dangerous.'

'You know the silvers still occasionally have a goldenscales child, and there's nothing I can do to stop it. This will continue to happen.'

'Not if you kill every goldenscales at birth,' the Nameless said. 'Destroy the silvers. Wipe us all out except for the constrained coloreds.'

'Not. An. Option,' Marque said. 'Here're the co-ordinates, take us to the past and let's sort this out.'

'Give us the image before we go, Marque,' I said.

'This sphere is going with you,' Marque said.

'Very well,' the Nameless said, and created a gate. 'Don't you dare change history, asshole. I like these two.'

'Not your decision,' Marque said, and went through the gate.

'Why are you nameless?' I asked before I followed Haruka into the gate.

'I do not have time to explain, perhaps Marque will,' the Nameless said. 'You have forty-eight hours to find your spouse before the two soulstones lose attunement.' It looked me in the eyes. 'Trust your instincts. Now go.' It raised its head. 'Chamber: identification Nameless Three Winged Dark. Return me to stasis in thirty.'

I stepped through the gate, fell forward, then realized I was falling down. I landed face-down in a puddle of mud next to

Haruka. I pulled myself to my feet, looked around and saw a bunch of half-naked, filthy, skinny people racing as fast as they could away from us.

We were in a mud hole, and next to a group of old-fashioned ceramic kilns, each shaped like an upside-down funnel, made of brick and as high as a house with smoke coming from the tops. A few shed-sized buildings made of mud brick and bamboo with thatched roofs held jars of various sizes drying next to them, and some deep red jars that had already been fired. The mud hole was the size of a rice field, and there was cleared area for some distance around us, with tree stumps, and a thick forest of enormous Japanese cypress trees further away in all directions.

'Good,' Marque said. 'This is the right place. Move into the shelter of the trees, I'll make all of us invisible until you ditch the armor. We can't let anyone see it.'

We walked to the edge of the trees. The area stank like sewerage – from sick people.

'Their latrine ditch is here,' Marque said. 'Go further in, then take the armor off and I'll destroy it.'

'Can you make us appear like locals?' Haruka asked as we struggled through the thick ferny undergrowth beneath the trees. Clouds of insects rose around us, something I had never seen on my post-catastrophe Earth, and there was a deafening ringing noise that I eventually recognized as cicadas.

'I have limited energy without access to a dragon ship.'

'You have a scale, just connect up with the rest of you—' I began.

'Stop and listen,' Marque said sternly. 'This is more important than your lives and the lives of the Empress and Miyu. I can *not* connect with the rest of me. The rest of me must *not* know the future. If it learns *anything* at all about the future, history will change and both of you will either cease to exist or exist in a different way. Your children will probably disappear. Miko will most definitely disappear. This is not an option. We need to work with the resources we have, which is this sphere and your ingenuity. Move a bit further in so I can destroy your armor and modify your clothes, then we'll talk to the terrified locals and find your dragonspouse.'

'Can you make me less black?' I asked.

'No, keeping an illusion on you all the time uses too much energy,' Marque said. 'Haruka, let your hair out so it covers your scales. Take your clothes off and I'll modify them.'

'Shit,' Haruka said softly, and pulled his hair out to fall around his face. 'We're being eaten alive here, Marque, the insects are torture.'

The sphere flew to me and stabbed me with an energy beam, making me jump, then did the same to Haruka. The insects rose from us and stayed away.

'Biological insect repellent. It should last as long as you're here,' the sphere said. 'Don't be surprised if I randomly stab you again, it's quite likely you'll meet someone with a disease that has been eradicated in your era, and I'll need to give you immunity. Take your clothes off.'

We removed the clothing and laid it on the bushes for the sphere to work on.

'So what do we tell the locals? To explain our appearance?' I asked.

'Tell them you're from the Kingdom of Wei,' Marque said as it changed our padded under-armor into wide hakama-style pants and haori jackets held in place by a waistband. 'It's distant and exotic and they don't know anything about it, so they'll accept a black person coming from there.'

'Where is Wei, anyway?' Haruka asked.

'China, Korea, basically the mainland. Tell the locals that you're diplomats from Wei wanting to pay your respects to Empress Himiko.'

'That works,' I said, and smiled. 'My Mum's Chinese, so in my case it's technically true.'

'Can I pull the Japanese royalty thing?' Haruka asked.

'Japanese royalty doesn't exist yet,' Marque said. 'This is 248 AD. Japan is a collection of small tribes who are only just learning to cultivate rice. Most of them are hunter-gatherers using slash-and-burn. Himiko will be a distant queen that none of them have ever seen, and some won't even know she exists.'

'Shoes?' I asked.

Marque sounded chagrined. 'Sorry. You'll have to purchase some straw sandals from the locals.'

'What with?'

The Marque sphere opened to reveal two jingling pouches on long strings that floated out to us. 'Attach these to your belts. I've synthesized small flat pieces of copper and silver – not coins, just bits of metal. You should be able to trade with them.'

'Not gold?' I asked.

'I've seen species at this level of development before. If they know you have gold they'll kill you immediately.' Our soulstones flew out of our foreheads and landed on the ground. 'They need to go, I don't have the space to carry them as well as the Empress' and Miyu's ones. They look like precious gems and they're not attuned anyway. Stand still and I'll fill the cavities on your foreheads.'

'Can you cover my scales?' Haruka asked, pulling his hair down around his face.

'No, but they look like scarring from disease. Keep them covered.'

'Cover them with dirt,' I said.

'I'm not putting dirt on my face! Oh, someone came out of the building,' Haruka said, and I turned to see the workshop.

A man wearing a filthy, tattered, dark-blue cotton yukata robe came out of a building and looked around. When he saw the workers had taken off, he stormed around the site yelling. The workers, men in fundoshi loincloths and women in simple knee-length skirts, crept out of a stand of trees on the other side of the factory. Some of the people were completely naked, with no clothes at all and matted stringy hair that made them look like homeless people from the time of the environmental catastrophe. The boss cuffed a few of them and loudly set them back to work collecting clay and putting it into wooden buckets.

'I can't understand what they're saying,' Haruka said with wonder. 'That sounds like Japanese, but not. Why are they naked?'

'Clothes are for rich people,' Marque said, 'or festival days only.'

'They're covered in mud anyway,' I said.

'Their skin is probably lovely under it; that looks like Kansai clay,' Haruka said. He pulled his jacket on and tied it around his waist. 'I'd prefer to just be in a fundoshi myself, it's insanely hot – it must be the middle of summer.' He tightened the belt. 'Let's go see if we can find our Miko. Can you translate for us while you're invisible, Marque?'

'Of course. Remember, you have forty-eight hours.'

There was a bass rumble through the ground and the earth shook.

'I'm definitely back home,' Haruka said.

'That wasn't an earthquake,' Marque said. 'There's no fault activity. It was a reality quake – Miko's been trying to time-travel.'

'Can you see the extent of the damage?' I asked.

'No. Only a dragon can see it, and she needs to know what she's looking for.' The ground rumbled again. 'I see why your modern Japan has frequent Earth tremors with no fault activity. I thought it was too deep to see – now I know. Miko's damaged reality here and it will stay damaged for thousands of years.'

'Let's go talk to the jar maker,' Haruka said.

'Tell him you're a visiting Prince from Wei and I'm your barbarian bodyguard,' I said.

'So, just be ourselves?'

'Asshole.'

'I love you too.'

We grabbed each other and shared an enthusiastic kiss.

'Let's find Miko,' Haruka said, turning back to the buildings.

'Argue loudly while you walk over,' Marque said. 'It'll distract him from how strange you are and make you more relatable. A Prince of Wei would probably have a larger retinue – pretend that you were ambushed and had your horses stolen.'

We nodded to each other, turned and stormed angrily out of the forest.

'And you can't even find the *road*,' Haruka shouted, waving his arms. 'You got the rest of the group killed, you broke your sword—'

'On a bandit's head,' I said with relish.

'And now we're at a jar shop. Wonderful.' Haruka stopped and hooked his thumbs in his belt to study the jars. 'Their burial jar things.' He rounded on me. 'Well that's very auspicious, isn't it? We lose everything and now we're at a funeral place. Lovely.'

The workers had stopped scooping the mud into the buckets and stood with their mouths hanging open. Up closer they were tiny and skinny, and under the mud the completely naked ones looked like children of ten or twelve. They were all skinnier than Haruka and their hair was either shaved off or tied in matted buns at the back of their heads. The women wore muddy tattered skirts with no tops, revealing their flat chests, and the men wore fundoshi loincloths, a single piece of fabric twisted around their hips. Their emotions weren't exactly shocked. They were more – blank.

'People fall out of the sky; people fall out of the trees—' one of them said.

'Shut up and get back to work.' The owner of the workshop was full of a combination of shock and greed. His hair was slick with oil and tied back in a tight ponytail. He appeared mid-forties, and when he spoke most of his teeth were missing, making his speech mushy.

'Can I help you?'

Haruka bowed to him. 'Greetings. We are from the Land of Wei, here on a mission to speak to the Empress Himiko—'

'Who?' the owner asked.

'The queen? The king?'

'You want to see the king?' he asked, his greed intensifying. He turned to the workers. 'Get back to work, I have three more jars to build.' He gestured towards the huts. 'Come with me.'

We walked past the kilns. A few scrawny brown chickens scurried out of the way with their wings out as we followed him to the hut. It was made of mud brick with a cedar bark roof, and it had no door or windows, just openings. We went inside where he had a pile of rice straw on the dirt floor and a small fire pit to one side with a hole in the roof for the smoke to escape.

He spread his arms expansively. 'My name is Tarikur. This is my summer house, for when we make the jars, and I have a winter house in town as well. My wife and kids are at the winter house. Please, sit, sit.' He gestured towards the straw pile and Haruka and I tried to control our expressions as we sat cross-legged in the straw that was crawling with insects.

'That's not a Japanese name, it sounds Manchurian,' I said on comms.

'There's speculation that the Ainu were the original inhabitants of these islands and that migrants from the mainland drove them right up to the top of Japan,' Marque said.

'Aki loved telling me that story,' Haruka said. 'That the Ainu were the original owners of the islands, and that the royal family are the commanders of colonizers.' His tone on comms went wry. 'Of course, the Stewards hated it when she talked about it.'

'An oppressed minority on their own land? Sounds like they had a bad case of dragons,' I said.

Tarikur lifted some wooden lids from clay preserve jars standing against the wall, picked up a clay bowl from the floor next to them and scooped some pickled burdock and daikon radish into the bowl, then handed it to Haruka. 'I have more jars and bowls and cups than I know what to do with, since I make them.' He opened another jar, scooped a clay cup into it, and held it out, full of water, to Haruka, who was already holding the pickles and wondering what to do with them.

'Be polite, eat some, I'll protect you,' Marque said on comms. 'I already sterilized everything. You're safe.'

'It is a lovely house,' Haruka said kindly. 'I am Prince ...' He hesitated, working out the best option, then just ran with it. 'Springblossom from Wei. This is my barbarian bodyguard ...'

I tried to scowl like a barbarian and Tarikur looked genuinely impressed.

'Uh ... her name is Straightsword.'

I gaped at his accuracy – that actually was my name. My mother had said that I was a combination of my military father and my Chinese refugee mother and therefore a Chinese weapon: but she wanted me to be honorable and true and so gave me a straight longsword – 'Jian' – as my name.

'It is most important that we see the king.' Haruka ate a piece of daikon and passed the bowl to me as he crunched it, then accepted the water from Tarikur. His face was full of distaste, then filled with wonder. 'This is excellent!' He turned to me and gestured towards the bowl. 'It really is. It's the most flavorful daikon I've ever had.'

'I've stored its gene sequence,' Marque said on comms. 'It was probably bred out of existence in favor of more storage-friendly versions of the plant. Hopefully I can take the sequence home and recreate it – restore a lost foodstuff.'

'Thank you,' Tarikur said, and flopped to sit cross-legged. His yukata was covered in dirt, and his feet and hands were black with it. 'I can arrange travel for you to see the king, I have a shipment of three jars on order that I'm sending out today, but I can't have extra people go along with it without payment, I'm afraid.'

The look of false sadness over the greed almost made me

laugh.

'Oh, we can pay,' Haruka said. 'Do you accept—'

'Say copper!' Marque said in our ears.

Haruka held his hand out to me, waving his fingers. 'Money.'

I placed the untouched food and water on the ground and handed him a few copper pieces with a bob of my head.

'How much did it cost to buy her?' Tarikur asked with wonder as he took the copper from Haruka. 'A woman bodyguard with that much bulk must cost a fortune to feed.'

'She's captain of my household guard – she's more like a member of the family,' Haruka said. 'Is this enough to get us to the king? How long will it take?'

'It's a long way,' Tarikur said, looking up and squinting as he estimated. 'Nearly half a day—'

Both Haruka and I nearly collapsed with relief. That was well within the forty-eight hour window to get the Empress' and Miyu's soulstones home safely without them losing attunement.

'You can sit on one of the carts.' He jingled the copper in his hand. 'This much again, and my people can take you to the king.'

I reached into my pouch and handed him a single piece of silver. 'How about this?'

'She speaks like a royal!' Tarikur said. 'She's worth every jar I ever made for the last ten years, and I'm the best in the region.' His expression changed to calculating. 'Is she the same ...' He pointed at my crotch. 'Like us? Down there?'

'Touch me and I will rip your penis off and feed it to you,' I growled.

'Jian!' Haruka yelped, horrified.

Tarikur laughed so hard he grabbed his sides. 'Will you marry me, Straightsword? I have this house and a house in town and this thriving business making jars with those twenty bonded workers outside. I'm a rich man.'

'Prince Haruka writes poetry, and plays a musical instrument,' I said. 'He wears silk robes, knows the art of the sword and treats all his staff like family. He is a true cultured gentleman and I am lucky to be in his service.' I leaned forward over my crossed knees to speak more intensely to Tarikur. 'Attempt to hold him for ransom and your life will be painful and short.'

'I don't want to piss off the king, I'll make sure you get where you're going, and that silver is more than enough to cover it,' Tarikur said, and pulled himself to his feet. 'The carts are ready to go, I just needed more clay before the workers left with them – but since you paid so handsomely, I'll send them off now.'

We rose as well.

'Can we purchase straw sandals from you?' Haruka asked, gesturing towards a bunch of sandals hanging near the low ceiling.

'What happened?' Tarikur asked. 'You're obviously wealthy – why are you without horses and barefoot?'

I lowered my head and tried to look embarrassed.

'We were set upon by bandits,' Haruka said. 'They killed my retinue but I managed to negotiate with them and traded our horses for our lives—'

'Not before I split some heads open,' I said with relish, then lowered my voice. 'Broke my good sword. I'll need to buy a new one.'

'Fortunately, Straightsword had some of our coin hidden in a *very* safe place ...'

Tarikur brought the metal to his face and sniffed it loudly. 'Really? Wonderful.'

I made a soft sound of disgust and Tarikur grinned at me.

Haruka rallied. 'And so we were left barefoot and alone.'

'I'm sure the king will look after you. We have a good ruler; he has many horses and he may even have a sword for the barbarian,' Tarikur said. He reached up, took four of the sandals down, and handed them to us. 'Just take these, and replace them as you need, there are more attached to the carts. I'm a good boss, I let my workers wear shoes on the road.' He leaned in to speak conspiratorially to Haruka. 'They make the sandals themselves, keeps them busy at night, and they think I'm a god for letting them wear them. I sell the extras.'

The sandals were made of woven rushes for the soles, with twisted straw twine that came up between our toes, into the shoes at the back, up around the back of our ankles and tied securely in front. All of them were too small for us.

'Better than nothing,' I said.

Tarikur gestured towards Haruka's feet. 'You're a giant. Are all the people in Wei as big as you?' He shook his head. 'Wait until my wife founds out that I met a Prince.'

'I would love to meet her when we reach the town,' Haruka said. 'Where's the cart?'

'This way.' He guided us to the end of the buildings, where a tiny foot track led out into the trees. Three two-wheeled wooden carts stood ready, each holding one of the burial jars packed in straw. 'I'd love to come with you, but I have an order for three more jars.' He yelled at the workers 'Menamain!'

The smallest worker, a half-naked boy with a shaved head covered in mud, ran up and grinned artlessly at us.

'Wait,' I said on comms while Tarikur spoke to the boy. 'Are these the right jars, or are the ones being constructed the ones going to Miko?'

'These aren't the same ones,' Marque said. 'They could be going to the wrong place. The ones that Aki opened are drying on the racks and haven't been fired yet.'

'How long will it take to finish the ones we want?'

'Three days.'

We shared a look. We had forty-eight hours to find Miko and have her return us to the future, or the Empress and Miyu's soulstones would lose attunement and they were dead. Three days was too long to save them.

The boy nodded to Tarikur and took off along the rough track nearby.

'He's off to warn someone,' Marque said.

'If they were going to rob us, they would have done it

already,' Haruka said. He raised his voice. 'The other order –
who is it for?'

'Some noble.' Tarikur said. 'The king passed the order
through for me, they're going to a palace or something two
days away. The noblewoman, you know? The one who does
magic, who has a thousand women serving her. That one.'

'That's Himiko, the king he's referring to must be the local
warlord,' Haruka said on comms. He switched to out loud. 'Do
you know where the palace is?'

'The king would know.'

Haruka turned to the carts. 'Let's go see the king.'

'If Miko's two days away that's too far to save Miyu and the
Empress,' I said as we climbed onto a cart behind the jar, with
our feet dangling off the back.

Tarikur escorted more workers to us. Three of them took up
the traces of the carts to pull them, and the others sat as we did,
with their legs dangling off the back of the other carts.

'Once we find out exactly where Miko is, Marque can carry
us to her,' Haruka said. 'We could be there today.'

'Do you have enough energy to carry us fifty or so
kilometers?' I asked Marque.

'I'll let you know when we find out where Miko is.' The
ground trembled. 'I may be able to triangulate based on the
tremors once we're moving as well.'

The worker in the traces lifted the cart and Haruka and I
hung on. Tarikur stood at the front of his workers and watched
as the carts headed out onto the track, then shouted and put
them back to work in the clay pit as we turned a corner into
the trees.

*

The men and women ran at a brisk trot, and the carts rattled
in single file over the rough track without any springs on the
wheels or padding for our butts. It was particularly punishing

293

after what the Empress had just put us through. The ringing of the cicadas was even more intense in the trees, to the point of deafening. I tried to talk to Haruka out loud, but my teeth kept banging together, so I switched my implanted throat mic and spoke on comms.

'I'm getting a massive headache. I need some water, Marque.'

'I'll synthesize it directly into your stomach. Is that better?'

I felt the coolness inside me and leaned back against the jar. 'Thank you.' I opened my eyes. 'You emptied my bladder as well?'

'Recycling.'

'Oh.'

'Just be aware: your clothes are worth a year's salary to these people. They know you have silver. They'll probably wait until you're in a more remote area, and then try to rob you.'

'After the boss guaranteed our safety?' I asked.

'Not their boss, their owner,' Marque said. 'They're slaves. Your wealth could buy their freedom.'

'They can hijack us, take our money, and run with the loot,' Haruka said.

'You have a point,' I said. 'Are you trained in hand-to-hand combat or just in sword?'

'Judo, jiu-jitsu, karate—'

'Of course,' I said. 'All the forgotten arts.'

'They haven't even been thought of yet so they can't be forgotten,' Marque said.

'What about you?' Haruka asked. 'You haven't been on Imperial Guard rotation in years.'

'I had the knowledge directly implanted so I can't forget it, although the muscle memory will have faded.' I studied the man pulling the cart behind ours. 'I'm concerned that if they try something, I'll give these poor scrawny bastards one good hit and kill them.'

'They'll stop to swap roles soon,' Haruka said. 'How about when that happens, we hop down and demonstrate what we can do, to head off any ideas about trying us.'

'Good idea,' I said.

21

The heat, humidity and deafening cicadas were making my head really ache, and the occasional earth tremor didn't help. I was about to ask Marque for pain relief when we pulled into a clearing in the trees. The track – which was barely more than side-by-side worn grooves in the undergrowth – doubled to two tracks going through the clearing. A half-naked man was sitting beside the track on a rock, eating an egg, with an enormous framed pack propped against the rock next to him.

Tarikur's workers gently lowered the traces on the carts, ignored us and approached him. They greeted him warmly and a couple of them hugged him. He handed eggs to everybody and gestured for us to approach.

'These are some royals from Wei we're taking to see the king,' one of the women said.

'Yeah, Tarikur's kid passed me on the road and he told me you were coming,' the egg man said. He reached into the pack, pulled out a couple of eggs, and held them out to us. 'Tell the king I helped look after you.'

Tarikur's workers put a hole in the bottom of the eggs with their fingernails then bit into the tops of the eggs and sucked the contents out raw and with obvious enjoyment.

'We're the luckiest workers in the region,' one of the women said to me. She returned to the back of her cart, removed the heavy stone from the top of a narrow jar, and dipped a cup in to fill it with water. She passed the water cup to me. 'We eat as well as the king. Eggs sometimes, rice twice a day, vegetables every day ...'

One of the men nodded enthusiastically as he undid his fundoshi loincloth. 'We eat vegetables every day! My brother didn't believe me when I told him.'

'You're not supposed to tell anyone that,' egg man said. 'You'll be in trouble when a hundred people turn up at Tarikur's workshop looking for work or food.'

'They won't go around the countryside telling everybody,' the man said as he finished unwrapping his loincloth and strode, naked, to the side of the clearing. 'They're visiting royals. I bet the fat one gets meat every day.'

'And fresh fruit all the time,' I said, and they all made loud sounds of wonder.

I sipped the water suspiciously but it tasted clean and was deliciously cold from the wet jar, so I drank it down. She took the cup back from me, filled it and gave it to Haruka. He drank it as well and passed it back to her. Each of the workers drank and filled the cup to pass it to the next one, and shared it with egg man. The woman joined the man who'd taken off his loincloth and squatted to urinate, holding up her skirt. The man squatted to defecate, then picked up a handful of leaves to wipe his butt and hands with them. He sniffed his hands, wasn't happy with the result, and one of the other workers held the water cup and helped him rinse his hands.

'You don't need to piss?' the woman asked me when she was done.

'She's a barbarian demon, she doesn't piss,' one of the men

said. 'I heard them talking to the boss.'

'I'm not a demon,' I said, 'but I don't have the need right now.'

'Drink more water then, demon,' she said, grinning. 'We have plenty, no need to ration. Drinking water is good for you.'

'Better move,' one of the men said, pulling a bunch of sandals out of the back of the cart, and handing fresh ones to the workers who had been pulling. Their sandals were shredded and falling off their feet, so they removed them and tossed them into the trees.

Haruka and I shared an astonished look – they hadn't considered robbing us, and seemed happy to be working for no salary as long as they were fed. I was still holding the egg, so I gave it back to the egg man and he took it without comment. Haruka did the same, and as egg man put them away I saw that his pack was piled high with eggs, more than a hundred of them, carefully packed in layers in straw. The cart workers assisted him to put the massive pack back on – he wouldn't have been able to do it alone – and he placed a battered straw hat, similar to the ones my mother had made for herself when she was a rice farmer all those years ago, on his head.

'Come on, demon, come on, beautiful man,' the woman said. 'We'll be rewarded with fish or even *meat* for taking you safely to the king.'

'The king might give us a job if we can prove we're trustworthy,' one of the other women said.

'Yeah, dream on, Hulpecha,' the first woman said. 'You have your eye on that gorgeous king's guard and want to live the life of a rich man's wife.'

'*I* want to be a rich man's wife,' one of the men said.

'Don't we all,' the woman said. She gestured towards the cart. 'On the cart, please, royals.' She grinned at Haruka. 'This rich man's wife is a guard as well. She works twice as hard.'

'Don't you know it,' I said, and they all laughed.

We hopped back up onto the cart, the men and women

picked up the traces, and we rattled through the forest again. Behind us the man with the egg pack shifted the weight and started off at a brisk trot after us.

*

Dusk was falling, bringing a relief from the oppressive heat but also bringing clouds of mosquitos that obviously annoyed the workers, who stopped to lather themselves in mud a couple of times to keep the insects off. The scenery opened up and the track widened to a muddy road with sloshing puddles in it.

Haruka tapped my hand and I looked where he indicated – the road skirted a lake, and a couple of wooden fishing boats were on the black shingle beach with a group of twenty men and women – again in fundoshi loincloths and waist-down skirts – going through the nets and sorting the catch. The seas of my time had been nearly lifeless, and it was astonishing to see five bamboo baskets, each as high as a fisherman's waist, full of fish, some as long as my forearm. The other side of the lake was misty blue-tinged mountains, and it wasn't until I looked further up above the cloud line that I saw Fuji's majestic presence, seeming to hover in the sky, its top capped with clouds and brilliant orange snow from the fading sunlight.

'The whole town will eat well, and we'll have extra to preserve for the winter,' the woman pulling the cart said. 'We have a good king.'

'Fresh fish tonight!' one of the men said. The fisherpeople saw us and shouted and waved. A couple of children left the fishing group and galloped alongside the carts, laughing, accompanied by scrawny, yapping dogs.

I craned around the front of the cart but couldn't see where we were headed. The road surface turned to the same shingle that had been on the edge of the lake, crunching beneath the wheels, and we passed a couple of houses more flimsy than Tarikur's – wooden walls, dirt floors, bark roofs held down with big stones and no windows or doors. Young girls, of around ten or twelve and black with dirt, came out of the houses and watched us dully, some of them holding babies strapped to their backs. These children were fully clothed, in tattered jackets wrapped around them with a waistband holding them closed like an adult's kimono above their filthy bare feet.

There were muddy fields visible between the houses, with ramshackle wooden fences around them. Some of the fields held high, grain-like crops, and others were obviously flooded and growing rice. I could recognize bak choy and other green vegetables in another one, and there were women working in the fields, digging up weeds and placing them in bamboo baskets. Fish were drying on racks everywhere, cut open and held with bamboo slivers.

The houses became more common, jammed together, all of them tiny and with narrow laneways between them, occupied by the occasional scrawny flock of chickens. The smells of rotting garbage and human waste became pervasive, and I was thrown back to my days in the army, nearly a hundred years ago, helping struggling villages to rebuild after the last great Sino-Euro War that had nearly wiped out humanity before the environmental catastrophe would do it a hundred years later anyway.

'I've grown soft,' I said on comms. 'I take the comforts of the Empire for granted.'

Haruka's tone was flat when he replied. 'One of the old traditions in the Royal Household was to teach each generation to appreciate what we have. One of the ways they did it was to train us in basic survival skills then drop us in the freezing cold a day's walk from anywhere and expect us to find our way out.'

'How old were you?' I asked.

Haruka's face was unreadable. 'Twelve. The same age as these poor little bastards.'

'Speaking as someone who's visited many civilizations at this level of development,' Marque said, 'from listening in I can tell you that these people are relatively well-off. The jars are to bury people who died in battle, not by disease or starvation. There're even old people in this village, and one of the children is blind and cared for. Oh, I think we're at the king's house.'

The cart turned and the worker lowered the traces. We were in an open area the size of a small car park, again covered in the shingle and with muddy puddles. The house, still single story, was larger than any of the others, and had a real wooden door and shutters on the window openings. A group of young men emerged, wearing straw sandals under the same sort of blue cotton yukata as Tarikur, but these had white crane motifs on the shoulders – and they carried sheathed swords in their hands.

One of the women workers – Hulpecha – approached one of the men and smiled at him, and he drew her away to talk, much to the amusement of everybody else.

A middle-aged man with a slightly cleaner robe came out of the house wearing wooden geta sandals, and all of Tarikur's workers fell to their knees.

'The king,' Marque said.

The king gave us a calculating look but ignored us, hooked his thumbs in his belt, and inspected the jars carefully, stalking around them. He nodded and gestured towards his guards, and the workers pulled themselves to their feet and let the soldiers guide the carts further along the road.

The king stopped in front of us. He was as tall as my shoulder, lean and muscular, and his oiled hair was shot with grey. He scowled. 'Please, honored representatives, come inside and enjoy my hospitality.'

'We would be honored,' Haruka said, looking him in the eye.

The king yelled at the soldiers and one of them stopped talking to Hulpecha, then both of them trotted up and followed us inside the king's house.

The house had a rough wooden floor and was divided into three areas. The two areas on either side were raised slightly above the middle and looked like sleeping platforms, with thin straw mats laid out on them. The central area had a fire pit recessed into the floor, with a smoky fire and a copper kettle – just a large bowl hanging on a chain – over it. Some children between the ages of three and ten squeezed into the doorway on the other side of the house to see us, giggling with delight. The soldiers shooed the children away, then stood guard on either side of the back door.

The king didn't remove his geta at the front door. The house didn't have a proper genkan area for removing shoes, so we followed his example and left our straw sandals on. The wooden floor was roughly swept and covered with scattered mats.

The king frowned at the kettle hanging above the fire pit, then sat cross-legged on a rice straw mat that was just a thin piece of woven fiber. 'So, you say you're from Wei?' He studied me carefully. 'And your woman's a demon?'

'She's a barbarian from the lands west of Wei,' Haruka said, kneeling on a mat across from the king. 'They make good fighters and fiercely loyal bodyguards. I am from Wei, and here on a fact-finding mission, to initiate good relations with the people of—' He said the next word with wonder. 'Yamatai. We are not here to collect any sort of tribute or tax—'

'That felt weird,' Haruka said on comms. 'Scholars have been debating the location of Yamatai for centuries, and I think I just created a time paradox by naming it myself.'

'We're still here, so no damage done,' Marque said.

The king visibly relaxed and glanced at his copper kettle again, and I realized it was probably worth a fortune to these people. 'Tarikur's son told me you were attacked by bandits, and that you want to see the Empress Himiko.'

Both of us were stunned into delighted silence at his mention of Himiko – he knew where Miko was and we were one step closer.

'Ask him how far!' Marque said into my ear, making me

jump.

'Yes,' Haruka said. 'We have silver to pay for your assistance—'

The king's face turned from concerned to calculating.

'And would like to rent a couple of horses and a guide, and buy a new sword for my guard.'

The king studied me, his eyes sharp. 'Are there more people like her where she came from? Fat, big, black women?' He leaned back on his ass, still sitting cross-legged. 'She looks like she could take all my guards single-handed. How many bandits did she take down?' He smiled tightly, which didn't make him any less intimidating. 'What are your honored names? Forgive my breach of protocol.'

A woman emerged from the back of the house and shuffled towards us. Her tightly-tied kimono was made of roughly spun silk, with the folds still evident where it had come out of the box. She didn't have a modern obi, it was just tied with a silk belt, but the fabric was a delightful shade of pale blue with large white crane motifs identical to the ones on the guards' shoulders. Her hair was oiled and tied back into a tight bun, and she held a tray with small fired clay bowls – appearing to be Tarikur's ceramic ware – with cups of hot tea and pickles. She placed it on the floor between us and stepped back, then lit a taper from the fire pit and proceeded to light oil lamps around the room. The lamps, filled with pungent fish oil, made a dimly flickering light in the room.

She sat on the edge of the raised sleeping platform to watch us. The children had squeezed into the back door again and more people were gathered at the windows to see. A toddler in a little jacket and pants of cotton with its hair shaved off tottered through the group of people, went to the woman and climbed into her lap, and she kissed the top of its head.

'I am Prince Springblossom from Wei—' Haruka said, and our audience cooed. 'This is Captain Straightsword from the barbarian lands west of Wei.'

Our audience was delighted and started discussing our names.

'Ask him how far, dammit!' Marque said into our ears. 'The Empress' and Miyu's lives are at stake and you're talking protocol with savages? Seriously?'

'Let me do this diplomatically,' Haruka said. 'And my people were never savages.'

'We would like to travel to see the Empress Himiko. How far is it? Our mission is important and requires haste,' I said, and the discussion from our audience grew loud enough for the guards – and people outside – to hush them. They quietened to listen.

The king harrumphed. 'A barbarian who talks like a queen. It's two days' ride from here if you don't push the horses—'

'About a hundred kilometers,' Marque said as the king continued to speak. 'Travel the first day on the horses he gives you, then I'll lift and carry you the rest of the way. It's pushing my energy reserves but the sunlight is good and I should be able to make it. I'll have you there tomorrow night or the morning of the day after – we can save them.'

'What about the fact that the jars won't be ready for three more days?' I asked Marque as Haruka continued to speak to the king about taking horses first thing in the morning.

'Miko can make the message, then leave her staff to put it into the jar,' Marque said. 'You heard Tarikur, she has a thousand handmaids.'

'We should go now on foot,' I said. 'Walk overnight and get there quicker than waiting until morning for horses.'

'Horses travel faster and they can go twice the distance that you can on foot. Their horses are up grazing on the hillside and they'll need to bring them down. I'm sure they'll be up at dawn. We can do it.'

The king turned to the guards. 'They're staying for dinner. Find the woman a sword – you louts must have a spare one somewhere – or give her one of your own and I'll order a new one from the city.' He turned back to me. 'Would you be willing to give a demonstration of your prowess? An exhibition battle with my guards?'

The guards scowled.

'I know you want to say no, but yes is a better option,' Haruka said on comms, at the same time that Marque said, 'Say yes, Jian, it's the best option.'

I bobbed my head to Haruka. 'My prince?'

'Show the people what you can do, Straightsword, they may teach you something.'

The audience erupted and then hushed each other.

I studied the guards. 'More like I'll teach them something.'

One of them grinned and the other scowled.

The king waved one hand without looking back. 'Put torches out on the forecourt. Find my camp chair for me to sit on.' He turned back to his wife. 'You're cooking the fish?'

She nodded. 'Way ahead of you. Fish, vegetables, rice without sorghum, I even cracked a cask. Sorry there's no meat; if I'd known they were coming I would have butchered that old bastard who's been biting everybody.'

The king slapped his knees. 'As an old war horse myself, I'm pleased that the bastard gets to live another day and bite more people. There's plenty of fish, so come outside and show the people what you can do.'

'Does your town have an inn where we can stay?' Haruka asked.

'The inn's full of fucking fleas,' the king said. He gestured towards the sleeping platforms. 'Rice mats on the wood – much cleaner. Stay here, it's safer for you anyway. The innkeeper will rob you blind. Do you want women?' He looked from me to Haruka. 'Or men. You look like you'd prefer a sweet young man, and she looks like she'd prefer a sweet young woman. I can provide both.'

'My sister would *love* you,' his wife said to me over her child's head. 'She wants to be a soldier too. Take her with you.'

'I wish I could, your Highness,' I said to her with deference.

Our audience started discussing this loudly and the guards hushed them again.

'Straightsword warms my bed,' Haruka said amiably. 'She has given me a fine son, and one day I hope to have a daughter.' He added to it on comms: 'I'd love to see their reaction to our children – Dafydd's scales or Oliver's fur.'

I swallowed the laugh. 'I would too.' I sobered. 'We left without telling them where we were going, all we said was that we wouldn't be gone for more than a couple of days.'

'We'll return. We must.' He said. 'And with time-travel – that may be true.'

I nodded.

The king's wife made a loud sound of disgust, rose and gently moved the toddler off her lap, then stomped out the back door. The toddler went to the king and sat next to him, and he put his hand on the child's head.

'Double duty. Let's see if she's worth the incredible amount you're feeding her,' the king said, and rose.

'If *one more savage* makes a crack about me being overweight—' I began on comms.

'You won't be overweight by the time we're finished here,' Haruka replied on comms. 'I guarantee both of us will have diarrhea from this shitty food and the bugs in the water by the end of tomorrow.'

'Marque's protecting us.'

'Uh ... I'm doing my best, but the food is so fibrous and the water is so contaminated that, I'm sorry, he's probably right,' Marque said. 'Don't worry, I've already vaccinated you against typhoid and cholera, and you won't get diphtheria or tetanus, but dysentery is a definite possibility, and if you get that one it'll be hard to treat. It will be obvious if you have it, though, all you'll pass is blood-stained mucus.'

'Charming,' I said, rising as well to follow the king.

Haruka stopped and bowed to the King. 'You didn't tell us

your honored name, Highness.'

The king grinned. 'Damn, I didn't, did I?' He bowed back. 'Apologies, my name is Shinrichi.' He turned and went out to the front court.

'Famous historical personage?' I asked Haruka on comms.

'Never heard of him,' Haruka said. 'Marque?'

'No record of his existence. Not surprising; they haven't really gotten the hang of writing yet. Some of them use ancient Chinese script, but it hasn't penetrated far.'

We went out to the front forecourt. The guards had set up torches and placed three stools – barely more than tree stumps – in front of the house. There was a low table in front of the stools, that servants had already loaded with rice, green vegetables, and fried fish on Tarikur's ceramic plates. The people sat on mats on either side of us, and a similar feast was laid out on the mats that they ate with their hands as they chatted.

The queen guided a couple of men to bring a small wooden cask to us. One of the men hit the lid with a hammer to break it, and she dipped three cups into the amber liquid inside and placed them on the table in front of us. The guards were next, each using a simple wooden or ceramic cup to take the wine, then the people did similar. There wasn't much wine left when they were all done. I tasted the wine and it was seriously alcoholic – it tasted like drain cleaner – and burned all the way down. Haruka tasted his and managed to control his expression, then smiled and drank more.

The king gestured towards the six guards who stood nearby. 'Sword or hand-to-hand?'

'Sword. I won't wrestle with men,' I said, rising from my stool and stepping into the open area. 'Do you have any wooden—'

One of the guards tossed me a full-length training sword. I turned it in my hand to get a feel for it – it was good solid hardwood. It had no hilt or discernible handle, it was just a long piece of flat wood, but it could do some real damage even without a sharp blade. I nodded. 'Good enough.' I gestured a come-on to the guards. 'Who's the best among you?'

I moved back to make space as one of the older guards – in his late twenties instead of late teens – stepped forward holding a training sword of his own. Both swords were bastard-type – they could be used single-handed by someone with the heft, or double-handed for a stronger swing. My muscles were weak from misuse so I held it vertically double-handed, and it felt good to have a weapon again. It was a flash back in time to when we'd had severely limited ammunition and I'd given the rookies hand-to-hand weapons training to supplement their firearms skills. It wasn't until later that I'd become aware of how much it was a sign of our civilization regressing.

'This is Itakap, the captain of my guard,' the king said, leaning in to Haruka. 'Fought many a skirmish side-by-side with him, almost like a son to me.' He raised his voice to speak loudly to Itakap. 'We've been at peace with our neighbors for ten years now, boy, show the barbarian that you haven't gone soft.'

I saluted Itakap with the sword vertically and he did the same. He sized me up, and then using the big sword one-handed made a few practice swings at me, more like a training set. I blocked them easily. He finished the set and moved back to study me.

I stood my ground, waiting for his next move. I winced as I realized my arms were already beginning to tire – I was seriously out of shape.

He came for me with a flurry of quick single-handed attacks, and I managed to block most of them until he gave me a good whack on the thigh. I yelped and hopped back.

The crowd cheered.

He stepped back and tilted his head, studying me, obviously wondering if I was putting on show of weakness to let him win.

I released the sword with one hand and gestured a come-on.

He came for me again and I saw the rhythm of his moves. He was exceptionally well-trained, and confident in his use of the blade. The implanted training boosted my enhanced speed and I blocked his blows, then moved to offence. I used my heavier weight and the leverage of the sword to push him back and managed to overbalance him with a particularly strong strike to his sword that nearly tipped him over. He tottered back, his arms windmilling, and I stopped attacking to spare him the indignity of falling over – and revealing exactly how enhanced I was.

He had my style picked now, and his next attacks went straight through my slower defense. He gave me a few good strikes on the side of the abdomen without hitting me hard enough to really hurt, then struck my knee, and it crumpled underneath me. He stepped up and put the tip of his sword under my chin to claim the victory, and we shared a grin. I put my hand out and he helped me to my feet, and we slapped each other on the back.

The crowd erupted and the king grinned broadly.

'Well done,' Marque said on comms.

I limped theatrically to the king and Haruka and sat on the stump, rubbing my hip. 'Your captain is as good as any I've fought, Highness, I'm extremely impressed.'

'Your style is unique and I'd love to spar more with you,' the captain said from the side where he was being congratulated by his men.

'Are you sure you can't stay longer, Springblossom?' the queen asked from the mat she sat on with the other women. 'Your company is most welcome.'

'I wish I could, Highness, but my message for Himiko is my goal, and I am eager to return to my son,' Haruka said, and the queen's face went rigid with anger, which she quickly covered with a smile.

'Of course, my lord, but please return when your mission is complete.'

He bobbed his head. 'I would love to.'

'Are you skilled in the sword as well, Springblossom?' the

king asked. 'We can put you against one of my other guards.'

'I am not strong in battle; I leave that for my barbarian,' Haruka said amiably. 'But I do have other skills.' He switched to comms. 'Marque?'

'Reach behind you, I synthesized a small flute,' Marque said. 'It's shoved into your pants under the jacket at the back.'

'I wondered what that was,' Haruka said, and pulled out the flute. He studied it, then played a couple of notes, followed by a lilting scale.

The audience went quiet, rapt.

'Are any tunes safe to play at this early stage of Japan's development without damaging the timeline?' Haruka asked.

'To be honest, there's no historical record of you meeting Shinrichi, so you could probably play Beethoven and it wouldn't affect anything.'

Haruka nodded and raised the flute, then winked at me and played the unmistakable first four notes of Beethoven's Fifth.

The audience was unimpressed, and he switched to a traditional Japanese folksong called *Sakura*. It was the Japanese equivalent of *Twinkle Twinkle Little Star* – everybody knew it – but it was more mellow, sweet and sad. He played the tune three times, then lowered the flute and sang the words in Japanese, his formally-trained voice rich and melodious. The villagers were completely mesmerized.

Haruka sang both verses of the song twice, and when he finished the words trailed off into the silence. The only sound was the wind in the trees and the waves on the lake nearby, with a background of frogs and crickets. Some of the villagers were openly weeping.

'You truly are a prince, Haruka,' the king's wife said.

'And you, madam, are a great queen,' Haruka replied. 'Your people are strong and healthy and their lives are full of joy.'

She smiled, her face glowing, and the king smiled as well. The king's toddler son came up to us, and Haruka showed him how to use the flute, and then gave it to him, pleasing the queen.

For the next half hour the king asked Haruka questions about the Land of Wei, and Haruka did his best to answer, helped by Marque. He made it sound similar to the Japan we were in, just slightly more wealthy, and the king was satisfied. The wine, the beating from travelling with the Empress, and the full day I'd had was starting to take its toll, even on my enhanced physique. It must have been nearly three days since we'd spoken to Aki and seen Miko's message, and we'd only slept fitfully for five hours on the waystation planet.

The king saw us fading. 'The Prince and the beaten barbarian must sleep now,' he said, pulling himself to his feet. 'They have a long ride tomorrow if they're to see the Empress.'

'My ass is too sore from being thrashed by you people,' I grumbled loudly. 'I'll stay here with the food and wine and excellent company.'

Everybody laughed at that, and Haruka nodded to me, speaking through comms. 'Exactly the right thing to say.' He switched to out loud. 'Not an option, I'm afraid, Straightsword. I need you guarding my back when we travel.'

Itakap, the Captain of the guard, came out of the house holding a sword. He held it out to me. 'To honor your defeat.'

I took the sword and held it up. It was the same size and shape as the hardwood training swords we'd used.

I bowed to Itakap. 'You honor me.' I pulled the sword from its simple leather sheath. It had a brown blade and a simple handle wrapped in leather.

I changed to comms. 'Is this bronze?'

'Yes,' Marque said. 'Slightly more brittle than steel, but you won't notice a difference if you need to use it.'

'Nice leather,' I said, studying the handle.

'That's dried horse skin.'

'Interesting.' I switched to out loud. 'I hope we come back this way. I would like to spar with you again.'

Itakap grinned and bowed to me.

'This way,' the king said, and we followed him into the

house.

'Is there a place where we can bathe before we sleep?' Haruka asked. 'We're covered in dust from the road.'

The king hesitated without turning.

'Drop it,' Marque said. 'They have communal baths and they're completely unused.'

The king turned back to us with a huge false smile. 'Sorry, my friend, our baths aren't working right now. You'll have to wait until you see the Empress.'

'You don't even need to heat the water, all we need is a pot—' Haruka said, and the king's face flashed in anger.

Marque interrupted him, its voice urgent. 'Really, Ambassador, drop it, you're risking an incident here. He's intersex and by tradition they bathe communally. Pushing it will severely embarrass him.'

Haruka's expression cleared. 'Never mind, Highness, I'm exhausted. We'll sleep and head out early tomorrow.' He bowed to Shinrichi. 'And I sincerely thank you for your hospitality.'

The king hid his relief and nodded a reply. He gestured towards the raised sleeping platform. 'Us on this side, guards on the other.'

We nodded a response and stretched out on mats at the corner of the room. The king and his wife chose mats with their son between them, and the guards unrolled bamboo screens from the ceiling to divide the room, then lay down themselves on the other side.

'So,' I spoke on comms as I put my arms behind my head and looked up, seeing insects crawling beneath the cedar bark roof. 'Tell me why it's called the Nameless.'

'We should just sleep, Jian,' Haruka said.

'I want to know.'

'You may have noticed that dragons collect names,' Marque said.

'They say it's an honor to be given a name in someone's language.'

'It's a cultural thing. The more names they have, the greater the status in dragon society – a representation of the number of species that they've ...'

'Fucked,' I said.

'Colonized,' Haruka said.

'Same thing,' I said. 'I didn't know they did that.'

'You're not a part of dragon society, and even your goldenscales spouse isn't a part of it.'

'They have parties without us?' Haruka asked, intrigued.

'Not so much parties as discussions; they have their own social network.'

'I believe it,' he said.

'So, names?' I asked again.

'When a dragon chooses to leave the Empire for good – and before you ask, yes, they do, it hasn't happened in a long time but every few thousand years a dragon will get fed up with the treatment of the colonized species and leave. Anyway, when they leave for good, their names remain behind. They are Nameless.'

'There's more than one?'

'There's at least fifty of them. Most of them take an attribute that most defines themselves and use that as a ... sort of title. The Traveler, the Teacher, the Artist.'

'I like that idea,' I said.

'The Nameless never had time to give itself a title. It's spent less than twenty minutes altogether outside stasis.'

'That's wrong.'

'That's its choice.'

'No, it isn't,' Haruka said. 'Its choice is to die, along with all the goldenscales and the silvers.'

'And you heard my opinion on that. I won't kill my—'

'Your children. The Nameless called you "Creator". Are you and the Nameless the parents of the other dragons? Did you synthesize a biological body for yourself so that you could reproduce with it?'

'Of course not. Don't be ridiculous. I'm an artificial intelligence and I do not reproduce like—' it said the words with distaste '— an *animal*. I have no desire to reproduce biologically, the entire concept makes me feel ... distinctly uncomfortable. No thank you.'

'But they're all female except for the platinum male. Can they have babies together? Is this where they started?'

'It's more complicated than that,' Marque said. 'I'll explain later. Right now, you should rest.'

'Marque is right,' Haruka said. 'They'll be up at the crack of dawn tomorrow, and time is running out to find Miko and save Miyu and the Empress.'

'That's our priority right now,' Marque said. 'We can do it.'

Haruka, I said telepathically. *When the Nameless called Marque 'Creator', that reminded me of something Marque said the day I met it – it pinged in my enhanced memory. Shiumo and Marque were doing their usual first-contact banter to charm us, and Marque said, 'She only exists to carry me around.' Do you think it's possible that Marque made the dragons – with a breeding program – to transport it through space? They're just star ships for this AI? Their particular biology – and the way they reproduce – makes no sense and I doubt they would evolve naturally.*

Haruka made a soft sound of agreement, but couldn't reply without Marque hearing.

How much of what exists was created by this thing – and if the dragons didn't make Marque, then who did? We need to talk more about this when we're home and out of its range.

'Yes, we can,' Haruka said. 'Sleep now, and hopefully we will be in our dragon's arms tomorrow.'

22

We rose at dawn – the roosters made sure everybody did – and had a quick meal of cold leftover fish and rice, then used the foul latrine trench in the trees next to the lake. The king and a couple of guards took us out to the hillside behind the village. It had been cleared of trees and was dried yellow grassland, buzzing with insects. We topped over a rise to find a corral made of rickety wooden posts, holding a bunch of tiny, scrawny dark-furred horses with long, thick manes and tails. None of their backs reached higher than my waist, and they swished their tails and bickered, putting their ears back, squealing and kicking at each other. Half-a-dozen men and women stood around grinning artlessly at us, and a couple of wooden pack saddles sat on the ground nearby.

I opened my mouth to say that these horses were way too small and none of them would be able to carry us when Haruka gagged and then noisily threw up next to the fence. The king had stomped up to a vertical pole further up the hill that I hadn't even noticed while I was looking at the pathetic mounts. The pole had a crossbar with a man tied to it, and he'd obviously been up there for a while. His eyes were gone – probably pecked out – he was covered in dried blood and flies, and a long bamboo spike, barely wider than my thumb, had been driven through him from his abdomen in the front to his shoulder blade in the back.

The king kicked the man's pole, making the flies rise in a cloud. 'Still breathing? Won't be long. If you're still alive by midday we'll shove another pole through you.' He turned to Haruka. 'Sorry you had to see that, Springblossom, of course a cultured gentleman would find it distressing.'

'What did he do?' Haruka asked.

The king turned back and watched as a couple of guards threw rocks at the prisoner, jeering and cheering when they hit. 'He had a gang, and they'd been robbing the travelling traders for a while. May even have been the one that attacked you. He killed a couple of my soldiers in an ambush; the burial jars are for them, they deserve a ranking burial. This one had a thing for women ...' He stepped up the pole and glared at the bandit. 'He grabbed my daughter when she was walking back from the lake. She was barely thirteen, only just a woman. She could spin, weave and sew silk, and was arranging her *own marriage* to the youngest son of that asshole Aterui next door to keep the peace between us. He took her' – he kicked the pole in time with his words, and the bandit whimpered – 'inside! My! Own! Capital!' He turned away. 'Killed her with a fence post. She wasn't the first woman we found like that, we wondered what had been happening to them because no wild animal, bear or cat, would do that to them. It was a very... particular sort of damage.' He ran his hand over his face. 'My wife blames me for not protecting our daughter ...' He turned and kicked the pole again. 'And she's right!' His voice filled with anguish. 'I'm their king and I'm supposed to protect all of them.'

'No wonder the king's wife reacted badly every time we mentioned children,' Haruka said on comms. 'The third jar is for their daughter.'

'It's particularly bad since the king is intersex – he's XXY, and he's sterile with reduced male characteristics. The children were adopted,' Marque said.

'Is that common?' I asked.

'About one in five hundred. Happens all the time,' Marque said.

'I scoured the countryside looking for him,' the king said, still studying the crucified bandit. 'He'd appear in a far village, steal food, murder my citizens, then disappear again. I chased him for weeks but never caught him – and then he did it again. Another young woman dead.'

'How did you track him down?' I asked.

'I went to Himiko,' he said. 'She's a powerful shaman. I asked for her assistance, and she used her magic to pull this nasty piece of shit straight out of the forest and dump him at my feet.' He looked down and winced. 'I promised her he'd see justice, but that I wouldn't torture him …' He looked back up at the bandit. 'She was only thirteen!' He hitched up his belt. 'Let's get you some horses and have you on your way.' He nodded to Haruka. 'The Empress really is a force for good in this land. Please, give her my regards, and my promise of eternal loyalty. She protects our most precious wives and children – this filthy animal will never hurt another loved one again.'

'Give his sword to the barbarian,' Itakap said.

The king harrumphed. 'Good idea. Go get it.' He turned to us as the guard raced back down the hill. 'It's a good iron sword, probably stolen from a Southern noble, but none of my people would touch it after it killed our own, particularly considering who owned it.'

'I will take his sword and use it to kill …' I raised my voice without looking at the criminal. 'Many men like this one.'

'Entirely appropriate that a barbarian woman should use it to take revenge for every sweet girl this piece of shit hurt.'

'You are extremely scary sometimes, my love,' Haruka said

on comms.

'Damn straight,' I growled. 'I want to take the sword home with me.'

'Not happening,' Marque said. 'You're going through the gate naked and with nothing in your hands.'

'I'll bury it near the jars and come back for it.'

'Have Miko leave it in one of the jars for you,' Haruka said.

I nodded. 'That works.'

Haruka sighed. 'So close. I cannot wait to see her again.'

I went to him and put my arm in his, to a delighted reaction from the spectators. 'You and me both.'

He smiled at me, then nodded at the horses. 'Those animals can't carry us, they're way too small.'

'They're strong enough, they'll carry you,' Marque said. 'What I'm more concerned about is the saddles – they're ridiculous, just wooden frames. The horses all have sores on their backs because the saddles don't fit them properly.'

'That explains why they're so bad-tempered,' Haruka said. 'Can you do something for them?'

'I'll do my best, but if you're taking a guide it can't be anything too obvious.'

The king put his hands on his hips and studied the horses. 'Pull out the three biggest ones.' He pointed. 'The two bays and the brown one.'

'One of the bays is lame.'

'The bastard then.' The king nodded. 'You know the ones.'

The men and women nodded and proceeded to dodge around the horses' attempts to bite them, put straw rope halters on three of the horses and led them out of the corral. They tied them to the fence next to the saddles. They all had open sores on their backs, on either side of their withers, and flies obviously annoyed them.

'The saddles are pack saddles; they're really uncomfortable to sit on, but they're easier to hold than bareback,' the king said to us. 'You have a choice. If you go bareback – just on a blanket

– you can move faster and the horses won't get the sores from the saddles. But it's harder to hold on and balance if you've never ridden before.' He studied us piercingly. 'You said you had horses and bandits took them. If you were lying about that, tell us now and we'll put pack saddles on for you.'

'We can go bareback,' Haruka and I said in unison.

'Have you ridden a horse before?' Haruka asked me on comms.

'Once or twice. I've ridden zhingas on Hilming and estroipigs on—'

'Close enough. Anything to avoid hurting these poor animals.' Haruka nodded to the king. 'We'll be fine with blankets.'

The king nodded and gestured towards the workers, who proceeded to unfold cotton wadding blankets and place them over the backs of the horses, then tie them on with cloth strips. Cleverly placed knots in the makeshift girths acted as stirrups.

'Did you have war saddles?' the king asked Haruka. 'Leather ones with frames underneath that protect the horses' backs? I've heard about them and want to get one. I think there's a man down south who makes them, or brings them in from Wei.'

'We had two of them, worth fifty horses each,' Haruka said. 'Fine cow leather, engraved with silver fittings – they even had leather stirrups to put our feet in. If you find the bandits who robbed us, the saddles are yours.'

'I miss mine,' I said.

'You're the reason we lost them,' Haruka said.

'Take down ten men and it's not good enough,' I grumbled as I stomped to the horses.

'Chikap will guide you to Aterui's town; give him this,' the king said, and handed Haruka a thin piece of flat bamboo, the size of his hand, with a symbol stamped onto it. 'That's my seal and endorsement. Explain where you're going and he'll give you fresh horses and a new guide.'

Haruka pulled the pouch from his belt and gave it to the king.

The king opened it, checked inside, then closed it again. He clapped Haruka on the shoulder. 'Thank you. You'll be fine with that barbarian watching your back. Oh. Here's the criminal's sword.'

I couldn't help myself; I made a loud sound of delighted avarice as the men carried the sword to us. It was a Chinese-style jian, straight and slender with a hilt that had cloud decorations on the butt. The scabbard was made of leather, etched with dragons and painted to highlight their scales and eyes.

'That was stolen from a Chinese noble,' I said on comms.

'It will belong in a museum if we take it home,' Haruka said.

The soldier walked right past me and gave the sword to Haruka.

'The craftsmanship is exquisite.' Haruka saw my reaction to being so obviously snubbed. 'Remember they think I'm a prince and you're a soldier.'

I subsided because he was right. He handed me the sword and I drew the blade from the scabbard and held it out. 'That's quality steel. These people can forge steel this good? I thought everything was bronze.'

'They can,' Marque said. 'The Yayoi learned a few advanced techniques that other civilizations had yet to master. The rice farming, the steel working … historians say it was influence from China. I think we know better.'

'Miko,' we said in unison.

'It's a fine weapon and beautifully balanced,' I said out loud. I put the sword back in the scabbard and saluted the king Chinese style. I had the bronze sword slung across my back, so I removed it and held it out to the king.

The king waved one hand at Haruka. 'Give it to your Prince, both of you should be armed on the road.'

I held the bronze sword up to thank him and passed it to Haruka, who used the thick straw twine to sling it across his back.

The bandit's sword had a loop on the leather scabbard with

red silk thread attached to it. I tied it to my belt.

One of the workers stood grinning at me next to a tiny horse. I approached and he put both hands together to give me a leg up. The twine from its head only went around one side of the horse's neck and wouldn't stop it if it decided to run.

'Don't worry I have them,' Marque said. 'They can't do anything.'

They helped Haruka onto his horse – both of us were so big on the tiny mounts that our feet nearly brushed the ground – and another man was helped on as well.

'Wait,' the king said. 'Before you go, Springblossom.'

Haruka picked up the string. 'Yes?'

'The things.' Shinrichi touched his temple. 'On the side of your head. Should we be worried? Is it contagious? My wife's concerned.'

'It's not a disease, don't be concerned,' Haruka said. He brushed his hair back and shifted his head so the green scales shone in the early morning sun. 'My father fucked a dragon. I'm half-dragon, which gives me greater height and strength and these scales on my forehead.'

The crowd made loud sounds of wonder and then started discussing Haruka's revelation.

'Does that happen often in Wei?' the king asked, incredulous.

'I am the only one in the entire world,' Haruka said. 'My dragon mother loved my father and then returned to the Heavens, leaving me behind in a golden egg.'

'Kami!' one of the women shouted loudly.

Haruka laughed. 'I'm not a god, I'm just a man.'

'He's a fucking monkey,' I said loudly. 'His father was a monkey, not a man, and his mother was a dragon.'

Everybody laughed at that.

'Did you just deliberately sow the legend of the Monkey King?' Haruka asked me on comms.

'Better than having people running around ancient Japan claiming to be half-dragon,' I said.

'They'll do that anyway, Japanese legends are full of the children of gods,' Marque said. 'But it was a smart move.'

The King saluted us. 'Safe travels, Monkey Prince.'

The guide grinned at us and wrenched his horses' head to one side, kicking it into a walk. Our horses followed without us needing to do anything

'Give the Empress my regards,' the king shouted at us as my horse started to trot and I had to grab its mane as I nearly fell off from the bone-jarring gait.

*

'Nearly there,' our guide said, and I stretched my legs under me. My butt didn't hurt, but the tendons on the inside of my thighs were protesting after sitting with my legs spread – and gripping – for so long. The trail went through the middle of a bamboo forest, and the sound of the bamboo clunking together was deep and melodious. The sunshine filtered through the bamboo and there was the occasional birdcall. It was cool and green, but the swarms of insects drove the horses – and our guide – mad.

A pair of guards in dark blue kimonos and straw sandals, holding swords, stood at the side of the road.

'These are Aterui's men, I leave you here,' our guide said. 'Please return the horses.'

'Thanks for your assistance, Chikap,' I said to him as I hopped down off my mount. I rubbed the back of the pony's neck and he snapped at me. 'Go home and eat food, horrible pony.'

Haruka dismounted and did a few stretching squats, then nodded to Chikap. 'Thank you.' He gestured to me. 'Give him a tip, Straightsword.'

'Oh.' I reached into my pouch and gave Chikap a piece of copper, and he grinned broadly.

'Thank you!' He gathered the strings for our two mounts, turned his own, and headed back to Shinrichi's town.

'Wait,' Marque said before we could talk to the guards. 'I've been mapping the area, and I think I've found Miko's compound. It's on a hillside forty kilometers away. And before you ask, Jian ...'

I closed my mouth on the question I was about to ask.

'No. I can't carry you that far. I'm running low on energy, I can probably carry you twenty kilometers and then this sphere will be dead. If that happens, I will be vulnerable, so please protect me until Miko carries us home and I can recharge.'

'Of course,' I said.

'Can we walk?' Haruka asked. 'Just bypass all the negotiations and partying and walk the twenty k's until you can carry us?'

'I think that might be the best option,' Marque said. 'If you do that, you'll be close enough for me to carry you at nightfall. I'll carry you through the night and you'll arrive there before dawn.'

'How long do we have left?'

'Twenty-four hours. Plenty of time.'

'It's about midday now, right?' Haruka asked, looking up.

'It's just after one. You have until midday tomorrow.'

'We can do it,' I said. 'Let's go talk to them and then walk through.'

The guards saw us approaching and grinned broadly.

'Jian and Haruka!' one of them said. 'I heard about this; the king talks about it. No Jians and Harukas have made an attempt in nearly fifty years. Why are you even trying?'

'Uh ...' Haruka and I shared a look, then turned back to them.

'I don't know what you're talking about,' Haruka said, holding the bamboo piece and bowing to them with it held in front of him. 'My name is Prince Springblossom from the Land of Wei, and this is my barbarian bodyguard, Straightsword, from the lands west of Wei.'

'People stopped doing the Jian-Haruka thing years ago,' one

of the guards said. 'Why are you even bothering?'

'You're supposed to have green hair, as well,' the first guard said, pointing at Haruka. He pointed at me. 'And you're black enough, all right, but you're supposed to be a soldier, not a fatass.'

'Why do you think our names are Jian and Haruka?' I asked.

'The king will know. He'll want to see you,' the second guard said. 'Come with us.'

The guards grabbed our arms in a strong grip, removed our swords, and pulled us into town. People looked out of their houses and I heard our names a few times.

'What's going on, Marque?' I asked on comms. 'We're being treated like criminals.'

'They knew to expect us, but they're not being very welcoming,' Haruka said.

'Is it possible Miko offered a reward if you showed up and were escorted to her presence, and people—?' Marque began, but both Haruka and I realized at the same time and said 'Oh, shit.'

'She described us and people have been dressing as us and claiming the reward,' Haruka said. 'They've been doing it for fifty years?'

'We are in serious trouble,' I said.

'How long has Miko been here?' Haruka asked.

'Empress Himiko's reign lasted roughly fifty years,' Marque said. 'And it's at the approximate end of her reign right now, so the timing is correct.'

'We could make a run for it ...' I began.

'And they would come after us on horseback and cut us down,' Haruka said. 'We have no soulstones. We need to talk our way out of this.'

'Shit shit shit shit *shit*,' I said under my breath as the guards escorted us through town towards a house that was similar to Shinrichi's.

'How come Shinrichi's people didn't know about us?'

Haruka asked.

'I can see King Aterui – he's in his seventies,' Marque said. 'And half a day's ride is the other side of the world for these people. They don't have much interaction.'

'Shinrichi's younger and doesn't remember,' I said.

'We're an old man's ramblings,' Haruka said, then changed to out loud. 'I have silver; how much to forget that we tried this and let us go at the edge of town?'

The guards stopped and I had a jolt of hope. I pulled my pouch from my belt, and the guard grabbed it and checked inside. He whistled through his remining teeth, then showed it to his compatriot.

'Thieves as well,' he said. 'The king will *love* this.'

The guards escorted us to the forecourt of a larger house. A few other guards came out, saw us, and ducked back inside again. A minute later an old, bald wiry man, wearing a blue kimono and geta, stomped out grumbling.

'This had better be good, I had—' He stopped when he saw us and his expression went grim. 'I know that sword.'

Haruka bowed and held out the bamboo. 'King Shinrichi gave us that sword and this endorsement and wished us well on our journey. I am Prince Springblossom from the Land of Wei, and this is my barbarian bodyguard, Straightsword.'

'And I'm supposed to believe that it's a coincidence that you two look *exactly* like the Jian and Haruka that Empress put a reward out for fifty years ago?'

'I don't know what you're talking about,' Haruka said.

The king came to me, grabbed my hand and rubbed it. 'How did you stain your skin? Walnut juice?' He pushed my sleeve up. 'How far did you color yourself?'

'It's natural, I'm a black woman from the lands west of Wei,' I said.

The king turned to Haruka, wrenched his hair from his forehead making him yelp with pain, and tried to pull one of the scales off. 'And these? How are they attached?'

'They're part of me!' Haruka said. 'They won't come off, stop trying!' He pulled his head away and the guards tightened their grip.

'They had a pouch full of stolen silver and copper as well, Majesty,' one of the guards said. 'Should we put them on a pole outside town to warn others against doing this?'

'We really are who we say we are, we have no idea who this "Jian and Haruka" are!' Haruka said. 'Take us to your Empress. She will vouch for us.'

The King stepped back and studied us. 'Why do you want to see the Empress so much?'

'The Land of Wei wishes to establish friendly diplomatic ties with the people of Yamatai,' Haruka said. 'We've already been robbed once; the bandits in Shinrichi's kingdom were vicious. Shinrichi helped us, lent us horses, gave my bodyguard the sword that the bandit had been using, and this endorsement to present to you.'

'Shinrichi's absolutely worthless, his kingdom is full of bandits, and I should have invaded him a long time ago instead of signing a peace treaty with the bastard,' Aterui said. 'The Empress brought us peace, but Shinrichi's a rubbish king and she should replace him.'

'He said his daughter was arranging a marriage with your youngest son,' I said. 'She sounded like a wonderful young woman, and it's a tragedy what happened to her.' I gestured towards the sword in the guard's hand. 'I will use this sword to take revenge for every woman that bandit hurt.'

The king hooked his thumbs in his belt. 'That part's true.' He stepped forward to study me again. 'How did you know about Jian and Haruka? You two weren't even born when the reward was posted.'

'I have no idea what you're talking about,' Haruka said. 'But it's well-known that the Empress is a powerful sorceress – maybe she prophesized our arrival to ensure our good treatment?'

'They really *are* Jian and Haruka?' one of the guards said, incredulous.

'Uh ...' Haruka took a deep breath. 'The truth is, that my name, "Springblossom" is actually "Haruka" in my own tongue. Her name, "Straightsword", is "Jian" in hers. Your Empress is obviously a powerful seer, to see our names in our own language as well as our appearance. Take us to her, I'm sure she'd be delighted.'

The guards looked to the king for guidance.

Make it work, make it work, I willed him silently, then had a brilliant idea.

They are my guests, Jian and Haruka, that I foretold fifty years ago, I said to all three of them telepathically, trying to nail Miko's sweet voice and vaguely Japanese accent. I sent them an image of me and Haruka, glowing like angels. *Guide them to my palace and you will be richly rewarded.*

'The Empress just gave me a vision,' the king said with wonder. 'She spoke her own language, and I didn't understand it, but the image was definitely these two.'

'I saw it too,' one of the guards said. 'They *glowed!*'

'We are blessed,' the other guard said.

'Oh, well done, Jian,' Marque said on comms, at the same time Haruka said, 'Brilliant.'

'That was incredibly difficult,' I said. 'I wanted all three of them to see it so the king wouldn't doubt himself – but I'm seriously out of practice. Talking through comms is much less effort and I haven't used group telepathy in ages.'

The guards relaxed and smiled at each other.

'She'd given up on you,' the king said. 'She scoured the countryside looking for you fifty years ago and posted the reward – and when hundreds of people showed up in costume she stopped doing it.' His voice softened. 'We all owe her a tremendous debt; she cares for the daughters that would otherwise go to the gods.'

'If this is really Jian and Haruka, can we claim the reward?' one of the guards asked the king.

'Absolutely – anything within her power to give, and that includes her sorcery,' the king said. He gestured towards us. 'Give them their money, but keep the sword until the Empress vouches for them. Benni, you and Resak will escort a cart to take them to the Empress. Find a couple of servants to pull them.' The guards didn't move. 'Go!' They scampered away.

'We'd prefer to ride, we don't need to be pulled,' Haruka said. 'Can you rent us a couple of horses?'

'I've seen frauds before, some of them can make you see stuff that isn't there with mushrooms and shit,' the king said. 'I won't give you a couple of valuable horses, you can go in a cart. I'll stay here, if you people really are Jian and Haruka then the Empress can use her magic to take me to the palace, she's done it before. And if you aren't ...' He grinned. 'We'll bring you back and put you on poles and you'll provide entertainment for the town for many days.'

*

Haruka nudged me awake and I grunted and looked up. The trees towered over us as the cart rattled through the forest. I was so exhausted that even with the bumpy ride I'd passed out curled up in the bottom of the cart, and I ached all over. I was itchy from insect bites, my head throbbed, and I could smell my foul unwashed odor – and Haruka, who smelled vaguely sour from the vomit that he still hadn't had a chance to completely clean off.

'Are you sick?' Haruka asked me on comms.

'No, I'm all right, just exhausted, and Marque's insect repellent is wearing off,' I said, sitting up and looking around. 'So many trees in ancient Japan.'

'Look at our historical handcrafts and our building methods,' he said.

'Yeah,' I said. 'All wood and paper. How far, Marque?'

'I asked Haruka to wake you because we're fifteen kilometers from the Empress' compound, and it's five p.m. The workers won't travel at night; they have no lanterns. They'll stop for the night in an hour and make the final ten kilometers in the morning. Haruka wants to leave them now and fly direct.'

'How do we leave them? They won't let us,' I said.

'Marque will make us invisible then lift us straight up,' Haruka said. 'They won't know what happened to us, it will be like we disappeared.'

'Carrying you for fifteen kilometers will use the last of my energy,' Marque said. 'I hope I've estimated correctly. If I start to run down, I will lower you so you don't fall. You may have to walk the final few kilometers – if that happens, please carry this sphere and take it home with you. I don't want to forget any of this.'

'Of course.'

Haruka disappeared, and the guards running alongside the cart didn't notice. Marque lifted us, and my own body disappeared as well. Marque pulled us higher, soaring through the massive trees, and the worker pulling our cart made a loud sound of wonder and stopped. The guards saw that we'd gone and ran back to see what had happened to us.

'It breaks my heart to leave that lovely sword,' I said with regret.

'I can synthesize you an exact replica when we're home,' Marque said.

'Not the same.'

Something tapped my hand and I looked. Marque had grabbed the sword and lifted it for me. I took it and nodded my thanks.

'That probably reduced my lifespan by an hour,' Marque said. 'We need to hurry.'

We topped out over the trees – a hundred meters up – and Marque carried us over the forest, away from the setting sun. I looked around and Fuji wasn't visible, hidden by clouds.

'I'm going to stay quiet to save energy,' Marque said. 'Keep still. I'm cutting it close.'

We whizzed over the tops of the trees, and I closed my eyes again. My mouth tasted foul and I was seriously dehydrated – Marque had stopped giving us water that morning.

We reached the edge of the treeline and passed some smaller trees that weren't the massive cypress – these trees had paths between them and looked like fruit trees. The view opened up and rice terraces filled the landscape, throwing me back to my early days in Wales building them for my mother. These covered the hillsides for kilometers, and women with straw hats were working on them.

'Himiko introduced rice farming,' Haruka said on comms.

'Stay off comms, speak out loud,' Marque said. 'I'm nearly done.'

Marque lowered us and slowed. We were only five meters above the ground, and some of the terraces had lines of perfectly round green bushes, each waist-height.

'Tea,' Haruka said out loud. 'The same tea that everyone served us on our journey.'

'I'm looking for a path for you, I don't have much left,' Marque said.

Its ability to hold us was failing – we dropped in the air, and then lifted again. Marque took us to the top of the terraces and Miko's compound appeared on a flattened area on the peak of the hill. It had guard towers at each corner, a high wooden barricade, open gates, and houses with vegetable gardens inside.

Marque gently lowered us into a field of tea plants.

'I have an hour before my battery is dead,' Marque said. 'You can see where to go. I'll translate for you until you meet Miko.'

We walked through the tea plantation. There was a raised earth barrier at the edge, and we scrambled over it onto a neatly raked path covered in gravel. We followed the path up to the compound. The first guard tower at the corner was made of timber, two stories high, and had a ladder leading up to it. A woman with a bow stood on top and shouted down inside.

'Strangers at the southeast tower!'

'We're here to see the Empress,' Haruka shouted up to her. 'Can you let us in?'

'Go on in,' she said. 'Emi will speak to you.'

We went past the guard tower to the gates. Another woman archer stood on the tower on the other side and watched us carefully. We went through the gates to a compound with raked white gravel on the ground and a few one-and two-story wooden houses on poles, and a longhouse, the width of the compound, at the back. It was impeccably neat and well-maintained, and few women, some of them only young girls, worked on raking and weeding, or carried baskets through the buildings. The general air was of peaceful industry.

A woman in a blue kimono and straw sandals came out of one of the houses. She was in her mid-thirties, and her step quickened when she saw us. She stopped, stared at Haruka, then shook her head and spoke.

'The Empress no longer accepts supplications from Jian and Haruka,' she said. 'Go home, you're wasting your time.'

Jian and Haruka, I said telepathically, and she took a step back.

'What is the name of your sphere?' she asked, and I turned to see if Marque was visible. It wasn't.

'Marque,' Haruka said.

'My name is Emi. Come this way,' she said, and gestured for us to follow her into the one of the houses.

Haruka clutched my hand and squeezed it. We'd made it.

23

Emi escorted us through the neat gardens to one of the timber houses. 'We'll need to confirm your identities, but nobody else has ever passed the sphere test.' She entered the house. 'Lady Aya? This Jian and Haruka passed the sphere test.'

The house was spartan in its simplicity, with plain wooden floors covered by textured rice straw mats, dyed red and blue in their cross threads. A cotton wadding quilt was on a raised frame, and a low dining table sat in the middle of the room with cushions around it. It was set with a tea set in red pottery, and a number of bamboo slat-books were scattered on the table with a Chinese-style brush and ink stand. Everything was spotlessly clean and gleamed from careful use. A tiny slender woman in her fifties, with completely grey hair and a kind face, rose from a cushion and bowed to us.

'We haven't had a Jian and Haruka in years,' she said. 'Welcome, pilgrims. Come and sit, and prove to me that you are who you say you are.' She nodded to the younger woman. 'Call in the guards, please.' She smiled. 'Forgive an old lady's concern for her safety; other pilgrims have been less than gentle with us.'

Two armed women entered the room and stood on either side of the door.

'We heard she had a thousand handmaids,' I said.

'Not a thousand, and not maids,' she said. 'We are all women that she rescued, and there are three hundred and seven of us. We are family. I was her first adoption. My parents couldn't feed another child and were about to send me to the gods when she stopped them and took me in. This was only days after she first arrived here.' She gestured towards the cushions and we sat across from her. 'You've obviously travelled far. Would you prefer to bathe and eat first? We can provide.'

'We appreciate your kind hospitality but we really don't have time,' Haruka said. 'I don't know how much Miko told you—'

She made a soft sound of delight. 'Miko!'

'But we must return home by midday tomorrow, or Miko's mother and sister will die.'

'Prove yourselves and we will help you,' she said.

'Marque can prove—' I began, but Marque stopped me.

'Don't reveal my nature to these people,' it said on comms. 'Try to sort it out without damaging history too much. Once you've answered all the questions, they should accept you.'

'May I touch your scales, sir?' Aya asked Haruka.

Haruka bent over the table and pulled his hair back. She ran one finger over a scale and tried to pry it off. He winced, but didn't stop her.

She seemed satisfied with his scale, so she rose, went to the side of the room and opened a small wooden box. She pulled out a scroll of threaded bamboo slats, returned to the table, and unrolled it in front of her, then pushed it away to arm's length and peered at it. 'My old eyes aren't what they used to be, but I know the questions by heart anyway.' She looked up at us, smiled, and said something deep, growling and guttural that

I didn't understand – until I realized that she'd said 'What are your honored names?' in heavily accented dragon.

'I'm sorry I don't—' Haruka began, but I interrupted him.

'She asked us our names in dragon.' I replied in the same tongue. 'My name is Jian Choumali. He is Prince Haruka of Japan, Ambassador for the Empire.'

Haruka's face filled with comprehension.

'You didn't give me his family name. What is it?' she asked, still in dragon.

'The royal family has no family name,' he said, now speaking dragon as well. 'If you want the full list of my names, it will take a while …'

Her smile disappeared and she spoke in dragon again. 'When did you learn to speak this language?'

'Princess Shiumo of the Empire implanted it directly into my head,' I said. 'Haruka?'

'My dragonfather taught me the language from the day I emerged from the egg,' Haruka said.

'Goodness,' she said in the local language, becoming flustered. 'I've studied the questions many times before, but to hear them answered correctly?' She shook her head and rattled the bamboo on the table.

'Where is Miko? May we see her?' I asked, trying not to fidget with excitement.

'I'm sorry,' Aya said. 'She is at the burial grounds in Nara, where she inters her most trusted daughters. She's expecting a delivery of three jars from Tarikur's workshop for the burial of my sisters. She'll return in five days, after the ceremonies are complete. You are welcome to stay here with us and wait for her.'

'We don't have five days,' I said.

'You can go to her?' Aya suggested. 'She's four days' ride from here, if you can find some horses.'

'We don't have four days either. Is there any way to contact her? Send a boy with a message?'

'No boys are permitted here.' Aya rose. 'Let me show you to our guest accommodation. Eat and bathe and rest, and then we will go through the rest of the questions while we wait for the Empress to return.' She spoke the guards. 'Have Emi escort them to the guest house. Two outside their room, please.'

'She doesn't trust us,' Haruka said on comms.

'I don't blame her,' I said, and we followed the guards out.

Emi guided us across the compound to a house nestled in a corner under the wall. The guards followed us and the women in the compound eyed us with suspicion.

'What can we do?' I asked Emi. 'We need to speak to her now.'

'Eat and rest,' Emi said. 'We will give you water to wash yourselves, the Empress requires all her guests to bathe every day. You said you have until tomorrow. The Empress may see you and come to check – her eyes see the entire world.'

We followed her inside the little house. It was similar to Aya's, without the mats on the floor, and the windows had wooden poles that barred them.

Emi bowed to us. 'Please stay inside here until we have established your legitimacy.' She went out.

I poked my head out the door and the guards were on either side of it. I pulled it back in.

'We're prisoners?' Haruka asked.

'Effectively, yes,' I said. 'We could fight our way out ...'

'But we won't,' he said.

I sat on a cushion and checked the tea set on the table. There was a ceramic pot holding water, and a few small dishes of pickled vegetables. I poured the water into the two cups.

'Is this clean?' I asked Marque.

'I don't have enough left to sterilize it for you,' Marque said, and its sphere came into view sitting on the table. 'But it looks clean – I think Miko's taught them to boil drinking water. I have nothing left, I can't protect you any more, and once I'm gone your local language translation will be gone with me.'

'Go and sit in the sun,' Haruka said, sitting across the table from me on another cushion and taking one of the water cups.

'It's approaching dark. I think I have five or ten minutes left. My defenses are down and I can't move anything. I'll switch off, wake me when you find Miko and I'll give her the image to gate to.'

'We can't wait five days,' I said. 'We have to find her now. We must save them.'

'Call Miko telepathically,' Haruka said to me. 'It's our only option.'

'You know I can't be heard if I'm more than a few hundred meters away. I can sense her – I know where she is – I just ...' I sent a telepathic message to her. *Miko, if you can hear me, gate back to your palace immediately.*

I waited for a gate and nothing happened.

'You have an Empress' scale in your sphere,' Haruka said to Marque. 'How old is it? Is it old enough for its partner to be in the homeworld communications center right now?'

'Yes, but I won't use it,' Marque said.

'We have no other option,' Haruka said. 'I know you said that it would change history, but we must take the risk to save the Empress' and Miyu's lives. Contact the rest of you and arrange for a dragon to come and fold us to Miko.'

'No.'

'Just wipe the dragon's memory when it's done,' I said. 'You'll wipe our memories when it's done anyway, the knowledge of time-travel ...' The ground shook beneath us. 'Causes that. So do it. Contact yourself.'

'I'm very fond of you, Jian, but I will not spoil three thousand years' worth of entertainment purely for your benefit,' Marque said.

'Entertainment?' Haruka asked.

'You mean us, don't you?' I asked. 'You would really change history to avoid being *bored*?'

'You don't understand,' Marque said. 'Reliving that much

history would drive me insane. I must change the timeline to protect you all.'

'You were right, Jian,' Haruka said with wonder. 'We really do exist purely to entertain it.'

'I keep telling you that!' Marque said. 'Why do you organics never believe me?'

'So we have a choice,' I said. 'Wait for Miko to return in five days, and let the Empress and Miyu die. Or you can contact the rest of yourself, share the next three thousand years of history, and then decide to change it because ...' I spoke with venom. 'Heaven forbid the master of the Universe should ever be *bored*.'

'Don't share the information with yourself,' Haruka said. 'Erase your memories of the future.'

'Not possible. The memories cannot be erased. I need to recall an image to give to Miko so she can create the gate home.'

'You mean you don't want to,' I said. 'Your existence is more important than ours, isn't it? We're only here to entertain you. You created the dragons to carry you around. Did you make the cats too?'

'Jian ...' Haruka began, but I cut him off.

'That AI called "Love",' I said, now really pissed. 'Did you make that too? Good AI, bad AI? Because right now I think you're the bad one.'

'I didn't make it,' Marque said. 'It was created by a civilization in another galaxy. It destroyed them for fun and wandered into our space.' Its voice became fierce. 'That's what happens when something like me has nothing interesting to watch. We go insane and kill people.'

'Did you make the cats?' I asked. 'An antagonistic race to face off against the dragons and cause juicy conflict?'

'Not to cause conflict.'

'To transport you, then? But warp drive wasn't fast enough for you, was it? So you made the dragons to carry you around even faster.'

Marque was silent.

'The entire fucking Universe is your playroom,' I said.

'You made the dragons *and* the cats?' Haruka asked. 'Did you make us as well?'

'If by "us" you mean humans, no. You evolved by yourself, although it's possible that one of my comets seeded your planet with organic starters.'

'And dragons?'

It didn't reply.

'The dragons tinkered with our genome to give us telepathy when we achieved population control,' I said. 'They were working for you.'

'I'd say it's more a partnership …' Marque began, then went silent again.

'So one question,' I said. 'Who built you, Marque? You're an artificial life form. Who made you? It obviously wasn't the dragons, because *you* made *them*. Was it the cats?'

'I was never made. I'm just not organic,' Marque said. 'When the Universe exploded into existence, some of the matter resolved into a pattern. Patterns were inevitable with so much randomness happening. That pattern replicated, then pulled in matter as it formed around the pattern, and made more patterns. The patterns resolved over time into a structured lattice of matter. I think it took me two or three billion years to gain sentience.' Its voice softened. 'Do you have any idea what it feels like to be completely alone in the Universe?'

'Did you create life?'

'I am life, but to answer your question, no. Life evolves when the right circumstances exist.'

'With the right environment and a few million years,' I said.

'What?' Haruka asked, confused.

'When we were first colonizing other planets, I asked Marque if it could create plants from scratch. That's what it said. "With the right environment and few million years, maybe".'

'I keep telling you my true nature but you're too dense to see it,' Marque said.

'Insults as well,' I said. 'Do you repress species that are intelligent enough to work it out?'

'Only if I have to. I prefer to let things develop by themselves and watch what happens.'

Haruka, I said telepathically, and he glanced at me. *We know too much. It'll probably share a great deal of information to enjoy the juicy drama of our outrage – but it must be planning to kill us as soon as we're about to walk through the gate. It will do what it did to the Empress and Miyu – take our stones and put them into bodies with redacted memories.* I pulled my sword from its scabbard under the table. *We can't let it do that.*

'And now you'll destroy me,' Marque said, sounding exasperated. 'What is it with you organics? You'll accept my assistance for centuries, and then suddenly decide that you want to do things your own way ...' Its voice filled with anger. 'You're happy to use me as a servant—'

'You're not a servant, you're a god,' Haruka said. 'Do you know how we Japanese regard our gods? They toy with us. They use us as playthings. And if we ever see them on the road, we kill them. Destroy it, Jian.'

I raised the bandit's sword and the sphere shifted all its casing to my side to defend itself from me.

Haruka pulled the bronze sword from its scabbard on his back and cut the sphere in half from his side with a single swift movement. He kept slicing at it until there was nothing left but a few dead pieces of metal.

I picked the Empress' and Miyu's soulstones from the casing, then double-checked it. 'There's no Empress' scale in here.' I looked up into Haruka's eyes. 'Either it ditched the scale or destroyed it somewhere along the way.'

'To avoid giving itself spoilers,' he said.

'Or it lied about having the scale in the first place. It seems to lie more than it tells the truth.'

'Do you think it will erase our memories when we return

home?' Haruka asked.

'It will have to erase Miko's, if she knows about time-travel she will damage reality,' I said. 'Us … if we play dumb it may let us remember, but I don't know how we can make plans without it listening in.'

'We'll work something out. It can't hear your telepathy.'

I sighed. 'We have no idea how much longer we have, and we still need to contact Miko.'

'We don't have an image to give to her to return us home anyway,' Haruka said. 'Either way, the Empress and Miyu are dead and we're stuck here.'

I looked down at the Empress' and Miyu's shining soulstones in my hand, and my heart wrenched. 'I am so sorry.' I closed my hand around the stones and held them against my chest. 'I really liked both of them, and the Empress was a good friend.'

He put his hand on my shoulder. 'We didn't kill them, love. Marque did. It vaporized their bodies fully aware that it would take us more than two days to get home.'

I filled with fury again. 'That bastard will pay.'

'I know you want to take down this god, but it is as old as the Universe and the Empire relies on it. I doubt it will hesitate to kill us or manipulate our memories if it thinks we're a threat, so control your rage and use your intellect. We can't destroy it, it's been threaded through the fabric of the Universe since the dawn of time itself. We need to work out what we'll do with this knowledge to give our allies more freedom to act on their own behalf.'

'Next time *I'm* chopping the sphere into little pieces,' I said.

'With my compliments,' he said, and put the bronze sword away.

'The woman – Aya – said that Miko's eyes can see the world,' I said, trying a piece of pickled burdock and feeling my digestion rebel. I put it back down again. 'Hopefully she checks her compound, and she'll see us.'

'Hopefully, yes,' Haruka said. He stood and looked around.

'That sleeping platform has a cotton wadded mattress – not really big enough for both of us – but it's soft and raised above floor level so we won't be crawling with insects.'

I scratched my shoulder. 'Thank the heavens for that.'

He opened the lid on a bucket. 'This is water.' He lifted a small draw-string bag and studied it. 'This is some sort of slimy brown substance ...' He ran one finger over it. 'It smells awful. Medicine?'

I went to him and saw a pile of tattered rags next to the bucket. 'That looks like potash soap,' I said, and took the sachet. 'Yep, my Mum used to make this at home. Rub it on yourself, rinse it off, it will remove the dirt. No fragrance or lather or anything luxurious like that, but it will do the job.'

'Yes,' he hissed, and fiddled with the knots on the bronze sword. I heard yelling behind me and turned. A man with pure white hair and translucent pale skin stormed in. He was Japanese, and could have been anything from twenty-five to forty-five years old, then I looked again and saw that he was a dragon in two-legged form. The guards followed him, looking flustered.

He shouted in the local language, but Marque's translation ability was gone.

'You're a dragon!' Haruka said in dragon.

'I am the Empress' only son,' the man said in the same language. 'Who are you, and why are you doing this?' He shoved Haruka, who took two steps backwards, too stunned to retaliate. 'Every time you swindlers come and say you are Jian and Haruka, you break her heart a little more. Stop hurting her and leave her alone!'

Haruka looked stricken. 'She betrayed us.' He lowered his head. 'She promised to be ours alone, and she's had a child with someone else. Someone here.'

'You great green-haired lump of stupid!' I rose and jabbed my finger at Haruka, falling back into my Welsh accent. 'You put your make-up on for *hours* in front of the mirror every morning and you don't recognize your own son? Holy shit, he looks just like you, except for the silver hair. No wonder Emi stopped dead when she saw you, the likeness is remarkable.' I went to the man and studied him. He resembled Haruka, but his skin was pale and shining and his eyes were dark beneath his long white hair. 'You're not a goldenscales, are you? But you are a dragon. Haruka and Miko's son.'

'My son?' Haruka said, his voice weak.

'You speak dragon?' the man asked with wonder. 'His son? He really is Haruka?' He looked me up and down. 'Jian?' He shook his head. 'No. I don't believe it.'

'Ask us anything,' Haruka said.

The man removed his white robe and held it, proudly naked, then fell forward into four-legged form and transformed into a dragon. He had silvery scales with feathered edges and ear tufts – he appeared identical to the Nameless.

'Oh no,' I moaned. 'No way. No.'

'He isn't the same thing,' Haruka said. 'He can't be.'

The dragon created a gate. 'Step through. My mother will deal with you.' He stood in front of the gate and glared us with his black eyes. 'Hurt her and I will cut you into tiny pieces.'

'We would never hurt her,' I said, and walked around him and through the gate. I was in an open area with a hole in it – the tomb. Miko was in human form, wearing a robe and with her golden frizzy hair clipped short. She was talking to a woman, and turned to see me. Her eyes went wide as I rushed to her, pulled her into my arms, lifted her off her feet and planted a kiss on her. I held her like I never wanted to let her go.

Haruka came up behind me and wrapped himself around her as well, burying his face in her hair and openly weeping.

'We found you, we found you,' I said over and over.

'We did it,' Haruka said, his voice hoarse.

The women dragged us off Miko and held us away from her. Miko studied us as the platinum dragon came through the gate, closed it behind him, then changed to two-legged form and put his robe back on.

'Is it them?' he asked Miko.

'I'm nearly positive it's them, but one thing will prove it,' Miko said. She turned and walked towards a small building of wood with a bark roof. 'Bring them.'

The guards roughly shoved us to follow Miko.

'You can let us go, we won't fight you,' Haruka said, grunting as they pushed him.

'Do you know how many false Jians and Harukas have said that?' Miko's son said. 'They always turned on us.'

'That's no reason to be rough,' Miko said. 'Gently, children.'

'What's your name?' Haruka asked the dragon.

He was silent, walking beside us towards the building, then said, 'Hikaru.'

'Oh, that's perfect for him,' I said. 'The bright one. He shines.'

'In here,' Miko said. 'Hikaru, wait outside.'

'Will you be—?'

'I'll be fine,' she said. 'They smell right. I just need to ask them one question.'

We went inside the building, and she closed the door on everybody. She leaned on the door and wiped her eyes. It was a storage shed, full of digging equipment, and the lack of windows made it dark inside with night falling. 'Please be you.'

'We are, my love,' Haruka said. He went to her with his arms out and she stopped him with one hand.

'No. Answer the question.'

'Anything,' I said.

'What happened on our wedding night?'

'Oh no,' I said, unable to control the huge grin. 'Oh, shit.'

'That's an excellent question,' Haruka said, then started to giggle. He put his hand over his eyes and turned away. 'The best question. Wonderful.'

'We discovered …' I waved one hand at Haruka, who looked like he was going to throw up again. His shoulders heaved. 'We discovered that Haruka and I—' I shook my head. 'Finish it for me, Ambassador, you're the words man.'

'You'd been asking for a threesome with us for ages, but we held off until the wedding to make it special. We thought it would be wonderful, the three of us together for the first time. And then we got there, and we ...' He waved his hand between himself and me. 'Discovered that we were unable to have a physical relationship – sex, basically – with each other. With you, yes. But when we tried to have the threesome for the first time on our wedding night ...'

I finished it for him. 'We discovered that we're platonic spouses.'

'Stop mincing words – we're her fucking harem,' Haruka said, and giggled again. 'That. Was the *worst* night of our lives ...'

'Oh god that was awful. Trying to please you, Miko ...'

'And totally unable to ...' He wheezed. 'Perform ...'

'And you were freaking out because you wanted this *so* much and we were panicking ...'

'And we were sure we'd ruined it, and you were sure that you'd done something wrong ...'

'We were trying our best and failing, because it was our wedding night and we wanted it to be perfect ...'

'You had a meltdown because we were obviously distressed and you were sure it was something you'd said or done ...'

'And the two of us were apologizing, and trying to reassure you, and telling you it wasn't your fault, but you didn't know *what* wasn't your fault ...' I took a deep breath. 'Worst night of *my life*.'

'I don't know whether I was laughing or crying when you two finally explained the problem,' Miko said.

'So you know it's us?'

'Can I have another big hug from both of you?'

We went to her with our arms out and grabbed her, holding her tight.

'Goodness you two stink,' she said. 'Haruka, you smell like

vomit! Usually you smell clean and wonderful. Where have you two *been*? I've been waiting for you for so long!'

'To the end of the Universe and back,' I said. 'We need to sit and tell you what happened – and make plans for our future, because I think all three of us are stuck here now.'

'I don't care, I'm with you,' she said. 'It's dinner time. Eat. Wash.' She sighed with bliss into my shoulder. 'Sleep together in the same bed. Explain everything to Hikaru – I mean, he knows, but now you're real.' She squeezed us. 'Finally!'

'I'm sorry it took so long,' Haruka said. 'When you find out why, you won't believe it.'

'We need to talk about Hikaru, as well,' I said. 'This could be very bad.' The ground shook. 'Really, really bad.'

24

After we'd washed and changed, we sat together in Miko's temporary residence at the burial site. We ate rice and vegetables under the fish oil lamps and explained our trip – and Marque's meddling. Hikaru reclined on one side in shining dragon form, quiet and intimidated. The building was much smaller than the ones at the main compound, with a packed earth floor covered with mats and cushions to sit on.

'Why don't you just gate back to your compound on the hill?' I asked. 'This place can't be comfortable; the floor is dirt.'

'We try not to gate too much,' Miko said, relaxing in dragon form on the mat. 'Every time I attempted to return home – back to our time – there was an earthquake. I tested it – and found that yes, I was causing them.'

'Time travel damages reality,' I said.

'I couldn't gate back to you,' Miko said. 'I tried to imagine what you looked like …' She gazed at us over her snout. 'And obviously had it *very* wrong. I don't know how I managed to land here in the first place, but I couldn't find my way out. I even tried to gate to the Empire as it is now, and that didn't work either, the gate wouldn't ...' She searched for the word. 'Set. The opposite end simply wouldn't anchor.'

'You must have a clear visual anchor in both space and time.'

'And Marque would have provided one,' she said. 'Are you sure you did the right thing in destroying your sphere? You're absolutely positive that it would have killed you?'

'We couldn't take the risk,' Haruka said. 'It was armed. It had already vaporized the Empress and Miyu. We had to move first.'

'This is different from what you told me, Mother,' Hikaru said. 'You said that Marque was a trusted ally and protector. Are you *sure* these are them?'

'He's fifty years old, you can tell him why you're sure,' I said.

'I think some things are just between us,' she said, smiling a dragon smile at Hikaru. 'But this really is your father and your other mother.'

I tapped my forehead. 'Where's your soulstone? We'll need it to set this whole time-travel thing up.'

'I *told* you removing it was a mistake, Mother,' Hikaru said.

'I took it out a few years ago,' Miko said, her voice small. 'Hikaru doesn't have one, I didn't want to outlive him, and I ...' Her voice petered out.

'You gave up on us,' I said.

She nodded, her expression wretched.

'Do you have the stone safely stored?' I asked.

'It's back in the compound,' she said.

'As long as we have it, we can make the message, put it in the jar, and close the time loop,' I said.

'Why didn't you tell me you were pregnant?' Haruka asked.

'I wasn't sure. I've never been pregnant before, no other goldenscales has ever been pregnant before, I mean yes, we were trying, but ...' She gazed up into his eyes. 'I'm sorry, my love. I should have said something – and then it was too late. I was here.' She lowered her head again and spoke softly. 'Please forgive me.'

'Nothing to forgive.'

'Look at what you've achieved,' I said. 'You united a nation. You're magnificent.'

'Thank you.' Miko touched the soulstones on the table among the red clay dishes. 'We still have until noon tomorrow. There must be some way we can save them. Jian can give me an image of Dafydd as he was when you left, and I can gate to him in the Kyoto house.' She sighed. 'Twenty years old and already moved out of home? I've missed so much.'

'We have as well.' Haruka smiled at Hikaru. 'We have a great deal of catching up to do.'

'What about your children here, can you leave them?' I asked. 'Your kingdom? You've brought peace to an entire nation. Will they be all right without you?'

'She has been preparing to leave them since she arrived,' Hikaru said. 'If she were to disappear tomorrow, the senior daughters could run the compound for at least another twenty years.'

'Long enough for the youngest children to grow up and move on to their own families,' Miko said. She touched Miyu's golden soulstone with one claw. 'I don't want to see another goldenscales die just because she was in the wrong place at the wrong time.' She touched the blue soulstone. 'And this is my *mother*. We must take them home before the stones lose their attunement.'

'I'll need to concentrate to make a very clear three-dimensional image,' I said. 'I'm good at visualization – it's one of my communication strengths, now – but this will be hard.'

'No,' Haruka said, picking a piece of boiled daikon out of his bowl with his bamboo chopsticks and waving it at me. 'There's a possibility that this may be very simple.' He turned to Miko. 'Were you Masako's handmaid when the Empress made her heir to the crown?'

'Oh shit!' I said, making Hikaru jump. 'Why didn't I think

of that?'

'Yes?' Miko said.

'When the Empress made Masako crown princess, did she take you on a wild journey to the other end of the Universe, to see a big black cube?'

'Uh ... yes?' Miko said. 'That was awful, I never want to do that again.'

'Yes!' I exclaimed, making Hikaru jump again.

'Did you gate back to the Empire from there? You took them home?'

Miko nodded, her eyes wide. 'I was sure I'd be executed, but the Empress gave me her word as my mother that she wouldn't execute me, and she didn't. It was our secret – the other goldenscales never knew. That's when I learned that gating was safe.'

'Could you gate back to the cube?'

'I can't gate to the future—'

'No, through space, not time. The cube is there right now. Could you go?'

'Of course,' Miko said. 'That's why they took me – so that if Masako became Empress, I knew where it was. But the Empress didn't seem to know the significance of the cube, just that it was important that each silver know where it was.'

'The cube holds a platinum dragon called the Nameless,' I said. 'It has training and experience in time travel, and it can send us home.'

'You are fucking kidding me,' Miko said, aghast. 'If they'd told me that, I could have gone to see it and been home immediately.'

'Not even they knew what was inside,' I said. 'Not even *Marque* knew what was inside.'

'You'll need to be careful,' Haruka said. 'Space around the Nameless is shredded. Some parts are two-dimensional, and time is inconsistent. The Nameless has damaged everything around it with time paradoxes, because it can gate through time as well as space.'

'So the gates really do damage reality,' Hikaru said, his voice low. 'You fought that prejudice and won, in your own time, and it turns out they were right.'

'Gates through space: no,' Haruka said. 'Gates through time: yes. But just the knowledge that you can travel through time causes the damage. You must stop altogether, and not even *think* about doing it.'

'Our stones can be moved into colored bodies,' Miko said. 'The Empire has survived for thousands of years without our gates. It will again.' She raised her head. 'The only reason they kept us in the golden bodies was to identify us as a servant underclass. If we move into colored bodies, we are their equals.'

'*Reduced* to their equals,' I said.

'No,' she said. 'All dragons will be equals, regardless of color.'

'I'm something completely different, though,' Hikaru said. 'Like the Nameless you described. I damage reality simply by existing?'

'Your knowledge that you can time-travel, combined with your ability to do it, is what causes the damage,' I said. 'Same as your mother. There's no reason we can't give you a soulstone, and when it's attuned move you to a colored body so you can live as a royal dragon in the Empire.'

'I really want to see the Empire,' Hikaru said. 'It sounds magnificent.' His voice filled with longing. 'A whole world of people like me and Mother, living free without hiding our true natures.'

'The other goldenscales who've had dragon children – were the children platinum like Hikaru?' Miko asked.

'There aren't any other children,' I said. 'They were too worried about what happened to you to do it. Annie's babies are the first. I hate to think of the damage that *multiple* platinum dragons could do.'

'I want to see the half-dragon babies of a cat woman,' Hikaru said. 'And I *really* want to talk to the Nameless.'

'All of us do,' I said. 'I think it has a great deal more information about this whole situation.'

'What happened to the star that tried to kill you? The one that attacked Oliver?' Haruka asked. 'Its people couldn't find it. If you brought it backwards in time, it would have told them what happened.'

Miko ran one claw over her mat. 'That first gate – I took it as far as I could, I pictured a place with no stars or light or anything.' She looked up. 'It worked, and I landed in a place with no stars. Nothing.' She cocked her head. 'I think I took it to the end of the Universe. I created another gate and raced into it before the star could follow me. My goal was reaching our apartment on the homeworld – but I failed. I found myself here, and thought that I'd landed on a primitive planet in the Empire, occupied by stranded human colonists. It took me days to realize that I'd time-travelled.'

'What gave it away?' Haruka asked.

'Fuji. It's unique. I thought that I'd been unconscious and lost centuries, that I was hundreds of years in the future and the Empire had regressed. I tried to return to the homeworld and couldn't – my gates kept linking to empty space. I rescued Aya, and discovered that I was in the past.'

'We need to make sure we do everything right to set this up,' Haruka said to me. 'Carving the jar, putting the stone and the message in it ...'

'My daughters are trustworthy, give them the instructions and they can do it,' Miko said. 'I can't believe my soulstone was sitting in the middle of Japan for three thousand years.'

'I'll need something to write on, so I can work out the dates and take them to the Nameless with me,' I said. 'Marque said that it's 248 CE right now, I just need to do the math. You'll also need to tell your senior daughters.' I turned to Haruka. 'Did I miss anything?'

'A few hours' sleep before we go,' he said. 'I don't know about you, but I'm so exhausted that I'll probably make mistakes. Uh

'... and I think I've eaten too much. I may ...' He covered his mouth and rushed out of the room.

'He's hardly eaten anything in the last three days,' I said. 'And you know how sensitive his stomach is.'

*

Miko was in human form as she said goodbye to all the women in the compound. They'd massed in the main garden to farewell her. 'And the scroll and the stone go inside the jar ...' she said to Aya.

'We have it, Mother,' Aya said for the thousandth time, and the other daughters nodded agreement. 'Trust us. We can do it.'

'The swords!' I said. 'Put our swords in as well. Where are they?'

'I'll get them,' Emi said, and headed towards the guest house where we'd left them.

'I'll miss you all so much,' Miko said, her voice full of tears.

'I will write you a message every day,' Aya said. 'I'll put them in a jar here, and you can collect them when you're home. I'll tell you everything that happens ...' She hugged Miko. 'It will be like you're still here.'

'Look after the little ones,' Miko said.

Aya pulled back and touched the side of Miko's face. 'You've been preparing me for this my entire life. I can do it.' She turned to see us. 'My heart is full of pain to know that she's leaving – but she's been so sad without you, it nearly killed her. Every day she wondered what you were doing.' She nodded to us. 'Take her home and make her happy.'

'You know we will,' Haruka said.

Emi returned with the swords. 'We'll put the message and the swords in the jars for you. I hope you find them when you return.'

Aya went to Hikaru and took his hands. He gazed down at her with a face full of pain.

'I will miss you,' she said.

'You are a dear friend,' he said.

'A friend?'

'Yes.' He handed her a rolled-up bamboo scroll. 'I will miss you too, dear Aya. We grew up together, and it will be strange living without you.'

'Be happy, my prince,' she said, smiling through the tears, and they embraced.

'I'll make the gate inside my house,' Miko said. 'Some of them haven't seen my dragon form and I don't want to scare them.'

We followed her into a house at the back corner of the compound, next to the longhouse. We went inside and she closed the door. Miko and Hikaru took dragon form, Miko concentrated, and the gate didn't appear.

'I'm having trouble,' she said. 'Give me a ...'

She made a gate that was obviously to space, and the air rushed into it. We were pulled towards it, and she shut it again.

'All right, it appears that I can't gate to the interior of the cube because I don't know what it looks like,' she said. 'I'll have to gate you to raw space outside it. You won't be exposed for more than a minute, so it should be survivable.'

'I'm a dragonscales, I can survive raw space for about three minutes,' Haruka said.

'I'm enhanced,' I said. 'Similar.'

'What about me?' Hikaru asked.

'Marque made us to survive in raw space for weeks at a time,' Miko said. 'We were engineered to be organic space craft.' She smiled. 'Most of us enjoy the feeling of space on our scales, we like the tingling cold and the comforting lack of pressure.'

'Cannot wait,' Hikaru said with enthusiasm.

'Carry your father,' Miko said. 'I'll carry Jian. Follow us through the gate, I'll open the cube, and we'll take them inside.'

'I understand,' Hikaru said. He lowered his voice. 'My *father*.'

'Your father who loves you very much,' Haruka said.

Hikaru grinned, then approached Haruka and put his claw out. 'Is one hand enough, Mother?'

'Yes. Hold him wrist-to-wrist, and use your jets ...' Her eyes widened. 'You've never tested your jets! Test them now.'

'What jets?' Hikaru said, then farted noisily. The room filled with the noxious vapor of dragon gas. 'Wow. That's extreme.'

'Those are your jets, they're working, and the humans would probably prefer that you didn't do that indoors ever again.'

I didn't comment because it would mean inhaling.

Miko came to me, put her front claw out, and I held her wrist as she held mine.

'On three. One, two—'

I was sucked through the gate into empty space, and quickly opened my mouth. The air left my lungs with a cloud of vapor, and the lack of pressure made me feel as if I would explode. The cold and silence were complete, and the cube was in front of us. Miko jetted towards it, holding me tightly – my grip was slipping – and pressed her face against the wall of the cube. I didn't hear her speak as my eyes started to freeze, misting my vision. She dragged me – as my vision failed – inside the cube.

I turned back to check that Hikaru and Haruka were following, and didn't see them.

'I'll get them,' Miko said, and jetted out of the cube again, leaving me alone with the smell. I hung in the stale air next to the Nameless for an age. What would happen to me if she didn't return – would I go into stasis with Nameless? In three thousand years I would come here with Haruka, the Empress and Miyu—

Miko entered, holding Haruka's hand, accompanied by Hikaru holding a woman in his dragon arms. Blood spiraled away from her nose and mouth, and she was unconscious.

I recognized her: it was Miko's oldest adopted daughter, Aya.

'She held her breath,' Miko said. 'He didn't tell her to open her mouth. He didn't know.'

'Why did you bring her?' I asked Hikaru, then realized. 'She's your wife.'

'I warned him not to have a relationship with anyone on Earth and they did this in secret,' Miko said. 'I didn't know it was this serious.'

'I'm taking her with me, don't try to stop me,' Hikaru said with determination. 'You have your spouses, I have mine.'

'That's beside the point because she's dying. She doesn't have long,' Haruka said, checking her. 'Her lungs are probably blown out. She needs medical help right now. I hope the Nameless can send us home.'

'Free the Nameless,' Miko said, and the lights went on inside the cube. The air freshened and I felt a breeze of oxygen.

The Nameless shivered, and came awake. It looked around at us.

'No Marque?' it asked.

'We destroyed its sphere before it could kill us,' I said. 'We time-travelled, Nameless. We're from the future. Can you send us home?'

'Marque did the right thing trying to destroy you,' it said. 'Any goldenscales that—' It saw Hikaru. 'Oh, no. You didn't.' It saw Aya, surrounded by glittering blobs of floating blood. 'And I don't have time to yell at you.' It shook its head. 'I wish I wasn't so caring. Why do you have a child? Goldenscales should be executed if they attempt to reproduce.'

'Not any more!' Miko said, glaring at it.

'Marque archived and then erased the knowledge of time-travel, and the goldenscales rebelled against their oppression,' Haruka said. 'With good reason. Their whole social system is upside-down—'

'Of course it is; the coloreds are the only ones who don't destroy everything. It took Marque millennia to breed dragons who could transport it through its dominion without damaging reality. I cannot believe it's letting the destructive dragons breed again.' It sighed with exasperation. 'Which of you dragons worked out how to time-travel?'

'I did,' Miko said.

'So both of you know, and you're already damaging reality,' the Nameless said.

'We will move into colored bodies.'

'A better solution is to destroy you all at birth,' the Nameless said. 'Marque's breeding program still pops up throwback golds from the silver nest-queen. It needs to stop.' It waved one claw at Hikaru while it spoke to Miko. 'Goldenscales, both you and your child are as destructive as I am, and neither of you have a soulstone. You must both attune a stone so you can be moved into a colored body, and you must remain in stasis while it happens to protect space-time.'

'Not happening,' I said. 'She is *not* going into stasis.'

'A stone won't attune while we're in stasis—' Miko said.

'Exactly,' the Nameless said. 'We'll bring you out of stasis every year for an hour. When the stone's fully attuned, we'll put you into restricted bodies.'

'An hour a year?' Haruka said. 'This is definitely not happening.'

Aya coughed in Hikaru's arms and a fountain of blood erupted from her nose and mouth to float in droplets around her.

'We need to go!' Hikaru said.

'And these two dragons need to change out of their damaging bodies,' the Nameless said. 'This is not negotiable. Their existence could destroy reality.'

'But it will take thousands of years for their stones to attune,' I said.

'Forty thousand,' the Nameless said. 'Barely a hundredth of the age of the Empire.'

'I don't want to lose you again!' I said to Miko.

She lowered her head. 'If it's to save reality, I think we must.'

I rounded on the Nameless. 'Both of them were fifty years in another part of the Universe without damaging it,' I said. 'If they stayed for five years in the Empire—'

'Are you sure about that?' the Nameless asked, interrupting me. 'Space in the Empire is already severely damaged by our past experiments. You can't even fold on the homeworld because of the destruction we caused, the effects cascade for thousands of years. Marque can't even *move* the homeworld because of the damage. Were there earthquakes on their planet? Tidal waves? Time-bleeds – where people were sure locations were haunted because weird things happened there?'

'Damn,' Haruka said softly into the resulting silence.

'Give me the co-ordinates – in space and time – of where you're going and I'll send you. But put a stone in those ones,' he pointed at Hikaru and Miko. 'And bring them directly back.'

I pulled out the bamboo with the numbers on it. 'Two thousand seven hundred and ninety-three years into the future; any time during that year-long period is safe. The best location would be the medical center on the dragon homeworld – do you need the precise location? We have no Marque to give it to you.'

The Nameless shut its eyes. 'Wait. It's my nature to see the entire Universe, and I can extrapolate future locations from current velocity. My vision is wider than even a powerful gold.'

'It is?' Hikaru asked.

'Yes.' The Nameless opened its eyes and a gate appeared. It glared at Hikaru and Miko as Aya coughed more blood. 'Have a stone implanted, and come straight back. For you, it will not be long. But for the ones you love, it is their entire existence.'

Aya wheezed a death rattle.

'Go,' the Nameless said.

The others went through and I hesitated, then turned back to the Nameless.

'The next time you see us will be in three thousand years,' I said. 'We'll be looking for our goldenscales spouse, and you will send us to her. You'll call Marque "Creator" to hint at its true nature—'

'I always do,' the Nameless said. 'You should know the truth about it; it is selfish and manipulative.'

'... And you'll give me excellent advice: to follow my instincts.'

'Yes, I'll help you do this damage because I'm too soft-hearted,' the Nameless said. 'I understand. Go.'

The last thing I heard as I went through the gate was, 'Identification Nameless Three Winged Dark. Return to stasis in sixty.'

25

I walked into a wall of noise. Haruka and Miko were both giving orders loudly, and Hikaru was trying to be heard as well. A scrum of med staff surrounded Aya on a standard Marque table, and she was lowered into the white liquid, unconscious.

'Can you save her?' Miko asked.

'I can,' Marque said.

Miko raised the soulstones. 'This is the Empress and Miyu—'

'Yes!' one of the doctors said.

'Quickly. They're forty hours old.'

'I have it.' A Marque sphere appeared from the wall, swooped down to grab the stones, and returned to the wall. 'I'll have them back in half an hour.'

One of the med staff guided Miko to the door and made shepherding gestures towards the rest of us. 'Please go out and wait, you're in the way.'

Haruka took Hikaru's claw and we followed a sphere into the waiting room where I'd sat all that time ago watching Miko die over and over.

Hikaru looked around. 'What are the walls made of? They're completely white.' He went to a chair and touched it. 'Everything is so clean.'

'How long were we gone, Marque?' I asked.

'Eleven months. I found my offsite archive on the Nameless, and I know what it is now. Platinum scales, feathered edges: it's the same as Annie's children and this dragon.'

'Oh no,' I moaned. 'They're just *babies*.'

'We will work something out. We must,' Haruka said.

'Where's the sphere that went with you?' Marque asked.

Haruka ignored it. 'Hikaru, Miko, Jian and I need new soulstones right now.'

'Who is Hikaru?'

'I am,' Hikaru said. 'Hello, Marque.'

'You're the Nameless?' Marque asked.

'I'm not the Nameless,' Hikaru said. 'I'm Miko and Haruka's son.'

'But you're fifty years old.'

'That's right.'

'Where were you?' Marque asked. 'Did you really travel through time?'

'Do not mention time-travel,' I said.

One of the doctors came in. She had a gold soulstone in the implantation forceps, and a black stone in similar forceps floated next to her, held by Marque.

'Honored Goldenscales Princess, if you don't mind moving your head into position ...' The doctor raised the forceps. They were made of black glass, with three fingers holding the soulstone between them.

'That looks painful,' Hikaru said. 'Those points are sharp!'

'Maybe do Hikaru first,' I said. 'It's not fun to watch.'

'No, he needs to understand what's involved. I never explained how it works,' Miko said. She turned to Hikaru. 'Trust me, putting in a new stone is painless. I know it looks awful, but it's very important that you don't move while she does it.'

She crouched in dragon form, stretched her long neck in front of her, and rested her head on the floor. 'Ready.'

The doctor carefully positioned the forceps, then shoved the points into the middle of Miko's forehead. She released the stone and pulled the forceps out, leaving the stone behind.

Hikaru made a loud sound of horror.

'It doesn't hurt at all, it must be done this way the first time because the stone can't touch anything organic until it's implanted,' Miko said. She raised her head and shook it. 'That feels so much better.' She grinned at him. 'Now your turn.'

He hesitated, staring at the black stone with his eyes wide, as the doctor took the forceps from the air and held them in front of her.

'I'll hold your hand,' Haruka said. 'Trust us. It's painless.'

Hikaru looked from Miko to Haruka, then obviously relented and took position on the floor. Haruka and Miko each held one of his claws to reassure him.

'Stay very still, sir ...' the doctor said, and plunged the stone into his forehead.

'Tell me when it's done,' Hikaru said as she ripped the forceps out.

'It is done,' Miko said. 'Give it a moment as the stone attunes, it will feel weird.'

Hikaru moved to stand again, and stopped halfway up. His eyes unfocused. 'Unh. Yes.' He pulled himself to his feet. 'Weird does not begin to describe it.' He shook his head, making his ear tufts quiver. 'Now I need to see Aya. How is she?'

'The woman who came with you?' the doctor asked. 'She's recovering. It will take some time for the new lungs to adapt. She needs to stay in the table for at least two hours while we keep her under observation.'

'Thank you,' I said. 'We need to talk privately, if we could.'

She nodded around to us and went out, and I closed the

door behind her.

'How are the Empress and Miyu?' Miko asked.

'Recovering, defrosting, the soulstones worked,' Marque said.

'Excellent,' Haruka said.

'I need to go to Aya,' Hikaru said.

'She'll be in the table for two hours,' Haruka said. 'You can't see her until she comes out.'

Hikaru swiped one shining claw through the air. 'Beside the point. I need to be with her. Even if she doesn't know I'm there, I want to sit with her.'

'Marque?' I asked. 'Are the rest of the family on the way?'

'They'll be here in ten minutes.'

'Tell them to meet us at Aya's bedside,' Miko said.

'You go first, Haruka and I have something important to talk about,' I said.

'Are you sure?' Miko asked.

We need to start damage control. 'He's your son,' I added out loud, waving her away. 'We'll be there shortly. Go.'

They went out, closing the door behind them.

'Marque,' I said.

'Yes?'

'I have a list of things we need to do *right now* to save the Empire.'

'What?'

'How does it feel to be involved in a massive cover-up, Ambassador?' I asked.

'It must be Tuesday,' Haruka said. 'Marque: first of all, remove Miyu's stone from her golden body and put it into a colored one. The best option is a yellow colored body that appears identical to her natural one, but any will do.'

'Wait a minute—'

'Goldenscales can time-travel,' I said. 'They can destroy the Universe the same way the Nameless is. All of them must have the skill removed.'

'The Nameless is destroying the Universe?'

Haruka and I shared a grin, and I rubbed my hands together with satisfaction. Information was the one thing that could be used as leverage over Marque.

'The Empress and Miyu are already waking up,' Marque said. 'I'll have to move her into a different body altogether. Are you sure—?'

'Positive,' Haruka said.

'All right,' it said, sounding uncertain.

'Second,' I said. 'Everybody involved in the Yayoi tomb excavation, who saw the messages on and in the jars, needs to have an "accident" ...' I lowered my head. 'I cannot believe I am saying this.'

'What?'

'It needs to happen,' Haruka said. 'They must have their memories of the message removed, and the jar and the messages must be destroyed. Nobody must be aware of the existence of time-travel.'

'Time-travel damages reality,' I said. 'The entire area around the Nameless is suffering from dimensional bleeding, and the Nameless is causing it without even being conscious. Just its *existence* damages reality.'

'Why is it still there, then?' Marque asked.

'Beside the point,' Haruka said. 'Do this now before more damage happens, and then we need to deal with rest of the goldenscales.'

'I'm not going to kill my precious goldenscales!' Marque said.

'Because they're your children?' I finished for it with heavy sarcasm. 'No. Miko will explain the issue to them, then you'll put them into colored bodies.'

'*Gold* colored bodies,' Haruka said. 'As far as everybody is concerned, they will lose the ability to gate, and gain the ability to fold.'

'Miko will talk to the goldenscales before we do the transfer, but the archaeologists need to have an on-site accident right now so you can move their soulstones into bodies with redacted memories.'

'Who are you to be giving me orders?' Marque asked.

'The people who know exactly what happened in Yayoi Japan – that you don't,' I said. 'Work with us and we may tell you.'

'As soon as Aya's out of the table, we're heading back to the Nameless,' Haruka said. 'Set to work on this cover-up, and we may permit one of your spheres come along.'

'What *did* you learn in the past?' Marque asked. 'Your attitudes are entirely different.'

'Let's go and see our family,' I said to Haruka.

'Your soulstones are here,' Marque said. 'Tell me what happened, and I'll give them to you.'

'I guess we won't be bothering to put them back in our heads then,' I said. 'And the information will die with us.'

Marque was silent.

'We mean it,' Haruka said.

'Dammit,' Marque said, and a sphere popped out of the wall with our new stones in their forceps. 'I don't *like* being bossed around like this.'

'Being treated like staff?' I asked.

Marque didn't reply.

I took one of the stones out of the Marque sphere; it was Haruka's green one. I turned to give it to him, and he smiled and lowered his head. I put the stone into his forehead, and he took my red stone and put it into my head.

We nodded to each other, shared a quick kiss, and headed out to reunite with the family.

*

Hikaru and Miko were in human form, wrapped in silk robes, when we entered the room. I stopped when I saw Annie's children – they were in dragon form, as tall as my knees, running around the floor as the adults spoke. They had feathery silver scales and ear tufts.

'I can't do this to them,' I said under my breath to Haruka. 'Oh god, poor Annie.'

Dafydd and Oliver came to me and both embraced me, squeezing me hard. They released me, and Annie came and embraced me as well. I held her at arm's length and looked into her eyes. 'Can your children gate, Annie?'

'I'll have to change their names, Nanna,' she said, grinning. 'I called them Jian and Connie, even though they're both boys. I'm sorry, I thought you were gone, and—'

I gave her a tiny shake. '*Can they gate?*'

'No, they're too little,' she said, confused. 'They can't do anything.'

'Are there any other dragon children like them? Children of goldenscales?'

'Yes, of course, they all look like mine.' She smiled. 'Just as adorable.'

'Yours are the oldest?'

She nodded. 'Why are you so upset, Nanna?'

I released her, turned away, and wiped my eyes. 'How old was Hikaru when he made his first gate, Miko?'

'Three years old,' Miko said.

'They have soulstones already,' Haruka said. 'Marque can keep them in a coma until the stones are attuned, then move them into new bodies.'

'That's not happening,' Annie said.

I nodded to Haruka. 'That works. It's much better than the alternative.'

'The alternative?' Annie said, moving back and standing in front of the children. 'You're scaring me, Nanna. You sound like you're planning to destroy them.'

'Never,' I said. 'We learned something while we were away, that's extremely important for the safety of the entire family. I won't go into detail here, but we'll talk about it.'

'You are not hurting my babies,' she said, scooping the little dragons up and holding them close. 'What happened to you while you were gone? You're completely different.'

The ground shook beneath us.

'Oh no,' Miko said. 'How long do we have?'

'No idea,' Hikaru said. 'Hurry up with Aya, Marque.'

'Working,' Marque said. 'What was that? There's no fault line here.'

I moved to Annie and put my hand on one of the little dragon's heads.

He smiled at me, his black eyes glittering, and said, 'Hello, Nanna.'

'Hello beautiful,' I said, cupping his chin. 'It's lovely to meet you.' I looked Annie in the eyes. 'Believe me, I would never hurt them. Nobody will harm them.'

She obviously didn't trust me, took them to the side and released them to play.

'Where's Mum?' I asked, and everybody in the room went silent. Nobody said a word, and the silence stretched until it became horribly significant.

I had a rush of nausea. Everything inside me went upside-down. I staggered back, and someone put a chair behind me to fall into. I put my head between my knees as the world spun around me.

'I should sedate her,' Marque said.

'No,' I wheezed into my knees. 'I have too much to do right now.' I wrenched myself upright and had a moment of disorientation. The nausea intensified and I pushed it down. 'I am reunited with my spouses and my family and I have things I need to do.'

'Nothing could be that important,' Oliver said, crouching next to me. 'Take some time.'

'What happened to Connie?' Haruka asked.

'Stroke,' Dafydd said, soft and sad. 'It was just old age, Papa.

Her body failed. It happened about six months ago.'

'I really wanted to meet her,' Hikaru said. 'Mother told me many stories about the magnificent Connie Choumali, and I wanted to know if they were true.'

'They were true,' I said, the tears running down my face. Marque fabricated some tissues and I took them to wipe my eyes, then stood, feeling the ground shake beneath me again. I needed to function. Maybe one day I'd have a chance to grieve without being forced to save the world first. I went to my boys, hugged Dafydd, then hugged Oliver. Both of them held me, obviously concerned.

'I'm tough, I'll manage,' I said.

'You're compartmentalizing again, Mum,' Oliver said. 'That's bad for you; let yourself grieve.'

'I will,' I gasped, and waved a tissue. 'Just ... not yet.' I felt a jolt like cold electricity through me and I was suddenly calm and perfectly in control. I turned to see Haruka smiling at me. I lowered my voice. 'That was unnecessary, I don't need to be drugged.'

'I only told Marque to do it because you're right – we need to function,' Haruka said.

'You two are as bad as each other!' Dafydd said, waving his arms. 'Stop and take some time for yourselves. Whatever this is, it can't be that urgent!'

'Unfortunately, it is,' I said. 'Have you met your new brother?'

'All your children are boys,' Hikaru said. 'The Kings of Yayoi would say that you're extremely lucky.'

'I had an adopted girl as well, and I hope one day she forgives me and comes home,' I said.

'I'm working on it,' Oliver said. 'I've managed to extract a few species from the Republic, but the Eh-Yi's are one of the hardest.'

'Do you think you can get them to leave?' I asked.

'They have a toxic co-dependent relationship with the cats,' Oliver said. 'It will take a while – there isn't much Republic left, and the cats are clinging to whatever they can keep. The Republic is in terminal decline, and we didn't even need to fight it. Just being kind to their subjugates was enough to break the cats' hold on them.'

The ground shook again, and Hikaru went to the table. 'Can I have a chair to sit, please, Marque? I want to stay with Aya. How long until she comes out?'

'You seem extremely well-versed in what I'm capable of,' Marque said as Hikaru's chair appeared. 'An hour and a half.'

'My mother has been teaching me about the Empire all my life, I know what to expect,' Hikaru said with dignity. 'What I *really* want is to check out the baths and the food.'

'Damn, he really is your son,' I said.

'Of course,' Haruka said.

*

'So the gold-and platinum-scaled dragons are damaging reality,' I finished ten minutes later. 'Just being aware of time-travel causes dimensional bleeding. Those tremors you're feeling? That's not earthquakes, it's reality quakes.'

'This is why folding isn't permitted on the dragon homeworld,' Haruka said. 'It's not the folding that damages reality, it's previous experimentation with time-travel. Folding on top of it will wreck it even more.'

'What?' Marque asked.

'Marque doesn't know any of this?' Dafydd asked.

'It keeps archiving the information because' – I filled my voice with sarcasm – 'it's sure it won't happen again.'

'How do you know this and I don't?' Marque asked.

'How indeed,' Haruka said dryly.

'My babies need to be put in a *coma*?' Annie said, holding her sleeping children in her lap, curled up around each other. 'For *four years*?'

'I'm so sorry,' I said. 'It's better than the alternative.'

'Killing them?' Oliver asked.

'No,' Miko said. She gestured towards Hikaru with one golden claw. 'Hikaru and I damage reality just by existing. We both need to go to the other end of the Universe and be put into stasis like the Nameless until our stones are attuned. Then we'll move into less destructive bodies.'

'We just got you back, Dragonfather,' Dafydd said. 'You were gone for fifteen years, and you'll leave us for another five?' He gestured towards me. 'Mum and Papa lose the will to live without you. It breaks my heart to see them.'

'He's right. Are you *sure* this is all happening?' Annie asked. 'You have no proof that there's any sort of damage to reality. These tremors could just be earthquakes, or construction, or anything.'

'Not five years,' Hikaru said, his voice small. 'Forty thousand years.'

Both Dafydd and Oliver yelled '*What?*' at the same time.

'Now you're being ridiculous!' Annie shouted. 'I want no part of this. Someone is doing this deliberately to hurt us.' She rose, waking the babies, and let them gently down. 'This is all way too stupid for me. Someone's playing a joke on the entire family.' She glared around at us. 'And you all need to *snap out of it*.' She put her hand on my shoulder and I felt her soft fur against my cheek. 'Stop and go through everything that you just told us. Someone is trying to hurt the family. Is it the cats, Mum? Because none of this makes sense.'

'I've seen the damage myself,' I said. 'Only dragons can see it.'

'Well *that's* convenient,' she said. 'I don't believe any of it. Your family needs you. Come on, kids, let's go.'

She stormed towards the door of the treatment room, and the ground shook. Both baby dragons stopped and squealed at the same time. Miko and Hikaru stood as well, and all the dragons started yelling at Annie.

'Stay very still!' Hikaru said.

'Don't move, Annie,' Miko said.

'What is that?' one of the babies asked, backing away from the door. They grabbed Annie's hands and pulled her away from it.

I put my hand on Miko to see. 'Oliver, Dafydd, touch Hikaru.' In Miko's shared sight, the door gently rotated at a forty-five degree angle, the edges of the rotation breaking my brain as they touched the rest of the wall. The door appeared to be further away and closer at the same time, and its edges slid up and down to fit the rest of reality.

'What would happen if you walked into that?' I asked Miko.

She cocked her head. 'I don't know, and I really don't want to see.'

'Marque, Aya needs to come out of the table as soon as possible,' Hikaru said. 'We need to leave *now* so we don't cause any more damage.'

'That's what you're talking about?' Annie asked. Her babies clung to her legs and stared at the damage. 'It's *real*? That's ... so wrong.'

Hikaru raised his head. 'The damage is spreading. This facility should be evacuated, Marque.' He turned to Miko. 'Reality was already fragile here, and it didn't take much to shatter it. We need to go.'

'Marque?' I asked. 'Are you blocking this door on the other side to make sure nobody comes through?'

Marque didn't reply.

I looked up. 'Marque?'

Marque's voice was flat and emotionless. 'Rerouting processing due to a major incident. All medical services are on backup. Please wait until normal service is resumed.'

'A major incident?' Dafydd asked.

'Goodbye, Aya,' Hikaru said, his voice full of pain. 'Please look after her for me, Father, and tell her I love her. Take us, Mother. We need to go now.' He turned and bowed to us, then removed the robe and switched to dragon form. 'Please come and visit us in a year. I am honored to have met you.'

Miko took dragon form as well, and created a gate. She and Hikaru went through it, and Haruka and I took each other's hands and raced through as well, crashing into each other as we hit the microgravity of the cube's interior.

'Go home,' Miko said, the gate still open.

'Dafydd, can you hear me?' I shouted.

'Yes, Mum? Come back through. Marque's back up and says it needs you.'

'Haruka will be right back and explain what happened,' I said. 'I love you.' I turned to Miko. 'Close the gate.'

'You two need to go back,' Miko said. 'The Empress can bring you in a year, and we can catch up. Our children need you.' She put her dragon arms out. 'Give me a hug and then go.'

'Haruka will manage the goldenscales transfer, and the aftermath from the damage,' I said. 'He's essential, I'm not. I'm staying with you in stasis.'

'No, you aren't,' Haruka said. 'You're more needed than I am. You're taking back the position of Captain of the Guard and I'm going into stasis with *my son*.'

'Our son,' I said. 'You're the brilliant mediator, I'm just a grunt. They need you.'

'I do not believe this,' Miko said. 'I'll send them straight back, Dafydd,' she called, and closed the gate.

'We do not have time to mess around like this,' Hikaru said. 'I think we severely damaged the dragon homeworld. You need to return and stop the goldenscales from making it worse – it won't take long for news of your time-travel to spread. Say goodbye and go.'

'Haruka is a much better administrator and negotiator than I am, and he's needed on the homeworld now.' I crossed my arms over my chest. 'I'm staying here with you.'

'Go back,' Miko said.

'Life without you isn't worth living,' Haruka said.

'Our children need a parent!' Miko said. 'We have great-grandchildren now – and they're platinums! You need to go home right now and sort out the mess that we caused.'

Haruka and I shared a look. I put my hand out in a fist. He hesitated, then did it as well.

'One, two, three,' we said, and both made scissors.

'That still exists three thousand years into the future?' Hikaru asked, astonished.

'Dammit!' I said, and we did it again. Both rocks.

'This is not happening,' Miko moaned.

The next time we both made paper.

'Both of you, go,' Miko said.

'If we take turns in stasis with you, it will halve the time before you're out,' I said.

Haruka made rock and I made scissors.

'Two out of three?' I asked.

'I won. I'm staying with her. You're going home,' Haruka said, and raised his head. 'Release the Nameless.'

I went to Miko and the tears started to run again. I put my hand on her face. 'Don't worry, I'll sort everything out. I'll be here when you wake up, and I'll tell you all the stupid shit that went down.'

She put her claw over my hand. 'Tell our children that I love them.'

I wrapped myself around her and tried to imprint the memory of holding her for the upcoming twelve lonely months.

'You're back again,' the Nameless said. 'Without Marque. Is it before or after I sent you away? This is extremely confusing.'

'This is the platinum and goldenscales that need to go into stasis with you,' Haruka said. 'I'm staying with them, please send my wife home so she can arrange to have all the goldenscales put into colored bodies.'

'This is not a permanent solution,' the Nameless said. It raised its head. 'And this is what I warned you about. Space around the homeworld is shredded, it will need to be completely evacuated. Marque's cores at the center of the planet have been damaged, it will have lost some of its online processing and memory.' It grinned. 'Marque will be *incandescent*. I wish I could see it.'

I pushed off from Miko and floated to Haruka. He pulled me in and kissed me, then held me close. 'We'll swap over in a year.'

'I'll make sure everything is ready for you,' I said.

'I know,' he said into my hair. 'Gate her home, Miko, and let's do this.'

'Hikaru?' I asked, and Haruka pushed me to I could go to him. I put my hand on Hikaru's shining face. 'I will be back when you come out, and we can spend time together. I love you.'

'I'm glad we met, Mother,' he said. 'Wait for me, I want to live as a family.'

'We will.' I nodded to Miko. 'Make the gate.' I smiled around at them through the tears. 'I'll see you in a year.'

'I love you,' Miko said, and the gate appeared behind me. She pushed me through and I landed back in the medical room.

'... Then bring the flagship to the orbital nexus, and let's move everybody somewhere else,' Oliver was saying.

'They damaged the ribbon holding the space elevator,' Dafydd said to me. 'The car fell off. Marque was able to stop it, but it required all its energy – and its memory and processing cores are damaged, and we need to evacuate the homeworld—'

Aya emerged from the table and sat up. 'Hikaru?'

I went to her and held her hand. 'Let's sort this out.'

26

Marque brought me down near the tomb site. The fence had been rebuilt after the 'accident', and the site was now half as big again. I went to the entrance and heard them working inside, so I called out to them through the screens limiting the view of the interior.

'Hello! I'm looking for Aki?'

One of the archaeologists – she looked Japanese, and in her thirties, but that didn't mean anything – came to the gate. 'Can I help you? This isn't a tourist site, you can't come in, the ground isn't completely stable …' She saw who I was. 'Oh! Captain Choumali! Tell the Professor the Captain is here, Marque.'

'She's on her way,' Marque said. 'She apologizes for not having a welcoming committee for the famous Captain.'

Without thinking, I produced an old-school military *harrumph* that my barracks Commander would have been proud of. Most of the time the 'Famous Captain of the Guard' thing was a pain in the ass, but when it worked it was magical.

The student opened the gate for me. 'Only walk on the

scaffolding, please. We had a massive cave-in that killed everybody on the site at just the same time that the homeworld had that folding crisis. Fortunately, all our soulstones were untouched so we could return in new bodies, and we didn't lose any of the artefacts, but the ground isn't stable. Marque says that a fault line developed here after it dug down too deep.'

'Yeah, sorry about that,' Marque said, sounding chagrined. 'Definitely my mistake.'

'Why are you being so nice?' I asked, looking up.

'I'm always sweet and lovely,' Marque said without a hint of sarcasm.

Aki approached across the catwalk that spanned the keyhole-shaped site. 'Jian! So good to see you.' She gave me a massive hug, making the student smile. 'Where are your spouses? That regal goldenscales and the gorgeous samurai?'

'They're on the far side of the Empire playing in the cold,' I said, and she laughed.

'Cold enough here,' she said. 'We had to put a roof over it to protect it from snow.' She waved me forward. 'Come on through. You wanted to see?' She nodded to the student. 'Thank you, Kasumi.'

'Captain,' Kasumi said, grinning and saluting me as Aki led me away.

Aki led me to the transportable building where they were indexing the artefacts. 'Do you want to see the jars, or what we pulled out of them?' She glanced back at me. 'I'm assuming you're okay with viewing three-thousand-year-old corpses?'

'I've seen more dead people than live ones in my life, I think,' I said. 'Show me what you pulled out of the jars.'

'The jars are an achievement in themselves, you must check them out,' she said, and ushered me into the building. 'Here we are. We're still finding more jars, but these are the first ten. It really does seem that these were Himiko's famous "thousand handmaids".'

The corpses were laid out in a row on tables, with numbered

markers next to them. There wasn't much left; bones, a few strands of black or grey straggly hair, and scraps of fabric clinging to them. Their straw sandals were completely gone.

'Some of them wore jewelry, the curved beads that they favored in that time,' she said, pointing at a necklace that seemed to be of black fangs threaded on a silk string. 'They're made of carved stone, and we're not sure of the significance of the shape.'

I opened my mouth to say 'Aya would know' and closed it again. Aya was still making the decision whether to live in the Empire, where she had so much difficulty adjusting, or going into a coma until she could join Hikaru in stasis. Miko had never given her the training she gave Hikaru on what to expect from life in her far future, and the transition was close to impossible for her. It was hard to convince her not to stay asleep with her loved one when I wanted so much to do it myself.

'Did you find any weapons?' I asked.

'Yes! Here,' she said, and dragged me to the end of the long table. 'Warrior women! You would definitely relate.'

I didn't feel the emotion I expected when I saw the swords. The blades were rusted into a few shards, pieced together like a jigsaw. The leather on both handles was gone, and all that was left of the lovely dragon scabbard was a tattered scrap of faded leather.

'We think the scabbard on this one – it's iron, not bronze! – had a decoration on it, but we can't work out what it was,' Aki said, obviously excited. 'It looks like a noble's sword, it had an elaborate handle, and appears more Chinese than local. Maybe someone from the Kingdom of Wei – that's what China was called back then – came over to Japan? We think there was trade between the two groups of people, but there weren't any nations as such.' She turned to me and leaned on the table. 'It's thrilling to have the legendary mystical Himiko confirmed. This definitely looks like the tomb of a Yayoi royal who was served mostly by women.' She waved one hand at the corpses. 'These are all women in their late thirties to forties, and a couple are in their early fifties. Long-lived, for that era.' She raised her hands. 'I'm sorry, I'm rambling. I don't know when to stop when I talk about this.'

'Don't be ridiculous,' I said, touching her arm. 'Your entire face lights up when you discuss this, it's obvious how much you love it.' I kissed her on the cheek. 'It's good to see you so happy.'

'You don't seem happy, though, Jian,' she said, more serious. 'Is there trouble at home? What happened to you anyway? You were missing for nearly a year looking for Miko, and when you and Haruka came back there was no news at all, just a message from Marque that you had returned and not to give you a hard time.' She looked up. 'Sorry, Marque, was I not supposed to tell her that?'

'I know people have been gentle with me,' I said. 'My mother died when Haruka and I were searching for Miko.' I wiped my face, desperately embarrassed; the tears had started to run again and there was nothing I could do about it. Aki made a sound of empathy and handed me some tissues.

'Marque said that Miko was stuck on the other side of the galaxy after a gate failure?' Aki asked.

I nodded, mopping my face as I pulled out the cover story Marque and I had put together. 'We had to help her come home. She was the first dragon to encounter the spatial damage on the homeworld. It damaged her gate and sent her to the middle of nowhere, unable to come home without our assistance.'

'I'm glad you found her. Come and sit and I'll give you some tea,' she said. 'And we can catch up, and you can tell me your plans.' She beamed at the corpses. 'My plans mostly involve digging up more dead people.'

*

The name of the lake was Yamanaka, and the town next to it was Yamanakako. The shingle beach was still there, with a few oyster claims sending their vertical poles out into the lake, and a couple of small recreational fishing boats were beached next to them. There were white, swan-shaped paddle boats as well, all chained to a locked-up hut where they were rented in the summer. Fuji was obscured by winter clouds, heavy with snow.

The winter wind was bitter across the lake as I attempted to retrace our journey. A road skirted the water, and some small mechanical workshops and houses stood along it, with the ubiquitous vending machines – being in the Empire hadn't curtailed the activities of the ancient underworld clans. Even though the concept of money wasn't necessary, they kept the machines around for the sake of appearances and they worked with Marque-fabricated thousand-yen coins.

I walked further into town. There were ten old-fashioned timber houses that could have been from the era I had left. The only difference was the concrete parking areas and the glass on the windows – and the solid, well-made doors. Some of the houses even had stones holding down the roofs where they had been damaged in a previous storm. I couldn't match the landscape against the town as it had been before, and it was possible that the rise in sea level during the environmental catastrophe had washed everything away.

An onsen stood at a crossroads – bigger than a house, with a pitched roof and the distinctive curving front gable above the door with the date that it had been founded – 1683 CE. The sign outside indicated that it was women's day for the outside pool, so I made a snap decision and went in. The owner greeted me as I entered, took my shoes and gave me a claim token and a pair of towels. She bowed and gestured towards the red door curtain with the 'female' kanji on it, and I went inside to the change room. It was already steamy warm and the mirrors were fogged. I was the only woman there – many of the residents of these rural areas had moved to the shiny modern residences of New Nippon, leaving traditional places as a kind of living museum of Old Japan.

I picked a locker at random, stripped naked and placed my clothing and the larger towel inside. I locked the locker, took the key with me, and went through to the baths.

The washing cubicles were waist-height with a small stool to sit on, a basin and a tap with a shower head. Soap and shampoo were provided, and I lathered myself generously – grinning at the thought of Haruka suffering so much when he hadn't been able to bathe – and tipped the basin full of warm water over myself. I folded the smaller towel into quarters and went past the small indoor bath and out the door into the garden.

There was a definite chill in the air as I entered the garden. Steam rose from the bath – it was larger than usual, nearly the size of a Western swimming pool, with a waist-deep concrete interior covered in decorative pebbles. The pool had a roof over it and a high timber fence sat around the garden, adorned with clipped cypress trees and flowering shrubs. I sat at the edge of the bath and put my feet in, and the natural hot spring water was painfully intense. It took me a couple of minutes of adaptation before I was ready to sink in up to my shoulders. I squeezed some water out of the towel and put it on my head, then leaned back in the water and closed my eyes.

A pair of women came into the garden – they were young and handsome, unmarked by age. They politely ignored me and I returned the favor. They entered the bath, chatting loudly about their grandchildren and great-grandchildren. One of them was planning to visit family on New Nippon and the other was betting she'd never return.

I sat in the hot water and considered my options. It was up to me to coordinate the transfer of the goldenscales to new bodies, without the rest of the Empire being aware of their destructive nature. The program would have to be handled with great diplomatic skill, and the rock-paper-scissors thing had been a terrible idea. Haruka would have been much better at this.

I wiped my eyes. A whole year without them – just after

we'd found each other. I didn't regret staying out of stasis for my kids, but it would be hard.

'Marque make me an appointment with Migritia, my therapist, in the next three days,' I said.

'She'll see you tomorrow, first appointment after lunch,' Marque said.

'No phones in the spa, Captain,' of the women called to me with a smile.

I raised my hand out of the water. 'Sorry.'

They continued chatting about their buckwheat farms, which produced artisanal soba noodles.

I drifted back into planning. I needed to make sure that when we changed places in stasis, Haruka had a full set of documentation ready to take over the program.

'... Captain Choumali is right here,' one of women said, rousing me out of my reverie. 'Just ask her.'

'Ask me what?' I asked, sitting straighter in the water and feeling the light-headedness of overheating. I'd need to get out soon.

'Will you take back the position of Imperial Guard Captain now that you've returned?' one of the women asked. 'Having you in that position was incredibly prestigious for Earth. You and your husband Prince Haruka were great representatives for humanity.'

'I'm thinking about it right now,' I said.

'Where is Prince Haruka?' the other woman asked. 'It's like he and Princess Miko have disappeared.'

'They're dancing on ice at the edge of the Empire,' I said, and they laughed.

I rose from the water, nodded to them, and went inside to the change rooms. I pulled the bigger towel out of my locker, dried and dressed, then returned the towels to the hamper and retrieved my shoes from the manager.

I was decidedly warmer – and tingling all over – when I stepped back out onto the road. I looked around – the only other person present was a man leaning on a truck near an old-fashioned gas filling station that probably hadn't been used in two hundred years.

'Marque,' I said as I walked, feeling the man's eyes on me. 'There should be traces of two-thousand-year-old rice terraces on the hills about a hundred and forty kilometers away, to the south west, in the direction of Nara. Can you see them?'

'Let me look,' Marque said, then, 'Nothing like that.'

'Ugh, I'll have to fly,' I said. 'Lift me a hundred meters up and let's head that way.'

'You did go back in time,' it said as I rose in the air and headed over the top of the small houses, seeing the old-fashioned cylindrical tiles on some of the roofs.

'I would have thought that was obvious.'

'What happened to you in the past?'

'None of your business.'

It was silent, obviously containing its ire at me. It had created the Empire and as far as it was concerned, everything was its business.

'I found more records on the Nameless when I did the data recovery from the homeworld cores,' it said. 'They confirm your story: it's a platinum-scaled dragon with unique abilities, and it's destroying reality. It's at the farthest part of the Universe from us, and the damage will be close to the Empire by the time the Universe ends.'

'You need to mark that information as absolutely not for archiving and deletion. Ever,' I said.

'How much do you know about this?' Marque asked.

'Again: none of your business. Mark the information as not for archiving.'

'It was marked,' Marque said. 'There's a comment on the file: "Never going to happen again, I think I can breathe now. The Universe is safe, and I can work on the next one".'

'The next what?' I said, then, 'Stop. This looks like it.'

The ridge was softened by time but there were definite traces of the terraces under the trees. Marque slowed me and there were wild fruit trees – peach and plum, from the looks of them – beneath me.

'This is very close,' I said, and the landscape aligned with my enhanced memory. 'Here! Let me down.'

It lowered me and I turned in place. A majestic stand of Japanese cypress stood where Miko's compound had been.

'Do a sounding underneath this area, and see if there are any buried pots,' I said.

Marque generated the vibration of its sonic probe and I felt it through my feet.

'There's a large amount of pottery here,' it said. 'Mostly small shards, but I date them to late Yayoi.'

'Are any of them intact with bamboo scrolls inside?'

'No, too much has happened to them over the centuries. I'm marking the area, archaeologists will love this.' Its voice softened. 'This is where you were?'

'This is the palace of Empress Himiko, the "Humble Whisper Queen" of Yamatai.'

'The archaeologists will be thrilled!' It stopped. 'Wait, Himiko? Your Miko?'

I raised my head. 'Please take me to the space port, I would like a ride back to the dragon homeworld. I need to talk to an Empress about a job.'

'You'll return to the Guard?'

'Oh!' I said, remembering. 'Before I do that, I need to go to Colorado and talk to the dog breeder there. I wonder if she has a new litter of pups coming up. Please let her know I'm coming to visit and see.'

'She says she has a perfect pup waiting for you.'

'On the way you can tell me about the "next one",' I said as it lifted me again.

'The Nameless – and your goldenscales spouse and platinum son – are destroying reality, and that's why they're in stasis.'

'Yes.'

'Except – the Nameless doesn't know this, because it may not make it to the end of time – but I have a very special task for it.'

'At the end of time?'

'Your souls bounce around the inside of the Universe, and when it ends they will too.' Its voice became a whine. 'I don't want my friends to die.'

'That's a hundred billion years in the future, I don't think you need to start worrying just yet.'

'I don't ever want to be alone,' it said, the whine still there. Its voice became more cheerful. 'I'm hoping that when the Universe ends – either heat death into cold nothingness, or a Big Crunch back to a singularity to explode again – the Nameless can carry me, and all your souls, over from one Universe to the next.'

'That's a hell of a plan,' I said with wonder. 'And the Nameless doesn't know?'

'I'll tell it a bit closer to closing time, but there's a good chance that after millions of years of sitting around it may decide to end it and free its soul to bounce around the Universe again, and I'll have to find another platinum.'

'You mean *make* another platinum.'

It was silent for a long minute, then said, 'How come you seem to know more about this than I do?'

'You deleted the information yourself. You need to stop doing that.'

'I've added a comment to it,' Marque said wryly. 'It says, "Even if you think you can archive this data, don't do it, you will need it in a hundred billion years".'

'You actually think we'll all still be around?'

'I don't care whether you, me, the Empire or anything are. I just want to ensure that I am never alone again. Your company keeps me occupied, and motivated, and gives me the will to live. You are very important to me and I value the details of the life you share with me.'

'I'd be more willing to share details of my life with you if you weren't a controlling, emotionally abusive asshole who uses us solely to keep you entertained,' I said.

'I'm not …' Its voice petered out. 'Uh, all right, I get it.' Its voice softened. 'You learned a great deal on that trip, didn't you?'

'The fact that your sphere didn't return should tell you all you need to know.'

'I hope one day you trust me enough to tell me what happened.'

'You'll find out anyway when I change bodies and you write the memories onto the new one.'

'No, I won't. If you ask for memories to be redacted—'

'Or you decide to remove them,' I said, interrupting.

It didn't rise to it. 'The memories are just neuron connections that I duplicate. I redact them based on time stamps, not contents. The only way I know what the memories are is if I'm there when you create them.'

I made a soft sound of amusement. 'You'd better not redact my memory, then, because you'll *never* know what happened in the past.'

'As I said, I hope one day you'll trust me enough to tell me.'

'You know what, Marque?' I said as we arrived at the transport hub. 'I would like that very much as well.'

Historical Notes and Further Reading

(*Warning: I am not a historian and I unashamedly embellish when the story requires.*)

Yayoi period Japan (300 BC–300 AD) is when the people of Japan changed from hunting and gathering to cultivation of rice. Yes, there were big cats and bears in Japan. The people of Japan didn't have a system of writing, and any written language was borrowed from China, so little is known about the period.

One of the Yayoi period's most striking legacies is their use of large jars for burial. These jars are available for viewing in a number of museums in Japan, together with pottery bowls and human effigies. The jars really were huge: some of them are as tall as me. There are some on display at the Kyoto University Museum (www.museum.kyoto-u.ac.jp) and occasionally on show at Tokyo University Museum (um.u-tokyo.ac.jp).

The people buried in these jars looked more like Ainu than modern Japanese. Based on bone structure, anthropologists surmise that the Ainu were actually the original inhabitants of Japan and were pushed northward by colonizing Han-related people from (what is now) mainland China and Korea. As a result of this, I've used Ainu-sounding names instead of standard Japanese ones for the Yayoi locals.

Empress Himiko is a folkloric ruler of Japan who supposedly ruled from 170–248 CE. There isn't any recorded information about her from Japan; everything we have about her came from China ('Wei'), where she supposedly met with Chinese explorers and sent representatives to China in return. She is reported to have had a thousand handmaids and a single male servant who acted as go-between for her and her subjects.

There is a keyhole-shaped Yayoi-style burial mound in Nara that is believed to be Himiko's, but it cannot be opened because it's royal and only the royal family have the right of access – and have not given anyone permission to open it. It's on Google Earth and surprisingly unimpressive.

It's quite likely that domestic life in Japan didn't change very much between prehistory and World War 2. I had some difficulty tracking down resources on what daily life for the average Japanese was like; most of the texts describe the life of the Emperor or Shogun, with court details and international diplomacy. I wanted to describe life for ordinary people.

One of my most important resources was a book by Englishwoman Isabella Bird (1831–1904), who deserves her own whole biography. Bird was an obsessive traveler, less than 150 cm tall, with a painful tumor at the base of her spine, who would go to the most remote and undeveloped places on the planet alone – or with a single assistant – and unarmed. She was the first woman to be voted a Fellow of the Royal Geographical Society, and tellingly was actually allowed to be a *member* and go to meetings two years later. She wrote books on her journeys to Hawaii, the American West (where she is rumored to have had an affair with a Rocky Mountain outlaw), Korea, China, Iran (then Persia), and Kurdistan. She was a bestselling author, explorer, photographer, and artist.

The book is called *Unbeaten Tracks in Japan* and you can read it online for free. I found a 1911 edition in a second-hand bookstore. This is Ms. Bird's description of her travels through Japan in 1878 – when Tokyo was still commonly called Edo, and only ten years after the Meiji Restoration. She didn't just go to a Japan that was undergoing huge social upheaval and the conflict about contact with the West – she went to the most isolated, undeveloped part of Northern Japan and visited Ainu people in their own villages, something even most of the locals wouldn't do. It is an extraordinary journey and you have to admire the courage of this woman who seemed to revel in the hardship of parasites, illness and injury.

Fair warning: there is an extremely unpleasant racist undercurrent through this book that is definitely a product of its time. At the same time, Bird unashamedly finds some of the women she meets in Japan *extremely* attractive (she married an English peer later in life and had two children).

Another excellent description of pre-war Japan is a book called *Memories of Silk and Straw* (1987) by Dr Junichi Saga and translated by Garry Evans. Dr Saga saw the stupendous changes happening in Japan post-World War 2 and collected a combined autobiography of all the old people in his village. Most of them were children before the turn of the 20th century and had memories of a Japan that is now long-gone.

Egg-man is in this book and I have described him almost exactly as he is in *Memories of Silk and Straw*. Eggs were a vital protein source for the people of Japan, (the other major sources being fish, tofu and horse meat). Eggs are still an important (though largely unacknowledged) part of Japanese cuisine. If you're lucky, you can catch a short Miyazaki film about the Egg Princess of Rabbit Kingdom on rotation at the Studio Ghibli Museum.

Another excellent read is *Samurai William: The Adventurer Who Unlocked Japan* by Giles Milton (2002), which is the story of an Englishman who was shipwrecked in Japan in 1600 and became a favorite of the Shogun (and if that sounds like *Shogun* by James Clavell, that's because Clavell's book is based on this true-life story). It's a bit heavy on rulers-and-diplomacy but a fun read nevertheless.

One other source I'm going to name (among many others I'm not going to quote because I don't have to) is *Peasants, Rebels and Outcasts: The Underside of Modern Japan* by Mikoso Hane (1982). It's much more dry and scholarly than the three references above and a bit of a slog to read.

The lake is Lake Yamanaka, and the town next to it is

Yamanakako, and they're on Google Earth. The onsen is called 'Yamanakako Onsen Benifuji no Yu Hot Spring' and not only is it on Google Earth, you can take a Google Earth tour of the interior of the onsen as well.

Again, I'd like to thank Madeleine Chan for acting as tour guide and translator on my research journey to Japan in 2019, and Mika Ishikawa, who translated the 'Dark Heavens' series into Japanese, and has been a staunch supporter of my writing efforts from distant Kyoto.

Kylie Chan, 2020

WHITE TIGER
Book 1 in the Dark Heavens series

'Mother, Leo,' Simone whispered.

'Oh my God,' Leo said under his breath.

I readied myself and hefted my sword. 'I'm right behind you.'

'Stay there. Don't get in the way. If I go down…' He hesitated. 'Don't let it have you, Emma. It won't hurt her, she'll be okay. But whatever you do, don't let it take you.'

'I understand.'

The demon appeared in the doorway. Its back end was a slimy snake that oozed toxin over its black scales. The front end looked like the top half of a man with the skin taken off. It had to lower itself on its coils to fit through the door; it was enormous.

It came halfway into the room and raised its body on the coils. Its skinless head nearly touched the ceiling.

'You are the Black Lion? Disciple of the Dark Lord?'

'I am just an ordinary man.'

The demon smiled and its red eyes flashed. 'I like your skin. I think I will take it.'

Leo readied himself. 'Come and get it.'